Scars Series

NIKKI SPARXX

The Scars of Us

Mending Scars

For more information

www.facebook.com/NikkiSparxxAuthor

Cover Design: Cover to Cover Designs

www.covertocoverdesigns.com

Photo Credit: Simon Barnes Photography

https://www.facebook.com/HOTSNAPZ

Model: Andrew England

Contents

Mending Scars

NIKKI SPARXX

Prologue

Kaiya

I've heard people say that time heals all wounds, but I think that's bullshit. All time did was allow the wounds to scar, leaving a permanent reminder of your suffering. The emotional pain might fade away, but a little piece of it always lingered, taunting your happiness, and never letting you forget.

Now love was a different story. I believed love could heal all wounds, but only if you let it; only if you trusted it. Unfortunately for me, I couldn't trust anyone, at least not completely. The one person in the world who I was supposed to be able to trust unconditionally ruined that for me. Now, the only person I could trust was myself, and even that was questionable most days.

Every day, I looked in the mirror, hating everything that stared back at me. Every single feature reminded me of him, of the person he made me to be. I hated what he'd done to me, hated the scars he'd branded on my soul. I wished I could erase them, but they were embedded so deeply into my being that I didn't think even love could heal them.

I never thought I would ever experience love, until I met Ryker. He turned everything upside down the first time I'd laid eyes on him, and neither of us would ever be the same.

Chapter One

Kaiya

I glimpsed at the clock, which blinded me with glaring red light. As usual, my nightmare woke me way before my alarm was set to go off. Exhaling a sigh of resignation because of the ungodly hour, I rose out of bed and ventured to the bathroom.

Unable to look at myself after my reoccurring dream, I avoided turning on the light, not wanting to see my reflection in the mirror. Even a glance at my pale skin, blue eyes, and dark hair would almost guarantee a breakdown that would take hours to recover from. Avoidance was probably not the best method to deal with my issues, but it was one of the only ways I knew how.

After fumbling around in the dark while doing my business, I made my way to the kitchen to make a cup of tea to steady my nerves. Sleep was futile, and lying awake in bed with my thoughts was a disastrous idea, almost as bad as looking at myself in the mirror.

Padding down the hallway of my apartment, I stopped at my brother, Kamden's, open door. Sometimes, I crawled into bed with him when I couldn't handle the nightmares, but I didn't want to wake him tonight. He needed his rest, and I needed to be less selfish. I hated being so dependent on him, but I needed him, more than he would ever know.

Kamden was the only person from my family that I still spoke to, the only person that I remotely trusted. But even after everything he'd done for me, all that he'd sacrificed for me, I still couldn't trust him fully; I'd never be able to trust anyone completely.

Walking the rest of the distance to the kitchen, I began the process of shutting down, blocking out my thoughts, closing out everything around me. Withdrawing into myself was another coping mechanism, numbing myself, pretending that I was fine and didn't care so that my emotions would be unable to break me—they were the enemy. I doubted that I'd be able to function in society otherwise.

After I made my cup of tea, I headed to my office. Immersing myself in my work was easier than addressing my problems and acknowledging my issues. The numbers and figures made sense, and had a purpose, unlike my thoughts and emotions. I had control over the spreadsheets, tables, and documents, dictating everything that happened within them. I needed to have that power, needed to control as much as possible since I was constantly on the verge of unraveling.

After working on several projects for a few hours, I was interrupted by Kamden. "You sleep okay? "he asked, yawning as he leaned against the doorframe.

I gave him a look of disbelief before sarcastically answering, "Wonderful."

"Why didn't you wake me? You know I don't mind."

"It's not fair for me to wake you every night over a stupid nightmare." I replied brusquely, directing my attention back to the spreadsheets on my screen.

Walking over to me, he placed a hand on my shoulder. "Your nightmares aren't stupid, Ky. You can't—"

Cutting him off, I snapped, "I don't want to talk about it, Kamden."

Raising both hands in surrender and stepping back, he softly replied, "Okay, Ky. You know I'm here for you if you need me."

Sighing, I rose from my seat. "I'm sorry, Kam. I didn't mean to snap at you. I'm just exhausted."

"I know. That's why I don't mind if you come into bed with me—you need your rest."

"Not at the expense of yours. I hardly fall back asleep anyway."

Opening his arms to me, he responded, "I want to do all that I can to help you. Always remember that."

I easily fell into his embrace, enjoying the security of his arms. Kamden always made me feel safe, which was a fleeting notion for me most days. "Thank you, Kam."

Hugging me tighter, he replied, "No problem, little sis."

Ringing from down the hall interrupted our exchange. "I left my phone in my room—I better grab it."

Releasing me from his arms, he trotted out of our office. After a few seconds, I heard him greeting our mother. *Great.* His footsteps echoed from the hallway, increasing in volume along with his voice as he neared closer to where I stood.

"Hang on, Mom," Kam spoke into the phone. He pressed his screen before directing his attention to me. "She's asking for you—will you talk to her?"

I gave him a *really* look. "No."

"Kaiya," Kam chastised in an annoyed tone.

"Kamden," I mimicked in the same manner.

He sighed as he pressed his screen again and put the phone back to his ear. "Sorry, Mom, she already left for work," he lied.

I mouthed, "Thank you."

Rolling his eyes, he turned and went back down the hallway as he made small talk with our mom. Following after him, I decided to get ready for work. I almost ran into him when he abruptly stopped in the corridor right before his door.

"What?" he gritted into the phone, his whole body tensing in anger.

I scooted around to face him, locking eyes with his narrowed, enraged ones. His nostrils flared as he inhaled deeply before seething, "You can't be serious."

"What?" I mouthed anxiously. My heart raced, my anxiety peeking from beneath my walls in anticipation of what my mother was telling Kamden.

Jaw clenched, he shook his head.

Shit, this must be bad. Breathe, Kaiya, breathe. You're safe, you're with Kamden—he won't let anything happen to you.

Hanging up the phone without another word, he clutched the device in his shaking hand.

"Kam, you're scaring me. What's wrong?"

He blew out a breath of frustration as he ran his free hand over his buzzed head. "You should sit down for this, Ky."

My pulse pounded ferociously under my skin, my blood thrumming through my veins with fear. "What is it, Kamden?"

"Ky, I really think you sh—"

"Tell me, Kamden!" I shrieked, beginning my spiral out of control. My thoughts turned to the darkest of places, to where my nightmares were rooted. *Please no, please don't let it be him.*

Kamden sighed before stating, "Kaleb is being evaluated for release."

No… no, no, no!

Tears poured in rivulets down my cheeks as my lungs seized, my breath leaving me instantaneously at the sound of his name. My legs gave out as my stomach roiled, and my vision blurred. Kamden caught me before I crashed to the floor, and then blackness descended on me.

Light slapping on my cheek roused me from darkness. My eyes fluttered open to Kamden, whose face was creased in concern. His blue-gray eyes locked on mine before he sighed in relief. "Don't scare me like that."

"I didn't plan to pass out," I retorted as I sat up. I shut my eyes tight and pressed my fingers on the bridge of my nose as dizziness spread over me..

Kamden gave me some space, scooting over closer to the edge of my bed. "I told you to sit down, but you're so stubborn."

I scoffed as I rolled my eyes, not acknowledging his comment otherwise. He was right, but I wasn't going to admit that.

Noticing I was in my bed, I scrunched my face in confusion as I asked, "How long was I out?"

"Not long. Ten minutes, maybe."

I glanced at the clock, my stomach dropping at the sight of the time. *Oh shit, I have to get ready for work!*

"Don't even think about it, Ky. I already called your boss and let him know that you're taking a sick day."

"But—" I attempted to argue.

Kamden moved closer to me on the bed. "No buts. You need to rest. You're in no condition to do anything after that incident. Plus, you haven't been sleeping well either. Your boss said that you could work on your projects from home today." His tone was stern, but nurturing, the concern in his voice evident.

"I'm fine, Kam. Really, I am," I said, attempting to get out of staying at home with my thoughts all day, especially following the bomb that had been dropped on me.

Kamden gave me a knowing look as he replied, "We need to talk about this, Kaiya. You can't just avoid everything all the time. It's not healthy." Averting his eyes, I concentrated on a stitch of fabric on my comforter as I picked at it. *He knows me too well.*

"I can't," I whispered as tears began to surface.

Kamden grabbed my hands, cradling them in his larger ones. "Kaiya, look at me. I'm here for you—don't shut me out. I only want to help you, to do what's best for you. Please talk to me."

A rogue tear fell from my lids as I looked up at him. More threatened to follow as I angrily questioned, "How could they let him out, Kamden? After everything he did to me, how could they release him? He's a fucking monster!"

"I know. He's only being evaluated—he's not out yet. I'm going to do everything I can to make sure he doesn't get released. There has to be someone I can talk to at the hospital." His eyes narrowed in determination, his tone resolute as he spoke.

Biting my lip, I nodded as my tears began to flow freely. "He'll find me, Kam. He'll come back for me. What if he—"

Kamden shifted next to me, his body tensing. Gripping my chin, he forced me to look him straight in his eyes. "He'll never touch you again! I'll kill him before I let that happen," he growled in fury. "No matter what happens, I'll protect you, Ky."

Unable to speak, I nodded again. The tears continued to rain down my face as Kamden wrapped his arms around me. Clutching the back of his shirt in my hands, I trembled against him as I sobbed uncontrollably into his chest.

Kamden ran his hand through my hair as he attempted to console me. "Shh, I'm right here, *sorella.* I'm not going anywhere—you're safe with me."

I don't know how long I cried for, but Kamden never complained. Continuing to hold me, he murmured words of comfort, which helped pull me back from the abyss that always attempted to swallow me whole when I thought about Kaleb.

Pulling away, I wiped my swollen eyes with my palms. I looked up at Kam, who smiled softly at me, his face full of understanding. *Thank God for him.* I weakly smiled back, still fighting against the waves of emotion threatening to drown me. Even after eight years, Kaleb still managed to affect me so intensely. I hated it—hated him.

"Are you hungry? Do you want me to make you something to eat?" Kamden asked, his tone tender and loving. *The perfect big brother.*

Wrapping my arms around my legs, I wiped my nose against my pajama bottoms. I probably looked like a horrific mess with puffy eyes and red, splotchy skin. "I don't think I could stomach anything right now. The thought of him always makes me sick."

"Well, let me know when you're hungry. I'll make you something,"

Kamden offered as he rose up off my bed, making his way towards my door

"Don't you have to go to work?" I inquired curiously, the space between my eyebrows bunching together in confusion.

"I called in, too. I wanted to make sure you were okay for the rest of the day."

"Kam, you didn't have to do that. I'm fine," I lied. I was far from fine, but I didn't want to tell him that. He'd only worry more.

His lips curved up as he leaned against the doorframe. "I don't mind. Let me know if you need anything."

As he turned to walk out, I stopped him, "Kam, wait."

He stuck his head back through the doorway. "Yes?"

"Thank you."

Giving me a genuine smile, he responded, "Anytime, *sorella.*"

Smiling, I watched as he pulled the door behind him, leaving it open just a crack. I couldn't stop the warm feeling that filled me whenever he would use that term of endearment. Since I could remember, he'd called me *sorella,* which meant sister in Italian. Both sides of our family had some ancestry in Italy, and we had learned some words from our grandparents. Kamden was four years older than me, and had always been protective over me. He'd been even more so after the *incident*—especially since he almost didn't make it in time.

Laying back in bed, the warmth from Kamden's words began to fade away as memories of Kaleb came rushing back. Reminiscing about my childhood almost always reminded me of him because he was so interwoven with my past.

Curling up under the sheets, I attempted to dispel the thoughts of *him.* Clenching my eyes shut, I tried to focus on something else, but it was almost impossible since his face was so familiar to me—I'd never be able to forget it, no matter how desperately I wanted to.

Bolting out of bed, I headed to Kamden's room. He was sitting at his desk with his laptop open, staring intently at the screen. Turning in his chair, he directed his attention to me, "Everything okay? Do you need something?"

Gnawing at my bottom lip, I nodded. "Can I lay with you?" I hated asking him to do that, hated being such a burden to him, but having him near me was the only way I would fall asleep after hearing about Kaleb.

"Of course, Ky. Anything you need."

I silently walked over to his bed as he made his way to join me. Lifting the comforter, he slid onto the mattress and scooted back to allow me to slide in next to him before covering us with the blanket. Surprisingly, it didn't take long for sleep to find me in the warm security of Kamden's embrace.

Chapter Two

Ryker

Carefully untangling myself from the naked woman clinging to me, I eased out from under the sheets and got out of her bed. I picked up my clothes from the floor, and slipped them on soundlessly before heading to the door.

Sneaking out, I softly closed the front door, so I wouldn't wake up the woman… *Abby, I think.*

Whatever, her name didn't matter, but I doubted she'd care whether I remembered or not based on the night we'd had.

A slight pang of guilt threatened to surface as I trotted down the stairs from just leaving like that. I shook my head, reminding myself that all women were the same—they couldn't be trusted. I learned that from experience, and I'd be damned if I let myself be manipulated again.

Hopping into my Chevy Z71 truck parked in her apartment complex lot, I checked the time: 3:26 A.M.

Thank God, I don't have to wake up early.

My first class at the gym tomorrow wasn't until two, so I could sleep in. I had some fitness regimens and nutrition plans to work on before then, but I could squeeze them in when I woke up or in between classes if I needed to.

Once I arrived back at my apartment, I undressed and went to bed. My muscles were loose, my body relaxed from my release as I lay on my mattress. The woman from earlier was almost completely forgotten as I drifted off to sleep.

The gym was abnormally packed for a Thursday afternoon when I walked through the doors to start my shift. Our peak times were usually the evenings and weekends, so I was surprised to see so many people. Most of the machines were occupied by a mix of men and women, however, the majority of people were male muscle heads like me. Hardly any weights sat in their spots on the racks that lined the wall, and the clang of all the equipment echoed throughout the building. I also had many new faces in my Intermediate Kickboxing class, including some hot women.

I had to remind myself not to get involved with clients. Hooking up with them was bad for business, especially since I was one of the lead trainers. But it was difficult not to get sucked in by them, given some of the fine specimens that were at the gym regularly.

After my class ended, I went to my office to finish a fitness plan for one of my clients. I had finished most when I woke up that morning, and I just needed to put the final few touches on this last one. The man was an overweight lawyer who was trying to impress his paralegal mistress by losing weight and toning up. *Yeah, right.* The guy got short of breath every time he walked up the stairs to the upper level of the gym. He would need many sessions before he even came close to his goal, which was for him to lose fifty pounds in six months. If he followed the strict diet and exercise plan that I'd set, it could be possible, but it would take a level of commitment that I didn't think he possessed. Most people lacked the drive to stick with a fitness regimen long enough to see results.

Once my client, Harold Banks, arrived, fifteen minutes late, we

began the session with stretches to warm up his underused muscles. We briefly talked about one of his newest cases, a woman who had been in a car accident involving a drunk driver, as we stretched. After that, I took him to walk on the treadmill. He had already broken out into a slight sweat from the stretching and stairs, so I set his treadmill on low to start. I chose a medium pace for my machine, wanting to motivate but not discourage my client.

During our run, I noticed an unfamiliar face out of the corner of my eye. A woman, who looked to be my age, maybe twenty-five or twenty-six, hopped on a treadmill two machines away from mine. She seemed to be tuned out to the world around her, not seeking any attention like many of the other women here as her head bopped lightly to whatever was playing in her earbuds. Something about her immediately intrigued me; I couldn't put my finger on what it was, but I wanted to figure it out. I had to stop myself from leaving Mr. Banks to go talk to her.

Her dark hair was pulled up in a high ponytail that swished back and forth as she briskly jogged. Even from this angle, I could see that she had gorgeous eyes, the color similar to that of bright, Caribbean waters.

Images of her beneath me, eyes closed, lips parted as she moaned my name while I filled her with my cock ran through my head. I wanted to run my hands all over her, feel the soft skin of her tits, ass, and thighs under my rough, tattooed hands.

After glancing at me out of the corner of her eye several times, the woman stumbled, gripping the handrails to keep herself from falling and being thrown off the machine.

Jumping off my treadmill, I rushed to her side to help her. Grasping her by the waist, I pulled her up and against me as I turned off the power. Her chest rose and fell rapidly against mine as she struggled to breathe, her hands clutching my shoulders for support. *She feels good in my arms; natural.*

"Are you okay?" The concern in my voice surprised me. *Why did I care?*

Abruptly, she pulled away from me, like she had been stung by my touch. Her face reddened, probably from a combination of embarrassment and adrenaline. Keeping her eyes averted from mine, she meekly replied, "Thank you. I think I'm okay."

Sticking my hand out towards her, I introduced myself, "Ryker Campbell."

Her eyes flitted back and forth from my face to my hand before she timidly placed her hand in mine, peeking up at me through thick eyelashes. Her dazzling eyes mesmerized me as they locked on mine. She gently squeezed my hand as I caressed hers with my thumb. "Kaiya Marlow."

Her skin is as soft as I thought it would be. I wonder if she's that soft everywhere.

"That's a unique name. I've never heard it before. I like it."

Her full lips turned up into a small, shy smile. "Thank you."

We stood there staring at each other for a few seconds, as if in a trance, before I realized we were still holding hands. Kaiya must have noticed too because she pulled her hand from mine as her gaze darted around nervously, her skin flushing deeper as her smile widened. *She's beautiful.*

Heavy breathing from behind me redirected my attention to my struggling client. Sweat trailed from his receding hairline down his reddened face before dripping off his chin. Turning back to Kaiya, I stated, "I have to get back to my client. Are you sure that you're okay?"

"Yes. Sorry for embarrassing myself and interrupting your workout."

Chuckling, I responded, "Really, it was my pleasure. Nice meeting you, Kaiya."

Her voice cracked, catching in her throat as she replied, "You too."

Even though I didn't want to, I reluctantly turned around and went back to Mr. Banks. "Ready for weights, Mr. Banks?"

He nodded enthusiastically as his labored breaths continued. Laughing inwardly, I slowed his treadmill to a stop. He clutched the rails as he caught his breath, then stumbled off and trailed behind me towards the weight room.

As we walked, I looked over my shoulder, my gaze traveling back to Kaiya. She was still standing on the treadmill, unmoving as her eyes met mine, then instantly darted forward again. I smirked as her eyes flitted back and forth several more times before she secured her stare in front of her.

Glad to see I'm not the only one affected.

After Mr. Banks' session ended, I briskly walked back to the cardio room to see if Kaiya was still on the treadmill. Slowing my pace as I neared, I tried to act cool and unaffected as I entered the space. Unfortunately, she wasn't there, and I couldn't stop the disappointment that filled me, my shoulders sagging slightly and my mouth turning down into a frown.

What the fuck is wrong with me ? She's just some girl. They're a dime a dozen.

Shaking off the unexplainable feelings, I focused back on work, turning around and leaving the room without a backwards glance. I didn't need to be distracted by some chick, especially when there were plenty of others that could take her place. I knew I'd be able to find one at the bar later.

My next class was in thirty minutes, so I went to my office to work on some more fitness plans. On my way back, I caught sight of Kaiya talking with one of the regulars at the gym, Kamden.

I'd never seen her with him before, but this was the first time that I noticed her at the gym. They seemed very comfortable with one another, which caused a spark of jealousy to flare within me. *Of course she has a boyfriend. Look at her.*

Tugging on her ponytail, Kamden laughed with Kaiya. Her smile lit up the room, and I couldn't help but wish I'd caused it.*Stop thinking like that!* I veered the other way before I did something stupid I'd regret, like starting a fight in my workplace over some girl I barely knew. *Get a hold of yourself.*

I exhaled a sigh of relief once I entered my office. I set my attention on my fitness plans, class schedules, and workout routines. I actually needed to figure out some new exercises for my self-defense class tonight.

As I attempted to drive away my thoughts of Kaiya, a knock sounded at my door. Turning around, I faced Kamden and the woman that was currently occupying my mind. *Great.*

I plastered my fake, customer service smile on as I greeted them, "Hey, Kamden. How can I help you and your… friend?"

"This is my sister, Kaiya. Kaiya, this is Ryker. He's a personal trainer here at the gym."

Sister? A genuine smile spread across my face. *She's only his sister.* I noticed the slight resemblance between them now, but Kamden's eyes weren't the same color as Kaiya's.

"We've met already," Kaiya said as she tried to hide a smile.

Kamden looked back and forth between us, "When?" His tone was full of confusion, along with some apprehension.

"I slipped on the treadmill, and Ryker was there to rescue me," Kaiya answered as her eyes met mine. The corner of my mouth curved up as her cheeks flushed with color again. *I'd like to make that whole body flush. Over and over again.*

Clearing his throat, Kamden broke whatever haze Kaiya had put me in. He narrowed his eyes, glaring at me as he gruffly said, "I just added Kaiya to my membership. I wanted her to meet some of the staff since she'll be working out here now."

"Great. Please let me know if you need anything," I replied, excited that I would be seeing more of the beautiful woman in front of me. I wondered how long it would take to get her in my bed.

"I will. Thank you, Ryker," Kaiya replied with a shy smile, causing my stomach to knot at the sight.

What the fuck? Snap out of it, man!

"We better get going. See you around," Kamden said as he led Kaiya out. Turning to look over her shoulder, she gave me another coy smile as she walked out the door.

I was unable to fight the grin that spread because of hers. *I'm so fucked.*

Chapter Three

Kaiya

Looking out of the window at the passing traffic, I bit my lower lip to contain the smile on my face. Butterflies performed elaborate, acrobatic routines in my stomach throughout the whole ride home after my encounter with Ryker. No matter how hard I had tried, I couldn't push him from my thoughts. My mind had been preoccupied with the muscular, tattooed trainer ever since I laid eyes on him on the treadmill.

"You're in a good mood," Kamden observed, glancing at me out of the corner of his eye as he drove.

I shrugged my shoulders. "It was good to relax and get out of the apartment for a little bit."

"Well, I'm glad you enjoyed it. Did you like it better than your other gym?"

"Yeah, there's more equipment and space. And I like having someone to go with—makes me feel safe." I replied nonchalantly as I turned my attention to him.

"Good. Aren't you glad I made you call in sick today?" he asked with a smile of satisfaction

Chuckling softly, I punched his arm lightly as I responded, "Yes. Thank you. I needed to relieve some stress."

"Anytime. Let me know when you want to go back."

"How 'bout Saturday?" I asked, trying to hide my excitement. I told myself that my enthusiasm wasn't because of a certain sexy-as-sin trainer, but the knots in my stomach expressed otherwise.

What the hell is going on with me? I never get like this.

When he "rescued" me from careening off the treadmill and injuring myself, I was shocked that his touch didn't make me feel the normal panic I get whenever I come into contact with someone. I actually liked his touch. His strength made me feel safe, and I knew he wouldn't let me fall.

Once we arrived at our apartment, I headed straight for the bathroom. Eager to wash the sticky sweat off my skin, I wasted no time in undressing and turning on the shower. The warm water helped wash away some of the imaginary filth that still clung to me from the news about Kaleb's release earlier in the day, allowing me to relax a little.

I was thankful that Kamden dragged me out of bed to go to the gym. Working out cleared my head, something that I desperately needed in my life. Typically, I worked out at a smaller gym, but Kamden insisted I start going to his after finding out about Kaleb. Even though he'd never admit it, I knew he feared what could happen if Kaleb really did get released.

A shudder ran through me as my thoughts veered back to *him*. Squeezing my eyes shut, I immediately blanked my mind before replacing the horrid images with the first thing that came to my head—Ryker.

My eyes snapped open as confusion set in. *Why did he pop into my mind?* I tried to shake him from my thoughts, but his dark, messy hair, inked muscles, and deep, brown eyes were hard to ignore.

There was no way I could get involved with him, even if it was only a hook-up. I didn't need to get him tangled up in my web of issues. Guys that looked like him didn't fall for average-looking girls like me, anyway. They went after blonde bimbos with fake tans and boobs. At least that's what I told myself.

Sighing, I stepped out of the shower after giving my hair one last rinse. I plodded to my bedroom, avoiding the mirror once again. *Definitely can't look at myself for a while after this morning.*

I quickly dressed before heading to the office to get some more work done before tomorrow. I was the Project Coordinator for a huge marketing and public relations firm in Boston. I handled client invoices, contractor payments, ordered supplies, managed inventory, and created presentations, spreadsheets, and documents for meetings.

Kamden and I lived in the Riverside area of Cambridge, a small town about five miles outside of Boston. After I had graduated from college, we moved out here away from our mother, who lived in Bridgewater, MA.

There was no way I could stay there—not after everything that had happened while in that house.

Don't think about it, Kaiya. Think about something else.

Ryker's face appeared again, but I didn't try to shake his image away this time. Instead, I focused on his gorgeous features, especially his strong jaw line, golden skin, and full lips. Everything about him screamed man, and warmth began to simmer in between my thighs as I thought of him.

Damn, I need to get laid. I'm getting turned on by just thinking about a guy. A ridiculously hot guy, but still.

Grabbing my phone off the bed, I scrolled through my texts until I found the conversation I was searching for. I quickly typed my message before sending the impulsive query.

Me: U busy tonight?

Not surprisingly, I received a response within a few minutes.

Bryce: I think I can fit you in :) same time same place?

I hesitated for a few seconds before typing my reply.

Me: sounds good see you then

Bryce: :)

Bryce was a friend I'd met in college. Despite my standoffish demeanor, Bryce had continued his attempts to break through my walls and befriend me. Eventually, I had given in, unable to resist his good-natured personality and humor. Not to mention, he was extremely attractive—his hazel eyes were set upon a tan face that was framed by tousled, honeyed locks.

I'd never gone into detail with Bryce about my past, and thankfully, he'd never pressed the issue of my "issues." It had made our arrangement so much easier, and had allowed my need for control to flourish. He had always gone along with everything that I'd wanted, never questioning my stipulations when it had come to sex.

Those rules were absolutely necessary for me to have sex with someone, and most guys wouldn't put up with all of my OCD demands. I had been pretty promiscuous in high school, but after the *incident,* I'd changed. Everything had changed.

I'd spun into a downward spiral, sinking into a depression that encased me, shielding me from the ugliness of the world. Kamden had barely left my side, never relenting as he attempted to coax me out of the hole of despair I had buried myself in.

When I'd emerged, I was irrevocably altered, and I knew I would never be the same again. I had been emotionally scarred beyond repair, left a fractured shell of who I once was—all because of *him.*

Kamden had been the only light in the darkness that constantly enveloped me following what had happened. He and my best friend, Nori, had never let me give up, never let me sink too far back into the chasm deep in my soul. Even now, they still helped keep me grounded, helped keep me tethered to sanity.

Thinking about Nori reminded me that it had been a few days since we'd last spoken. Given the events of the day, I decided to text her to fill her in:

Me: Bad day today

Nori insisted that I let her know when I had rough days, being the mother hen that she was. She had been that way since we'd become friends in middle school, and I loved her for it, even if it was annoying at times.

My phone chimed with Nori's response:

Nori: I'm sorry :(want to talk about it

Me: Not ready yet

Nori: Tomorrow night? Girls night?

Me: Maybe

Nori: :)

Even though my reply was noncommittal, we both knew I'd be at her house tomorrow night, ready for a night of dinner and dancing. Dancing was another thing that helped clear my mind. The sound of the music and movement of my body allowed me to drown out everything else as I became one with the beat.

I headed down the hallway to my office to finish some of the spreadsheets I was working on before ordering take-out for Kamden and myself.

When we finished eating, I informed him of my plans. "I'm meeting Bryce at the bar."

I received his typical disapproving look as he responded in a parental tone, "Be careful."

Giving what I hoped was a reassuring smile, I said, "Always."

I'd never explained the details of the arrangement Bryce and I had, but Kamden knew; big brothers always knew stuff like that, no matter how old you were.

When I arrived at the bar Bryce and I typically met up at, I was surprised that he wasn't there yet. He was normally early.

I took a seat at the bar as the bartender walked over to me. "Hey, Ky. The usual?"

"Please." I looked around nervously before directing my attention to my phone, checking if Bryce had sent a message that he was running late, but there was none. *I wonder where he is.*

"And for you?" the bartender asked, peering around me at another customer.

"Jack and Coke," a deep, luscious voice said from behind me.

I stiffened before turning around and coming face to face with

Ryker. He unabashedly appraised me, causing heat to simultaneously flood my cheeks and the juncture of my thighs. "Uh, hi," I squeaked nervously. *Fuck, just kill me now.*

Ryker chuckled, obviously amused by my awkwardness. As he laughed, I caught a glimpse of something gleaming in his mouth.

Is that a tongue ring? Oh, God, it is. So fucking hot.

"Can I buy you a drink?" he asked as he moved closer to me, almost pressing his firm body against mine. His arms caged me between him and the bar, causing me to inhale deeply from the sudden proximity. His scent was amazing, a combination of man and clean. I had to stop myself from begging him to touch me.

"Actually, I, um, I'm meeting someone here," I stammered.

His eyes imperceptibly narrowed; I wouldn't have even noticed if I hadn't been so fixated on his face.

Is he jealous? No way.

"Everything okay, Ky?" the familiar sound of Bryce's voice interrupted.

Ryker's eyes stayed locked on mine, even though my "date" had obviously arrived. His arms remained in place, even when I broke eye contact to look at Bryce.

"Yeah, I'm fine. Ryker's a trainer at the new gym I'm working out at now." I replied, attempting to keep my voice steady, even though Ryker's closeness unnerved me.

Bryce stepped towards to us, keeping his gaze on Ryker as he approached. He warily stuck his hand out in greeting, "Bryce. I'm Kaiya's boyfriend."

What?

"No, you're not!" I impulsively defended. *Shit.* I wanted to slap my hand over my mouth because of my outburst.

Ryker's eyes met mine again as his lips curved up in a sexy smirk. Pulling his arms away, he moved back, taking most of his delicious scent with him. Some of it lingered for a few seconds before fading away I almost audibly sighed from the loss, but stopped before I made a bigger fool of myself.

Get a hold of yourself, Kaiya!

"Maybe I'll catch you at the gym," Ryker said coolly as he grabbed his drink off the bar. Looking at the bartender, he continued, "Put her drink on my tab."

Then, he walked away. *What just happened?* I turned around, not wanting to be caught ogling his retreating form. Grabbing my Cranberry Vodka, I quickly downed it as Bryce stared at me.

"What?" I asked defensively.

"Nothing," he replied with a knowing smile. He turned toward the bartender, leaning on the bar as he ordered another drink for me and a beer for himself.

Rolling my eyes at him, I headed for a booth near the bar while Bryce waited for our drinks. A few minutes later, he slid into the seat next to me and handed me my drink.

"How've you been?" he asked.

"Pretty good," I replied distantly. That was always my answer, and Bryce knew not to pry. "How about you?"

"I've been swamped at work, but the money's good." Bryce was an investment banker, and earned an envious salary, but he was always stressed out. That stress translated surprisingly well in the bedroom, making our sex intensely passionate as he took his aggression out on me.

After several more rounds of drinks, I was more than ready to head back to Bryce's apartment. I had been torturing myself as I watched Ryker flirt with various women around the bar as they draped themselves all over him. He caught my gaze more than once, giving me his seductive grin every time and causing my stomach to tighten.

"You ready to go, baby?" Bryce whispered in my ear as he trailed his fingers over my thigh. We both had a nice buzz going, making us overly touchy and affectionate. His mouth trailed down the side of my neck, pressing kisses as his hands began to roam over my body.

"Yes," I nearly moaned as I tilted my head to give his lips better access to the sensitive skin of my neck.

Bryce disentangled himself from me before helping me out of the booth. As he led me to the exit, my eyes locked with Ryker's once again. His deep eyes were hardened, his smirk absent from his beautiful lips as he took me in. He paid no attention to the slutty blonde draping herself all over him as he watched me walk away. I couldn't fight the guilt and disappointment creeping into my stomach as we left.

I followed Bryce back to his condo. As soon as the front door shut, I was on him instantly. I tugged at his clothes, needing them off so I could feel his skin against mine. I needed to feel something other than the emotions plaguing me constantly, needed his touch to drown out everything else.

Pushing him down the familiar hallway to his bedroom, I freed his body from his shirt. Even his toned form had nothing on Ryker, whose immaculately chiseled muscles bordered on perfection.

Stop thinking about him!

As we burst through the bedroom door, I fumbled with the belt on his jeans before unbuttoning them as Bryce's lips claimed mine. Our hands urgently worked together to take the rest of each other's clothes off as we fell onto his bed.

Bryce rifled through his bedside nightstand until he pulled out a condom. He eagerly ripped open the wrapper before sheathing his hard length, pressing it against my entrance within seconds.

Ryker's face came into my mind when my eyes fluttered shut as Bryce slowly pushed inside me, groaning as he filled me.

God, I wish it were him inside me right now.

Thrusting at an almost perfect pace, Bryce knew exactly how to please me, knew exactly what I wanted. My eyes closed in pleasure as Bryce's hands threaded in my hair and tugged lightly, pulling my head back to expose my throat.

My lids snapped open as I roughly remarked, "Bryce."

Apologizing, he immediately let go, "Sorry, Ky. I forgot."

Not responding, I tried to focus on the sensations of Bryce stroking inside me. Increasing his pace, he continued to plunge in and out of my slick, hot sex. I could feel my climax approaching as his large cock pounded against my walls. *Almost there.*

I pushed against Bryce, notifying him that it was my turn to take over. I always controlled when I came, needed to have that power over my body. *No one will ever take that power from me again.*

Bryce rolled us until he was on his back and I was mounted on top of him. Beginning to rock against him, I closed my eyes as I pictured Ryker. A moan escaped me as I thought of his luscious mouth, visualizing his tongue ring tracing over every intimate area of my body.

I imagined his rough, tattooed hands caressing my skin as his cock filled me, thrusting inside me over and over, our bodies intimately tangled in hot, sweaty ecstasy.

It didn't take long for me to find release. Normally, it took a while for me to relax and let go of everything, but thinking about Ryker filled me with hot desire. My body trembled as Bryce gripped my hips and thrust upwards, groaning out seconds later as he came.

Once we caught our breath, I lifted myself off Bryce and began to gather my clothes.

Bryce watched me from the bed as he questioned, "Why don't you stay the night?"

I almost ignored the ridiculous question—he knew my rules. Then, I remembered we both had a lot to drink, and it might have slipped his mind.

"You know I can't."

"No, you just won't," he sighed angrily.

This time, I did ignore him. I didn't want to fight with him. What we had was the closest thing that I had to intimacy; I didn't want to ruin that. I cared for Bryce, even if I didn't know how to show it.

Once I finished getting dressed, I said, "I'll call you later, okay?"

"Yeah, okay," he replied sadly as he rose off the bed. Throwing on a pair of gym shorts, he led me to the front door before walking me outside to my car.

"Thank you for a great night." I politely remarked as I pressed a kiss to his cheek.

"No problem. Anything for you, Ky." His eyes were sad as they looked into mine, but he still gave me a smile.

Bryce shut the door for me after I got in my car, then headed inside his condo. As I drove home, thoughts of Ryker still dominated my mind, confusing the hell out of me.

Chapter Four

Ryker

Sitting on the edge of the latest conquest's bed, I ran my hand through my hair. I blew out a breath of frustration as I tried to rid my thoughts of Kaiya. I'd been picturing her while fucking the blonde bimbo that lay next to me.

Why can't I get her out of my head?

Remembering the confusing jealously I felt when I saw that prick with his lips on her neck and his hands all over her body, I angrily stood. I got dressed and quickly left the apartment, not caring if I woke up the girl in the process. I just wanted the night to end already.

Clenching the steering wheel as I drove home, I was still tense, unsatisfied even though I had come while fucking the blonde. I basically had just gone through the motions, too preoccupied to enjoy the other woman. My mind was wired with thoughts of Kaiya, wondering if she was fucking the guy that she left with. *Why do I care?*

Once I got home, I showered, needing to relax. I still didn't understand why she affected me the way she did—she was nothing special.

Yeah, keep telling yourself that.

As the water rained down on me, I thought of her full tits, curvy hips, and long legs. *Fuck, I want to be in between them so bad, filling her with my cock and making her cry out my name.*

Even after the shower, I still couldn't get her off my mind. I kept picturing my hands tangled in her long, brown hair while my mouth tasted those full lips. *Maybe I just need to fuck her so I can get her out of my thoughts.*

Falling into bed, I tossed and turned restlessly, unable to fall asleep. The covers tangled around me as I moved back and forth, constricting my body uncomfortably. Kicking them off, I finally settled and stared at the ceiling. It took what seemed like hours before I finally drifted off, and Kaiya still hadn't left my mind.

Work on a Friday always dragged on and on, especially with a hangover. After Kaiya had left the bar last night, I had gotten wasted with the blonde before we'd gone back to her apartment. I was now paying for it at work.

I'd known better than to get hammered when I had to work the next day, but the whole encounter with Kaiya had fucked with my thoughts. My draw to her perplexed me, and I wanted to know why I thought of her so often.

Forget about her, already.

That would be difficult if I was going to be seeing her at the gym. Kamden frequently worked out, and I assumed that Kaiya would be coming with him, based on her physique. I could tell that she exercised regularly.

Her body is almost flawless. That ass, those tits… fuck, stop it!

I attempted to focus on work, but it was almost impossible with my pounding head. I only had a few personal training sessions scheduled, but I had several group classes for the day, which were going to be hell to get through since I felt like shit.

Later that day, I received a text from one of my friends, Drew:

Drew: Club tonight you in?

Fuck, I had to work tomorrow, but I wanted to get my mind off Kaiya. Maybe the club would be better than the bar had been—lots of women, loud music, and plenty of distractions.

Me: Yeah what time bro?

Drew: My place @ 11

As I knew it would, the day took forever to end. When I'd finally made it to Drew's apartment, I had almost forgotten about Kaiya—almost. She had continued to linger in my mind, but after a few drinks and a woman beneath me, thoughts of her would be gone.

It was midnight when we entered the club. Drew, and two of our other friends, Dane and Logan, headed straight for the bar, and we ordered our first round of drinks.

"Are you stalking me?" a familiar voice giggled.

I turned towards the sound, unbelieving that I'd run into her two nights in a row.

Kaiya stood about five feet away from me. She had on a dark, denim skirt that barely grazed her thighs, and a black, one shoulder shirt that hugged her body like a second skin. Her flushed cheeks and flirtatious smile told me that she probably had a nice buzz going already.

Can I get a fucking break?

"Is this the guy you were talking about, Ky?" a pretty redhead slurred as she bumped into Kaiya, causing her to stumble into me.

Her hands gripped my biceps as mine instinctively grabbed her waist to steady her. Her tits grazed my chest as she struggled to maintain her balance, and I pulled her against me to keep her from falling. "Falling for me again? Do you do this often? Twice this has happened since I met you," I teased. *Damn, she smells good.*

Looking up at me with those entrancing eyes, she smiled shyly, her cheeks flushing more.

She pulled away as she replied, "We're both a little drunk. This is my friend, Nori. Nori, this is Ryker."

"He *is* the guy you were talking about," Nori squealed loudly.

"Nori!" Kaiya responded with a combination of annoyance and embarrassment as she smacked her friend on the arm. Turning back to face me she apologized, "Don't mind her—she's drunker than I thought."

I smirked as I crossed my arms over my chest, "So, I'm not the guy you were talking about?"

"No! Yes… I mean… no." she stammered, her face reddening more.

I chuckled, pleased that I affected her like she had been affecting me. "Where's your boyfriend?" I asked as I moved closer to her, uncrossing my arms.

"I told you he's not my boyfriend," she answered in a slightly exasperated tone as she rolled her eyes.

"He looked like your boyfriend last night."

"Well, he's not. But even if he was, it wouldn't be any of your business." She put one hand on her hip and jutted it out to the side.

"You're right. I'm sorry for prying," I apologized as I took another step toward her. "Can I buy you a drink to make it up to you?"

A smile fought its way onto her lips. "You bought me a drink last night."

I laughed, "I can't buy you another one?"

"I really shouldn't. One of us has to drive home, and Nori's pretty drunk already." she replied as she bit her bottom lip, drawing my attention to it. *Damn, I want to suck that in my mouth, taste her at least once.*

The guys chose that very moment to walk up. Drew interrupted, "Getting started without us?" He checked out Kaiya and Nori. "Who are your new friends?"

"Guys, this is Kaiya and Nori. Kaiya, Nori, these are my friends, Drew, Dane, and Logan."

"Nori. That's a unique name—I like it," Drew commented. *Did I sound that lame when I said it to Kaiya yesterday?*

Nori coyly smiled, giving Drew a flirtatious look. *Well, I guess it works.*

Drew continued, "Can I buy you a drink, Nori?"

Nori giggled in response, "Sure."

Drew sidled up next to Nori before waving down the bartender and ordering their drinks. Dane and Logan had ventured further down the bar, where they talked to two brunettes.

I turned my attention back to Kaiya. "So, can I buy you that drink?"

She looked conflicted, internally debating her options before smiling up at me. "Just one more—Cranberry Vodka, please."

Turning around, I waited for the attention of the bartender. Nori giggled as Drew led her away toward a couch in a dimly lit corner of the club.

Kaiya shook her head and laughed as she watched them. "Maybe I don't have to worry about giving her a ride home."

The bartender came over, and I ordered our drinks, "Cranberry Vodka and a Jack and Coke."

As we waited, I snuck a glance at Kaiya, unable to keep my eyes off her. She darted her gaze away when our eyes met before fidgeting nervously, twirling a strand of her long, brown hair around her finger. Her eyes found mine again, and I could practically feel the connection buzzing between us.

Once we got our drinks, I grabbed Kaiya's hand before leading her through the crowd of people to where Nori and Drew were tangled on the couch making out.

"Oh my God, Nori!" Kaiya laughed.

Either they didn't hear or didn't care, because they continued to devour each other as we sat on the opposite end of the couch.

"I can't believe her," Kaiya remarked before taking a sip of her drink.

"Looks like fun—maybe we should try it," I suggested as I cocked an eyebrow..

Kaiya playfully glared at me while still sipping her drink, which was already halfway empty. "I'm not that drunk."

Teasing her, I called out, "Waitress! I need more drinks over here!"

Laughing, she smacked me on the bicep, "Stop it. I already told you only one more drink—I need to drive home."

"You could come home with me," I seductively suggested.

Desire filled her eyes, but she resisted, looking away as she shifted in her seat. "In your dreams."

"They won't be dreams for long. I'll have you soon," I promised.

"Oh, really? Good luck with that," she replied sarcastically with a clipped laugh.

I placed my drink on the small table in front of us before leaning toward Kaiya and asking, "Is that a challenge?"

Flirtatiously smiling at me, she replied, "Maybe."

Inching closer to her, my leg brushed against hers as I draped my arm on the back of the couch behind her head. She stiffened, but didn't pull away.

I dipped my head next to hers as I gruffly whispered in her ear, "Challenge accepted."

Pulling away slowly, I trailed my lips along her jawline as my hand lifted to brush a strand of hair out of her face. Ever so slightly, she turned her head when I neared closer to her mouth, barely grazing my lips with hers.

The slight touch broke her resistance—she crushed her lips against mine as she pressed her body closer to me, even though we were already almost on top of each other. My hands brushed her bare thighs as I moved her to straddle my lap, draping her legs over mine. Slipping past her lips, my tongue sought permission to thread with hers, which she eagerly gave.

Her taste was borderline addictive. I couldn't get enough as I savored the hot sweetness of her mouth. Her hands roughly ran through my hair as we relentlessly consumed one another.

My hands gripped her ass, pulling her against my growing hard-on. She moaned before abruptly breaking the kiss, hopping off my lap like it had caught fire.

"I'm sorry, I can't," she gasped, her lips swollen and face flushed.

Before I could even reply, she turned and ran into the crowd.

Chapter Five

Kaiya

What the fuck are you thinking, Kaiya? I mentally scolded myself as I left the club. You can't get involved with him!

Replaying the events in my head, I wondered what the hell just happened.

Did that really just happen? Did he really just kiss me? He tasted so good, and that tongue ring—oh my God.

When I got in my car, I immediately locked the doors.. I doubted that Ryker would follow me, but it was almost one in the morning in downtown Boston, and a girl could never be too safe. I sent a text to Nori:

> Me: Sorry had to leave I'm in the car do you want me to wait for you?

Sighing, I leaned my forehead against the steering wheel, inhaling deeply and exhaling as I waited for her reply. About five minutes had passed before my phone dinged with her response:

> Nori: No I'm good r u ok?

> Me: Yeah

I knew I'd hear from her about it tomorrow, but I just wanted to go home and sleep. I wanted to forget about how foolish I had acted. *Damn alcohol.* I was definitely not looking forward to seeing Ryker at the gym tomorrow.

"Kaleb, please stop," I begged as tears ran down the sides of my face.

He didn't respond as he continued to run his hands all over my naked body, covering me with his own larger one. I knew he wouldn't stop. No matter how much I begged, he never did.

He began to remove his clothes, still keeping me pinned with his legs, causing me to sob harder.

"Please, Kaleb, no!"

His eyes already looked detached, like he was no longer there, no longer in control.

I started to squirm and fight beneath him. My fear reached a desperate peak, strangling the air from my lungs and knotting my insides from what I knew was about to happen.

His hand reared back before he swiftly brought it across my face with a biting slap. My cheek stung, but I didn't stop fighting. I couldn't stop, couldn't let things progress any further if I wanted to maintain some semblance of my sanity. I thrashed and kicked beneath him before he pulled out a knife.

I froze as he held it to my neck, daring me to keep fighting him. "Are you going to behave?" he snarled in anger.

I never understood what I'd done to make him so angry with me.

"Yes," I whimpered, afraid to move too much and trigger him.

"That's my girl," he said lovingly, showing a sliver of his normal self before shifting to the hard, evil person I had encountered so often. His personalities changed like the flip of a switch.

His brows furrowed, his muscles tensed, and his eyes went cold again as he hungrily eyed my naked flesh.

He kept the knife pressed against my throat as his free hand traced the curves of my breasts. I trembled from a combination of disgust and pleasure, my body betraying me as it gave in to the sensations from his soft touch.

My cries became louder as he removed the knife, biting down on the handle as he put it between his teeth, His hands trailed over my stomach and chest again before he reached for the hem of his faded, black tee. "Please, Kaleb, don't," I begged, hoping he would stop, even though I knew he wouldn't.

"You made me do this," he mumbled around the knife in his mouth. "By giving away what's mine."

Gripping the bottom of his shirt, he began to pull it upwards. When it came up to cover his face, I used the distraction to get away, pushing him off me before kicking and scrambling out from under him.

I almost made it to the door before he caught me and tackled me to the floor. I screamed as we wrestled on the carpet of my bedroom, obtaining cuts and nicks from the knife as I fought him off.

Overpowering me, he pressed the knife against my throat. "Now I have to punish you. I don't like to punish you, but you leave me no choice."

His eyes hardened as he pushed the knife deeper into my throat. Pain didn't register from the adrenaline running through me, numbing my body as my heart pounded wildly. I only felt the trickle of blood warming my neck, the only indication that I had an injury.

"No, Kaleb, please stop. I'm sorry!" I screeched desperately, my body rigid with fear and panic.

Just then, the door flew open, and Kamden charged in. His face was masked in rage as he ripped Kaleb off of me. The knife flew out of his grasp, clanging as it fell to the hardwood floor. Both men dove for the knife, struggling for it as they rolled repeatedly with their hands clasped tightly around the weapon.

Blood trailed down my neck as I sobbed at the top of my lungs. My screams ripped through my injured throat as I curled into myself, clenching my eyes shut as I prayed for everything to be over.

I sprang up in bed, gasping for air. Sweat dripped from my skin as I continued the screams from my nightmare.

Kamden rushed in seconds later, enveloping me in his arms on my bed. "It's okay, Ky—it was just a dream. He's not here. You're safe," he cooed, trying to comfort me.

Chest heaving, I drew in ragged breaths as tears rained down my face. Instinctively, I reached for my neck and checked to make sure there wasn't an open wound. I felt the familiar raised scar but nothing else—no blood, no gash.

My eyes rose up to meet Kamden's, pausing on the long scar across his chest before our gazes locked.

"I'm sorry. I'm okay, you can go back to bed," I said, barely above a whisper.

"Are you sure? I can stay if you want," he offered, wiping the tears from my face.

Even though I didn't want to be selfish, I knew I'd never fall back asleep without him. "Please," I murmured.

Kamden softly smiled as he slipped under my comforter. Turning on my side, I propped my hand under my pillow as Kamden draped his arm over me.

Even with his familiar embrace and warm breath on the back of my neck, I couldn't fall asleep. Choking back a sob from the images that I couldn't get out of my head, my body involuntarily shook with fear.

Kamden turned me over so that I faced him before he rubbed my back softly, slowly lulling me to sleep in the safety of his arms.

Kamden had let me sleep late before finally waking me up to get ready to go to the gym. My mind was conflicted over the idea, both loving and hating the fact that I was going to see Ryker.

Once we walked into the gym, I thought I was going to throw up from the nerves that had built up in anticipation of seeing him.

What am I going to say to him? Will he even talk to me again?

I didn't see Ryker as we walked into the cardio room, and relief and disappointment simultaneously flooded me. I hopped on an elliptical, not wanting to have another freak accident like last time, as Kamden headed to a treadmill across from me.

I put my earbuds in before starting up on the machine, letting the music block out the world around me. I didn't even notice Kamden come up next to my machine until he tapped my arm.

I reflexively startled, my body jerking before I focused on him. Pulling my left earbud out, I asked, "What's up?"

"I just wanted to tell you that I'm going to the weight room."

"Oh, okay. I'll be here."

As he left, I saw him stop to talk to Ryker. *Shit.*

Ryker glanced in my direction, and I immediately darted my eyes away.

My eyes kept finding him as he continued to talk to my brother. After they finished, he headed towards me, no doubt wanting an explanation for last night. The knots in my stomach intensified the closer he came, and I had to stop myself from running away.

You'd definitely look like a crazy person then.

I pulled out my earbuds when he reached me, preparing for the inevitable. "Hey," I lamely greeted.

"Hey, yourself. What happened last night?"

Sighing, I averted my eyes from his as I replied, "I'm really sorry about last night. It was a mistake, and I—"

"A mistake?" he interrupted as he crossed his arms over his broad chest, obviously offended.

I swallowed the huge lump that had grown in my throat before I answered, "It's just that I can't get involved with you—with anyone." *Even though I want to.*

"Why not? If you're worried about commitment, don't. I'm not the commitment type," he replied flippantly.

"Oh, so, you just want a one night stand?" I asked incredulously. When he cocked his eyebrow up with a smirk, I continued, "No, thanks." Rolling my eyes, I started to put my earbuds back in so I could ignore him. *Did he really think I was that easy?*

"We'll see about that," he smugly responded before playing with his tongue ring. My eyes immediately went to his mouth. *Fuck me.* "Have a good workout."

Baffled, I watched him stride away, wondering what the fuck just happened—again. Placing my headphones back in, I resumed my exercise as I tried to forget about Ryker. *Yeah, good luck with that.*

Thoughts of having sex with him filled my head, and I seriously contemplated having a one night stand with him. *Maybe that would get him off my mind.* My mind warred as it debated the pros and cons, and unfortunately, the cons outweighed the pros. I'd have to tell him all of my rules before we even got naked, and he probably wouldn't want to have sex with me after that since most guys didn't want to fuck with rules involved. I was lucky that Bryce was so understanding, otherwise I'd be stuck with a vibrator to get off.

But the thought of Ryker's body pressed against mine, of feeling him inside me, of tasting and touching every inch of his skin, was almost enough to change my mind—*almost.* I had to stay in control, not be ruled by my emotions; I couldn't let them overtake me. Opening myself up to Ryker, even just to have sex, could have irreparable consequences that I was incapable of dealing with.

Once I finished on the elliptical, I went in search of Kamden. As I passed some of the exercise rooms, I saw a flyer that read:

Kickboxing/Self-defense classes
Sundays, Tuesdays and Thursdays at 7:00 P.M.
Sign up at the front desk

Maybe I should look into that, especially since Kaleb might get released.

I shook my head, immediately attempting to dispel my thoughts and block out my emotions before they started to take over. I couldn't afford a public breakdown, especially in front of Ryker. *I'd never be able to come here again.*

Kamden was doing squats when I walked in, but he stopped when he saw me.

"You finished?" he asked, wiping the perspiration from his brow with a towel. He handed it to me when he was done.

"Yeah, but I can wait for you if you're not ready." I took the towel from his hand, which was soaked with his sweat. *Gross.*

"I only have a few more reps."

"Okay, that's fine. I'm going to get some water."

As I waited, my eyes scanned the room anxiously. I tapped my foot nervously on the floor as I looked around. I told myself that I wasn't looking for Ryker, but that was a lie. I wanted to see him one more time before we left, but I didn't. *It's probably better this way—the less of him, the better. Now if only I could get him off of my mind.*

Once we got home, Kamden's phone rang. "It's Mom," he informed.

"I'm not here," I said, dropping my purse on the table by the door and heading toward the bathroom to shower.

Rolling his eyes, he answered the phone, "Hey, Mom. No, Kaiya's not here." He paused for a few seconds before angrily snarling, "What?"

The tone in his voice stopped me dead in my tracks. *Oh no. What now? He couldn't have gotten out that fast, could he?*

My heart beat furiously beneath my chest, fear clenched my lungs, making it almost impossible for me to breathe as a panic attack began to take hold. *Breathe, Kaiya. In, out, in, out. Don't have another breakdown.*

"No, Mom, it's not great! He should be left to rot in there forever for what he did to Kaiya!" he yelled before abruptly hanging up his phone.

It began ringing a few seconds later, but Kamden rejected the call. He smiled sympathetically as his anger began to recede, and his eyes softened when they met mine.

Pushing my emotions down, locking them away inside me, I numbed myself, preparing for the worst.

"Just tell me," I impatiently insisted.

Kamden sighed before speaking, "Kaleb's release was approved, pending a six month observation period."

Fear tried to take hold of me again, clawing at my walls, but I forced it down. I needed to be stronger if I was going to survive this whole ordeal. "Can we stop it?"

"I'm going to try. I want to go up there as soon as possible, and I think it would be best if you came with me."

"Kamden, I can't." Shaking my head, I wrapped my arms around myself for comfort. "I can't be that close to him."

"You know that I wouldn't ask you unless I thought it was absolutely necessary. I think that if you remind them what happened, tell them how much what he did has affected you, I doubt they'll give the final approval on his release."

I sighed. "I'll think about it. I can't guarantee anything though. I can barely keep it together with him miles away."

"You're stronger than you think, Ky." He placed a hand on my shoulder. "I know you can do it," he voiced confidently as he gave me an assuring smile.

Uncomfortable focusing on myself, especially when it involved Kaleb, I changed the subject, "I need to shower. I'm all sweaty."

Turning around, I didn't give Kamden a chance to make me talk about the issue any further. I heard the phone ringing again when I entered my bathroom.

Stripping my clothes, I avoided the mirror as I stepped into the shower. I kept my body turned away from it the entire time, letting the water rain over my skin, hoping it would wash away the emotions trying to break through.

After I stepped out of the shower, I made the mistake of looking in the mirror. Dangerously drawn like a moth to a flame, I inched closer to my reflection, knowing the aftermath would be disastrous. Even though it was my face, all I could see was *him*staring back at me—his eyes, his nose, his mouth, his… everything.

Shuddering, I gripped the counter, trying to pull away, to disentangle myself from the trap I'd fallen in, but the damage was already done. My heart thumped wildly in my chest as I struggled to breathe. My lungs familiarly tightened in anxiety. I couldn't think, couldn't talk myself down, when all I could see was him.

Taunting me, he smirked menacingly as he vowed, "I'm coming for you, Kaiya. This time, I will have you."

"No. No, no, no!" I shrieked in horrified panic. Fear heated my skin, strangled my veins, and rooted itself deep within me as Kaleb responded with intermittent yeses and maniacal laughter.

Impulsively, I grabbed my blow dryer before repeatedly bashing it against the mirror, causing it to splinter and crack. I angrily screamed as I continued, making my throat burn until it became raw. Small pieces of glass began to shoot outward from my blows as I spiraled out of control, hammering him with all my force. Stinging pain registered on my face, but I was too beyond gone to care.

"Kaiya, stop! Stop!" I heard a voice yell before large, strong hands gripped my arms. The blow dryer clanged to the floor as I fought against whoever was holding me, throwing myself back into a bulky mass before slamming us into the wall.

Squirming against the body, I struggled as I tried to kick, punch, and scratch whoever was holding me.

"Kaiya, it's me! It's Kamden. Stop!" he yelled urgently.

Kamden?

Chest heaving with ragged breaths, I looked back at the fractured mirror, seeing Kamden's distorted reflection holding me. I began to relax against him once I realized I was safe—that it wasn't *him.*

Kamden eased his hold on me before gently rubbing my arms.

Slowly turning around to face him, I rasped, "I'm so sorry, Kam."

"Don't apologize. You have nothing to be sorry for. I threw too much at you at one time." Looking toward the mirror, he continued, "I'll have to get that replaced."

"Maybe it's better if you don't," I suggested. When he gave me an inquisitive look, I explained, "I try to avoid looking at it all the time anyway."

He nodded before cautiously lifting his hands up to my face. He turned it side to side, examining my skin. "Let's get you cleaned up—you've got some cuts."

As he walked to the sink, I raised my hand to my face, tenderly touching the areas that were now starting to burn with pain. Blood dotted my fingers when I pulled away, and I couldn't believe how fast I had lost control.

Kamden came back before leading me to the toilet. He sat me

down before kneeling in front of me with cotton balls, peroxide, and antibiotic ointment.

"This is going to sting," he warned.

I flinched slightly as he gently cleaned my wounds, and once again, I was awed by how amazing he was. *I don't deserve him, but God knows I need him.* I would've never survived everything without him.

When he was finished, I began to clean up the mess of bloody cotton balls and glass shards on the floor while Kamden went to grab the broom. As I looked at the fragments on the floor, I thought of how much they resembled me—shattered pieces of what they once were. I didn't want to be like that, didn't want to be a broken shell anymore. I wasn't going to keep letting Kaleb dominate my life—I was going to take control.

When Kamden came back, broom in hand, I stood and faced him. "I'll go."

"What?" His eyes scrunched in confusion before searching my face.

"I'll go with you to the hospital. I want to do everything I can to make sure he doesn't get released."

"Are you sure? After that episode, I don't thi—"

Interrupting, I replied, "I want to. I want to take control of my life. I don't want to be afraid to live anymore. And I want to take self-defense classes at the gym—I want to be prepared in case he does get released. I want to be able to fight back."

Smiling proudly, his huge grin lit up his stormy eyes. "Okay, *sorella.* I'll be with you every step of the way. Anything you need."

Returning his smile, pride swelled within me as I hugged him. *You can do this. You will do this.* And with that, I took the first step to becoming whole.

Chapter Six

Ryker

Shock didn't begin to express how I felt when Kaiya walked into my self-defense class on Sunday night. Class didn't start for another fifteen minutes, and she was the first one there. Her eyes reflected the same surprise that I felt as her body stiffened in uncertainty, like a deer right before it bolts away from danger.

"Hey," I greeted. "Welcome to Self-Defense."

"You're the instructor?" she asked in disbelief.

"I am," I grinned.

Mumbling something indiscernible, she set her gym bag down on the hardwood floor against the wall before making her way toward me. As she neared, I saw small cuts on her face, and I couldn't explain the anger that filled me at the thought of someone hurting her.

"What happened to your face?" I all but spat. *Calm down.*

Her eyes widened, my question taking her off guard. "Why do you care?" she retorted defensively.

Why does she have to be so stubborn? "Just tell me. It's suspicious that you want to start my self-defense class after getting those cuts on your face." *Yeah, that's the only reason I want to know.*

Her face relaxed as her features returned to normal. "Uh, my cat scratched me."

Her voice lacked confidence. I didn't believe her for a second, but I didn't want to press the matter. If I wanted to get closer to her, have any kind of chance with her, I needed to gain her trust. I couldn't push her away by interrogating her, even though I really wanted to know what happened.

"I think you need a new pet," I joked.

She gave me a small smile as she fidgeted nervously with her hands. But without missing a beat, she changed the subject, "I've never taken a class like this before. Can you tell me what to expect?"

"Well, we start off with warming up on the bags," I answered, gesturing to the standing punching bags along the walls of the room. "I demonstrate different combinations you can use, and you perform them on the bags. Having the foundation of knowing basic punches and kicks will help you in any situation because you can't predict what an attacker will do. I want to give you as many tools as possible to help you defend yourself, and kickboxing is a great platform for that.

"Then, we have an open request forum. I take requests from the class and show techniques on how to defend yourself in specific situations, which you will then practice with me or one of the other instructors."

Her eyes widened apprehensively, showing fear from my words. I had to stop myself from trying to comfort her. *Why do you care?*

"Everything okay? You look conflicted."

"Maybe this isn't for me—I don't like to be touched, especially by strangers."

Interesting; she didn't seem to mind me touching her the other night. Well, until the end. I wonder what the story is behind that. I shoved my concern for her away as I stated, "If you don't like to be touched, you need to know ways to prevent it from happening, to protect yourself from the people that don't care what you want."

Uncomfortably sighing, she asked, "Can you work with me? I don't think I'll be comfortable with anyone else." Her eyes widened, her cheeks flushing red as she stammered, "Only because I already know you. Not because I want you to touch me or anything."

I chuckled before replying, "Whatever works for you—I want you to be comfortable. If you're not comfortable, then you're less likely to come back."

She nodded before exhaling a heavy breath. "I'm really nervous."

"Don't be—we'll take it slow. I try to give specialized attention to all the students based on their strengths and weaknesses. I'll help you every step of the way."

A small smile graced her beautiful lips, causing my stomach to tighten.

"Thank you. I really appreciate it," she said softly.

"No problem—just doing my job. Go ahead and get stretched out before we get started." I turned to walk away, but stopped and asked, "Do you have gloves?"

"I didn't know I needed them. Can I still take the class without them?"

"Yeah, I have some. They're old and worn, but they'll work until you get some of your own," I said as I walked to the small closet in the corner of the room. Rifling through my storage of kickboxing supplies, I found some gloves that I thought would fit Kaiya's small hands.

When I exited, Kaiya was bent over, touching her right foot gracefully with her fingers as she stretched. Her ass was to me, and I couldn't help but imagine entering her from behind, sinking my dick inside her pussy as I pounded against that sweet ass.

Fuck, stop. Focus—you're about to teach a class.

I cleared my throat before I spoke, my voice slightly cracking, "Here are the gloves."

Straightening, she turned and took the gloves from me, barely brushing her fingers against my palm. "Thanks."

Giving her a slight nod, I turned away and walked back to the supply closet again, trying to distract myself from thoughts of Kaiya and sex.

Minutes later, the other students began to trickle in, along with the other instructors, Mark and David. They were there to give the students real life models to practice with, ensuring they became accustomed to what a typical man's body feels like when they attack since a man's weight and strength were huge factors in overpowering women. All the techniques I taught would be almost useless if they didn't have training utilizing them against a man.

After I had demonstrated the first combo, I walked over to Kaiya to see if she needed help while the others started. She attempted the maneuver, but her form was off. Way off. She'd probably never been in a fight before.

"I'm doing it wrong, aren't I?" she asked, blowing a strand of her hair off of her face in frustration.

I laughed lightly, "Not completely. You're doing a lot of things right, but your form is a little off. Let me show you again."

Repeating the combination again, I said the moves aloud for her to hear. "Jab, punch, palm strike, elbow, elbow, knee, front snap."

"What's the difference between a jab and punch?"

"Well, a jab is basically just a quick punch using your front hand. A punch is thrown from the back hand, and has more power than a jab," I demonstrated as I answered her.

"Okay, jab is front hand, punch is back hand," she said, copying my moves.

"You got it. Let's try the combo again."

As I showed her once more, I could see her mimicking me out of the corner of my eye.

"Remember to always keep your hands up to protect your face when you're not punching. One good hit to the head and it'd be over for you."

Bringing her fists up in front of her face, she asked, "Like this?"

"Yes. You also need to twist your body when you punch—it gives you more momentum, thus giving you more power. Try again."

Doing as I requested, she executed the combo, hitting the bag more forcefully.

"I do feel more power that way," she commented enthusiastically.

"With any method of self-defense, just a small adjustment usually can make a huge difference, whether it be positive or negative. Any mistake could result in injury, while perfect execution of a technique could save your life."

"I'll make sure to remember that. Thank you."

"No problem. Switch legs and keep going, alternating each time."

Nodding, she changed her stance to her left leg before starting again. Each time she completed the combo, her movements became more fluid, her hits delivering more power as they connected with the bag. I couldn't stop the smile that spread as I watched her. The determination was evident on her face as her eyebrows furrowed in concentration. Plus, the fact that she was getting all sweaty and flushed turned me on—a woman was so sexy when she worked out.

Once we finished several more combinations on the bags, we switched to freestyle techniques.

"Five Minute Freestyle! Give it all you got!" I announced.

Everyone knew what that meant, except Kaiya. As everyone started pummeling their bags, I walked over to her, surprised to see that she was already punching and kicking her own bag.

Her eyes locked with mine, causing her to miss landing her punch and stumble slightly. Her already flushed cheeks reddened more as she gave me an embarrassed smile. "I don't know what I'm doing."

"You're doing great. Just keep doing the moves you learned today however you want for the next five minutes. Don't stop, no matter how tired you are."

She turned her attention back to her bag before slowly repeating several of the combinations I had taught today. I couldn't wait to see her once she got more comfortable, once she let go and allowed that warrior to break through that I glimpsed every so often when she argued with me.

Once the five minutes were up, I gathered the group on one of the mats. "Awesome workout, everyone. Before we start the self-defense techniques, I want to introduce Kaiya. She just started working out here and is testing out our class. Please give her a warm welcome."

The other students greeted Kaiya, who blushed profusely from the attention while glaring at me playfully. She waved her hand to everyone as she shyly said hi.

Redirecting everyone's focus back to the class, I asked, "Anybody have an attack you'd like to practice defense against? Even if we've already learned it before."

One of the older women raised their hand. "Can we practice when a guy traps you on the ground? That still scares me, and I think we can never have enough practice with those escape techniques."

Murmurs of agreement flowed through the class, except Kaiya, who remained quiet and still. When our eyes locked, I could see the apprehension and anxiety in her strained face.

"Okay, everyone pair up with your usual partners," I said before making my way to Kaiya. "I need to catch you up on some basics before we start the escape techniques, okay?"

Nervously nodding, she replied, "Okay, sure."

"Before we start anything, there's one thing that I must stress. Always protect your face—do not get knocked out. Most attackers will immediately try to punch you and knock you out before anything else. If you're unconscious, they can do whatever they want to you—kidnap, rape, or murder you. Got it?"

She gulped before meekly replying, "Yes."

"Okay, the first move I'm going to show you is called the Shrimp. You mu-"

"The Shrimp?" she laughed, interrupting me.

"Yes, the Shrimp. Let me finish," I chastised playfully before continuing. "You must master this move before we can start any other techniques. Lie down."

Surprisingly, she did as I requested without argument. *That's a first.*

When she was flat on her back, I instructed, "Bend your knees. Good, now, when you're being attacked, you need to determine which direction you are going to try to escape from. If you want to go to the right, your right leg is going to remain planted to the floor, along with your left shoulder. If you want to go to the left, then it's the opposite—got it?"

"Yeah, I think so."

"Which way do you want to practice first?"

"Um, the right."

"Okay, keeping your right foot on the ground, I want you to push

your body back with it, twisting while picking your left foot off the ground. As you slide backwards, keep your left shoulder pressed to the ground while lifting your right shoulder up until it is directly above the left. Your body should form the shape of an L. We refer to this as shrimping out. I'll demonstrate first, then you're going to try."

I modeled the technique slowly several times, showing both directions before directing Kaiya to try. She executed the move very sluggishly at first, but after multiple attempts on each side, she finally was able to fluidly carry out the maneuver.

"Congratulations, you've mastered the Shrimp." I smiled, slightly teasing her.

Returning my smile, she asked, "What's next?"

"Now, I'm going to walk you through the steps to get away when an attacker traps you on the ground."

Lying down on the floor, I continued, "Get between my legs and press against me as close as you can."

"Wha… what?" she stammered, her cheeks flushing pink.

She's so sexy when she blushes.

"Kneel in between my legs." I paused, waiting for her to do as I said. "Now, scoot up and press your pelvis against me." *Fuck, it's so hard to be professional with her this close to me. All I want to do is rip her clothes off and fuck her.*

Giving me a skeptical look, she slowly inched her way towards me until we were barely touching. I sat up and gently grabbed her by the hips, pulling her flush against me. Her lower body was cradled by the inside of my thighs, and her knees were framing the outside of my hips. "Like this," I stated.

Her blush deepened as our eyes locked. Having her pressed against my dick caused it to start to harden.

"What now?" she asked, her voice cracking slightly. I didn't know if she was turned on or just responding to the sudden feel of me.

"Now, place your hands outside my shoulders. This is the most common form of attack against women, and it usually escalates from this position, so it's best to stop it as soon as possible. The first thing you want to do is brace your hands against your attacker's shoulders, keeping your arms straight, like this." I demonstrated. "This hinders their movement, and prevents them from coming down on your body. Notice how off balance you are?"

"Yeah, but you're like ten times stronger than me. How am I supposed to keep a man off me that's stronger and heavier than me?"

"You only need to keep them off you for a brief time. Once you have them in this position, use the Shrimp technique." I modeled, pushing into the formation and propping my elevated foot against her hip. "Let me show you again."

I demonstrated the move again before moving on to the next step. "Now, keep your foot on their hip as you slide your hands down to your attacker's elbows, like this," I said as I grabbed her elbows. "Next, twist back to the center, bringing both knees up and pressing both feet against their hips. The typical reaction for an attacker is to pull away, so when they do, slide your hands down to their wrists, bring your feet up, and kick the shit out of them. Then, run away and find help."

I sat up, and we both pulled apart. "Any questions?"

"Where should I kick?"

"Anywhere— the groin, stomach, and face are the most vulnerable and effective targets to kick. Are you ready to try?"

Exhaling, she gave me a quick nod, "Yeah, I'm ready."

"I'm going to walk you through everything, so don't worry. Lie down and open your legs," I instructed.

Briefly hesitating, she did as I requested.

"I'm going to get between your legs now, okay?"

When she nodded, I scooted up, placing my knees on the outside of her hips as I draped her legs on my thighs and pressed up against her. My mind briefly transported us to my bed, where she would be naked, open and ready for me, waiting for my dick to slide inside her.

Concentrate on the technique. You'll have her soon.

"Now, I'm going to try to come down on you. Stop me by bracing your hands against my shoulders." I started to move my upper body down toward hers, and she threw her hands up, stopping me by grabbing my shoulders. "Good, now shrimp out and place your foot on my hip."

That move was more difficult for her to execute, so we practiced it several times until she felt like she got the hang of it before moving on to the next step. The constant contact and rubbing had hardened my cock more, but Kaiya didn't say anything. I knew she felt it by the way she tried to adjust when it pressed against her, causing her face to redden.

"From here, slide your hands down to my elbows and move back to the center while bringing both knees up and putting your feet on my hips."

"Like this?" she asked as she trailed her hands down to my elbows and propped her feet on me. Her touch was light as her skin grazed mine.

"Yes, now slip your hands down and grip my wrists as I pull away. I'm going to move my head to the side so you can practice kicking upwards. Go ahead and kick."

We practiced the routine a few more times, and Kaiya moved more fluidly each time. I could tell she was becoming more comfortable with me as her body relaxed throughout the exercise. As class ended, I gathered everyone on the mat again before I closed. "Great class today, everyone. I love the enthusiasm, and I want to thank you for your active participation. Remember, we can't predict exactly how an attack will happen, but practicing these techniques will definitely help in any situation. Always fight back—punch, kick, scream, scratch, anything to protect yourself. See you Tuesday."

Everyone filed out of the room, except Kaiya.

Glancing shyly as she approached me, she said, "I just want to thank you for working with me. Like I said, I don't do well with strangers touching me."

"No problem. See you Tuesday? For the next class?"

Biting her lower lip in contemplation, she didn't say anything for several seconds before she replied, "Yes. I'll be here Tuesday."

"Great, I'll see you then."

She turned to walk away, but I stopped her. "Wait." I wanted to keep talking to her. Something about her intrigued me, maybe the fact that she didn't just give into me like other girls.

"Before you go, let me give you my number, in case you need to get a hold of me for class or something." Reaching my hand out, I gestured for her to give me her phone.

Rolling her eyes, she questioned, "Do you give your number to all your students?"

"Only VIP ones," I joked. I didn't normally give out my personal number to students, but I wanted an excuse to get Kaiya's. I kept my hand out, and she finally placed her phone in my palm. Keying my number in, I called my phone so that I'd have her number, too.

As I gave her phone back, I said, "Let me walk you to your car."

"You don't have to do that—I'll be fine."

"Just let me walk you to your car," I insisted.

"Fine," she huffed before smiling.

So stubborn.

As we walked, I took the opportunity to try to get to know her better, hoping that would help in my quest to get her in my bed. I ignored the fact that I was interested in her, that I actually wanted to know more about her.

"So, do you and Kamden live together?"

"Yeah, just me and him. We've lived in our apartment together since college."

"Any other family?"

Her skin paled as her eyes widened. "No."

Okay, not a good topic. Maybe we have more in common than I thought. "What do you do for work?"

Her face relaxed, and color began to return to her cheeks. "I'm a Project Coordinator for a marketing and public relations firm in Boston."

"Sounds boring."

She looked offended, but laughed. "Thanks. Not everyone gets to work out for a living."

"It's pretty awesome," I admitted. We were nearing the exit doors, so my time with her was running out. "What do you like to do for fun?"

I opened the door for her as she answered, "I love to go dancing."

"I'll keep that in mind when I ask you out."

She laughed again; this had to be the most I'd ever seen her do so. I was getting somewhere, finally.

"Anything else that might help my chances?"

She stopped by a black, Acura TL before leaning against it, facing me.

"You don't want to get involved with me," she said with a half-hearted smile.

"Oh, yeah? Why not?" I replied as I stepped closer to her. *Always fighting me.*

Her eyes watched me warily. This close to her, I could see so many different hues of blue and green that made up the unique shade of her eyes. They really were beautiful. "I just… I have a lot of issues."

"Don't we all?" I asked in a rhetorical tone. *I know I do.*

She chuckled softly, "Not like mine."

"You tell me yours, I'll tell you mine." *What am I saying? I don't want to her to know about my past—do I?*

"That's never going to happen," she replied matter-of-factly, an unspoken challenge present in her eyes.

"Never say never." I smirked while backing away. "Goodnight, Kaiya."

I didn't need to say anything else that I might regret, like telling her my whole life story. *Why does she make me feel so different? Why do I want to open up to her?*

Shaking her head, she smiled as she got into her car. As I turned around, I couldn't help but think, *Tuesday can't come fast enough.*

Chapter Seven

Kaiya

My body still thrummed with adrenaline from a combination of class and touching Ryker. It amazed me how just being close to him made me feel so alive, like I hadn't really been living until I met him. Honestly, I really hadn't.

Kaleb had made me afraid to live, afraid to trust anyone. But with Ryker, I felt there was a chance that I could open up to him, and that scared the living shit out of me. *If I couldn't even trust Kaleb, how could I trust Ryker?*

Shaking the thoughts from my head, I started my car to drive home. I didn't want to think about anything negative when I was feeling so good, when I actually felt… happy. I knew completing one self-defense class wasn't very significant for most people, but it was huge—absolutely huge—for me. One of the many steps I needed to take to reclaim my life and eliminate the power Kaleb had over me.

My stomach growled as I walked into my apartment, so I headed straight for the kitchen to look for something quick to throw together for dinner.

As I rifled through the refrigerator, I heard Kamden call out, "I ordered a pizza—figured you wouldn't want to cook."

His voice had increased in volume as he walked from wherever he was in the apartment into the kitchen. When I closed the refrigerator door, I turned to see him standing in the doorway. "How was class? Everything go okay?" he asked with concern.

"Yeah, everything went fine," I shrugged. "I was a little nervous at first, but Ryker worked with me one-on-one to make sure I was comfortable," I continued as I searched for the pizza, which I found right on the counter next to the refrigerator. *So observant.*

"Ryker's the instructor?" Kamden questioned. He sounded a bit bothered by the idea.

"Yeah," I said, my focus mainly on the pizza box as I stalked towards it. Opening the cabinet above it, I grabbed a plate and put two slices on it before putting it in the microwave. When I turned back around to look at Kam, I noticed his furrowed brows and tense jaw. "What?"

"Nothing, just be careful with him," he warned with a cautionary look in his eyes.

I voiced my thoughts aloud, perplexed by his warning, "Why?"

"I notice how he looks at you, Ky. He's a total womanizer, and I don't want you to be another notch on his bedpost." He crossed his arms as his voice took on that over-protective, brotherly tone I knew so well.

Wow, I so don't want to have this conversation. Thankfully, the microwave beeped, giving me the perfect opportunity to escape. As I removed the plate, I said, "Don't worry, Kam. I'll be fine—I'm not interested in Ryker." *Keep racking up those lies.*

"I'm serious, Kaiya," he sternly remarked, authority obvious in his words.

Placing the plate on the counter, I turned around to look at him—arms still folded tensely over his chest, eyes narrowed, mouth set in a tight, thin line. *He's really upset over this.*

"Kam, do you really think I'd be getting myself involved with someone, especially now? I'm barely holding myself together."

The angry expression on his face eased, his features softening as he walked toward me. "You're doing great, *sorella.* I didn't mean to get upset at you. I just don't want you to get hurt."

"I know, but you have nothing to worry about. I'm not planning to get involved with Ryker, okay?" For some reason, those words caused my chest to tighten uncomfortably. *Do I want to be with Ryker?* I couldn't deny the attraction to him, or the fact that I wanted to jump him every time I saw him, but did I want to be with him?

My stomach grumbled, interrupting my thoughts.

Kamden laughed. "You better eat—that thing sounds hungry."

I smacked him on the back as he turned to walk away. Picking up a slice of gooey, cheesy goodness, I opened my mouth to take a bite as Kam turned back around. "I'm really proud of you, Ky."

I stopped mid-bite as another genuine smile spread across my face. *I must be setting a record today.* "Thank you, Kam."

Wordlessly, he exited with a matching grin on his face.

After finishing my pizza, I went to my room and decided to call Nori and update her on everything that had happened since the club. She'd called and texted me a few times after that day, but I'd had yet to get back to her.

"Hey, girl. What's up?" Nori greeted when she answered.

"Hey. I wanted to apologize for bailing the other night."

"Don't worry about it. What happened?"

"Things moved too fast, too soon. I don't know what I was thinking." I fell onto my back on my bed with a sigh.

"Don't be so hard on yourself. He's a hot guy, I mean really hot guy, and you got caught up in the moment."

"I can't get involved with him, Nori. You know that."

"Why not? You can't let your past rule you forever, Ky."

I sat up, shaking my head in disbelief. I couldn't believe what she was saying, but she had a point. "I know, but a guy like Ryker wouldn't be interested in me—I have too much baggage."

"I'm not saying for you to get in a relationship with the guy. You have heard of having a good time, right? Nothing wrong with a little fun for once in your life. He doesn't need to know about your issues for you to have sex with him."

"I love how you think." I laughed.

"That's why I'm your bestie. Seriously though, you deserve to have some fun."

I blew out another breath as I lay back down. "Yeah, I guess." Wanting to change the subject, I brought up my class. "Hey, I started taking a self-defense class."

"That's awesome! I'm so proud of you, Ky."

"Guess who the instructor is?" I asked, biting my lower lip as I stifled a smile.

"No way! Ryker?" she shrieked, sounding like a teenage girl.

"Yep. I couldn't believe it. He gave me his number after class was over."

"Shut up! I think fate is trying to tell you something," she squealed giddily.

"Yeah, it's trying to torture me," I replied in exasperation. Having Ryker as my instructor didn't help in my efforts to try and stay away from him, even though I was seriously reconsidering that now.

Nori giggled, "I'll take that kind of torture any day. That man is delicious."

"He really is," I sighed dreamily. "It's been so hard to resist him."

"I can imagine. I don't think I'd be able to."

"Kamden says Ryker's a man-whore. He wants me to be careful around him," I said, deepening my voice to imitate his as I spoke.

"Of course he's going to say that. He's your older brother."

"Yeah, I know." I hesitated, doubting myself. "But what if he really is?"

"Who cares? That's what condoms are for," Nori responded as though it was obvious.

I snorted. "Nori!"

"What? You're not looking for commitment, and I doubt he is either. It doesn't matter if he's a man-whore. Sex is sex, and he looks like he'd be damn good at it."

"You're such a bad influence," I joked as I rolled over onto my stomach.

"Hey, you only have one life. I guarantee you'll regret it if you don't sleep with him at least once."

Would I? "Yeah, I probably would. He's the hottest guy I've ever seen." I paused, gnawing on my bottom lip in contemplation. "I don't know if I can do this, though. I haven't been with a guy, other than Bryce, since everything with Kaleb."

"I know. And, you don't have to do anything if you don't want to. I just want you to be happy; I don't think I've seen you as happy as when I've caught the two of you together, and when I've heard you talk about him."

"Really?" I asked, holding back a smile.

"Really. It's good to see you smile so much, and hear the happiness in your voice. Ryker may be just what you need to finally move on. And if not, at least you would get some really great sex out of it."

"Maybe. I'm not promising anything, but I'll keep an open mind. I better get ready for bed; I have an early day at work tomorrow—our weekly Monday morning meeting," I groaned unhappily.

"Ugh. Okay, text me tomorrow?"

"Okay, bye."

"Bye."

After hanging up with Nori, I got ready for bed. Kamden had removed what was left of the mirror sometime today, so I was relieved not to have to deal with that mess.

My phone chimed while I brushed my teeth. When I finished, I went to my bed to pick it up. When I swiped my passcode in, I saw that Ryker had sent me a text:

Ryker: sweet dreams

A smile spread over my face as I texted him back:

Me: you too :)

As I lay in bed, thoughts about my conversation with Nori kept me awake. Should I really get involved with Ryker? Does he really want me? Would I be okay with just a one night stand? Could I handle it?

The only thing that I was able to determine was that if I decided to go through with it, I would take things slow concerning Ryker. Neither one of us wanted a relationship, and I definitely wasn't ready to have sex with him, no matter how much I wanted to. So if it was going to happen, it was going to happen on my terms.

When I finally fell asleep, it was to images of Ryker's heavenly body over mine.

Let's just say that I really hoped that dreams came true. I needed a cold shower after the imagery from last night. I slept all the way until my alarm went off, which was unheard of for me. Usually I'd wake up from a nightmare.

Even though I had worked from home on Thursday, and went back to the office on Friday, I was behind on my work, swamped with documents and spreadsheets. Mondays were typically the busiest day of the week, especially since we had our weekly meeting to discuss happenings throughout the whole company.

Once I got home, I couldn't wait to go work out and relieve some of the tension from the day. I dropped my keys and purse by the door before trotting to Kamden's bedroom. Tapping on his open door, I peeked in. "Hey, you want to go to the gym?"

His eyes rose to mine from his laptop. The screen illuminated his handsome face. *Thank God he doesn't look like me.*

"Yeah, I was waiting for you. I need to talk to you about something first, though," he stated while closing his laptop.

Great, what now? "Okay," I said as I walked in and sat on his bed. He swiveled his rolling chair to face me before saying, "I set up an appointment to speak with the head of the hospital."

My mouth suddenly became dry from his words. I swallowed deeply before asking, "For when?"

"Six weeks from today— April 28. Do you still want to come with me?"

My first instinct was to say no, but I thought about my goal, about the baby steps I had made so far. "Yes. I want to do everything we can to keep him in there. I don't want him to be released."

Pride shined in his blue-gray eyes as he smiled at me. He turned and rifled through some documents on his desk. "Great. I think we still have the paperwork from the attack somewhere."

"I don't know—I haven't looked at them since we filed them. They should be in the filing cabinet unless you took them out."

"I'll look for them. Go ahead and get ready for the gym," Kamden said as he continued to search through the mess of papers on his cluttered desk.

I hopped up off his bed before going to my room to change. Fifteen minutes later, we were out the door on the way to the gym. Nervous, excited energy bounced through my veins as I anticipated seeing Ryker. *Play it cool, you're supposed to take things slow, remember?*

The drive to the gym seemed to drag on as my nerves continued to build up, making me feel like a kid on a sugar high. I practically skipped into the building, but my mood deflated when I realized Ryker wasn't there.

I didn't want to seem like a stalker by asking for him at the front desk, so I just assumed it was his day off—Monday probably wasn't a peak workout day. *Oh well, I'll see him tomorrow at class.*

Brushing off the disappointment, I headed to my usual elliptical. Kamden went straight to the weight room, but he joined me in the cardio room to finish up his workout before we left.

When we got home, I decided to call Nori again, needing to talk to her about what Kamden and I discussed before we went to the gym. After dialing her number, I cradled the phone between my shoulder and ear as I took out some of the leftover takeout from the other night. I could hear the surprise in her tone—I typically didn't call her two days in a row. "Everything okay, Kaiya?" she answered.

I chuckled, "Yes. But I have something to tell you."

"You did it, didn't you? That was fast, you whore," she teased, giggling.

My eyes popped in shock as I pulled two plates from the cabinet. "No, I didn't, Nori! I can't believe you think I'm that easy."

"I don't, but he's hot, and he seems very determined to have you from what you told me."

I sighed, a little disappointed. "I didn't even see him today." Pausing, I cleared my throat. "But that's not why I called. Remember I told you about Kaleb possibly being released?"

"Yes," she said, her playful tone from a second ago gone.

Setting the plates down, I went to sit at the breakfast bar. I released a deep breath before explaining, "Well, Kamden and I are going to the hospital to try to stop it. I wanted to see if you would come with me. You know, for support."

Without hesitation, she answered, "Of course, Ky. When?"

"April 28, six weeks from today."

"I'll ask for the day off when I get to the office first thing in the morning."

"Thank you, Nori. You don't know how much it means to me that you'll go." I let out a sigh of relief. I'd need as much support as I could get to get through all this.

"Aw, it's no problem, girl. I'd do anything to keep that bastard committed."

"Yeah, you and me both. I'll call you with more details later—I just got home from the gym, and I need finish dinner and shower."

"All right, talk to you later. I'm really proud of you, Ky."

"Thanks," I smiled. "Bye."

"Bye."

I exhaled another deep breath, easing more of the tightness in my chest. *You can do this. You're stronger than you used to be.*

I made a plate for Kamden and heated it in the microwave, but I didn't feel like eating anymore. Talking about the meeting and Kaleb caused unease to settle in the pit of my stomach, so I decided to skip dinner and take a shower.

As I walked to the bathroom, I repeated my phrases to myself, afraid that fear would try to take root inside of me because of the upcoming meeting about Kaleb. It would be the closest I've ever been to him since the *incident,* and that thought terrified the weak, fragile part of me.

The warmth of the water helped erase the tension in my muscles.

Working out had cleared my head, but after talking about the meeting with Nori, thoughts of Kaleb started to creep to the forefront of my mind again.

Shoving the thoughts back, I continued to chant my mantra and focus on the water trailing over my skin. Closing my eyes, I tipped my head back and let it pour over me as I let go of everything else.

Once I finished, I felt so much better. The weight of the situation had been alleviated, even if it would only be for a short time. I knew that as the date approached, it would be increasingly difficult to cope with everything.

Exhausted, I quickly dressed in my pajamas before falling into bed. Sleep found me quickly, pulling me under its veil seconds after my head hit the pillow.

"Kaleb, I don't like when you touch me like this." I flinched as he ran his hands over my skin.

"Why? You're mine, and I'm yours. I should be able to touch you wherever I want." Both his hands and voice were possessive and harsh as he continued to touch me.

Mom and Dad have always said that Kaleb was supposed to take care of me, but this feels wrong. Good, but wrong.

"Doesn't it feel good when I touch you like this?" Kaleb asked, interrupting my thoughts.

We were in my bedroom, on my bed with the door locked. Mom and Dad never questioned when they came up and found the door that way. Kaleb lay next to me, pressing his body up against my side. His fingers stroked my breasts before trailing down my stomach, eliciting a shudder from me.

"You're so beautiful, made just for me," he murmured against my ear before sucking my earlobe in his mouth.

"We shouldn't be doing this," I weakly protested as I squirmed beneath his venturing hand. My friends never talked about their brothers touching them this way, but his mouth was on my neck, and the combined sensations were making it hard to

think.

"Why? You love me, right?"

"Of course I love you, Kaleb, but—"

"Then, you'll let me do this. And you won't tell Mom and Dad."

His fingers had reached their destination, slowly caressing me and making me forget why I was objecting when it felt so good. My head lolled back against the pillow as Kaleb continued to touch me. Something that felt this good couldn't be wrong, could it?

When he was finished, I immediately covered myself with the blanket, clutching it to me as he stood up from my bed. He licked his fingers, like he did every time, and disgust began to replace the pleasure tingling through my body once the haze began to recede.

I fought the tears that threatened to spill over, not wanting him to see me cry. It would only make him angry, and he hurt me when he was angry—I didn't want him to hurt me more than he already had.

He walked toward me, leaning on the bed as he pressed a kiss to my forehead, causing me to cringe in response. "I love you, Kaiya."

As a tear escaped each of my lids, I quickly swiped them away before he pulled away and saw. "I love you, too," I replied, avoiding his gaze.

I didn't move until I heard the door shut. Then, I bolted out of the bed and into my bathroom, barely reaching the toilet before throwing up.

Once I finished vomiting, I hopped in the shower, turning on the water to the hottest I could stand it before scrubbing my skin until it was red, almost raw. Tears poured off my face, sobs wracking my body as I stayed there until the water ran cold.

Sitting up in bed, my eyes snapped open to darkness, the only light coming from my alarm clock. Sweat clung to my skin as I threw the covers off me, feeling as though they were suffocating me.

Much like my dream, I sprang out of bed to throw up in my bathroom. Disgust still permeated my body, my stomach still nauseated despite vomiting. Shakily, I stood, stripping my clothes before turning on the shower.

Stepping in, I turned the handle almost all the way to the left before scouring my skin in the scalding hot water as I cried. My body burned as the heated drops pelted me, feeling like molten lava dripping down my flesh. Sobs shook my body as tears trailed down my face and mix with the spray falling over me from the shower head. Nothing I ever did could totally erase the dirtiness that still remained whenever I had a flashback. *How could he do that to me? How could I let him? Why didn't I make him stop? God, I was so weak! I'm still weak!*

Slumping to the tile floor, I set my forehead against my knees, wrapping my arms around my legs. I sat there until the shower ran cold, letting the frigid water numb my skin. *If only I can get it to numb my brain and emotions, too.*

Chapter Eight

Ryker

Kaiya was more uptight than usual during class on Tuesday night, if that was even possible. She angrily hit and kicked the bag aimlessly, and I could tell that something was bothering her.

Sweat dripped down her face as I approached her. "Is everything okay?"

"I'm fine," she snapped, keeping her eyes trained on the bag, panting angrily as she continued to fiercely attack it. As I watched her, I noticed that she was holding her breath.

"Breathe, Kaiya," I urged, moving closer to her. "You need to breathe or you're going to pass out."

Her hands fell to her sides as she stepped away from the bag and took deep breaths. She began to pace in a small circle in front of me as she steadied her breathing.

"Are you sure everything is okay?" I asked again as I handed her water bottle.

She took the bottle, greedily drinking before taking more deep breaths. "Yeah, I just… I had a bad night last night, and it carried over into today."

I furrowed my brow. *I wonder what happened.*

"Well, take it easy, alright? I don't want you to overexert yourself."

She nodded before focusing back on the bag and repeatedly kicking the shit out of it.

There's that warrior.

After the kickboxing segment of class, I decided to work with Kaiya on different strikes since she was still so tense—she definitely needed to keep hitting something.

"I'm going to teach you where you should target different hits. First thing I'm going to show you is strikes that are best for the face—avoid directly punching someone in the face because you'll more than likely break your hand. Only use elbows, hammer-fists, and palm strikes when you are hitting the face."

I modeled a palm strike on one of our dummy bags, which had the upper body of a man, instead of the regular, cylindrical punching bag. I wanted Kaiya to target the specific areas of the body we were working on. I then repeated the same with elbows and hammer-fists, stopping for Kaiya to practice each one. I loved watching her body move and seeing sweat glisten over her skin. *Fuck, I want to feel that body beneath me.*

I didn't notice that Kaiya had completed the last move until she cleared her throat. When our eyes met, she smiled shyly and asked, "What next?"

Smooth. She caught you checking her out. Concentrate. Playing cool, I ignored that she had noticed me looking at her. "You can also use a double palm strike on an attacker's ears, which will completely knock off their equilibrium. Aim for right here," I instructed as I demonstrated on the dummy. "Right outside the ear. Slam as hard as you can."

We continued working on different strikes, and Kaiya's anger began to slowly fade as she released it on the bag. I didn't focus on her technique that much because I could tell she needed to blow off some steam, so I just let her. I knew she'd been hiding something beneath her guarded exterior, and whatever it was affecting her tenfold today.

When class was over, I stopped Kaiya as she was about to walk out, catching her at the door. I pulled her to the side as the remaining students squeezed past us and left. "Hey, you want to grab a drink? You seem stressed today."

"I really shouldn't," she replied as she pulled her bottom lip between her teeth, her tone indecisive.

"You always give me that lame excuse. Just one drink—you earned it after kicking the shit out of that dummy," I said with a grin.

She rolled her eyes as she fought a smile. "Should you be taking your students out on dates?"

"Oh, so this is a date?" I teased, raising my eyebrows as my smile spread.

"No! I… you know what I mean." She blushed as she darted her eyes away from mine.

"Yeah, you want me to take you out on a date." I smirked knowingly.

"No, I don't," she blurted as her eyes widened in embarrassment.

"Oh, really?" I challenged as I played with my tongue ring, knowing it unnerved her. I always caught her staring when I messed with it.

As I expected, her eyes darted to my mouth, and her lips parted slightly. With a knowing chuckle, I asked her again, "So, do you want to grab that drink or not?"

Her eyes snapped back to mine. "I need to shower."

"Do you need help? I'd be happy to assist you," I offered as I continued to toy with the barbell in my tongue.

Her gaze darted back and forth from my mouth to my eyes as she stammered, "No… I… I can meet you after I shower."

Yes. Smiling confidently, I suggested, "Phoenix Landing? In an hour?" Phoenix Landing was a popular, central bar in Cambridge, so I figured it was a safe choice.

Her words were rushed as she replied, "Sounds good. I'll see you there." Tucking a strand of stray hair behind her ear, she gave me a flustered smile before turning to leave. "Bye."

"Bye," I returned with a laugh.

Glancing over her shoulder as she walked out, her lips curved up more as our eyes locked. *I'm going to taste those lips again tonight.*

Rushing to close up, I quickly wiped down everything and locked up since my class was the last one of the night. I was anxious to meet up Kaiya, hoping to get another step closer to getting her in my bed. I blocked out the thoughts that passed through my head of actually wanting to spend time with her, ignoring that I wanted to get to know her. *No relationship—just sex. You don't have to get to know her to have sex with her.*

An hour later, I was waiting for Kaiya at the bar, leaning my back against it with a Jack and Coke in hand. After fifteen minutes had passed, I thought she had changed her mind and wasn't going to show. *If she's not here by the time I finish this drink, I'm leaving.*

As I took another sip from my glass, I glanced over toward the door. My lips involuntarily spread in a grin as I watched Kaiya walk in, wearing some tight jeans and a strapless, white top. Her hair flowed down her back before ending in big, loose curls, and I pictured myself wrapping my fingers in it while I bent her over and fucked her. Searching the room, her eyes roamed before locking on mine. A shy smile spread over her lips as she made her way toward me, those luscious hips swaying with each step. *She's so fucking hot.*

When she reached me, I snaked my arm around her waist, bringing her closer to me. I felt her muscles tighten beneath my touch, but she didn't resist otherwise.

Bringing her between my legs, I inhaled her sweet scent, a mixture of strawberry and vanilla, as I kissed her cheek. Her hands lightly pressed against my chest as I pulled back. "I thought you weren't going to show for a minute there."

"Me too. I almost didn't come." Her gaze darted down before coming up to meet mine as she shifted nervously.

"Well, I'm glad you did. It would've really hurt my ego if you didn't," I said as I rubbed my hands along her sides.

"I'm sure your ego is strong enough to survive," she replied dryly as she moved away to sit on the barstool next to mine.

"I don't think it stands a chance against you," I joked.

"Do women really fall for that?" she asked as she fought a smile.

"Most of the time. But they're not always the brightest."

Kaiya slapped me on the bicep as her eyebrows rose and her mouth opened in shock. "Ryker!"

"What? I'm being honest. Woman want honesty, right?" She stared at me, mouth agape for a few seconds before she shook her head and laughed.

"What do you want to drink? Cranberry Vodka?"

She thought a few seconds before replying, "No. Apple Martini."

"Damn, that bad of a day?" I commented before turning and getting the attention of the bartender. Once I ordered us a round, I focused my attention back on Kaiya, determined to figure her out.

"Do you want to talk about it?"

Her body stiffened slightly as she sipped her drink. "No. I don't want to think about it—I just want to forget."

I know that feeling. "I know plenty of ways to help with that."

Her lips tipped up. "I'm sure you do. I've heard about your reputation."

This is going to be good. I took a swig of my drink. "Oh, really? What have you heard?"

"Basically, you're a man-whore," she replied bluntly as she swirled her martini, avoiding my gaze.

I laughed. "I'm not going to lie—I've had my fair share of women."

Kaiya gave me a perplexed look before replying, "Thank you for being honest. I thought you'd lie about it."

"Why? I am who I am. I'm not going to pretend be anything that I'm not."

"I respect that. Not the being a man-whore part, but that you're true to yourself."

I took another drink, enjoying the warmth of the liquor as it slid down my throat. "How are you liking class?" I asked, attempting to redirect the topic away from my personal life. *Not ready to talk about that yet.*

Kaiya took another sip, leaving only half of her martini. "I like it. Everything can be a little overwhelming, but I'm willing to work through it."

"You'll get the hang of it. Why did you decide to take self-defense?"

Visibly swallowing, she cleared her throat before taking another long gulp, leaving only a small sip in the bottom of her glass. "Old demons."

"Care to elaborate?" I didn't know why I asked, I already knew she'd say no.

"No." She threw back the remainder of her drink before standing. "I'd better go. Thanks for the martini."

"Why don't you stay for another? I won't ask any more personal questions. Scout's honor." I said as I put my fingers together to make the hand gesture.

She snorted, "I doubt you were a Boy Scout."

"Why? Is it the tattoos?"

"No. I just can't picture you as one. You don't seem like the type that follows directions well."

"I don't. I was thrown out for kicking my scout leader."

She laughed. "You didn't."

"I did—guy was a prick."

Kaiya continued to laugh; she definitely didn't smile or laugh enough, and I wished she did more of both. When our eyes met, I repeated my earlier question, "Can I get you another drink?"

Even before she responded, the smile she was fighting gave me my answer. I ordered another round of drinks from one of the bartenders, then turned my attention back to Kaiya. Our gazes locked as a blush began to creep up onto her cheeks, painting her porcelain skin with pink.

"You're so beautiful," I said, just above a whisper as I leaned towards her. Her eyes focused on my lips as they neared hers, which parted in anticipation, as if waiting to reacquaint themselves with mine after so long.

Closing my eyes, I brushed my mouth against Kaiya's, enjoying the silkiness of her lips.

Her hands rested on my chest before sliding up and around my neck as she brought herself closer to me, pressing our bodies together. Winding around her, my arms enclosed her against me as my tongue intertwined with hers.

Fuck, she tasted so good—I could get lost in her for days, oblivious to everything else but consuming every part of her sweetness. One of my hands trailed up her back before cupping her head, tangling my fingers in her hair as the kiss intensified.

"You have a tab? Or do you want to pay cash?" the bartender interrupted, causing Kaiya to abruptly pull away from me.

Asshole. Glaring at the bartender, I grabbed the drinks. "I have a tab—Ryker Campbell."

Handing Kaiya her drink, I couldn't help but notice her swollen lips. My cock hardened more as I thought about Kaiya sucking me with those lips, taking my dick deep into her mouth before letting me sink myself into her pussy. *Fuck, I have to have her.*

As we drank, we told each other stupid bar jokes that we had heard over the years. Kaiya giggled loudly, her eyes glassy as she swayed slightly in her seat. Her cheeks had deepened to a light shade of red and she wore a drunken smile. She was definitely tipsy. "I should go. I have to work in the morning," she said halfheartedly.

"Why don't you come home with me?" I suggested with a crooked grin as I pulled her barstool between my legs.

"I can't," she replied as she leaned forward, bringing her face only inches from mine.

Closing the distance, I barely grazed her lips as I asked, "Why not? We both know you want to."

Pulling back a little, she put some distance between our mouths. "Those old demons I mentioned earlier—they haunt you forever." Before I could respond, she continued, "You don't want to get involved with me."

Resting my hands on the outside of her thighs, I rubbed my thumbs against them. "You've said that before. I know what I want, and I'm looking right at her."

She smiled sadly. "If you knew me, you wouldn't want me."

"Why don't you let me decide that for myself instead of fighting me all of the time? You don't even give me a chance to get to know you."

"I have to fight—it's the only way I can protect myself. I need to go," she snapped before grabbing her purse off the bar.

"Kaiya, wait," I called after her. Ignoring me, she pushed through the crowd, continuing to walk toward the door before exiting. I wanted to go after her, but I wasn't the type to chase a woman. My pride wouldn't allow that, so I just let her go, forcing myself to stay at the bar.

I ordered another drink, along with a straight shot of Jack. I downed it as a sexy brunette walked up next to me, her tits almost popping out of her skin-tight dress.

"Want some company?" she asked before biting her bottom lip seductively.

She wasn't what I wanted, but I didn't want to sit around sulking about Kaiya, so I pulled her onto my lap. "Sure, baby. Wanna get out of here?" I asked before tracing my tongue along her jawline.

"Yes," she practically moaned as she tilted her head. *Too easy.*

After I paid my tab, I followed the girl back to her place. We barely made it in the door before she started stripping her clothes off and getting on her knees in front of me.

Unbuttoning my jeans, she pushed me back against the wall next to her front door. She pulled my cock out before eagerly sucking it into her mouth, skimming it lightly with her teeth.

Grabbing her hair, I pushed my dick deeper into her mouth before starting to thrust in and out. I tried to lose myself in the sensations, but all I could think about was Kaiya and how I wished her mouth was around me instead.

Pulling out, I turned the woman around as I knelt behind her. I took a condom out of my wallet before rolling it over my cock and sinking myself into her, making her moan loudly in pleasure.

Gripping her hips, I imagined I was pounding into Kaiya instead of some random girl. I closed my eyes, envisioning her silken skin, perfect body, and beautiful face as my dick repeatedly stroked inside her.

My hips smacked against her ass as my pace increased, the image of Kaiya bringing me closer to release with each passing second.

Crying out, the woman's pussy tightened around me, her body trembling its climax before she lay slack on the floor, ass still up as I plunged deeper into her. My fingers dug into her hips as I slammed her harder against me, seeking my own release.

Groaning, I stilled as I came, panting heavily to regain my breath. Once I did, I pulled out from the unnamed woman.

She rolled over and spread her legs, opening herself to me. "Want to go again?"

My dick had already started to go down once I was reminded that she wasn't Kaiya. I slid the condom off me as I said, "Nah, I'm good."

She looked offended as I stood up before throwing the condom away and buttoning my jeans.

"What?" she angrily asked, her mouth setting in a hard line as she closed her legs and sat up.

"I said that I'm good," I replied as I turned and reached for the doorknob. I didn't even wait for her reply as I opened the door and left.

Chapter Nine

Kaiya

Bryce had been more than happy when I'd called and asked if I could come over. Even though I'd wanted to take Ryker up on his offer at the bar, I'd been too scared to go through with it. So instead, I pushed him away. *Chicken shit.*

As I put my clothes back on, Bryce commented, "I've missed you, Ky."

What's with him lately? He's never been so affectionate. "We saw each other last week," I reminded, my response cut and dry as I avoided his penetrating gaze.

"I know, I've just missed you," he said with sincerity as he sat next to me on the bed. He tucked a strand of my wild, sex hair behind my ear before caressing my cheek.

What do I say to that? "Thanks." It sounded more like a question than an expression of gratitude.

"Thanks?" he chortled without humor.

Squeezing the bridge of my nose with my fingers, I replied, "What do you want me to say, Bryce?"

He stood angrily as he said, "I don't know, maybe that you missed me too."

But I haven't. I've been too consumed with Ryker to think about anyone else. "I'm sorry—you know I don't do feelings well." I really didn't.

Sighing, he rubbed the back of his neck. "I know. Don't worry about it."

After Bryce walked me to my car, I drove home, thinking about the events of the night, wondering why I couldn't have just let go and lose myself in Ryker like I'd wanted to.

I didn't see Ryker again until class on Thursday. He wasn't at the gym on Wednesday when I went after work. I hated the gnawing feeling in my chest from not seeing him, and I thought I was going to explode once it combined with the knots in my stomach from the anticipation of finally seeing him again at class.

When I arrived, he was hitting one of the bags. Sweat glistened over his skin as he fluidly moved, doing intricate combinations while simultaneously delivering substantial force. His muscles bulged as he used them expertly, and I found myself drawing closer to him, enthralled by his power and grace.

Seeing me out of the corner of his eye, he stopped before turning, his lips curving up in a cocky grin, "Like what you see?"

Um, yeah. Ignoring his comment, I responded, "I'm just trying to see the correct form so I can get better. I suck at this stuff."

"Yeah, you're pretty terrible," he replied jokingly as he leaned against the bag. When I glared at him, he continued, "You just started—you're not going to be an expert from the get go. But honestly, you've been doing great."

I felt my cheeks heat—*seriously? Get a grip.* "Thanks," I replied before pausing. "I'm sorry about the other night."

He chuckled, "I think I'm having deja vu."

I smiled. "I'm just not good at this—whatever this is."

"A beautiful woman like you shouldn't have any trouble with guys."

Yeah, and they shouldn't have issues because of their brother molesting them either. "I'm not like other women. I've already warned you that I have issues."

"And I thought I made it clear that I didn't care." He pushed off the bag and came toward me. "I want to get to know you, Kaiya."

"I'm not looking for a relationship," I stated firmly, locking my eyes with his as I crossed my arms over my chest.

Ryker's lips tipped up in that sexy smirk. "I guess we have something in common then."

"I don't just want a one night stand, either," I blurted, surprised that I had voiced what I wanted. My stomach knotted uncomfortably as I waited to hear his response.

Those deep, beautiful eyes of his studied me, and I wished I could hear what he was thinking. "So, you want something between a one night stand and a relationship, huh?"

I sighed, "I don't know what I want. This is all happening so fast for me." *I want you, though.*

He kept our eyes locked as he said, "Well, when you figure it out, let me know. I don't want to keep pressuring you if you're not ready." His tone was sincere, but I still didn't trust his words.

"Thank you for understanding." The skeptical side of me wondered if he was trying to play me, telling me what I wanted to hear so that I'd give into him. But the smaller part of me, the optimistic side, hoped that it wasn't just an act. "What are we working on today?"

"I'll probably work with you again on the techniques we've done, but I also want to show you some blocks and other moves to keep you from getting in those situations."

I get to have that body pressed against me again? Yes, please. "Okay, sounds good," I replied, hiding my excitement.

As I turned to walk away, he asked, "Hey, do you want me to help you with some punches before class starts? I can give you some one-on-one attention."

Yes! Yes! "Sure, that's fine. I bought some gloves," I said, trying to pretend I wasn't jumping for joy on the inside as I pulled my new gloves out of my bag.

"Great, put them on and meet me at the bag."

I set my stuff down by the wall before slipping my gloves on. I don't know why, but just putting them on made me feel powerful and in control, like I could take on anyone. Even *him.*

When I came up to the bag, Ryker surprised me by walking around and standing behind me. Stiffening, my heart skipped a beat before going into overdrive, thumping wildly in my chest as I nervously asked, "What are you doing?"

"I'm going to show you how your body needs to be moving with each strike," he replied unaware of the panic overtaking me. He was so close that I could feel the heat from his body at my back. Pressing his large, muscular chest against me, he ran his hands over my arms, causing goose bumps to break over my skin.

For some reason, I wasn't scared like I would normally be if someone was this close to me. I was nervous as fuck, but not afraid. Excited, but not afraid. I still couldn't understand why Ryker was different, why he made me feel so many things other than fear. The only thing I knew was that I liked it.

His gloved hands covered mine as he instructed, "Relax—you're always so tense. Kickboxing is very fluid and is all about moving your body the right way."

Bringing our joined arms out by my sides, he shook them, trying to loosen my taut muscles. Then, he brought our hands up in front of my face as he positioned our bodies in the traditional fighters' stance. Extending our right arms out towards the bag, he said, "Do you feel how we're twisting slightly when we throw this jab? Every move needs to be like this, using your body as a power source. Our muscles are made to work together, just like when we lift something heavy or do other everyday tasks."

As he pulled my hand back in front of my face, he twisted our bodies more as we threw a punch with our left hands, slightly pivoting our hips inward. Feeling his sweaty, firm body pressed against me, especially the lower half, was so distracting; I could barely focus on what he was saying. "Kaiya?"

"Huh? What?" I felt like I was under some sort of spell.

"Did you feel how we used more movement with the punch over the jab? Whatever side is behind will require more force to correctly execute."

I couldn't speak, not with him flush against me like that, so I just nodded. We continued working that way until other members started entering for class. By then, my body was sticky with heat from a combination of hitting the bag and Ryker's proximity to me. All I could think about was how his bare body would feel tangled with mine.

Once we started kickboxing, I started to let myself go as I worked on the combo Ryker modeled. I loved hitting the bag—absolutely loved it. Even though I wasn't very good yet, it was an amazing outlet for my stress and anxiety, not to mention my anger. It felt good to release it, free myself from all my negative emotions, at least for a brief time. They always slithered back, snaking their way inside and tainting my soul with their poison.

After the kickboxing segment of class was over, Ryker and I practiced the technique that he taught me the week before. I wasn't as uncomfortable since I was becoming accustomed to his touch, so I was able to execute the maneuver better.

Constantly touching him electrified my skin, intensifying the sexual tension that was already present between us. My mind and my body warred—my body wanted to give in to Ryker while my mind protested, fearing that inevitably, I would be hurt by him.

I didn't trust my body, especially since it betrayed me so many times in the past. I knew that I needed to follow my head when it came to Ryker, to be smart and not give into my emotions and desires so easily.

Ryker broke through my thoughts, "Let's work on a common variation of this move since you seem to have this one down." He lay down on his back before continuing, "Straddle me."

"Excuse me?" I stammered nervously, feeling my cheeks heat.

"Straddle me. I'm going to show you how to escape if an attacker pins your arms to the floor."

I hesitated briefly before climbing on top of him. His body felt so right beneath me.

"Now, pin my hands by my head."

Doing what Ryker instructed, I leaned over, clasping my hands around his thick, tattooed wrists and pinning them to the ground.

"First thing you're going to do is simultaneously bring up your right knee while shooting your left arm upwards, like this," he said before modeling.

I felt his knee prop against my ass as he made me lean forward by jerking his left arm upwards. "Now, you're going to roll to the right and pin your attacker."

Swiftly rolling, Ryker had me pinned beneath him in seconds. "Once here, you can use the strikes I taught you last week to attack them. Elbows would probably be best from this position."

Even though he was wearing loose shorts, I could still feel his semi-hard, yet still impressive erection pressing into my lower abdomen, muddling my thoughts as arousal flooded me. *Focus, Kaiya.*

Ryker smirked at me; I was pretty sure that my desire was written all over my face. "You want to try? I already have you pinned," he pointed out as he lightly pushed his hips against me and pressed down on my arms.

Heat simmered between my thighs from the slight movement, from having Ryker's flawless form hovering over me. My eyes trailed over the intricate tattoos exposed from his tight muscle shirt, which spanned his chest and spread over his arms all the way down to his hands. I had to fight the urge to trace them with my fingers.

Ryker cleared his throat before huskily saying, "If you keep looking at me like, I'm not going to be able to do what I said earlier."

My gaze snapped up to his, and his eyes reflected the desire I felt. I wanted him so badly, wanted to tell him how I felt, but I couldn't. I had too much baggage that he didn't deserve to deal with; no one did. My voice cracked as I said, "Sorry. What do I do from here?"

"Jerk your left arm up while bending your right knee and putting it against my back."

I doubted that I would be able to move my arm, especially since his were double the size of mine and his muscles were so big.

Jerking my arm above my head, I caused Ryker's weight to shift forward as his arm went with mine, bringing his face only inches from my own. My eyes focused on his lips, the ones I had tasted only a few nights ago, and had thought about every night since.

Ryker's grip tightened on my wrists as he gruffly reminded, "Don't forget your knee."

Shit, concentrate! I brought my right knee up, pressing it into Ryker. "Now use that leg to roll us over."

Pushing with my right leg, I tried to roll us, but couldn't; Ryker was so much heavier than me. "I can't," I sighed agitatedly.

"Yes, you can, Warrior. Put those hips into it—use your whole body."

Doing as Ryker said, I bucked my hips, using my entire body for momentum as I pushed against him. Slowly, I was able to roll us over until I was mounted on top of him again. A smile spread over my face as I impulsively put my arms up in the arms and squealed, "I did it!"

Embarrassment took over my happiness as I brought my arms down, the heat that was in my core now rushing up to my face. I looked down at Ryker, who had a proud smile on his face as he chuckled, "Awesome job."

"Thank you," I mumbled.

We practiced a few more times, and the longer Ryker was touching me, the more my resistance crumbled. I probably would have let him fuck me right there on the mat in front of everyone by the time we finally finished. Not really, but I was seriously contemplating it.

After class ended, Ryker walked me out to my car. Leaning against the driver's side door, he praised, "You did really good today."

"You're just saying that," I replied as I rolled my eyes.

"No, really, you did great. You're progressing well—it usually takes people weeks to really get the techniques down."

"Well, thank you," I smiled. Our eyes met, and Ryker was looking at me with that sexy smirk that tightened my core while setting it on fire.

Uncomfortably squirming under his gaze, I spoke, "I better get going. I'll see you Thursday."

Ryker leaned in, and my lips parted in response to his closeness. I closed my eyes as I waited for his lips to meet mine, but instead I felt them on my cheek as he brought me into him and whispered, "Goodnight, Warrior."

As he pulled away, my voice embarrassingly cracked, "Goodnight."

Ryker stifled a laugh as he backed away, his eyes never leaving mine until he turned around and jogged back to the entrance of the gym.

As I sat in my car, I wondered how long I could resist him, if I would be able to at all. I didn't want to, but I couldn't think of an outcome that ended well. One of us would end up hurt, most likely me, no matter which way I looked at it. No one wanted damaged goods anyway.

As I started the car, I sighed and made my decision. It was best for both of us if we didn't get involved. No one would get hurt, and it was less complicated if I was going to continue taking classes. No matter how much my body wanted him, my head knew better, knew what was best to protect me from more pain. Now if only my heart would understand.

Chapter Ten

Ryker

Kaiya had been coming to class for a few weeks, and her technique and form had improved greatly. But when we practiced certain defense maneuvers, her body stiffened and her grip was tight, her apprehension evident in her tense muscles and wary eyes.

She had become more guarded, keeping some distance between us and pulling away when I touched her for too long. I tried giving her the space I had promised, but it was getting harder with each passing day.

The sexual tension between us had increased over the weeks. Every detail of her silky skin had been committed to memory from touching her so much, making me want her even more. Since Kaiya was only comfortable working with me, that meant constant, close contact, which I didn't mind at all, but she was always resisting, always fighting me, both in class, and in my personal advances. I could see the desire all over her face, especially in those eyes, but she always fought it, fought what I knew we were both feeling. *My little warrior.*

I hadn't realized I had so much self-control—I wanted Kaiya more than I had ever wanted another woman. Her resistance only made me want her that much more. Any other girl would've been in and out of my bed by now, but Kaiya was different—I couldn't do the same with her that I did with other women. That confused and irritated the shit out of me. My patience was running thin, and I wasn't going to keep playing games with her. *I'll have her soon.*

After working on the bags, I asked the group about what self-defense technique they wanted to work on. One of the students raised her hand. "Can we work on getting out of a choke?"

The other students voiced their agreement, but Kaiya stiffened. Her eyes widened, and her lips tightened as our gazes locked.

"Okay, get with your usual partners." While everyone else split up on the mats, I walked over toward Kaiya, keeping my eyes fixed on her. "Everything okay?"

"I don't know if I can do this." She looked away as she reached for her neck. She stopped herself and pulled her hand away before looking up at me. "I don't like having my throat touched."

My eyes went to her throat. A thin scar spread about two inches long against her pale skin. I had to be looking at it just right to see it, or else it would be undetectable in the natural creases and curves of her neck. *How the fuck did she get that?* I knew she wouldn't tell me what had happened, so I didn't ask… yet.

Rubbing her arms, I leaned down a little so that my face was in line with hers, forcing her to bring her downcast eyes to look at me. "We can take it slow. I'm only trying to help you learn how to defend yourself—I'm not going to hurt you." *I'd never hurt you.*

Even though she nodded, she still looked uncertain as she took a deep breath and shook out her hands.

"You can attack me first, and I can show you how to get out of it, like always."

"Okay," she replied softly. The other instructors had already started with the rest of the students, so I prepared to demonstrate the techniques with Kaiya. I lay down on the mat and patted my abs. "Get on me."

She glanced around nervously, biting her lip before finally straddling me, framing my torso with her legs. Even though we had done this several times before, she was still embarrassed and self-conscious. She nervously looked down at me as her cheeks turned pink, and I wished we were doing this without clothes on, just like I wanted to every time. "Now, choke me."

"What? No!" she exclaimed. "I… I can't do that to you." She crossed her arms over her chest.

"Just do it—you don't have to squeeze hard. I'm going to walk you through the steps to get out of the hold." I reassured as I softly rubbed the sides of her thighs.

Slowly, she brought her delicate hands down to my neck before applying slight pressure. "Too hard—can't breathe!" I gasped as I pretended to choke.

Inhaling a sharp breath, she instantly jerked her hands to away as her eyes grew wide. My body rumbled with laughter, and her eyes narrowed as she smacked me on the shoulder. "That's not funny, Ryker!"

I continued to laugh as Kaiya crossed her arms across her chest again, trying to stifle a smile. Once I stopped, I apologized, "I'm sorry. I was trying to get you to loosen up. I promise I'll behave. Choke me again."

The smile she'd been fighting broke through as she leaned over to grab my throat again. *I wish she smiled more.* She squeezed my neck, bringing my attention back to the exercise. "The first technique I'm going to show you is using your forearm. Bring it up and over, parallel to your chest," I said, modeling as I talked. "Then, slam it down across their forearms and push. Usually when someone is being choked, the attacker is just out of reach. This move will make them come closer to you, so you can grab them, like this, and force them off you." I easily tossed her off me onto the mat.

"Yeah, it's easy for you—I'm lighter than you." She rolled over and sat up as her eyes looked over my arms. "Plus you have all those muscles. How am I supposed to overpower you? Or any guy for that matter?"

"Let me show you again, and I'll explain how. Get back on me," I instructed as I lay back down.

Straddling me again, she closed her hands around my neck. *Fuck, I love how she feels on top of me.* Images of her riding me, head tipped back and eyes closed as she moaned my name played through my head.

"Ryker?" Kaiya softly spoke, snapping me from my thoughts. Our eyes locked and her lips curved up, drawing my attention to them. *Damn, I want to kiss her again.*

"Sorry." I cleared my throat. Bringing my arm up, I braced it against hers. As I pushed against them, I asked, "Feel how your weight is forced to shift when I do this?" When she nodded, I continued, "I'm not pressing that hard, so even if your attacker is stronger, the pressure will still affect their balance and move them close enough for you to grab something."

Pushing harder, I forced her arms to bend, bringing her closer to me. Our faces were only inches away from each other; I had to stop myself from closing the small gap to touch her lips, wanting to taste her after so long.

Her breath hitched as our gazes met; her eyes always revealed so much, even when she tried to hide everything away. Fear and longing swam in those bright, blue eyes, and I wanted to lose myself in them—in her.

Breaking the haze we were in, she darted her eyes away and hoarsely asked, "What next?"

What were we doing again? Oh, yeah. "You grab anything you can to help you push them off of you—face, shoulder, arm, clothes, anything."

"And if I can't get them off?"

"Then, you kick, bite, scratch, punch, whatever. Do everything that you can do to defend yourself. Usually, that will catch your attacker off guard, allowing you to get them off of you," I stated firmly.

Kaiya squirmed against me, and I realized that my free hand had found her hip. Slowly pulling away, I grazed the tips of my fingers over the skin exposed from her tank top riding up.

Shuddering a shaky breath, she pulled away before dismounting me. I propped myself up on my elbows. "Ready to try?"

"I think so," she replied. Her tone was unsure, but her eyes held a look of determination.

"We'll take it slow. Lay down." When she complied, I continued, "I'm going to get on top of you, okay?"

We locked eyes as she nodded. As I straddled her, I assured, "I'm not going to hurt you."

"I know," she softly replied with a small smile.

I'm making progress here.

"I'm going to put my hands around your neck now. Do what I just demonstrated to escape, okay?" I studied her face, waiting to make sure she was ready.

She gave me a clipped nod. "Okay."

I kept my eyes fixed on hers as I gently placed my hands around her neck, applying light pressure. My thumb brushed over the small, raised scar, causing anger to swarm me like a pissed off hive of bees. *I'd like to meet the asshole who did this in a dark alley.*

Kaiya began to implement the technique from beneath me, but she couldn't throw me off. After several attempts, she huffed in frustration. "See, I told you that I wouldn't be able to get you off of me."

"Remember to use your whole body," I suggested with a chuckle.

Her eyes furrowed in determination as we attempted the maneuver again. Once she forced my arms to bend, she used her hips to try and vault me off of her while pushing them up into my crotch. My cock began to harden, especially when she started moving side to side, trying to get me off of her. *Fuck, how does she do this to me?*

Stilling beneath me, Kaiya's eyes widened, and her creamy skin flushed as she panted heavily. "I'm not doing it right."

"Oh, you're doing something right," I winked.

Softly giggling, she redirected the topic back to the maneuver. "You know what I mean. I'm not getting you off."

"Not yet, but if you keep doing that you will." I said suggestively as my eyes roamed over her face.

Her lips quirked up even though she ignored my comment, keeping her focus on the training. "What should I do?"

I wanted to continue playing with her, but she was really trying to execute the move, so I focused back on my job. "As you buck your hips, use your arms to help you. Push me off at the same time you're pushing up with your hips. Use that momentum together in the direction you want to throw me. Let's try again from the beginning."

Sitting up, I waited for her to readjust before starting the routine over. This time, she was able to throw me partially off of her. I landed on her right side, my legs still over hers.

"If this ever happens, which is likely since you're so small, you need to go crazy once you're in this position. Do everything you can to hurt your attacker—hammer-fists, kicks, knees, elbows, anything. Do whatever it takes to push them the rest of the way off of you. Again," I firmly said, going back into instructor mode, trying to keep my attention off her sweaty skin and how it would feel as I fucked her.

We practiced the move a few more times, and I couldn't help but notice how she tensed every time I placed my hands back on her neck. I really wanted to find out why, to make sure no one was hurting her.

As I helped her up off the mat, I asked, "What happened to your neck?"

Jerking her hand away, her face tightened with anxiety as she snapped, "None of your business."

Turning away, she began to storm off towards her stuff. *Shit.* Following her, I said, "Don't be upset. I just want to make sure no one is hurting you." When I caught up to her, I pulled her to a stop and placed my hands on her shoulders. I lowered my head to look into her eyes, hoping she would see my genuine concern. "You'd tell me if someone was hurting you right? Even if it was Kamden?"

Shock replaced some of the anger in her eyes as she sighed in defeat. "I'm sorry. I just…" She looked away, shaking her head. "I can't talk about it. But no, no one's hurting me, especially not Kamden." She grabbed her bag and turned to walk away again. "Thank you for your concern, though."

Grabbing her hand, I stopped her. "I want you to know that you can come to me if you need help, okay? Not just as your instructor, but as a friend, too."

A warm smile spread over her lips. "Thanks," she replied softly as she squeezed my hand.

I pulled her closer to me, to where her tits pressed against me. A strand of hair had fallen loose from her ponytail, and it dangled in her face. Reaching to tuck it behind her ear, I caressed her cheek with my palm. Her eyes closed as she leaned into my hand, but she snapped them open and quickly pulled away.

Letting out a heavy breath, I dropped my hands to my side. "Why do you fight me so much? Why won't you just give in to what I know you're feeling?"

Her lips tightened into a frown, and her eyebrows furrowed. "I can't," she said barely above a whisper.

"Can't or won't?" I challenged, my voice thick with frustration.

Her eyes watered as she opened her mouth to speak, but she snapped it shut instead. She turned around and rushed out of the room, pushing past some of the other class members.

Fuck! Why does she have to be so stubborn? Clenching my fists, I punched the bag nearest to me, sending it into the wall about three feet away. I ran my hands through my hair, pacing as I debated whether or not to go after her. We were both too upset for anything to end well, so I decided against it. *Damn it.*

I didn't see Kaiya again until Tuesday, but we had texted back and forth a few times on Monday, after both of us had apologized for our actions during class Sunday.

Tonight, I was really excited, not only to see Kaiya, but also because I planned to have the students spar, which we hadn't done in a long time. I had been waiting until Kaiya demonstrated she was ready, and since she had made so much progress, I thought she could handle it.

Once all the students arrived, I announced, "Today's class is going to different. All we're going to do is spar."

There were a few groans along with some enthusiastic cheers. I had the other instructors hand out the sparring equipment as I grabbed some for Kaiya and myself before walking over to her.

She looked at me nervously. "Are you sure I'm ready for this?"

"Yes," I responded confidently. "But if you're not comfortable, we can work on something else or watch the others spar." I set the rest of our equipment down and then looked up at her for confirmation.

"No!" she blurted. "I mean, I want to, I just don't know what to do."

"We'll take it slow. A lot of things will come naturally since you've been practicing. Let's get you suited up," I said as I picked up a chest protector. "This is a hogu—it'll protect your chest and stomach from any hits."

Slipping it over her head, I turned her around to tie the straps behind her. *I'd like to tie her hands to my bed and fuck her senseless.* Grinning stupidly at the thoughts, I moved around in front of her, making sure the hogu was positioned correctly. She looked up at me and smiled. "What?"

I shook my head and chuckled, "Nothing." I bent over to pick up her head gear and handed it to her. After she pulled it on, I helped adjust it, making sure it fit comfortably.

Once she had everything on, including shin guards, her gloves, and a mouthpiece, I put my own equipment on. As we stood in the center of one of the mats, I instructed, "Use everything you've learned so far. I'm going to let you hit me for the most part, but if you let your guard down, I'm going to take advantage, okay?"

She nodded, but I could see the anxiety in her eyes. As I walked closer to her, I assured, "Hey, you know I'm not going to hurt you, right?"

Her response was muffled by her mouthpiece, "I know." She nodded once more. "I'm just nervous."

"Are you sure you want to do this? It's okay if you don't want to."

"I want to," she replied with confidence, a determined gleam in her eyes.

That's my girl.

Moving back a few steps, I gestured with both hands for her to come to me. "Let's see what you got."

Hesitantly, Kaiya advanced towards me, keeping her hands in front of her face like I had taught her. She threw a few punches that I easily blocked, but she nailed me with a roundhouse to my thigh. "Nice hit," I praised.

She attempted to hit me with another roundhouse, but I deflected it with my own leg, causing her to stumble slightly. Recovering quickly, she came at with more jabs and punches, but I was able to block them. She lowered her hands from her face to her chest, obviously tired from the constant movement—sparring was exhausting for anyone.

Jabbing her lightly in the forehead, right where her head gear went across, I reminded, "Hands up! Always protect your face."

Her hands shot back up right before she swung at my stomach. I jumped back to avoid her hit. "You need to get closer for shots like that. Get some water and I'll explain more about your technique."

After we both got a drink, I sat with Kaiya on the mat to let her catch her breath before we started the next round.

"You're doing great. The only thing I noticed is that you're not close enough for some of the hits you're attempting." I took a long swig of my water and watched as she brought her bottle to her mouth. I quickly looked away, not wanting to focus on her plump lips and remember how they tasted. "You'll tire yourself out by throwing and not landing them."

Sweat dripped down her face as she nodded. "Got it."

"Hey, loosen up. Have some fun—I'm giving you a chance to beat the crap out of me. I don't let just anyone do that."

"I feel so special," she remarked sarcastically, fighting a smile.

I tugged on her ponytail and nudged her playfully. "Smart ass."

Slapping my arm away, she laughed and pushed me back. "Jerk."

I chuckled before taking another swallow from my bottle and standing. "Ready for round two?"

When Kaiya nodded, I reached down to help her up. We took our defensive stances, and I motioned for her to come at me again. She came in closer before executing the basic one, two, three combination of jab, punch, jab to my stomach, but I blocked with my arms before pushing her away.

Her eyes narrowed in determination as she advanced towards me again, throwing an elbow to my face that I batted away with my forearm. She threw a jab to my chest and kicked me below the ribs with a roundhouse.

Grabbing her leg, I trapped it against my side before stepping closer to her, bringing our bodies together. Ignoring the feel of her against me, focusing on how to help her technique, I said, "If this ever happens, you need to start punching anything you can to make them let you go, but don't pull away—you could break your leg."

Kaiya's breathing was ragged as I kept her trapped against me, enjoying having her pressed against me. Reluctantly, I let go before backing away slowly. Kaiya took advantage of my lowered hands by throwing a hook to the left side of my face.

"Nice." I grinned.

A smile lit up her face, showing her pink mouthpiece. Bringing my hands back up, I waited for her to attack me. After she threw a few punches, her hands fell to her chest again.

I threw a back-fist to the side of her head. "Hands," I reminded. "One good hit, and you're done for. Remember the first thing I taught you: never get knocked out."

We went a few more rounds before I decided to work with her on defending against standing attacks. I had Kaiya remove her equipment, but I kept mine on so she could use more force when hitting me during the escape techniques.

"Many times, an attacker will come up and grab you from behind, trapping your arms and putting you in a bear hug. I'm going to show you some ways to escape while disabling your attacker. Come up behind me and wrap your arms around me."

Doing as I instructed, she grabbed me from behind, pinning my arms to the side.

"First thing that you want to do is crouch down, leaning over a little so that it's harder for them to lift you up. Most attackers will try to throw you or slam you to the ground—you can't let that to happen."

I bent down. "Now, you're going to stomp on their instep then shift to the right side, giving you some space to throw a hammer-fist into their groin with your right arm, like this. This should cause them to either completely let go or at least loosen their grip on you, allowing you to throw some back elbows into their stomach."

I softly elbowed her in the stomach a few times before turning. "Once you're in this position, I would recommend a couple of knees to the groin, and some elbows to the face, even a knee to the face because they'll probably be hunched over. Put all of your force into your hits so that you can knock them out. Want to try?"

After she nodded, I came up behind her, pinning her arms to her sides as I brought her body against mine. Her ass pushed against my crotch as she leaned over, and even though I was wearing a cup, I couldn't keep thoughts of bending her over and fucking her from behind out of my head.

She shifted then threw a hammer-fist into my crotch. I loosened my hold on her as she started to elbow me in the stomach before turning and kneeing me in the nuts twice. *Thank God for cups.*

Elbowing me, she connected with the side of my face, which thankfully, was protected by the head gear. Elbows were one of the worst hits to take, especially to the nose or mouth.

We practiced a few more times before I ended class. Everyone was drenched with sweat as we discussed their feelings about sparring, most of which were positive. Tired smiles lined everyone's faces as they talked about what they practiced.

As everyone left, I started gathering the equipment to sanitize before I closed up. "You need some help?" Kaiya asked.

"Sure. I just need to clean this stuff," I said as I grabbed the gym's disinfectant spray and some paper towels from their station in the corner of the room.

After we had sanitized everything, I put the equipment back in their containers before putting them up in the closet. "Thanks for helping me."

"No problem. I'll see you Thursday." Kaiya smiled as she headed for the door.

"Hey, you want to grab something to eat? My treat for your help," I offered.

She turned back to face me. "I can't—Kamden waits for me for dinner."

"Oh, okay. Maybe some other time," I replied coolly, trying to mask my disappointment.

Our eyes met as she nibbled her bottom lip. "Tomorrow?" she suggested, quirking up an eyebrow in question.

My lips curved into a grin, "Just tell me where and when."

"East Side at seven?"

Is she serious? I couldn't fucking believe it—Kaiya was actually agreeing to go out with me. "I'll see you there."

Her skin began to flush as she replied, "Okay. See you tomorrow."

Hastily, she turned and exited as I finished closing up. My stomach knotted itself as I thought about tomorrow night—I hadn't felt like this about a date in a long time. I had given up trying to make sense of how Kaiya made me feel—all I knew was that I wanted more, anything she would give me.

Chapter Eleven

Kaiya

Oh my God, did I really just do that? I couldn't believe how impulsive I was—what was I thinking? I was supposed to be keeping my distance from Ryker, not going out on dates with him. *But one date can't hurt, can it?*

My resistance was wearing down, especially when he was trying so hard to give me the space I asked for. I knew it couldn't be easy since we were always touching during class. I could see and feel his desire when we practiced all the techniques he taught me. And I'm sure he could see mine written all over my face.

I felt like I was going to throw up all day on Wednesday since I was so nervous about seeing Ryker that night. None of the figures on my computer screen at work were making sense, my mind too caught up in thoughts of him for me to get anything done. I decided to text Nori and get her thoughts on everything:

> Me: Ryker is taking me to dinner tonight :)
>
> Nori: Finally! I was waiting for you to grow some balls and go out with him

I laughed aloud as I text her back:

Me: Idk if this is a good idea :/

Nori: Stop overthinking like you always do just have fun :)

I smiled at her text but didn't reply back. I tried to focus back on work, to keep my mind off dinner, but it was almost impossible. My phone beeped, and I thought Nori had text me again, but it wasn't her:

Ryker: Can't wait for tonight ;)

There was no use trying to fight the goofy smile that took over my lips. Impulsively, I sent the first thing that came to mind:

Me: Me neither :)

Now I'm definitely not going to get any work done.

I anxiously sat on Nori's bed as she helped me with my make-up for my date. I had told Kamden that I was going to dinner with her, not Ryker. I knew he wouldn't approve, and I didn't want to get a lecture from him, not when I was feeling so good.

"Stop moving," Nori scolded as she applied my eye shadow.

"I'm sorry, I'm just so nervous. I don't think I can do this," I said as I started panicking. My palms started sweating as I wrung my fingers together.

Nori stopped what she was doing and put her hands on my shoulders. "Calm down. Deep breaths—in, out, in, out."

Doing as she said, I slowly inhaled and exhaled until I felt calmer.

Nori looked at me with concern. "You don't have to do this if you don't want to, Ky."

"You don't think I should?"

"No, I think you should. You've been giving that poor guy blue balls for weeks now."

"Nori!" I exclaimed as I smacked her arm.

"What? You have."

"I know." I let out a deep breath. "He's been pretty understanding, but I'm just scared I'll get hurt. If Kaleb, my own brother, my own blood, hurt me, then how can I possibly believe that Ryker won't?"

"You don't know for sure, Ky. You can't punish everyone for Kaleb's actions. He has mental issues. Look at Kam—he's never hurt you and never will, same with Bryce. There are some good men out there."

Absorbing Nori's words, I contemplated what she said. Even though she was right, my defense mechanisms wouldn't fully accept it. I could never completely trust anyone, her and Kamden included.

With pursed lips and a raised eyebrow, she shook the eyeshadow brush in my face. "So, am I finishing your make-up or not?"

Smiling, I nodded. Even with all the conflicting thoughts running through my head, I couldn't deny that I wanted to see Ryker. Maybe I could let everything go and just have fun for one night. Unlikely, but a girl could hope.

I was about ten minutes late, as usual, and Ryker was waiting just inside the doors. Dressed in a nice, black dress shirt and dark jeans, he had his sleeves pushed up, exposing the tattoos on his forearms.

Our eyes met as he gave me his trademark smirk. Heat flooded my entire body as I took him in, and I wondered why I kept resisting him—he was absolutely gorgeous and made me feel so many amazing things that I'd never felt before. *Because you're crazy, that's why.*

As I approached, he brought me into his arms as he pressed a soft kiss to my cheek. "You look beautiful," he complimented.

"So do you. I mean handsome—you look handsome," I stammered. *Great start.*

His chest rumbled with laughter as he kept me against him. Keeping my hand in his, he pulled away and led me to the hostess stand.

When the hostess directed her attention to us, she gave Ryker a flirtatious smile. "I was hoping she wouldn't show—my shift ends in fifteen minutes."

Jealously sparked through me as my eyes narrowed and my hand tightened around Ryker's. *Bitch. I'm standing right here.*

Ryker released my hand to wrap his arm around the small of my back, drawing me into his body. He pressed a kiss to my temple, causing her smile to fade as he said, "She was just running late, right, baby?"

Giving her a smug smile, I leaned into Ryker, placing my hand on his chest. "Two, please."

Her eyes thinned as she huffed and grabbed two menus. Ryker chuckled as she angrily stomped in her heels while leading us to our table.

"What a bitch," I said after she walked away.

Ryker laughed, "Jealous, huh?"

Yes. "No! She was just rude."

Ryker gave me a knowing look before directing his attention to the menu. The waiter arrived to take our order after a few minutes, then left to get our drinks.

Ryker grinned. "I have to admit, I was surprised you suggested this."

You and me both. "One of my rare impulsive moments," I joked.

"I like the impulsive side of you. You should let her out more often."

The waiter came back with our drinks, giving me an opportunity to change the subject. "We always talk about me. Tell me about you."

He propped his elbows on the table as he looked at me. "What do you want to know?"

"Anything—what about your family?"

"My parents died when I was in high school."

Shit. "I'm sorry. Do you have any other family?"

"I have a brother, but we don't talk," he replied coldly, his jaw tensing in anger.

I'm sure he can't be as bad as Kaleb. Fuck, don't think about him—change the subject. "How long have you been a personal trainer?"

The anger in his face receded as he answered, "A few years—I went to school for it, and was lucky enough to get a job right after I graduated."

"That's awesome—I can tell how much you love it."

"Yeah, it definitely has its perks. I basically get paid to work out."

And it shows. I smiled as I thought about his flawless muscles, how they felt when I touched them while we practiced, and how hot he looked when they gleamed with his sweat.

The waiter brought our food, interrupting my delicious thoughts about Ryker, who slyly grinned at me, as if he could tell that I was thinking about him. Blushing, I directed my attention to my food to avoid his heated gaze.

After we finished eating, we had a few more drinks before Ryker paid our bill. Once we reached my car, he wound his arms around my waist, pulling me flush against him as he kissed my cheek. "Goodnight, Warrior."

Unable to control myself, I turned my face, connecting our lips. My mind reminded me that this was a bad idea, that I'd just end up hurt, but I blocked it out, enjoying the feel of Ryker's hot mouth on mine.

I almost moaned when his tongue parted my lips, missing his taste after so long. His hands came up to cup my face as he pushed me back against my car.

Nibbling my bottom lip, he gruffly whispered against my mouth, "Come home with me."

I almost said yes—almost. Lord knows I wanted to, but that scared, broken part of me took hold, making me break away from Ryker as I breathlessly replied, "I can't."

Ryker's face fell, then set in frustration. His voice raised in anger as he stepped away from me. "That's what you always say, Ky. And we still end up like this every single time."

"I know, and I'm sorry. You just don't understand." I sighed as I hugged myself. *No one ever will.*

"Help me understand, then. I know you feel what's between us, so tell me what the problem is," he demanded as his eyes locked on mine.

"Me! I'm the problem! I'm too fucked up for this; for you!" I yelled, gesturing towards him before dropping my arms to my sides.

His eyes softened as he closed some of the distance between us. His voice reflected the gentleness in his eyes as he said, "Ky, no-"

I cut him off as I felt tears rimming my lids, "I have to go."

Once inside my car, I couldn't contain the tears anymore, and I ended up crying all the way back home. Thankfully, Kamden was asleep, so he didn't see my puffy, red eyes and blotchy skin. I didn't want to explain to him why I was crying after dinner with Nori.

As I lay in bed, my mind taunted me, *I told you this was a bad idea.*

Fuck off, I replied as I closed my eyes, hoping sleep would find me sooner rather than later.

Going to class the next day probably wasn't the best idea, but I didn't want to give up on all the progress I had made. I just needed to suck it up and stick with it, no matter if I had to suffer with my emotions. Plus, even though I had ruined things with Ryker, I still wanted to see him.

Things were more tense then normal between us, which I had expected. I didn't know how he could look at me, let alone touch me after how I treated him.

We practiced all of the escapes that he'd already taught me, reviewing everything to make sure I remembered the moves. I wouldn't have been able to focus on any new techniques with everything running through my mind, so I was glad that we were doing things I already knew.

Once class was over, Ryker asked me to stay behind. "I want to talk to you. I'm going to lock the doors—I'll be right back."

I wanted to leave, but he deserved an explanation for last night. I needed to just break things completely off with him, maybe ask to work with one of the other instructors, even though I didn't want to. *It's best for him. You'll just bring him down with you.*

When he walked back in, he surprised me by saying, "I have a proposition for you—if you can get one good hit on me, I'll leave you alone."

My head cocked in confusion as I stared at him, contemplating what he had just said. *Would he really leave me alone? Did I want him to?* I had just been telling myself to break things off, but I really didn't want to. "Just one hit?"

"Just one. And a good one, not some weak shit. Are you up for it?" His eyebrow raised in question.

My heart screamed no, but the fear rooted inside me said yes. I didn't want him to quit pursuing me, but I doubted that I'd ever be enough for him; he didn't deserve someone as fucked up as me. So, I went with what was familiar, what I knew, pushing him away. "Yes."

The smirk that was on his face fell slightly, but he played it off as he took up his fighting stance, holding his hands up to protect his face as he chuckled. "Good luck."

Narrowing my eyes, I mimicked his pose. He always wanted a challenge, so I planned to give him one. Or at least go down trying.

"Ready?" he questioned as he pulled off his shirt, exposing those immaculate, inked muscles. My eyes instantly traced over them, admiring every inch of his perfection. *Fuck.*

When I nodded, he advanced on me instantly, landing a soft slap to the right side of my head, toying with me. "Hands up!"

I picked my hands up, but I knew they'd be falling again soon. I always forgot to keep them in front of my face when I got caught up doing combos, and I tended to drop them more when I was tired.

Aimlessly, I threw punches and kicks at Ryker, all of which he dodged or blocked easily. After several attempts, I finally landed something, grazing his jaw with my fist. He cockily smiled in response as he pushed me out of the way, throwing me off balance as he got me with a light side kick.

Stopping, I struggled for air while wondering how he sparred so effortlessly, seemingly unfatigued while I was the opposite. I was utterly exhausted from just a few minutes.

Ryker's legs swept mine out from under me, causing me to slam to the mat on my back. The impact stung my exposed skin, the force from the fall reverberating through my bones and causing the air to vacate my lungs.

Covering me with his firm, sweaty body, Ryker mounted me, pinning me to the mat as my chest heaved with heavy breaths. "Are you finished?" he gruffly asked.

My heart pounded wildly but not from fear or panic. Ryker was like a pure shot of adrenaline mixed with lust that ramped up my entire being.

I struggled against him, not wanting to concede defeat. I had only been coming for about two months, so I didn't know that many defensive tactics to aid in my efforts, at least not with sparring.

Ryker grinned as he trapped my hands above my head on the mat. "Why do you insist on fighting what you feel for me? I know that you want me."

"No, I don't," I panted. That was a huge lie, maybe the biggest I'd ever told. I wanted Ryker more than I'd ever wanted anything before, and that scared the shit out of me.

"Oh, really? You don't want this—want me—to fill your pussy?" he challenged as he ground his ample erection against me.

Closing my eyes, I bit my lip as I stifled a moan. Ryker's firm body pressing against mine was like gasoline to the fire he always set within me, and I was so close to letting the flames consume me.

Ryker's hot mouth met my neck, causing the moan I'd been withholding to escape. His tongue slowly trailed over my skin before he brought his lips to hover over mine. "Admit it, Warrior. You… want… me."

Clouded by desire, I breathlessly groaned in response, "Yes."

He softly grazed my lips with his as he gruffly asked, "Yes, what?"

Voice laced with need, I replied, "Yes, I want you."

My words set off a passion within both of us. Ryker crushed my mouth with his, eagerly devouring me as his hands roamed over my body. His tongue parted my lips before tangling with mine, the barbell in his mouth adding to the amazing sensations from his kiss.

Instead of fighting him like before, I melted into him, wanting to feel him all over and in me. My hands ventured over the hard planes of his flawless muscles as he mercilessly kissed me, one hand tangled in my hair, the other skimming under my muscle shirt.

His fingers traced over my fevered skin, causing a slight shudder to run through me. All of my thoughts, insecurities, and compulsions were erased by Ryker's skilled mouth and hands. The only thing I could focus on was the divine sensations he elicited in me as he flooded my senses, making me lose all control in a completely different way.

His hands continued up my body, pushing my shirt up as they explored my skin. Breaking our kiss, he pulled the tank top over my head before reconnecting our mouths, which couldn't get enough of each other.

Finding the waist of his shorts, my hands tugged on them, needing to remove the remaining barriers blocking his skin from mine. I wanted to feel every inch of him all over me, wanted him to continue to drown out everything else with his touch.

Ryker growled as he swiftly removed his shorts before pulling at mine. "Fuck, baby, I've wanted you for so long."

Maneuvering my body, I allowed him to easily slide my shorts and panties down while I lifted my sports bra off.

His naked body was flush against me within seconds, his thighs opening my legs as his shaft pressed against my slick entrance. I moaned from the contact, wanting and needing more of what only Ryker seemed to be able to give me.

Slowly pushing into me, he blissfully filled me inch by inch with his massive cock. Arching against him, he sank even further into me, the entirety of him still not able to fully fit inside me. We both groaned as he seated himself within me, my pussy tight around him as he began to stroke inside me.

My nails dug into Ryker's shoulders as he nipped and sucked on my breasts. Each thrust was like heaven, giving me an immense pleasure that I'd never experienced before.

Wrapping my legs around his hips, I pulled Ryker deeper within in me, causing him to emit a sound that was a cross between a growl and a groan. "God, Kaiya. I've wanted you so badly, wanted to feel your sweet pussy clench my dick."

I moaned in response to his words, unable to think straight, let alone say anything comprehensible. He continued to relentlessly pound into me, bringing me closer and closer to ecstasy with each exquisite thrust.

Perfectly caressing my walls, his cock sent me into orgasmic oblivion. Tremors of bliss flowed through my body as Ryker extended my climax with his perfect strokes. Seconds later, he pulled out before streaming his warm release all over my breasts and stomach. The feel of his cum on my body added to my arousal, making me want him inside me again, filling me over and over.

As we both regained our breath, Ryker grabbed his sweaty shirt off the mat before wiping his cum off my fevered skin. Immediately I became anxious as realization of what we'd just done sank in. *Oh my God, I just broke all of my rules. We didn't use a condom. I'm on the shot, but still. How could I lose control like that?* "I have to go," I stammered as I abruptly stood, grabbing my clothes off the floor.

I awkwardly dressed as I continued to rush towards the door. *Shit, shit, shit. Wait until you get in the car to break down—don't let Ryker see you. Breathe, breathe, breathe.*

"Kaiya, wait. Where are you going?" Ryker called after me as I flew out the door of the kickboxing room.

Please don't follow me. I all but ran towards the main entrance but was stopped by the locked doors. *Fuck!* I pushed against them, even though I knew Ryker had locked them when everyone left. We were the only ones still there.

Tears began to drip down my face as I realized I had to face Ryker. *He's never going to want to see me again. Why do I have to be such a freak?*

Pressing my forehead against the cool glass of the door, I exhaled a shaky breath as I willed back the tears. *In, out, in, out. Breathe, breathe, breathe. Just tell him the truth.* Tell him the truth? What the fuck was I thinking?

Ryker interrupted my thoughts as he placed a hand on my shoulder. His soft voice surprised me as he asked, "What's going on, Warrior?"

Swallowing the huge lump in my throat, I apologized, "I'm sorry,

Ryker. I can't do this. We shouldn't ha—"

Interrupting me, his harsh voice was a stark contrast to the gentle one from a moment before. "Hey, don't worry about it. I got what I wanted. I told you I'd have you once, remember?"

My head snapped from the glass toward him, not believing what had just come out of his mouth. My jaw gaped open, my brain unable to form the words needed to express the emotions roiling within me. "You fucking bastard," I finally seethed as I slapped him. Hard.

Ryker's eyes thinned to tiny slits as his nostrils flared in anger. Silently unlocking the door, his muscles tensed, making his tattoos bulge as he held the door open.

Neither of us said anything else as I exited the gym, and I couldn't help but feel as if I left another broken piece of myself at his feet when I walked out that door.

Chapter Twelve

Ryker

What the fuck just happened? I stood staring at the doors to the gym, wondering what the fuck went wrong. Things went to shit in less than two seconds. I couldn't believe what she'd said after we just finished having sex, especially when it ranked up at the top of my list. I thought she was blowing me off until I saw her face.

Those watery eyes and tear-stained cheeks made me regret what I'd said. Every. Fucking. Word. It was all bullshit anyway. *Why did I have to be so fucking stubborn?*

I didn't understand what caused the pain in her eyes, but I knew what I'd said made it worse. I wanted to apologize, to take back the lies I defensively spewed out; anything to remove the hurt on her face. But, I couldn't, my words stuck in my throat for fear of her rejection.

Then, my warrior broke through. Anger replaced the sadness and mixed with the pain that always seemed to linger on her face. Her eyes hardened, and her lips thinned as she slapped me.

Yeah, deep down, my girl's a fighter.

I wanted to find out everything that made Kaiya who she was, to peel back every intricate layer and uncover what lay beneath her guarded exterior.

I knew her standoffish demeanor was a front that she put up to protect herself. What I wanted to know was from what. Obviously, someone had hurt her—I recognized that type of pain; the kind that embeds in your soul, and never goes away. I endured that scarring pain every fucking day.

I wanted to erase some of hers, even if it was only a sliver. I would take what she'd give me, if that was anything at all after what had just happened. *Damn, I fucked up.*

I couldn't help what I had said, especially when her words reopened old scars. "I can't do this."

That phrase had changed everything, altering my whole life when it was said to me four years ago.

"Ry, we need to talk."

"About what, babe?"

She exhaled a heavy sigh. "I don't know how to say this…" she trailed off as a sob broke through.

"What's wrong? Is it the baby?" I asked with concern as I took her hand in mine.

Jerking her hand away, she stood and clenched her fists. "I can't do this anymore!"

Confused and worried, I questioned, "Baby, calm down. What are you talking about?"

"This! Us! I can't stand the lies anymore!" She threw her hands out to the side.

"Lies? What lies? I've never lied to you before." I had no clue what she was referring to.

"The baby's not yours!" she blurted.

The air caught in my lungs, my heart stuttering in my chest from her words. "What?" I whispered as tears began to burn my eyes.

Her own tears trickled down her face as she coldly repeated, "The baby's not yours."

And to twist the knife she had plunged in my heart, she added, "Ethan's the father."

Fuck her. And him. The both of them could rot in hell. It was because of them that I was the way I am—hollow and numb, just going through the motions of everyday life without giving a fuck about anyone else. I never thought that I'd let another person in, but Kaiya was different. She made me want to feel again, to experience life again, kindling a long dead fire inside me. Now, I'd gone and fucked it all up.

I thought that having her once would be enough to satisfy my desire for her, just as it had with all the others. But, it didn't; if anything, it had made me want her more. Her sweet sex had become my drug, addicting me the moment I sank my dick inside her.

I watched her angrily storm off to her car before she got in and sped out of the parking lot. Locking the door, I tried to stash away my thoughts of her, unable to process anything with the smell of her still on my skin.

I was off the next day, so hopefully I'd be able to make sense of all the mess after I slept, but I had a feeling that I wouldn't be getting much sleep tonight.

As I had expected, I slept like shit. Tossing and turning all night, I was unable to get Kaiya off my mind. Memories of her moaning my name, digging her nails into my skin, and feeling her soft flesh against mine as her pussy clenched my cock taunted me as I tried to sleep.

Even though it was my day off, I was still going to the gym. I needed to release the pent up frustration from last night. I knew Kaiya wouldn't be there—she never worked out on Fridays, so I wouldn't have a chance to apologize to her. I'd tried calling and texting her, but she didn't answer any of my attempts. I was hoping to run into her at the club later where we had first kissed—she and Nori went there most Fridays. But I wasn't sure if she'd go after what had happened last night.

I was wound up even after working out, the stress of last night still weighing me down. *Why did I have to say those things to her? She'll probably never want to see me again.*

I sent a text to Drew to see if he wanted to go with me to the club:

Me: Club tonight?

After a few minutes, he responded back:

Drew: I'm down what time

Me: Your place 11

Drew: Cool

When I got to Drew's apartment, he opened the door and offered me a beer. "What's been going on with you? Still talking to Kaiya?"

I took a long swig of my beer and let it slowly roll down my throat before saying anything. "I kind of fucked it all up last night. She won't return my calls or anything." I sat down on the couch. "I'm hoping to see her tonight."

Drew popped the top on his own bottle as he leaned against the counter in the kitchen. "You really like her, huh?"

Taking another drink of my beer, I swallowed deeply. "Yeah—she's not like all the girls we run game on all the time."

"You think she'll be at the club tonight?" Drew asked as he came and sat on the end of the couch.

"I don't know. Kaiya says she and Nori go there almost every Friday, but I don't know if she'd want to go out after last night—she was pretty upset."

"Even if she doesn't, we can still get drunk and hook up with some hotties, right?" Drew said as he punched my bicep.

"Yeah," I replied halfheartedly before taking another long pull of my beer. I didn't feel like hooking up with anyone else; I just wanted Kaiya. *Don't be such a pussy. She can be replaced.*

I almost laughed at myself. I'd never find anyone else quite like Kaiya. She wasn't like the sluts that threw themselves at me all the time—there was more to her than that, something deeper that she didn't let anyone see.

After finishing off a six pack of beer, we left Drew's in separate cars. We arrived at the club a little after midnight. The club was so crowded that you couldn't turn around without brushing up against someone. Music blared as we waited at the bar to order drinks, and I searched the room for Kaiya. Within seconds, my eyes zeroed in on her. My jaw twitched and my fists clenched—she was completely wasted, dancing all over some guy in the middle of the dance floor.

My blood boiled as I angrily stalked through the crowd, making my way to where she was grinding herself against him.

Lightly grabbing her arm, I pulled her to me as I glared at the asshole dancing with her. "Fuck off," I seethed, holding back from knocking him out right there on the dance floor.

I turned my attention to Kaiya, who was swaying in her heels. I cupped her chin and forced her to look at me. "What do you think you are doing?" I growled.

Her glazed eyes narrowed as she angrily slurred, "Why the fuck do you care? You got what you wanted already, remember?" She weakly shoved my chest.

Fuck. I knew she wouldn't let what happened go so easily, but I didn't think it would have affected her that much.

My grip on her eased as I softened my tone. "Kaiya, I—"

She pulled out of my grasp, basically falling into the dickhead's arms. "Leave me alone, Ryker."

The bastard smugly grinned at me as he wrapped his arms around Kaiya, resting his hands on her ass. I balled my fists as I took a deep breath so that I didn't end up strangling the guy. I kept trying to tell myself that she wasn't mine, that I had no claim on her, but everything in me screamed that she was.

Fuck this shit, I'm leaving. I pushed through the crowd towards the exit, getting cussed at as I forced people out of the way.

When I reached my truck, I hesitated as I was about to get in. *Don't let that asshole punk you out and take your fucking girl from you. Go back in there and get her.*

My eyes scanned the room when I went back in. Kaiya and the tool she was with were in the same spot on the dance floor. As I wound through the mass of bodies, the guy leaned over to whisper something in her ear, then led her towards the back of the club.

Increasing my pace, I followed after them, shoving people that got in my way. *Fuck this shit.* I'd drag her over my shoulder if I had to; I wasn't going to let her do something I knew she'd regret.

As I reached the door, I stopped. *What are you doing? You're acting like some stalker. If she wants to hook up with some guy in the back alley of a club, then let her—she's not your problem.*

I tried to turn around, to walk away, but I couldn't. She meant more to me than that. I'd only wanted a one time fuck, but she changed things, made me want something more.

I pounded my fist against the door and cursed, "Fuck!"

As I warred with my thoughts, dull voices from outside interrupted my internal debate.

"Come on, baby, you know you want it," the jackass urged.

Really, guy?

"No. Stop, please," Kaiya pleaded, the desperation in her voice snapping something within me. Sounds of a struggle followed, and both fear and rage consumed me at the thought of someone hurting her, constricting the air in my lungs as my heart beat increased. I shoved open the door, sending it to slam against the wall as I stepped into the alley. Darting my head from side to side, I searched for Kaiya in the dim lighting behind the club, but I couldn't find her. *Where are you, baby?*

I heard shuffling to my left, along with the guy's voice again. "You've been all over me all night—I know you want it."

Following their voices, I rushed in the direction that Kaiya was speaking now. "Get off me!" she shrieked before I heard a slap.

I could see them in the distance now, on the other side of a dumpster. *Real classy, asshole.*

"Oh, you like it rough, huh? I'll give it to you rough, then."

I was about thirty feet away when he slapped her back, which sent me into a rage-filled run. *I'm going to kill that motherfucker!* Kaiya began to scream as he covered her mouth with one hand, pushing her back against the wall while using the other to grope all over her body. *I'm almost there, baby.*

Then, my warrior bit him. *Good girl.* He pulled away instinctively before rearing back again to hit her, but it was too late—I was already there.

Tackling him to the ground, I immediately began punching him, bashing his head into the asphalt with my fists. He tried to fight back, but with the combination of my training and his drunkenness, he was no match for me. Fury took hold, overpowering any other emotion as I continued to beat him until I couldn't recognize his face beneath the blood and bruising.

Then, I remembered Kaiya. Standing up, I turned to face her—she was huddled against the wall, arms tightly around herself, crying. As our eyes locked, we both began to move towards each other until I wrapped her in my arms.

Burying her face in my chest, her sobbing intensified. I held her tighter, pressing kisses to the top of her head. She clutched the back of my shirt in her hands as her body shook against mine.

"Shh, it's okay, now—I've got you, baby," I whispered into her hair.

"I'm sorry," she apologized through her sobs, the sound muffled against my chest.

"You have nothing to be sorry for—I'm the one who should be sorry. I shouldn't have said what I said last night, shouldn't have hurt you like that. I fucked up."

Looking up at me, she propped her chin on my chest as tears continued to stream down her face. Even with her smeared make-up and blotchy skin, she was the most beautiful woman I'd ever seen.

"Thank you for saving me."

I brought my hands to her face, stroking the tears off her cheeks with my thumbs as I looked into her eyes. "I'll always save you, Warrior. You just have to let me."

Her bottom lip trembled as she nodded. Her hands came up to cover mine as my mouth came down on hers. Unlike our other kisses, this one was gentle, but not less passionate—electricity surged through me as my heart rate up kicked up, just like it did every time.

When we separated, I placed my forehead against hers. "Ready to go?"

She pulled back, looking up at me with reddened eyes. "Yeah, I have to find Nori—she drove." Her voice was hoarse and knotted with emotion.

"I can give you a ride home."

She briefly hesitated, unsure as always. Reaching toward her, I waited for her to put her hand in mine. She threaded our fingers together while giving me a small smile as we started to walk towards the end of the alley.

Once we got in my truck, I could tell she was still shaken up. She trembled as tears rimmed her eyes, and a few escaped every so often to fall down her cheeks.

After starting the truck, I placed my hand over hers, hoping I could calm her some. "Hey, it's okay, it's over. Please don't cry anymore."

She squeezed my hand tightly. "You don't understand. I… I just…" she hesitated, cutting off her words.

"What, baby?"

Her eyes closed as she took a deep breath. "This just brought back so many bad memories."

Bad memories? "This has happened to you before?" I asked angrily.

"Not exactly," she sighed before pausing. Her eyes opened and met mine as I waited for her to continue. "I… I—" a sob broke through, cutting off her words as she shook her head.

"Kaiya, baby, tell me." I urged.

Our gazes locked, her eyes searching mine as tears streaked her cheeks. Stroking the back of her hand with my thumb, I said, "You can trust me, Warrior."

She continued to hold my gaze before speaking, her voice cracking, "I… I… I was abused when I was little."

"What? For how long?" I asked, my anger building back from her words.

Tears were raining down her face as she choked through her sobs, "As long as I can remember. He… he wouldn't stop. No matter how hard I tried… he always touched me. It didn't end until… until I was seventeen."

My body was on fire with rage, even more so than minutes ago when I saw that asshole hit her. Someone had hurt my warrior for years, making her live in fear.

"Who?" I gritted through clenched teeth.

Her skin paled, making the slap mark on her face stand out even more. I softly caressed the area on her cheek as her eyes closed and she exhaled a heavy breath.

"I can't," she whispered as she shook her head.

Even though I wanted to, I didn't question her further. She'd already opened up to me more than she ever had before, and she'd been through enough for the night. "You don't have to tell me now—whenever you're ready, I'll be here."

"Thank you," she murmured softly as she gazed down at our joined hands. "Oh my God! Your hands!"

Grabbing both of my hands gently, she inspected them before looking up at me sadly. Most of my knuckles had split open, and blood splattered the skin.

"It doesn't hurt, not yet anyway. This is a perfect example of why you should never punch anyone in the face. I just couldn't control myself."

She softly smiled as she pressed her lips to my fingers, careful to avoid my injuries.

How could anyone want to hurt someone so perfect?

Once she finished, she leaned over the center console to lay her head on my shoulder, keeping one of my hands linked with hers.

"I need your address for the GPS."

"19 Pleasant Street."

By the time we got to her apartment, Kaiya had fallen asleep. Carefully reaching to lift her in my lap, I cradled her in my arms as I stepped out of the truck. *Shit, I don't know her apartment number.* "What's your apartment number, baby?" I asked softly.

Stirring slightly, she mumbled, "Sixteen."

Once we made it to her door, I pushed the button for the doorbell. After several seconds, the door opened to a surprised Kamden. When he focused on Kaiya in my arms, his expression morphed from shock to anger as he reached for her. "What the fuck did you do to her?"

Stepping back, bringing her closer into my body, I said, "I didn't do anything. We need to talk."

He must have seen something in my face because he moved from the doorway to let me in.

"Where's her room?"

"I'm not letting you in her room," he stated gruffly.

"Then, I guess I'm holding her until we finish talking," I retorted as I looked down at her, sleeping peacefully. She was like an angel, and I couldn't believe someone had hurt her for so long.

When my eyes went back up to meet Kamden's, his anger seemed to have receded some. His jaw was no longer tense and his eyes softened as he gazed at Kaiya.

"Her room's this way," he sighed.

I followed him down the hallway to the door at the end. After we walked in, Kamden pulled back the comforter so I could lay Kaiya down. As I covered her, I pressed a kiss to her temple and brushed the hair back from her face. "Goodnight, Warrior."

She drowsily smiled as I pulled away. I shut the door before following Kamden back out into the living room.

"Care to explain what happened?" he asked, his eyes glaring as he crossed his arms over his chest.

"Some guy got too handsy at the club tonight. I took care of him."

He sighed in relief. "Thank you." He fell back onto the couch and covered his face with his hands. "I don't know what I would've done if something happened to her."

"Sounds like a lot has happened to her already." I stood in front of him and folded my arms over my chest. "Care to explain that?"

His gaze snapped up to mine as his body tensed. "You don't know what you're talking about!" he spat.

My fists clenched. "Was it you? Were you the one that abused her when she was little?" If he was, I was going to kill him.

He sucked in a breath, eyes wide with disbelief before furiously responding, "No! I would never do that to her!"

"Who was it, then?" I gritted.

"It's not my place to tell you—Kaiya will tell you when she's ready," he replied firmly.

We both silently stared at one another for I don't know how long before Kamden finally spoke, "Thank you again for protecting her."

I nodded, then headed for the front door, but stopped. Turning back around to face him, I asked, "Will you have her call me? I want to make sure she's okay."

He hesitated, shaking his head. "Look, you seem to have feelings for Kaiya, but I don't think you two should see each other anymore."

I squared my body, pushing my chest out. "Last I checked, Kaiya is a grown woman, and you aren't her father. She can make her own decisions."

He stood up with authority and stared me down with a death glare. "And last I checked, you're a womanizing asshole. I don't want my sister getting involved with you."

"Too late." I shrugged. "I'm going to see her, whether you fucking like it or not."

"Oh, really? We'll see about that." There was an obvious challenge in his tone.

"Yeah, we will," I responded. I turned and walked out the door, slamming it behind me. I was going to see Kaiya, and there was nothing Kamden or anyone could do to fucking stop me.

Chapter Thirteen

Kaiya

Noise from the kitchen woke me, and I winced from the throbbing pain in my cheek and head. *Why did I drink so much? I can't believe how stupid I was.*

As I slowly sat up in my bed, I thought about how Ryker not only came to my rescue, but listened to me when I needed someone—he actually seemed like he cared, despite what he had said to me the night before. *What changed?*

I dreaded facing Kamden—Ryker had to have brought me home, and I wondered what happened after that. *Did Kamden question Ryker? Did they talk about what happened at the club?*

Slowly, I trudged to the kitchen, where Kamden was making breakfast.

"Hey." I plopped down at the breakfast bar, preparing for the inevitable.

As Kamden turned to face me, his eyes focused on my cheek, then immediately set in anger as he stalked over to me.

"Did Ryker do this?" he growled as he gently grabbed my chin, tilting it to look at my face better.

"No!" I snapped, pulling back from him. "Ryker saved me from the guy that did—he stopped him." I looked away and wrapped my arms around myself.

Kamden placed his arms on my shoulders, looking at me with concern. "Tell me what happened."

Tears stung my eyes as I remembered last night. *Thank God Ryker was there to save me. I don't know what would've happened if he hadn't come after me.*

"I acted stupid—I got drunk and was all over this guy." My voice was barely above a whisper as shame and embarrassment got the better of me. "He wanted to take things further, and I didn't want to. He didn't like that, and got physical."

When I looked up, Kamden's nostrils flared in anger as he took a deep breath and gripped the side of the counter. "And?"

"Ryker intervened—he beat the crap out of the guy and brought me home."

"You told him about Kaleb?" He sounded irritated and confused as his eyes searched my face.

My muscles tensed slightly at the accusation. "Not everything. I just told him that I was abused when I was little. Not who."

"He thought it was me—I thought he was going to kick my ass." His stern expression and tone told me he was serious.

"What?" I laughed nervously.

"Seriously—he asked if it was me. He was pissed."

"Really?" *I can't believe he cared.*

"Yeah. I told him to stay away from you." Kamden crossed his arms.

"What?" I exclaimed angrily as I stood. "Why did you tell him that?"

"He's not good for you, Ky. He—" He relaxed his stance as he moved towards me again, but I held my hand up to stop him.

"That's not your decision, Kamden!" My voice rose as I narrowed my eyes at him. "It's my choice whether I want to see him or not!"

Kamden paused, giving me a perplexed look as a grin attempted to curve his lips. "You really like him, don't you?"

Did I? "I don't know… he makes me feel different." I sighed as I locked eyes with him. "Alive… like I'm not just a hollow shell anymore."

"Well, he didn't sound like he was going to listen to me, anyway. He wants you to call him." He smiled knowingly at me.

My lips tipped up, but almost immediately fell. "I can't believe he wants to talk to me after last night. I was all over that guy right in front of him, and I yelled at him in front of all the people in the club." I blew out a breath of frustration as I buried my face in my hands and groaned.

"I don't like the guy, but he obviously has feelings for you. He wouldn't have wasted his time otherwise. Ryker has no problem getting women."

That was an understatement. Ryker had told me that he had lost count of how many women he'd been with, and never slept with the same one twice. *I wonder if he'll be the same with me.* After Thursday night, I would've said yes, but given the events of last night, I wasn't so sure anymore.

"I know. I'm going to get some ice for my cheek and call him."

After grabbing a bag of frozen vegetables, I went back to my room and dug my phone from my purse. *Fuck, it's dead.* Plugging it in to the charger, I powered it up before dialing Ryker's number.

"Hey, Warrior."

A warm tingle spread through me at his words, causing a smile to spread over my face—I loved when he called me that. "Hey." I lay back on my bed, keeping the phone to the opposite side of where I was holding my makeshift icepack to my cheek.

"How you feeling?" His tone sounded genuine, like he actually wanted to know.

"Fine. My cheek and head hurt, but I'm okay. How are your knuckles?"

Ryker's laughter sounded into the phone. "You're the one who got attacked last night, and you're worried about me. They're fine, baby."

"Good." I paused for a few seconds, nibbling my bottom lip. "I'm really sorry about last night."

"Me too, for everything." He sighed into the phone. "Let's just forget about it and move on. Can I see you today?"

Some tension eased in my chest—he still wanted to talk to me after how I acted. "What did you have in mind?"

"Lunch? I don't have to go into the gym until two today. I can pick you up or meet you somewhere."

"You can pick me up. In an hour?" A goofy smile spread across my face as I stifled a girly squeal.

"I'll see you then. Bye, Warrior."

"Bye."

After I hung up, I rushed to shower and get ready in time before Ryker got there. We had a lot to discuss, especially the things he'd said to me after we had sex Thursday night—I hadn't forgotten them. Their harshness still stung me, and they were such a contrast to his actions last night that I was left totally confused.

I dressed in a deep purple sundress, then applied some foundation to the bruise on my cheek, but it didn't help much. The purple of the welt almost matched the color of my dress and looked terrible against my pale skin.

Ryker texted me when he was downstairs, and I peeked my head into Kamden's room to tell him about my plans.

"I'm going to lunch with Ryker. I'll be back later."

Kamden gave me a disapproving look as he cautioned, "Be careful."

I rolled my eyes. "I will."

Ryker was waiting for me at the bottom of the stairs. He looked amazing, as always, in a tight blue V-neck shirt that emphasized his muscles. He gave me his sexy grin until I got closer, then his eyes focused on my cheek. His eyebrows creased in anger as his smile morphed to a scowl. "That fucking bastard," he mumbled below his breath.

When I reached him, he pulled me into his chest, cradling my face as he examined the bruise like Kamden had earlier.

"I'm fine." I pulled away, uncomfortable with him looking at me so closely, afraid he would see what lay underneath if he looked too long.

"Ready to go?" Ryker asked as he joined our hands.

Giving him a small smile, I nodded. He led me to the passenger side of his truck, opening the door and helping me get in the raised cab.

"Where do you want to go?" Ryker asked when he got in.

"Hmm. What about Cafe Luna?" I suggested.

Cafe Luna was a quaint brunch spot that Nori and I went to occasionally. They had delicious paninis and breakfast, including a spicy chicken chorizo and black bean omelet.

"Wherever you want, baby," Ryker said as he started the truck.

It only took us about ten minutes to reach the restaurant. Ryker once again threaded our fingers together after helping me get down from his truck. *I really like this side of him.* A smile took over my lips as I glanced at him, but I quickly darted my gaze away when he caught me looking at him out of the corner of his eye.*What are you, like twelve? Quit being such a girl.*

We were seated in a booth right next to a huge window overlooking the street. People hurried past us on their cell phones, some talking on them as others stared at the screen while trying not to run into anything.

The waitress came up to our booth and took our drink order. After she brought our drinks and jotted down what we wanted to eat, I impulsively asked Ryker, "Did you mean what you said the other night?" I couldn't keep the question inside any longer—it had been nagging at me the whole drive.

The muscles in his jaw tensed as he swallowed. "No."

"Then, why did you say those things to me?"

He didn't say anything for several seconds, and I was afraid he was going to get up and leave me there, not wanting to deal with my bullshit anymore.

"Fear." He reached for his glass of water before taking a long drink.

Fear? What was he afraid of? "Fear?" I repeated, wanting him to clarify.

He gave a quick nod as he set down the glass. "I thought you were blowing me off."

"So, you decided to blow me off first?" I raised my eyebrow and rested my arms on the table.

"Look." He sighed. "I know I made a mistake, and I'm sorry I hurt you. I… I have issues." He leaned in, grabbing my hands and locking eyes with me. "I've been fucked over in the past, and it's hard for me to trust someone after what I went through." He sat back and shrugged his shoulders. "We all have our own demons."

"Yeah, but some demons are worse than others." I stared at my glass, tracing a finger along the rim.

"That doesn't make them any less easy to deal with for the person that has to live with them."

He had a point. Just because I felt my demons were worse, didn't mean that Ryker's weren't hard for him. I didn't even know what his were to be able to judge. I wouldn't feel right asking him to tell me since I kept so much from him all of the time.

I nodded in understanding. "So, where do we go from here?"

"I'm not sure." He released a heavy breath. "All I know is that I want to keep seeing you. That is, if you still want to."

"I want to, but I'm scared." I gnawed on my lip as I looked over his face. "What if you hurt me?"

Abruptly, he stood before coming to my side of the booth and scooting in next to me. He draped an arm around my shoulder, pulling me into him. He used his other hand to tilt my chin to look in his eyes.

"Honestly, Warrior, I'm scared, too. I haven't felt this way about someone since… well, a really long time. I promise I won't hurt you if you don't hurt me."

My heart fluttered. I wasn't completely sure I could trust him, but I was willing to take the chance. Life wasn't meant to be lived in fear, and I felt that moving forward with Ryker was taking another step to becoming stronger, to becoming whole.

Instead of answering him with words, I brought my lips to his, hoping that was enough of an answer for him. I wasn't good at expressing my feelings, but I hoped that the kiss demonstrated how I felt, showed that I was trusting him not to crush what was left of me.

When we finally parted, he said, "So, was that a yes?"

I laughed. "On one condition—no other girls."

Making a skeptical face, he teased, "I don't know if I can do that."

"Then, I guess I'm leaving," I joked, pushing him away from me.

Wrapping me in his arms, he chuckled. "I was just kidding." He brushed his lips over mine. "No other girls."

I pulled back and gave him a deal breaking glare. "Promise," I demanded.

Cupping my face, he held my gaze. "I promise—no other girls."

"You better not hurt me or I'll be forced to use my fighting skills on you." I lightly jabbed him in the stomach as I giggled.

"No, please don't," he playfully pleaded, acting fearful of my non-existent threat. We both laughed before he brought his lips to mine again, sending warmth through my entire body before it pooled between my thighs. My stomach tightened as his tongue entered my mouth, joining with mine to deepen the kiss. *Damn, he kisses so good.*

Throat-clearing caused us to break away from each other, but not before Ryker pressed one last soft kiss on my lips. We both directed our attention to the waitress, who held a tray in her hands.

"I'm sorry to interrupt, but your food is ready," she said politely.

Blushing with embarrassment, I avoided her eyes as she set our food on the table. When she left, I looked at Ryker, who chuckled at me and shook his head.

Once we finished eating, Ryker drove me back home. He made plans to take me to dinner once he got off work, and I couldn't fight the foreign feeling of happiness that overtook me. *Maybe Ryker is good for me.*

When I entered the apartment, Kamden came out of his room and asked me a million questions about Ryker and our date. Okay, maybe not a million, but way more than necessary.

After his interrogation, I tried to escape to my room, but he stopped me as I was walking down the hallway.

"Do you remember about Monday?"

"Monday?" I said quizzically. *What's Monday?* After a few seconds of contemplation, it hit me. *Our appointment. Kaleb. Fuck. Shit. Fuck.* "Fuck. I can't believe it's already here," I groaned.

"You okay?" Kamden asked with concern, rubbing his hand up and down my arm.

My stomach tightened uncomfortably. "Yeah, just nervous. I better call Nori and remind her."

"Let me know if you need anything—I know this is going to be tough for you."

"Thanks, I will," I replied before turning and heading into my room. Taking my phone out of my purse, I dialed Nori. She answered after the second ring. "What the fuck happened last night, Ky? You didn't return any of my fucking calls or texts. I was worried sick."

Shit. I forgot that I just left without a word—she sounded pissed. I sat on my bed as I apologized, "I'm sorry. My phone died, and it just slipped my mind this morning."

"Well, what happened? Is everything okay?" Her voice lost some of the venom that had been in it.

I explained everything that happened at the club last night, but I started with Ryker and I having sex on Thursday. I hadn't told her about it because I was so upset, but she needed to know everything to understand the events of last night. Nori didn't say anything for several seconds, then finally spoke, "So, how was it? I bet he was amazing."

That was an understatement. He was beyond amazing. "It was… unbelievable." I sighed dreamily as I flopped back on the bed. "He made me feel things I've never felt before, and gave me the best orgasm of my life. There just aren't words."

Nori giggled. "Wow, that's awesome, Ky. I'm really happy for you."

"Can you believe what he said to me after, though?" Thinking about it still hurt, and it was hard to push the thoughts away when they were so fresh.

"He's a guy. They aren't good with rejection. He thought you were blowing him off after literally just having sex with him—total ego killer.

Obviously, he didn't mean what he said or else he wouldn't have gone to the club looking for you, and he definitely wouldn't have saved you from that asshole. Actions speak louder than words, girl."

I picked at the ends of my hair as I released a sigh. "True. Words still hurt though."

"I can't believe you told him about Kaleb." Her voice was filled with disbelief.

"Me neither. I mean, I didn't tell him everything."

"Why did you tell him?"

That had surprised even me—I hadn't told anyone anything involving Kaleb except Kamden and Nori.

"When he saved me, I felt like I at least owed him some of the truth for my actions. And, even after what he said to me, I trusted him. Like you said, actions speak louder than words."

"Yeah, he seems like a great guy that just has some issues. If anyone should be able to understand that, it should be you."

I snorted. "Yeah, I'm sure his issues are nowhere even close to being as fucked up as mine."

"You never know, Ky. Maybe you should ask him about them."

"I don't like being asked about mine. He'll tell me when he's ready."

"Just like you will?" she countered.

Will I? "I don't know if I'll ever tell him—I don't want him to look at me differently."

"If he cares about you, he won't. Then, you'll know whether he's worth it or not."

"I'm not ready for that yet." I blew out a deep breath. "I don't think either one of us are. We just agreed to start dating. Baby steps, Nori, baby steps."

"You've made a lot of progress. I'm really proud of you, Ky. Seriously."

I smiled from her words. "Thank you. It's hard, but I'm trying. Oh, I almost forgot! Monday is our appointment at the hospital."

"I know. I thought that's why you were acting all crazy yesterday."

"Oh. No, I totally forgot. Kamden just reminded me." My smile began to fade as I thought about the appointment, my chest tightening in anxiety. I rubbed my hand over it, trying to ease some of the tenseness.

"I'm planning to come over to your apartment that morning and we can all ride together."

We talked a little more about Monday before we hung up. Heading to the bathroom, I searched for some aspirin since my cheek and head were still pulsing with pain.

I didn't realize how exhausted I was until I lay back down on my bed. Sleep found me within seconds.

I was extremely wound up at class on Sunday because of my impending visit to the hospital the next day. I was so not prepared to be in the same building as Kaleb. It also didn't help that I was unsure of how to act around Ryker in front of the other students and instructors. It was probably against policy or something for him to be with me, so I didn't want to get him into any trouble.

Ryker approached me as I was hitting my bag. "Everything okay?" he asked as he eyed me warily. *How could he always tell when something was bothering me?*

"Yeah, just a little stressed." *A lot stressed, actually.*

"Anything I can help with?"

"No—I'll be okay. Hitting the bag helps." I forced a smile.

Those warm eyes told me he knew better, but he didn't question me further. "Just don't overdo it, Warrior," he said as his lips curved up slightly.

After class ended, I waited for Ryker to close up before we left together. He walked me to my car, then crushed his lips against mine, stealing my breath as he passionately kissed me. *Holy crap.*

Pulling back slightly, we both gasped for air.

"I've been wanting to do that all night, that and so much more," he said, holding my face in his hands.

Our mouths reconnected in a frenzy as Ryker's hands roamed over my body. He hooked my legs around him, pushing me against the car as his erection pressed into my core. I might have moaned, I wasn't really sure since I couldn't process anything but the feel of Ryker all over me.

"Come home with me," he murmured against my lips.

Oh, how I wanted to—so badly. It probably wasn't the best idea given what I had to do tomorrow, but then again, it might be good for me to lose myself in Ryker before I had to deal with Kaleb.

"Okay."

Even though I answered him, Ryker didn't release me. He kept relentlessly devouring me right there in the parking lot. I couldn't have even told anyone my name once we finally stopped—that was how amazing that man kissed.

"My warrior finally gave in," he teased when we finally stopped. "You can follow me there."

As I drove behind him, I started to reconsider what I was doing. *I'm going to have to explain my rules—do I really want to go into that right now? What if he laughs in my face? Shit, why did I agree to this? Maybe I should just turn around and go home… no, I can't do that to him. I'll just have to tell him something came up and leave—that'll work.*

Once we were up in his apartment, I tried to give Ryker the excuse I came up with, but his mouth silenced mine, capturing my lips as soon as he locked the door.*Shit I can't lie to him—I'm just going to have to tell him the truth.*

Pushing him away, I disconnected our lips and locked our eyes. "We need to talk."

Chapter Fourteen

Ryker

"We need to talk."

No man wanted to hear those words, especially when first starting out, but Kaiya was standing right in front of me saying them. The last time I'd heard those words, things didn't end well for me.

"About?" I questioned as I searched her face. I rubbed my hand on the back of my neck anxiously. I had no idea what Kaiya was going to tell me—with her, it could be anything.

Sighing, she led me to the couch, and we sat down. "Before we have sex again, you need to know my rules," she advised me matter of factly.

Some tension lifted off me. I expected worse. *Rules? This is going to be interesting.* "Go on."

She exhaled a heavy breath. "One, I don't do foreplay—strictly sex."

Raising an eyebrow, I caught her gaze. "No foreplay?" *We'll see about that.*

"No foreplay. Two, my throat is off limits. I don't like having it touched."

Her hand had gone instinctively to her throat, covering her small scar. She still refused to tell me what had happened. I wondered if it had anything to do with the scar I'd seen across Kamden's chest when he worked out.

"Three, I have to control when I… when I go." she stammered nervously.

"Go? Go where?" I teased, trying to lighten the mood and pry out the words she was having such a hard time saying.

"You know what I mean, Ryker." She blushed as she avoided looking at me, staring down at her hands in her lap. She was so innocently sexy when she was embarrassed.

I sat back and shrugged, playing dumb. "No, I don't. You're going to have to elaborate."

Sighing with exasperation, she flung her hands out. "Come, okay? I have to control when I come."

Interesting. "You didn't seem to have a problem with that before." I smirked.

She glared at me and pressed her lips in a tight line. "Well, I have a problem now. If you can't accept my rules, then maybe we shouldn't do this."

Raising my hands in surrender, I apologized, "I'm sorry. Any more rules?"

"Just one more—I don't spend the night."

Leaning forward, I propped my elbows on my knees and rubbed my hands together. "Okay—anything else?"

"No. Are you okay with them—with this?" she asked as she gestured between us.

I considered her question, thinking about her rules. I knew all these stipulations for sex had to do with her abuse when she was younger. On one hand, I didn't want to push her away by disregarding her rules, but on the other, rules were made to be broken. And I wanted to break hers.

"For now." I grinned mischievously. We silently stared at each other for a few seconds. "But one day, I will break each of those rules—

one… by… one. And you're going to love every second of it when I do."

"I wouldn't be so sure about that," she weakly challenged as she broke away from my gaze.

Suddenly pulling her into my lap, I grasped her hips, pushing her down against my cock. She gasped as I grazed my lips against hers. I gruffly murmured, "I'm going to let you have your way now, Warrior. But trust me when I say that those rules will be broken—soon. I guarantee it."

I claimed her lips with mine, smothering any response or argument. The only sounds I wanted to hear were the moans and whimpers she was already making as my tongue entered her mouth and twined with hers. I'd been waiting all night to feel her, to taste her, to just lose myself in her—class had been torture since I couldn't touch and kiss her like I wanted to, and I was going to make up for it the rest of the night.

My hands rubbed along the curves of her ass before I gripped it and rose from the couch. Carrying Kaiya to my bedroom, I kicked open the door and walked to the bed, laying her down. I reluctantly separated our lips, tugging my shirt over my head before doing the same with hers, eager to feel her bare skin against mine.

Once the rest of our clothing was removed, my mouth easily found hers as I pressed against her on the bed, covering her flesh with mine. My hands ran up and down the curves of her naked body, enjoying the feel of her silken skin as I savored her sweetness.

I rubbed my dick against her pussy, causing her to writhe under me. "You're so wet for me already," I growled against her lips while I rocked against her.

She whimpered as I bit her bottom lip before sucking it into my mouth. Nudging against her entrance, I barely pushed the tip of my cock inside her before dragging it out again. Kaiya's moans became deeper and louder as I teased her, gripping her hips and readying to thrust inside her.

Slowly, I sank myself into her, enjoying the feel of how she stretched to accommodate me. Her body arched into me as I spread her thighs, pushing myself deeper into her warmth.

Once Kaiya was completely full of me, I pulled out before pounding back in again, causing her to cry out as she dug her nails into my forearms. Pumping in and out of her pussy, I increased my strokes, building up the pleasure within both of us.

Kaiya wrapped her legs around my waist before squirming under me, attempting to turn us over. As I told her I would, I let her flip me and have control. *This time.* I wasn't going to complain about having a hot woman riding me.

Her hair curtained around my face as she rocked against my cock, caressing it with her soft flesh. Biting her lip, she closed her eyes in pleasure as she rode me, driving my cock further inside her. *Fuck, she feels so good.*

Her fingers dug into my chest as her pace increased, her walls tightening around my dick as she neared climax. Throwing her head back, she cried out my name and her body shuddered in ecstasy, pulsing around me as she went limp.

Flipping her over, I repeatedly slammed into her, seeking my own release. Her pussy was freshly moist from her orgasm, making it easier for my cock to slide in and out of her.

The combination of her wetness and snug walls clenching around me finally sent me over the edge. I groaned as I pulled out, coming on the inside of her thigh as I buried my face in her neck. *So fucking good.*

We both lay there for a few minutes, catching our breath before I got up to grab Kaiya a towel. When I walked back towards her, she averted her gaze from my naked body and the flush on her face deepened.

As she took the towel from my hand, she commented, "We need to start using protection."

"Why? It feels so much better without it." I gave her a crooked grin.

She gave me a look, like the one a mom gives her child when she's trying to be mad at them, but couldn't.

"Besides, we've already done it without one." I shrugged.

She shook her head as she fought a smile, propping herself up on her elbows. "You better not have given me any STDs."

"I don't have any STDs. I've always used a condom."

"Yeah, I'm sure you use that line with all your women." Her expression and tone were full of disbelief.

Laying back next to her, I brushed some hair out of her face. "Seriously. I've always used a condom before you." *And her.*

She stared at me, searching my eyes for a sign that I was lying. She opened her mouth to say something, but changed her mind and closed it before getting up and picking her clothes up off of the floor.

"What's wrong?" I sat up on the edge of the bed while she moved around.

"Nothing," she brusquely replied, avoiding looking at me.

"Bullshit." I stood and walked over to her. Turning her around, I softly demanded, "Tell me."

After several seconds of silence, she sighed, looking down at the clothes in her hands. "I'm afraid that I'll be just one of the many women you've been with and that you'll just toss me to the side when you get bored with me."

Her words were like a jab to the gut. I didn't make it a secret that I went through women like a college frat boy, but Kaiya had to know things were different between us, that she wasn't just a hook-up. Hadn't I told her that? By the sad look on her face, she had no clue how I felt about her, that I didn't plan on using her like I did the others.

Taking her face in my hands, I lifted it until she looked at me. "I'm not gonna do that to you. You're not like the others, Ky."

"How do I know you're not just saying that?"

"Because I'm standing here telling you that I'm not. I'm a lot of things, but I'm not a liar. If I wanted just a one-time thing, I wouldn't have bothered with you after Thursday night, especially after the fight we had. I wouldn't be here with you right now—I would be with someone else."

Once again she searched my gaze with hers, looking for the truth in my words. Doubt and apprehension still resided within her eyes, which I expected given her past. I knew it would take more than just my words to make her believe me, so I showed her how I felt with the only way I could think of.

Leaning down, I softly pressed my lips to hers, hoping I could chip away at some of her walls. The clothes fell from her hands and her arms slowly glided up around my neck as she reciprocated my kiss, pushing her body against mine.

I grabbed the undersides of her thighs and picked her up, wrapping her legs around me as I took her back to the bed. As soon as we met the mattress, I entered her in one, swift thrust, rooting myself deep within her.

I wanted to take my time with her, show her that I meant what I had said, but that was so fucking hard with the way her body fit mine, perfectly molding to me as we tangled in sexual ecstasy.

Kaiya lifted her hips, making me sink deeper within her. I groaned against her lips before tracing over the bottom one with my tongue ring. She moaned, then sucked my tongue back in her mouth, eagerly consuming me while I fucked her.

My hands tangled in her hair as I devoured her, loving the taste of her hot mouth. Pulling on the soft strands, I caused her to gasp against my lips while I thrust slowly inside her, bringing us both closer to climax again.

I wanted to make her come, especially since she told me she needed to control it—that made me want to do it even more. I lowered my hands, slowly caressing each curve of her soft body, intensifying my strokes. "I want to make you come, baby."

She weakly protested, shaking her head, but she continued to kiss me. Fuck, I wanted to break her rules so bad, demolish every boundary between us, but I knew I couldn't do it all at once. We'd already broken this rule before, so it was a good place to start. "Please, baby, let me make you come."

After a few seconds, she whimpered in my mouth, "Yes."

I nibbled her bottom lip, then sat up. Her half-lidded gaze found mine as I hooked my arms around her thighs, gripping the delicate flesh in my hands as I began to pummel her.

"Fuck, baby, you're so tight around me. I love the way your pussy

hugs my dick," I growled.

Kaiya's eyes rolled back before she closed her eyes in bliss, fisting the sheets while I pounded into her. She was so close to coming; I could feel her tightening around me as she repeatedly moaned my name.

Then, her thighs began to tremble in my hands as she orgasmed. Tremors of pleasure racked her body as her walls throbbed around my cock, sending me into euphoria with her. I barely pulled out before I started coming, streaming my release all over her stomach.

Reaching over the side of the bed, I picked up the towel I had brought for her earlier before wiping my cum off her skin.

Once I was finished, I pulled her body to mine, wrapping my arms around her and pressing a kiss to the top of her head. "I know you don't completely trust me, but it's different between us. I'm not going to use you."

She kissed my chest, then looked up at me. I loved the flush I put on her skin from just having sex with her. "Prove it." Her voice was strong, but those beautiful eyes looked vulnerable.

My eyes playfully narrowed. "Is that a challenge, Warrior?"

"Yep. And I think it will be your biggest one yet."

Leaning down, I grazed my lips over hers. "Accepted."

When we finally broke apart, Kaiya rose off the bed, grabbing her clothes once again from the floor.

Once she finished getting dressed, I slipped on some shorts and walked her out to her car. "See you tomorrow?"

"Maybe." she smiled. When I raised my eyebrow at her, she giggled. "If you're lucky."

I scoffed as she got in her car. I watched her drive away before I went back up to my apartment. That night, I slept the best I had since Thursday.

Chapter Fifteen

Kaiya

Fear burrowed in my body, making every muscle and joint uncomfortably stiff as I sat waiting for the hospital administrator with Kamden and Nori. I hadn't been this close to Kaleb since the *incident*, and that was eight years ago. Nausea assaulted my insides as my leg bounced frantically, my hands gripping the armrests of the chair to keep myself from bolting out of the door.

Reaching over, Kamden placed his large hand over mine. "Everything's going to be okay, *sorella,*" he assured with a comforting smile.

Giving a tight, forced smile of my own, I nodded. I didn't want to speak, afraid my voice would crack if I did. *I can't do this. I can't do this. He's going to come out here and find me. He'll finish what he started. I have to get out of here.*

As I was about to make a run for the exit, Nori silently linked our fingers before squeezing my hand gently. "You got this, girl."

Squeezing back, I released a deep breath. *You can do this. Don't let him win. You can't let him get released. He'll hurt more people. He'll hurt you.*

Just then, the door opened, causing my head to whip around—an older man with glasses in a white coat walked in with a bunch of thick files in his hands. His gaze perused over us as he rounded the desk in front of us to stand on the opposite side.

Setting the files down, he introduced himself, "Good morning. My name is Dr. Samuel Owens, and I oversee things here at the Massachusetts Treatment Center."

The Massachusetts Treatment Center was a division of the Bridgewater Correctional Complex for sexually dangerous persons. Kaleb had been diagnosed with a combination of different mental disorders, including schizophrenia and narcissism, before he was committed for his long-term sexual abuse of me.

Kamden stood to shake the doctor's hand before introducing Nori and me.

The doctor spoke, his tone authoritative and clinical. "So, you're here concerning your brother's release?"

Kamden replied, "Yes, we wanted to see if there was an appeal process—we want to prevent it."

Dr. Owens looked perplexed as he responded, "I'm sorry, but his release is determined by his doctors and other hospital personnel."

Kamden's jaw ticked. "You don't take into account his victim's testimony?"

"We do—we review his whole file, including the progress he's made since being here. You do realize that it's been eight years since he was committed? People change." His tone was defensive and condescending. *Asshole.*

Kamden started to speak again, but I interrupted as fury took hold of me. My chair toppled over behind me as I angrily stood. "Do *you* realize what he did to me? What I had to go through for all those years?" Hot, angry tears began to stream down my face as my voice increased in volume. "Do you know what the aftermath is following something that traumatizing? Do you know what I've had to deal with for the past eight years? How afraid I am of other people? All because of him!" I screamed as my tears blurred my vision.

Kamden wrapped his arm around me, trying to comfort me as he pulled me into him. I clutched his shirt as I glared at the doctor.

His eyes softened some as he addressed me, "I'm sorry for what happened to you, but I can assure you that Kaleb is much different than he used to be. We wouldn't be considering his release otherwise. The treatment and therapy have done wonders for him, and his current medication has proven to be successful in controlling his behaviors."

I didn't respond—Dr. Owens would never understand. He had looked at everything logically, only taking into account what his research had dictated, not my feelings or opinions. Kamden, however, was a different story. He wasn't having any of the doctor's bullshit.

His grip on me tightened as he seethed, "Monsters like that don't change. They just find a way to adapt to their surroundings, to fool everyone into believing they're something that they're not." His voice cracked, and he took a deep breath to calm himself down. "Kaleb had me fooled for our entire lives. I… I never knew what he'd been doing to our own sister for all those years, and we lived under the same roof."

As I slumped into Kamden's seat, tears slid down my face. I began to zone out, the heated discussion between Kamden and Dr. Owens sounding garbled and distant. All of this talk about Kaleb and the fact that he was somewhere in the building started clawing at me. I clutched my head as images of him and memories of all the times he had violated me played in my head like a deranged slideshow made specifically to torment me. *I need to get away from him, need to get out of here.*

Shooting out of the chair, I bolted for the door, ignoring everyone's calls as I ran. All I could think about was getting out of there, of getting as far away from Kaleb as possible, especially since his release seemed more eminent based on what Dr. Owens had said. My legs pumped harder as I headed for the exit doors, and I almost collapsed in relief once I passed through them. Bracing my hands on my knees, I sucked in heavy breaths of air as I tried to compose myself.

Nori came through the doors shortly after I did. She wrapped her arms around me and held me until Kamden exited about ten minutes later. His hardened eyes and tight frown told me that the meeting didn't end as we had hoped.

The whole ride home was silent. Kamden tensely clutched the steering wheel with a white-knuckled grip as he drove. Nori held my hand the entire way, stabilizing my frenetic emotions, keeping me from coming completely unglued.

Once we got home, I headed straight for my room and shut the door. I could hear footsteps in the hallway directly outside, but no one knocked or entered.

Nori's muffled voice sounded through the door. "I'm worried about her, Kam."

"You think I'm not?" He sounded frustrated, and I could practically see him running his hand over his buzzed head.

"Well, what are we going to do?"

"I don't know," he sighed.

"Maybe you should call Ryker—have him come see her."

"No," Kamden raised his voice angrily. "He is not a part of this. He doesn't need to be involved."

Shutting my eyes, I blocked out the rest of their conversation. I wanted to see Ryker, but things were different now. Kaleb was going to be released, and then he would hurt Ryker because of me. My heart clenched, my stomach turning at the thought of Kaleb causing any kind of harm to Ryker.

I had to protect him. I couldn't let Kaleb hurt him. I'd never forgive myself if anything happened to him. Even if Kaleb wasn't involved, my unstable emotions would destroy both of us eventually, and I didn't want that for Ryker. He deserved a normal woman free of issues that could love him completely, that could give him more than I ever would be able to.

Tears surfaced as I thought about what I had to do. *Don't be selfish. Do what's best for him. He'll hate you, but at least he'll be safe.* I knew I never should've gotten involved with him. I just prayed that it wasn't too late to save him.

Chapter Sixteen

Ryker

Kaiya had been avoiding me for weeks, including missing class. I'd called and texted her several times with no response, so I was done. At least I was trying to tell myself that, but who was I kidding? I couldn't get her off of my mind, no matter how hard I'd tried.

I didn't understand what had happened—the last time I saw her, everything was fine. Well, except for that small argument, but I fixed that—at least, I thought I had. I could never tell exactly what she was thinking, so there was no way for me to know why she had started avoiding me.

Occasionally, I'd seen Kamden in the gym, but he avoided me like I had some contagious disease. I was getting fed up with him, almost reaching the point where I didn't mind causing a scene to get information about Kaiya.

I stalked toward him in the weight room as he executed leg presses. Hovering next to the machine, I looked down at him. "We need to talk."

He abruptly stopped and got off the bench. As if I was invisible and hadn't said a word, he walked away from me. *Fuck this, I'm getting* *some answers.*Determined, I followed after him and grabbed him by the arm.

His muscle tensed under my grip as he stopped. "Let me go," he seethed.

"Not until you tell me what's going on with Kaiya," I growled.

Turning his head towards me, he narrowed his eyes and snarled, "That's none of your fucking business."

Fuck, I'm not going to get anywhere this way. Maybe hostility wasn't the best approach. I softened my tone as I let go of his arm. "I just want to know if she's okay."

His hardened expression eased slightly. "She's fine," he replied, shaking his head. "Just forget about her."

Not possible. I squared my shoulders. "That's not going to happen."

"Why? There are tons of other girls out there."

I clenched my fists, trying to control the anger gripping me. "I don't want any other girls—I want her," I snapped.

"Well, she doesn't want you," he countered, shifting uneasily, avoiding my eyes as he swallowed hard.

"You're a terrible liar," I said before walking away across the gym to my office. I knew Kaiya wanted me, but something had happened to freak her out. I just didn't know if it was something I had done, or if another factor was in play.

"Fuck!" I cursed once I shut the door to my office. I couldn't figure out what was wrong if she refused to see me or talk to me. *How can I fix this when I don't know the damn problem?*

I picked up my phone to text her but changed my mind. *Maybe I should just forget about her and save myself all this trouble. She obviously doesn't care, so why should I?*

Exhaling a frustrated breath, I tossed my phone onto my desk. *Quit being a pussy and move on. Kamden is right. There are plenty of other women out there.*

Picking up my phone again, I typed a text to Drew:

Me: Bar tonight?

Drew: U know I'm always down

We planned to meet at the bar at midnight. It was one of our regular spots, and we always found girls to take home when we went there. These past few weeks had been the longest I'd gone without sex since high school, and it unnerved me because I'd easily changed my ways for Kaiya. *Look where that got me. I don't know why I trusted her.*

The place was packed when I walked through the doors. I pushed past dozens of people to get to Drew, who was already at the crowded bar talking to two women in short, tight dresses. They were both practically on his lap.

When he saw me approach, he lightly pushed them away to greet me, then ordered us a round of drinks.

One of the girls, a blonde, wasted no time before coming up to me and pressing her body against mine. "Hey, handsome."

"Hey," I replied as I fought the urge to push her away. I knew what I wanted, and it wasn't her. I shoved my thoughts away as I threw back the shot Drew ordered—I'd be fine once I had a few more drinks, then I could move on and go back to the way things used to be.

"What you drinking, baby?" I asked, letting my eyes travel the length of her body. *Not bad, but not Kaiya either.*

She gave me a sultry smile. "Cherry Vodka Sour." She licked her lips as she ran her finger down the front of my shirt.

After I ordered our drinks, I downed mine quickly and ordered another. I needed to get wasted fast in order to drive away the guilt that was starting to eat at me because of Kaiya. *You're not together. There's no reason to feel guilty.*

After several rounds, the girl, whose name I didn't bother to ask, was all over me, rubbing her hands down my chest and abs before cupping my dick through my jeans. "I want you," she slurred.

Drew laughed as the other woman sloppily kissed his neck. "They're good to go," he shouted jokingly over the music.

I chuckled before turning my attention back to the blonde in front of me. "Let's go then, baby."

As she pulled me toward the door, I called over my shoulder to

Drew, "Catch you later, bro."

She stumbled through the exit. *Classy.* I snorted at her and rolled my eyes. "Where's your car?"

She looked up at me—her glazed, blue eyes were nothing like Kaiya's. "I came with my friend. Can you give me a ride?" she replied as she bit her bottom lip. It was so sexy when Kaiya did it, but on her, it was too fake, like she was trying too hard.

"Sure, I'll give you a ride," I responded suggestively.

Once I started driving to her place, her hands roamed over my dick, rubbing it through my jeans. It began to harden under her touch reflexively, but she wasn't turning me on like Kaiya did so effortlessly. *Stop thinking about Kaiya!*

When we entered her apartment, she led me to her bedroom before pushing me down on the bed. Slipping clumsily out of her dress, she tossed it to the floor and tugged off my shirt. Her bra was next, freeing her tits as she slid down my body to kneel on the floor by the bed between my legs. She unbuckled my belt and undid my jeans before sliding them down to my ankles.

Her hand wrapped around my cock as she licked her lips, eying it hungrily before taking me in her mouth, sucking me deep in her throat.

The woman eagerly consumed me, stroking me up and down with her tongue, but she didn't feel right; she wasn't Kaiya. Even though I was drunk, I couldn't let go of how terrible I felt, how wrong this was. I was pretty sure at that moment that no one would ever feel as good as Kaiya did.

Propping up on my elbows, I told the woman, "Stop."

Ignoring me, she sucked my cock harder and dragged her teeth along it.

"I said stop," I repeated as I pushed her lightly on the shoulders.

My dick popped out her mouth as she gave me a confused look. Her face morphed to excitement as she got up and positioned herself on my lap. "Can't wait, huh? I want you inside me just as badly," she said as she grabbed my cock, readying to sink down on me.

Gently forcing her off me, I stood and pulled my pants up. "I have to go." I grabbed my shirt before exiting her room and heading toward the front door.

I could hear her footsteps behind me as I put my shirt back on. "Wait, why?"

Turning the handle, I replied, "I just do."

I left without waiting to hear her response, wishing I could rid myself of all the feelings caused by Kaiya. We'd only known each other a couple of months, but I couldn't deny that she had left her impression on me.

I found myself driving to her house, but I changed course when I realized what I was doing. I'd done the same thing many times since we stopped talking, but I could never bring myself to go through with it. *She'd probably just slam the door in my face.*

I drove home, where I showered the smell and feel of the woman off me before collapsing into bed. *What the fuck am I going to do?*

Chapter Seventeen

Kaiya

I'd spent weeks avoiding Ryker, and they were definitely taking their toll on me. Every part of me missed him, especially my neglected body, which craved his touch. I hadn't had sex since the night before the meeting with Kaleb.

I'd been ignoring him and Bryce. I hadn't returned any of their phone calls or texts, and I'd been skipping class. Before Ryker, I had hooked up with Bryce at least once every two weeks, if not more often. We hadn't had sex in over a month, and he had definitely noticed. He called and texted me multiple times daily.

I was waiting for one of them to show up at my door since I wouldn't return any of their calls or messages, but neither had. I guess both of them respected my privacy, but that selfish part of me wished that Ryker would come searching for me.

Avoiding Ryker meant I had to stop going to self-defense class, and that was definitely affecting me. My body harbored so much pent up energy and anxiety from not releasing it that I thought I was going to come out of my skin.

Knowing that Ryker didn't usually go to work on most days until the afternoon, I decided to go to the gym early one Saturday morning with Kamden. I had to get out of the house, had to release some of the frustration and nerves eating away at me.

As we parked in the lot of the gym, he asked, "Are you sure you want to do this?"

Looking among the cars, I searched for Ryker's truck, but I didn't see it. A combined sense of disappointment and relief washed over me, and I scolded myself for being selfish and wanting to see him. *You can't be with him. He'll only get hurt.*

Once we entered, Kamden wanted to stay with me while I exercised, just in case Ryker showed up. Rolling my eyes, I walked away from him to get on the elliptical. He didn't follow me, so I assumed that he went to the weight room.

After I finished, my muscles felt strained, sore from lack of use. I decided to use the sauna to help relax the tight tension, so I headed to the locker room to swap my clothes for a towel.

After I had the towel securely wrapped around me, I padded to the steam room, hoping that since it was so early no one would be in there. I'd been wanting to use it since we started coming to this gym. But the sauna was always filled with people, and I could never bring myself to go in, afraid of being alone with strangers with only a towel on.

Peeking in, I smiled—no one was inside. *Hopefully, no one will come in.* I went in and sat on the bench, already starting to perspire from the humidity within the room.

Closing my eyes, I leaned my head back and let out a breath as my body began to relax. A couple of minutes passed when the door abruptly opened, causing me to stand and grip my towel. When I focused on the person in the doorway, I blinked several times to make sure I wasn't dreaming.

"Why are you avoiding me?" Ryker angrily spat, closing the door to the sauna. His eyes ran over me as he crossed his arms over his broad chest. Clad only in a pair of gym shorts and no shirt, his skin gleamed with a sheen of sweet. He looked like he'd just finished working out. *Fuck me.*

"Are you really going to do this in here?" I snapped back as I clutched my towel to me.

His voice was gruff and matter of fact. "I have no other choice—you've missed class for almost three weeks now, and you won't answer my calls."

"I've been busy," I lied.

The truth was that I'd been sulking around my apartment trying not to think of Ryker, which was almost impossible. He dominated every thought, much like his presence did in real life.

Eyes narrowing in determination, he advanced toward me, causing me to back up into the tile wall. Surprisingly, I wasn't scared—Ryker never caused that kind of fear in me. What he made me feel was more of an exhilarating kind of the fear, the kind you get when you're about to do something like bungee jump or skydive, the kind that excites your soul.

Caging me between his arms, my already fevered skin heated more from his proximity as he pressed against me with his body. I hadn't realized just how much I missed his touch until his skin reunited with mine, making me feel as though a piece of me had been lost since we'd last been together.

Ryker's eyes met mine, and there was no denying the desire and longing in them. "Always fighting me, Warrior," he softly spoke as he caressed my cheek with the back of his knuckles. Leaning in, he grazed my neck with his lips. The combination of heat from the steam and his mouth began to blanket me in a heady fog, evaporating all thought and replacing it with lust.

"I've missed you," Ryker murmured against my skin before tracing the curve of my jaw with his tongue. My breath escaped in a low moan as he pulled my body closer to him, leaving no space between us while he continued to taste me.

My hands tangled in his hair, leaving my loose towel barely clinging to my sweaty skin. When he brought his lips to mine, I let go of everything, losing myself in him and how he made me feel.

He groaned in my mouth as our tongues met, tangling together seamlessly as he lifted me. My legs automatically wrapped around him as he pressed me up against the wall, his hardened erection pushing against my already heated core.

Ryker nipped at my lips as he ripped the towel from my body, tossing it to the floor as his callused hands reacquainted themselves with my skin. *God, I missed him. I don't think I'll ever be the same without his touch.* Finding my breasts, Ryker's talented fingers massaged my stiff nipples before his mouth claimed them. The blissful combination of his soft, wet mouth and hard, smooth tongue ring against my sensitive flesh caused a moan to escape from my throat.

Leaning my head back against the wall, I let Ryker consume me. He eagerly suckled my breasts, pulling each nipple with his teeth before caressing it with that amazing piercing again. *I love how he makes me feel—so alive… almost whole.*

"Ryker," I breathlessly moaned as I reached for his shorts. Slipping my hand inside, I found his cock and pulled it out, needing him to fill me.

He didn't hesitate—he never did. Gripping my hips, he thrust himself inside my slick sex as his mouth reclaimed mine. Sweat beaded on our skin as he roughly pummeled me against the tile, taking me closer to heaven with each stroke.

Ryker's thick shaft stretched my walls, the pleasurable pain spreading throughout every inch of my limbs. I reveled in how he made me forget everything else, immersing me in us and the beauty of how our bodies perfectly connected. He unraveled and completed me all at the same time.

"Fuck, I missed you, baby, missed the taste of your sweet skin," Ryker groaned against my lips.

I love it when he talks to me like that.

I forced him deeper inside me with my legs, tightening my hold around his hips. He growled his approval, increasing the pace and intensity of his thrusts as his cock blissfully ravaged me.

Ryker's lips left mine as he nuzzled his face into my neck and placed soft kisses along my skin. "I haven't been able to get you off my mind. I've been going crazy thinking about you, baby."

"Me too. I've missed you so much," I whimpered as I guided his mouth back to mine.

His strength amazed me, unwavering as he supported my weight while simultaneously using his body to fuck me senseless. Ryker continuously pumped into me, creating a sensual rhythm just for us as our bodies molded together in harmony.

Ryker pulled back and grasped my face in his inked hands. "Never again, Warrior." His voice was gruff and deep, laced with emotion. "Can't go through that again."

"Never, baby, never," I whispered.

His mouth crashed on mine again. Every press of Ryker's lips, every caress from his hands, and every stroke of his amazing cock pushed me closer to ecstasy. My body ached for it, needing release after craving Ryker for so long.

As if sensing how close I was, Ryker pounded harder into me, creating the perfect combination of pain and pleasure within my body. My nails raked across his back as I cried out in euphoria, my climax sending tremors of sensation throughout my limbs. My thighs trembled against his hips as his strokes intensified in both speed and strength, seeking his own release. Seconds later, he withdrew his throbbing cock from my sex before shooting his cum up between my breasts.

The sticky heat of the room was stifling, making it more difficult to breathe as we disentangled ourselves. Picking up my towel, Ryker gently wiped his release from my skin, snapping me out the sensual fog we'd created. Immediately, I felt self-conscious, causing panic to root within me. Anxiety began to tighten in my body, trying to seize every muscle in its grasp as it attempted to take hold.

Ryker's hand cupped my cheek. "What's wrong?"

My eyes snapped to his, trying to focus on him to pull myself out of my downward spiral. My chest heaved as it struggled to breathe, causing Ryker's eyes to crease in worry. "Breathe, baby, breathe. It's okay, everything is okay."

Breathe. In, out, in, out. The pressure began to relinquish as I concentrated on Ryker's face. Both of his hands clasped my face. "You with me, baby?"

I gave him a tight nod. My chest was still somewhat constricted, and my muscles were stiff, but the tension was slowly easing away.

"I'm sorry—I have to go," I stammered as I snatched the towel from Ryker's hand. I darted around him toward the exit while trying to wrap the cloth around me.

"You don't have to run from me, Warrior," he called out after me.

Ryker's words stopped me, only a few feet from the door. I felt him behind me as his arms wrapped around my waist, pulling my body against his. Pressing a soft kiss to my shoulder, he murmured, "Talk to me, baby."

My mouth dried up, the words stuck in my throat. I blinked rapidly, willing back tears. Ryker slowly turned me to face him and pressed our foreheads together as he released a breath.

"I know you've been hurt before, experienced things that no one should ever have to. Just know that I'd never do that to you. Ever. I know you're probably not ready to talk about it yet, but when you are, I'll be here."

And with those words, Ryker smashed a small hole in the barrier surrounding the broken pieces of my heart. My eyes watered as I looked away. "My demons are torturing me a lot lately. I'm having trouble dealing with them."

"You know I'm here for you, Warrior. You don't have to fight alone," he said as he caressed my cheeks with his thumbs. My eyes closed from the blissful sensation, wishing I could just stay like that with him forever.

Opening my eyes, my gaze locked with Ryker's. My voice cracked, sounding weak and small as I spoke, "You know how I told you that someone abused me when I was little?"

"Yes," he growled angrily.

"Well, that person was institutionalized, but he's being considered for release." I sighed deeply and looked away as the reality overtook me. "Kamden and I went to protest it. The whole thing overwhelmed me." My hands wrapped around my body, keeping the towel in place and the shiver coursing through my body at bay. "I… I hadn't been that close to him in years, and I didn't deal with it well."

Ryker enveloped me in a hug. "Why didn't you tell me? You shouldn't have dealt with that by yourself."

Laying my head against his chest, I confessed, "I didn't want to bring you into it. You shouldn't have to deal with my issues." *With my psychotic brother.*

Ryker pulled back, gripping me softly by the shoulders and leaning down to look in my eyes. "Don't start this shit again, Ky. If I didn't want to deal with your issues, I wouldn't be here right now."

"I don't want you to get hurt," I choked.

"Hurt? Why would I get hurt?" His eyebrows furrowed in confusion and his forehead creased as his eyes ran over my face, looking for an answer.

I swallowed the lump in my throat. "If my… he gets out, he'll come after me. He'll hurt you just for being with me."

He laughed—actually laughed. "Baby, you don't have to worry about me. I can take care of myself." He paused before his eyes steeled, his voice deepening angrily. "And if he lays one finger, one fucking finger on you, he won't be breathing for long."

My eyes searched his, looking to see if he was joking—he wasn't. This had to be the most serious I'd ever seen him. My heart swelled at his protectiveness, and my resolve to stay away from him crumbled.

Melting against him, I wrapped my arms around his waist, pressing my cheek to his muscular chest. "I'm not good for you," I whispered.

His body rumbled beneath me with a soft chuckle. "Oh, yeah? Why not?"

"I'm just not." I'd already divulged too much, and I didn't want to reveal anymore, afraid he'd leave if he learned the whole truth about me. *That might be best for him.*

Tilting my chin up, he stared deep in my eyes. "You are." His voice was firm, leaving no room for argument.

Then, he leaned down and pressed his lips to mine, evaporating all my fears and doubts and replacing them with hope. He made me feel as if one day, I could be complete, not the fucked-up, fractured version of a person that I was.

The door opened, causing me to jerk away from Ryker and tightly grip my towel around me. An older man walked in, giving Ryker and me a suspicious look as we darted around him and exited.

A laugh burst from Ryker as soon as the door closed. My heart beat fast as adrenaline rushed through me from almost being caught. I couldn't fight my own laughter when Ryker's was so contagious.

Draping his arm over my shoulder, he led me toward the locker rooms. We both were still laughing as he said, "That was a close one."

"Yeah, and whose fault is that? You're such a bad influence," I joked.

"Me?" His eyebrows rose incredulously as a playful grin tipped up his lips. "You're the one who makes me crazy. I can't control myself when it comes to you. Especially when I haven't seen you in weeks."

My stomach and chest bunched tightly from his words. I felt so terrible for avoiding him, especially when I considered how I just stopped talking to him with no explanation or reason. Who knows what was going through his mind that whole time; he probably thought he'd done something wrong, and it was really me and my madness.

"I'm sorry," I looked up at him as we walked. "I was only trying to protect you."

"I don't need you to protect me, Warrior. I just need you."

Need? Needing someone was way different than just wanting someone—did he really need me? I wasn't ready to go into that, and I doubted he was either, but I couldn't ignore the joy that fluttered within me at the thought.

We had reached the locker rooms, and Ryker stopped and faced me. "Are you going to stop fighting me now, Warrior? Or do I have to keep chasing you?"

I held his gaze with mine. "I don't want to keep running, but it's hard to let go of my ways. If we do this, it's not going to be easy."

"Easy is boring—you know I like a challenge."

My lips curved up in a smile. "Well, good luck because I'm definitely a challenge. I'll probably try to run again—will you keep chasing me?"

"Until you don't let me catch you anymore," he softly grinned, sending a tingle through my body.

I wasn't really afraid of Ryker hurting me any longer—I didn't think anything could hurt me as much as Kaleb had. I was more scared of myself, of what my emotions could do to him if I let him in. I might not have been ready to let him in completely, but I wanted to try to make things between us work.

"You'll stop chasing me before that happens," I teased, placing my hand on his chest as I dipped my face to hide the blush that touched my cheeks..

His finger tilted my chin up. "I don't think I'd be able to stop chasing you—you're like an addiction."

"That's really what I want to be compared to, thanks," I replied sarcastically as I moved away from him.

He pulled me back to him, not letting me get away. "That was a compliment." I raised an eyebrow and pursed my lips in doubt. He cocked his head to the side and tightened his arms around me. "Addictions give you a high unlike anything else, make you crave whatever it is you're addicted to. And, Warrior, I crave you."

His lips found mine, fueling the flames his words had started inside me. The kiss was greedy and hungry, filled with passion and longing. It spoke volumes without needing words. It was the kind that made your stomach knot while igniting your soul.

When we finally broke apart, I was breathless and flushed. The feelings that kiss evoked within me confirmed that it would be almost impossible for me to walk away from Ryker. I'd never be the same after him, and I wasn't sure if that was a good or a bad thing yet.

Ryker

When I saw Kaiya exit the locker room, I did a double take. I almost slapped myself to make sure I wasn't dreaming, but stopped so I wouldn't look like a fool. I'd seen Kamden's truck in the parking lot, but he came regularly without Kaiya lately so I hadn't expected to see her.

Seeing her made all kinds of shit surface inside me—anger, lust, happiness—I'd been pushing everything down because I didn't want to admit how much I missed her; I didn't want to feel the pain of her absence. I'd never been able to contain my feelings around Kaiya, and even after everything that had happened, I still couldn't. The sight of her crashed into me like a train, causing my emotions to start seeping out.

I wanted to turn and pretend I hadn't seen her; just head to the locker room as planned to shower after my workout, then go home. But I wanted answers—I deserved answers.

I rushed around the corner and caught a glimpse of her entering the sauna. I followed, about to enter when I hesitated, pausing as I turned the door handle.

What the fuck are you doing? You're acting like some stalker.

Letting go of the handle, I blew out a frustrated breath. I hated what I was feeling, a jumbled mix of confusion, longing, and anger.

Women don't do this to me. Grow some fucking balls and get over her. Move on.

I balled my fists and walked away, then stopped when I reached the end of the hall.

Fuck this, I'm getting answers.

I whipped around, then stormed back to the door and shoved it open, startling Kaiya in the process. She hopped up off the bench and clutched her towel, eyes wide with shock.

I couldn't help but check her out. Her body was a masterpiece, especially when it was covered in sweat and she was just in a towel.

Focus. Get your answers, then get out.

I closed the door. "Why are you avoiding me?" I questioned angrily, crossing my arms over my chest.

She narrowed her eyes at me, gripping her towel tighter. "Are you really going to do this in here?"

"I have no other choice—you've missed class for almost three weeks now, and you won't answer my calls."

God, you sound like a clingy girl.

Kaiya darted her eyes away, avoiding my gaze. "I've been busy."

Bullshit.

I couldn't take any more; even though I wanted answers, I knew I could get them later. It had been so long since I'd seen Kaiya, and my cock ached to be inside her again. Everything else could wait.

I approached her, making her back up to the wall. Placing my hands on the tile on either side of her head, I pressed against her.

Fuck, I've missed feeling that sweet body against me.

My anger receded as I stared in her eyes; the beautiful blue eyes I'd dreamed about almost every night since we'd been apart. I softly ran my knuckles down her cheek. "Always fighting me, Warrior."

Leaning in, I trailed my lips over the sensitive skin of her neck. "I've missed you," I mumbled as I moved up to her jaw, dragging my tongue along it.

I pulled Kaiya flush against me, causing her to moan. My hard cock twitched from the sound as she knotted her hands in my hair.

That's right—let go, baby.

My mouth crushed hers, claiming her lips. I groaned as I lifted her, devouring her like a man eating his last meal. Her legs wrapped around me as I pressed her against the wall.

Mine.

I nipped her swollen lips, tearing the towel away from her body and tossing it to the ground. I needed every barrier removed so I could feel her again after so long.

Grabbing her tits, I played with her nipples with both my fingers and mouth. Kaiya moaned as I went back and forth between the hardened nubs, alternating biting and sucking her perfect breasts.

"Ryker," Kaiya gasped as she tugged at my shorts. Her hand slid inside and grabbed my cock, then pulled it out.

Yes.

My mouth found hers again as I thrust myself into her slick pussy. I pounded her against the wall, savoring the feel of her tightness after being without it for so long. "Fuck, I've missed you, baby, missed the taste of your sweet skin," I groaned against her swollen lips.

She forced me deeper inside of her, tightening her legs around me.

I growled and pumped harder, needing more of the woman against me. I was going to fuck her until she couldn't take anymore; until we'd both had our fill.

Breaking away from her lips, I buried my face in her neck, then trailed kisses along the sensitive flesh. "I haven't been able to get you off of my mind. I've been going crazy thinking about you, baby."

"Me too. I've missed you so much," Kaiya whimpered, guiding our mouths back together

We consumed each other, unable to get enough as I continued to pummel Kaiya with my cock. The lust and passion between us intensified with every stroke, bringing us both closer to climax.

Being with Kaiya after not having her for weeks made me realize how much I missed her; feeling her skin, tasting her sweetness, and having her pussy wrapped around my dick again solidified my need for her.

Pulling back, I grasped her face in my hands. "Never again, Warrior; can't go through that again."

"Never, baby, never," she responded in a breathless whisper.

My mouth crushed hers, and I pounded harder into her. My hands caressed every inch of her skin, needing to feel as much of Kaiya as possible. I wanted to feel her tremble beneath my fingers when I made her come all over my cock.

Her nails dragged across my back as she cried out in pleasure. Her body shuddered her orgasm as I continued to drive deeper and faster into her. It didn't take long for me to find my own release since I hadn't fucked in weeks. Pulling my cock out, I came in between Kaiya's tits.

Fuck, feels so good.

After I set Kaiya down, I picked her towel up and cleaned my cum off her skin. Her body stiffened as I finished, and I knew something was wrong as her eyes spread wide.

I gently cupped her cheek. "What's wrong?"

Kaiya's panicked gaze met mine and her breaths became heavier and quicker.

Fuck, what is happening?

My heart started to pound as concern tightened my gut. "Breathe, baby, breathe. It's okay, everything is okay," I softly said, hoping to calm her down.

Her breathing slowed, and her body relaxed slightly.

I clasped her face in my hands. "You with me, baby?"

Kaiya gave me a clipped nod. "I'm sorry—I have to go." She snatched her towel from my hand and darted around me, heading for the door as she wrapped it around her naked body.

I turned around and called after her. "You don't have to run from me, Warrior."

I hadn't expected her to stop, but she did. Walking up behind her, I wrapped my arms around her waist and pulled her against me, then kissed her shoulder. "Talk to me, baby."

She didn't respond, but she didn't pull away either. I slowly turned her around to face me and pressed our foreheads together, then sighed. I'd never been good at expressing my feelings, but I couldn't deny what I felt for the broken woman before me. I wanted her to know that she could trust me; that I was there for her. "I know you've been hurt before, experienced things that no one should ever have to. Just know that I'd never do that to you. Ever. I know you're probably not ready to talk about it yet, but when you are, I'll be here."

Her eyes started watering as she avoided my gaze. "My demons have been torturing me a lot lately. I'm having trouble dealing with them."

I rubbed her cheeks with my thumbs, causing her eyes to flutter shut. "You know I'm here for you, Warrior. You don't have to fight alone."

After a few seconds, her eyes opened and met mine. "You know how I told you that someone abused me when I was little?" Her voice shook as she spoke, showing her fear.

Anger began to simmer in my veins. "Yes," I snarled, wishing I could strangle the person responsible for Kaiya's pain.

"Well, that person was institutionalized, but he's being considered for release." She exhaled a heavy breath and looked away. "Kamden and I went to protest it. The whole thing overwhelmed me."

Kaiya wrapped her arms around herself, obviously shaken up. "I … I hadn't been that close to him in years, and I didn't deal with it well."

My poor Warrior.

I threw my arms around her, hoping to comfort her. "Why didn't you tell me? You shouldn't have dealt with that by yourself."

She rested her head on my chest. "I didn't want to bring you into it. You shouldn't have to deal with my issues."

I pulled back, slightly offended. I gripped her shoulders and leaned down to make eye contact. "Don't start this shit again, Ky. If I didn't want to deal with your issues, I wouldn't be here right now."

Her voice caught, full of emotion as she replied, "I don't want you to get hurt."

My eyebrows bunched together in confusion as I scanned over her face, looking for answers. "Hurt? Why would I get hurt?"

"If my … he gets out, he'll come after me. He'll hurt you just for being with me."

Me, get hurt? Yeah, right. The motherfucker can try.

I laughed, "Baby, you don't have to worry about me. I can take care of myself." I paused as thoughts of him hurting Kaiya played in my mind. "And if he lays one finger, one fucking finger on you, he won't be breathing for long," I promised.

Her eyes searched mine for several seconds, then she leaned into me, wrapping her arms around me. "I'm not good for you," she whispered.

I chuckled. I was the one who wasn't good for her. "Oh, yeah? Why not?"

"I'm just not."

I grasped her chin and tipped it up, forcing her to look at me. "You are."

Leaning down, I pressed my lips to hers, ending any protest before it started. In that moment, it was just her and me—none of our scars, issues, or pasts—just Kaiya and Ryker.

Then, the door opened, causing Kaiya to jerk away from me. I grabbed her hand and pulled her around the older man that had walked in.

A laugh escaped me as soon as I shut the door. Kaiya started laughing, also.

God, I missed her laugh.

I draped my arm around her shoulders, leading her down the hall toward the locker room. "That was a close one." I chuckled.

"Yeah, and whose fault is that? You're such a bad influence," she replied, giving me a playful grin.

"Me?" I smirked, raising my eyebrows. "You're the one who makes me crazy. I can't control myself when it comes to you; especially when I haven't seen you in weeks."

Kaiya's expression turned serious as she looked up at me. "I'm sorry. I was only trying to protect you."

"I don't need you to protect me, Warrior. I just need you."

Whoa, getting a little serious now, aren't we?

I couldn't deny my feelings for Kaiya, but I didn't want to rush anything, especially when we both had so many issues. I just wanted her in my life, as much as she would allow.

I stopped as we reached the door to the locker room and faced Kaiya. "Are you going to stop fighting me now, Warrior? Or do I have to keep chasing you?"

Her eyes locked with mine. "I don't want to keep running, but it's hard to let go of my ways. If we do this, it's not going to be easy."

"Easy is boring—you know I like a challenge," I replied with a smirk.

Kaiya's full lips curved up. "Well, good luck because I'm definitely a challenge. I'll probably try to run again—will you keep chasing me?"

I didn't have to think about my answer. "Until you don't let me catch you anymore."

Her cheeks flushed pink and she ducked her head, placing her hand on my chest. "You'll stop chasing me before that happens."

I lifted her chin with my finger, making eye contact. "I don't think I'd be able to stop chasing you—you're like an addiction.

She frowned, moving a few steps back. "That's really what I want to be compared to, thanks," she replied sarcastically.

I grabbed her arm, pulling her back to me. "That was a compliment."

She cocked an eyebrow and pursed her lips.

Tightening my arms around her, I explained myself. "Addictions give you a high unlike anything else, make you crave whatever it is you're addicted to." I brought my hand up to her face and ran my thumb along her cheek. "And, Warrior, I crave you."

I leaned down and kissed her, claiming her lips hungrily. Her fingers dug into my back as I pressed against her. I wanted to make sure she understood that she was mine, that there was no one else for her but me.

When we broke apart, Kaiya was breathless and flushed. Her lips were swollen, and the look in her eyes told me everything I needed to know. Neither one of us was going anywhere—what happened in the sauna had changed things, and there was no more turning back or running. She needed me, and even though I didn't want to admit it, I needed her, unlike anything I'd ever needed before.

I just hoped I wouldn't get fucked over again.

Chapter Eighteen

Ryker

After finally fixing things with Kaiya, I felt like a huge weight had been lifted off my shoulders, and I was the happiest I'd been in weeks. It kind of fucked with my head how much she got to me, but she made me feel things I hadn't felt in a long time. The thought of being with her didn't give me the urge to run like it had with every other chick since that stupid bitch.

After working on the bags at Sunday's class, I decided to have the students work on techniques for what to do if they fell down during an attack.

"Today, we're going to work on ground defense. You can easily fall during an attack, whether it's because you were knocked down or because you tripped. What you don't want is for your attacker to get on top of you if that happens. The moves we are going to show you will prevent the attack from escalating, and can also disable your attacker if executed correctly."

Kaiya and I found a spot on the mat as everyone broke into their pairs. She smiled at me shyly when we locked eyes, and her face started to flush.

"Still nervous around me, baby?"

"No, things are just different now that we… that we're you know," she softly stammered.

"Having sex?" I blurted.

Her eyes looked around then glared at me. "Yes! We probably shouldn't be hooking up since I'm your student."

"It's frowned upon, but it's not forbidden. Don't worry about it, okay?"

"What if the other students find out?"

"Who cares?" I shrugged. "It's none of their business."

Her lips twitched as she fought a smile, but it broke through after a few seconds. "So, what's the first technique?" she asked, changing the subject.

I laid down on the mat. "If you ever get knocked down, the first thing that you need to do is turn on your side and pick your leg up to defend yourself. Most attackers will try to pin you from here." I shifted my body demonstrating what I was doing. "Your only concern is to avoid him from climbing on top of you and getting knocked out." I made sure to keep my eyes on hers. "Come toward me."

I stopped her when she got about a foot away from my legs. A few strands from her ponytail fell across her face and she quickly tucked them behind her ear. "Once your attacker is this close, you can kick them in the stomach or the groin. Hook your bottom foot here." I moved my foot to the back of her ankle. "Use all your force to kick them in the knee with your top leg."

We continued the technique until she got it. I'd go over it again and again just to make sure that nobody would ever hurt her again. Now that we were together or dating or whatever it was we were doing, I felt more protective over her. I didn't even want to think about the possibility of her being attacked, and just the thought of it laced my veins with rage. I wished she'd known how to defend herself when she was a little girl. *What kind of sick motherfucker would hurt her?* I shook away those thoughts and focused on her face.

Once class was finished, I closed up the gym and walked Kaiya to her car. "You wanna come back to my place?" I asked as I framed her against the driver's side door.

"I wish I could," she answered, her voice full of disappointment. "Mondays are hell for me. I have to wake up earlier." She placed her hands on my chest and traced over the tattoos showing with her fingertips. "If I go home with you, I won't get any sleep."

"Are you sure?" I leaned closer before trailing soft kisses along her jaw line.

She lightly moaned but still resisted. "I can't, baby. I've been slacking at work the past few weeks, and I really need to catch up."

"Okay." I nuzzled my face in her neck, getting as close to her as I could as I slid my hands in hers. Pulling back, I said, "Hey, don't make any plans for Friday night. I have a surprise for you."

"Oh, yeah? Will I like it?" she smiled coyly at me.

I pressed a kiss to her lips, then another to each side of her neck. "I don't know. I hope so."

When I pulled away, her eyes were closed as she wore a look of contentment. They slowly fluttered open as she smiled at me. "I can't wait."

Me neither. If everything went according to plan, I'd be breaking one of Kaiya's rules that night, getting closer to her in the process. "See you tomorrow?"

"Yes. Do you want to meet for dinner after I get off of work? I'll tell Kam that he's on his own."

"Sure, baby. I'll talk to you tomorrow," I replied as I opened the door for her.

As she drove away, my mind was racing in preparation for Friday. *Everything needs to be perfect.*

I picked up the earlier shift at work on Friday so I could get off with enough time to get everything ready for my date with Kaiya. As I was leaving, one of the receptionists stopped me. "Hey, Ryker, someone left a message for you."

No one usually calls me at work. "Who was it?"

"Um, I'm not sure." She rifled through some papers at the desk. "Some guy—he said something about it being important and for you to call him as soon as possible." She snatched a small paper from the mess and read the name aloud, "Ethan Campbell."

All my muscles tensed as anger gripped every limb, just the sound of that name infuriating me. I clenched my fists as I gritted, "If he calls back, tell him to never contact me again."

Storming out of the entrance, I didn't wait to hear a response from her. *Why the fuck would Ethan be calling me? He knows that I want nothing to do with him.*

Brushing the thoughts away, I focused on getting everything ready for my night with Kaiya. I sent her a text telling her to be at my place at seven. Just seeing her reply put a smile on face and wiped away most of the anger that lingered from hearing about Ethan.

I found out from Nori that Kaiya loved gnocchi from a little Italian bistro two towns over. She didn't get to go very often because it was out of the way and never had time to make the trip. So I made arrangements to pick it up for our date.

My palms were sweaty as I set up everything, which was strange for me—women never made me nervous. But Kaiya had me feeling like I was some high school kid about to take the hottest girl to prom.

When the doorbell rang, my heart rate kicked up as my stomach tightened in anxiety. *Chill out, it's just Kaiya.* Walking over to the door, I opened it and took Kaiya in. She was wearing a light blue strapless dress, almost the same shade as her eyes, and her hair was loosely curled.

"Hi," she smiled, her cheeks flushing as her gaze settled on mine. I didn't need words for her to know what was going through my mind at that moment, my eyes said it all.

"Hey," was about all I could manage before I had to clear my throat. *Smooth. How does she do this to me?* "You look beautiful." I leaned down to kiss her cheek before I brought her inside and closed the door.

Her eyes widened and an astonished smile spread over her face as she looked around my apartment. Candles and rose petals were scattered along every surface, including the table, which I had set with my best dinnerware, but that wasn't really saying much. Bachelors didn't have fine china.

Kaiya looked up at me, her eyes lighting up her whole face. "Ryker, you didn't have to do all this for me."

Leading her to the table, I pulled out her chair. "I wanted to."

I picked up her plate before taking it to the kitchen and serving the gnocchi on it. I returned and gently placed the plate before her. "It's not homemade or anything, but Nori said that this was your favorite."

She stared at it for several seconds, then darted her gaze to mine. "Is this from Luciano's?"

Grinning, I answered, "Yeah. I picked it up before you came."

Another wide smile spread over those beautiful lips. "Thank you."

I bent down to kiss her. "You're welcome."

I'd also bought a bottle of her favorite wine, the house Moscato from the restaurant. I poured us both a glass and sat down to eat.

Throughout dinner we talked about everything, from favorite movies to hobbies. Kaiya loved to read, and I, of course, was a workout junkie. I found out that she hated scary movies, loved the water and animals, except snakes, which she was deathly afraid of, and her favorite color was pink.

After we finished dinner, I cleared the table while Kaiya finished her third glass of wine. I could tell she was already a little tipsy by the flush on her face and her glassy eyes, which she had locked on mine as I walked toward her on the couch.

Setting her glass on the coffee table, she pulled me down next to her before leaning in and kissing my lips. "Thank you for dinner. Everything was amazing."

"No problem, baby. I rented some movies for us—which one do you want to watch first," I asked as I held them out for her to see.

Her lips bunched to one side as she looked over the DVDs. She decided on an action flick, which surprised me, but she surprised me on a regular basis. I never knew what to expect with her, and I loved that.

Kaiya cuddled into my side after I started the movie. About ten minutes in, she started trailing her fingers under my shirt, lightly tracing the ridges of my abs. Just that small touch was causing my dick to harden. She ventured lower, making my breathing slightly erratic as her delicate fingers played under the waist of my jeans.

"What are you doing, baby?" My hand skimmed under the hem of her dress, rubbing the delicate skin of her inner thigh.

"Nothing," she replied sweetly as she peered up at me, giving me a flirty smile.

"Oh, yeah?" Shifting her on to my lap, I rubbed my hands along the curves of her hips to her ass, squeezing the soft flesh lightly as I pressed her against me.

Her breath caught right before our lips met. Wrapping my arms around her, I pulled her tighter against me as I parted her lips with my tongue, letting her sweetness flood my mouth. I doubted I could ever get enough of her taste. She really was my addiction, making me want more and more.

Rising off the couch, I took us to my bedroom. My plan was in full swing as I set Kaiya on the bed. This wasn't just about breaking her rules—this was about getting her to open up to me, to connect with her on a deeper level. I wanted her to trust me with her body, let me show her how it was meant to be touched.

I pulled down her dress as she simultaneously tugged my shirt over my head. Laying her back on the bed, I trailed light kisses down her body, hoping to ease her into letting go, into losing herself in pleasure. I wanted to erase the memories constantly tormenting her, to replace her pain with happiness.

She squirmed under my lips as I ventured down, hooking my thumbs under her lacy thong as I pressed more kisses on her lower abdomen. Looking up at her, locking our eyes, I slid her panties off as I traced her skin with my tongue.

Once she was completely naked in front of me, I admired her bare form. *Fuck, she's gorgeous.* She had no idea how beautiful she was, how she caused an eruption of desire within me that was unmatched by anyone else. I wanted to show her exactly how she made me feel.

"Can I taste you, baby?" I pressed a soft kiss to her inner thigh.

Holding her gaze, I placed another kiss on the inside of her other thigh. She looked uncertain, unsure about giving me trust over her body. I wanted to shatter that doubt, reassure her that I only wanted to cherish her, not hurt her. "I won't hurt you, baby."

Using my lips to caress her skin, I traveled back up until I reached her mouth. Hovering over her, snug between her thighs, I darted my tongue out to trace her soft, lush lips before slipping my tongue inside.

A moan escaped her, vibrating the inside of my mouth as our tongues laced together. I pressed my erection against her bare, wet pussy, eliciting another sound of pleasure from her as she arched against me. I had to resist the urge to unbutton my jeans and sink into her right then, but I was on a mission, one that would hopefully bring us closer together.

Breaking the kiss to nibble her bottom lip, I gruffly spoke, "Fuck, you taste so good. I bet your pussy tastes even better. Lemme taste you, baby."

Whimpering, she writhed beneath me, shaking her head 'no' as I dragged my tongue along her jawline before sucking her earlobe into my mouth.

Shifting down, I moved my lips over her collarbone, pressing soft kisses as I continued lower. Reaching her breasts, I sucked one of her nipples into my mouth and played with it with my barbell. She jerked underneath me, fisting the sheets as I sucked her tits.

I moved to the other nipple before teasing it with my tongue. More moans escaped her as I repeated, "Let me taste you, Warrior. Let me show you how good I can make you feel."

After a few seconds, she finally groaned, "Yes, yes, yes."

Yes. I trailed my mouth back down, back between her thighs. I wanted to take things slow, wanted to savor Kaiya while crushing her fears and doubts.

Slowly, I traced my tongue along the outside of her delicate center before flicking her clit with it. Sucking the sensitive skin into my mouth, I slowly sank two of my fingers inside her tight opening. Her hands tugged my hair as she arched against my fingers, pulling them deeper within her.

After several seconds, I swapped my fingers for my tongue, thrusting it inside her snug entrance.

Her hands tightened in my hair as she pushed at me, crying softly, "Stop. Please, stop."

The pain in her voice immediately halted my actions. I sat up on my knees to look at her, and saw that tears were trickling down her face. I felt like a bucket of ice water had been dumped on me. *Fuck, I didn't want this to happen.* "Baby, what's wrong?" I asked as I moved from between her legs to by her side.

Sitting up, she brought her legs to her chest and wrapped her arms tightly around them. "I'm sorry," she sobbed as she buried her face in her knees.

I rubbed her back in gentle circles. "Ky, look at me. Talk to me, baby."

Peeking at me, she inhaled deeply before saying, "He… he used to do that to me. I… I can't."

Running a hand through my hair, I blew out a breath. I didn't want her to think about him, about what he did to her. All I wanted was to take away her memories of him, replace them with better ones, make it so she never hurt again.

"Ky, I know this is hard for you. I know that he hurt you, that he mistreated your body. I don't want to do that, baby. I want to erase what he did by showing you that your body was made to be cherished, not abused."

She propped her head on her arms as she stared at me, sniffling before she replied, "Some scars can never be erased."

"Lemme try, Warrior," I urged.

Exhaling, she replied, "I don't know, Ryker. I-"

"We'll take it slow—if you feel overwhelmed at any point, just tell me, and I'll stop. I stopped when you asked me a few minutes ago, right?"

"You promise?" she softly asked, locking our eyes again. I knew this was huge for her, to be able to trust someone not to hurt her. I wanted to kill that fucking bastard for doing whatever he did to her, making my warrior afraid of being intimate with someone.

I looked into those beautiful, blue eyes. "I promise, Ky."

Leaning in, I gently pressed my lips to hers as I cradled her face in my hands. Laying her down on the bed, I separated our mouths to feather kisses over her face and neck, leaving no area untouched by the soft touch of my lips.

Using the tips of my fingers, I lightly caressed her skin as my mouth followed. I ventured down over her tits and stomach before kissing her hips and thighs, avoiding her pussy.

Descending down her body, I enjoyed the taste and feel of her supple flesh. I stopped to massage her legs as I placed kisses on the inside of her ankle before switching to the other. Retreating back up, I ran my hands along her skin, causing her to writhe under my touch.

I spread more kisses along the sensitive area of her inner thighs, eliciting moans of pleasure from Kaiya. Nearing closer to her pussy, I dragged my tongue along the tender skin before stopping at the juncture between her thighs. "Do you want me to stop, baby?" I murmured huskily. I sure as hell didn't want to, but I didn't want her to feel forced. I'd never force a woman to do anything she didn't want to.

She only moaned incomprehensibly, lost in passion. I softly kissed her clit a couple of times before repeating my question. "Do you want me to stop?"

"No," she cried out, her voice thick with desire.

Yes.

My lips curved as my tongue darted out to taste her again. Her body jerked slightly as her hands found my head and brought me into her pussy. Kneading her thighs, I began to slowly devour her, my tongue dancing inside her.

My fingers found her clit, deftly massaging the bundle of nerves as my tongue played with it and sucked it in my mouth. A high-pitched moan escaped Kaiya as her body jolted in pleasure again. Her hands tightened in my hair as she pushed me closer against her, her body squirming as she neared climax.

My hands moved around to her ass, gripping the voluptuous flesh and bringing her closer to me as I delved back inside her. The more I had of her, the more I wanted, the taste of her sweet pussy feeding my addiction, intensifying my desire for her.

Her thighs tensed and trembled along with the rest of her body as she moaned in orgasm. I eagerly consumed her sweetness as it flooded my mouth, savoring the evidence of the pleasure I gave her.

Trailing kisses back up her slender torso, my hands caressed the curves of her body before I finally stilled, hovering over her. Lidded with desire, her eyes met mine as she seductively smiled, raking her hands down my abs before stopping at my jeans.

I held her gaze as I ground my erection against her. "Did you like that, baby?

Her hands began to fumble with my jeans as she bit her lip and nodded. Voice throaty with arousal, she answered, "Yes. I want you inside me, now."

I wanted to plunge my dick deep inside her, fill her until she repeatedly cried out my name, but I loved teasing her, loved unraveling her until she was overcome with desire.

"Oh yeah, baby? How bad do you want me?" I asked before grazing her nipple with my teeth.

Her hand slipped inside my jeans before grabbing my cock. "So bad," she moaned.

"You want me to fuck you, baby?" I murmured against her tit before sucking it into my mouth. *Fuck, she tastes so good.*

"Yes," she moaned, arching against me. I nipped at her breasts as she pulled my dick out and slid my pants down with her feet.

Guiding me with her hand, she pressed my cock against her slick opening.

"You're so wet for me," I growled as I rocked against her.

When she wrapped her legs around me, pulling me to her, urging me to enter her, I couldn't contain myself anymore. Gripping her hips, I thrust inside her, sinking my cock deep within her pussy as I captured her mouth with mine.

Kaiya's nails dug into my back as I pounded in and out of her. Moving my hands to her ass, I lifted her upwards. Her pussy clenched tighter around my dick from the slight movement. Her moans increased with each of my strokes. Finding orgasm, her body shuddered as she cried out my name, waves of pleasure finally overtaking her.

As she throbbed around me, I could feel my release approaching. I moved my hands around to spread her thighs, burying myself further inside her.

Pulling out, I shot my cum on Kaiya's breasts and stomach, loving how it looked on her flawless skin. I rolled off next to her before catching my breath and getting up to grab a towel for her.

As I stood at the edge of the bed, her gaze had traveled to my dick, and the lustful look in her eyes caused me to get hard again. "You want more, baby?"

She bit her bottom lip as she nodded. I was on her within seconds, and I spent the rest of the night showing her how her body was meant to be worshiped.

Chapter Nineteen

Kaiya

I left Ryker's at around three in the morning. He wanted me to stay, but I'd already broken one of my rules for him, and that was enough for me for one night. It scared me how easy it was for me to break them for him, but I was happy for once in my life, and I wanted to focus on that and all the other wonderful things Ryker made me feel.

My whole body felt amazing, like I had a full body massage that released all the stress and tension plaguing me. Ryker was definitely gifted, and he spent so many hours showing me exactly how talented he was. The way his rough hands were able to caress me so softly, how he used that delicious mouth to please me so expertly, and how every movement was used to show me how my body should've been treated all along blew my mind.

I slept late Saturday, exhausted from my amazing night with Ryker. When I checked my phone, I had several text messages from both Ryker and Bryce. I opened up Ryker's first, a smile involuntarily spreading over my face as I thought about him.

Ryker: Good morning beautiful

Me: Good morning

About a minute passed before he replied:

Ryker: You free today?

My fingers started typing my reply automatically:

Me: Yes :)

Ryker: Pick you up in an hour?

Me: Ok :)

Before I got out of bed, I looked at Bryce's message:

Bryce: Haven't heard from you in a while everything ok?

Me: Yeah I'm good

Bryce: When can I see you again?

Shit. I needed to tell him that I couldn't hook up with him anymore, but I felt terrible about it. He'd been there for me when I needed him, understanding when most guys would've blown me off. I hesitantly typed the text, but my thumb hovered over the send button. After several seconds, I finally pressed it.

Me: I can't see you like that anymore but I still want to be friends

My phone started ringing as Bryce's number popped up on my screen. I swiped the reject key and left my phone on the bed to get ready before Ryker arrived. I heard the phone ringing again as I hopped in the shower, but I ignored it. *Hopefully, he'll understand.*

Once I finished getting ready, I put on a pair of jeans and an off-the-shoulder tee before putting on some light make-up. I'd always been okay with using a small compact mirror because I didn't see every feature at once, so I didn't see *him.* Otherwise, who knew what I would go outside looking like.

As I went downstairs to meet Ryker, I looked at my phone and noticed that I had more missed calls and text messages from Bryce. I'd have to figure out how to deal with that later before it blew up in my face, but I was too excited about going out with Ryker that I pushed my worries aside.

He was waiting for me at the bottom of the stairs again, wearing a snug, white Henley shirt that looked ridiculously amazing on him, but he looked good in everything. Ryker would look hot even in a garbage bag.

Once I reached him, he picked me up in a hug. Slowly, he let me slide down his body before kissing me deeply. I was beginning to understand what Ryker meant about addiction, because he was becoming my own personal drug, especially when he kissed me like that, to where I felt it all the way in my toes.

"Ready to go?" he asked after he pulled away from me.

"Yes. Where are we going?"

"I thought we'd get some lunch in Boston before my surprise."

"Another surprise?" I questioned as a smile curved over my lips. *A girl could get used to this.*

He smiled as he helped me into his truck before wordlessly closing the door. When he got in on his side, he was still grinning from ear to ear. *What is he up to?*

"What are we doing?" I asked.

"I can't tell you, or it'd ruin the surprise. But, trust me, you'll like it."

He started the truck and started driving toward Boston. We grabbed a quick lunch at a local eatery before we drove toward the Boston Wharf. Excitement started to fill me as we neared—I loved the water, envied how it was so fluid and free, something that had always been an unattainable feeling for me.

When we headed toward the Central Wharf, I had a good idea of where we were going. "Are you taking me to the New England Aquarium?" I practically squealed in delight.

He didn't answer, but his smile told me my answer. I clapped happily and actually squealed in glee that time. Ryker began to laugh as the aquarium came into view and I couldn't wait to get there. I'd visited a couple of times when I was little, but I'd never been back.

Once we parked in the garage directly across from the aquarium, I basically jumped out of the truck and bounced up and down in excitement as I waited for Ryker. I had told him last night how much I loved the water and animals, especially ocean animals—he was definitely gaining some serious points with me.

After we got out of the elevator, he linked our hands together as we walked toward the entrance. My chest and stomach tightened happily from the gesture, and I felt all tingly inside. Ryker caused me to feel so many things that I'd never felt before, and I briefly contemplated whether any of the new feelings could be love.

The idea should've scared me, would've scared me before I met Ryker. Love was dangerous because it meant trust, and trust meant vulnerability. Vulnerability meant that I would be opening myself up to be hurt, and I couldn't afford to be hurt by anyone else; I'd never survive it. I always avoided commitment and attachment for that reason, but Ryker was starting to change my mind. He was showing me that trust could be earned, and that love might not be such a bad thing after all. It might be just what I needed to heal.

After Ryker bought our tickets, we started with the first area on the floor level, which housed harbor seals, penguins, and the Shark and Ray Touch Tank exhibits. The seals were outside, so we started there and worked our way in, spending extra time playing with the sharks and rays.

We made our way towards the back, going through the penguin and tropical fish exhibits. While we were looking at the fish, I noticed Ryker was texting on his phone. A smile tipped his lips as he typed, and I couldn't help but wonder if he was texting another girl. My happiness began to fade, and I hated the ugly twisting in my gut.

I almost pulled away when he grabbed my hand, but I didn't want to overreact and jump to any conclusions. I knew the gnawing feeling I had would eventually eat at me until I said something, but I wanted to try and hold it in until we got back to his truck.

Ryker guided me to the back of the first level, which housed more seals and sea lions. "We already saw seals," I said, irritated, my mood beginning to sour.

We stopped right outside the doors that led outside to the exhibit.

His phone chimed with a new text message and he took it out to look at it, causing irrational anger to take over me.

"I'm right here, you know. You could at least wait until I go to the bathroom or something to text one of your other girls," I spat before storming off.

His hand lightly gripped my arm and pulled me back to him. "What are you talking about, Ky?"

I snatched my arm from his grasp and accused, "You know what I'm talking about. I saw how you looked when you were texting—you were talking to some other girl."

"No, I wasn't—I told you there are no other girls, baby."

I scoffed. "Then, who were you texting?"

Just then, a guy in a diver's suit walked inside from a side door. He saw Ryker and greeted, "Hey, ready?"

I looked between them, perplexed about how they knew each other and what the man was referring to. Ryker then spoke, "Kaiya, this is Mike, a client of mine from the gym. He's arranged for us to have a personal encounter with the seals. That's who I was texting."

"Oh," I replied, my face heating from embarrassment. *Way to overreact.*

I was about to apologize when Mike interrupted, "Let's go—we're not even supposed to be doing this right now, so we have to do it quick."

Mike turned around and sped back through the door he came in, which had an "Employees Only" sign on it. I looked up at Ryker. "I'm sorry," I meekly apologized.

"It's okay. I kinda like that you were jealous," he teased with a smirk.

I rolled my eyes and followed after Mike. Ryker came up next to me before holding the door open and ushering me in. Mike waved us over to a desk before saying, "I've lost almost a hundred pounds thanks to Ryker. I would've never been able to do it without his training, so I owe him big time. This was the least I could do."

"I really appreciate this, Mike. Thanks," Ryker replied.

"No, thank you. I wouldn't have reached my goal without your help."

Ryker smiled proudly as Mike led us into an adjoining room. "Put these on and meet me back in the waiting area when you're finished."

He handed Ryker and me a pair of the pants that fisherman wear over their clothes when they walk in shallow areas of water to fish. They reminded me of rubber overalls as I slipped into them. Excitement began to fill me again, and I felt terrible for accusing Ryker of something he didn't do when he was planning something special for me. I locked eyes with him as I apologized again, "I'm really sorry. Thank you for this."

He wrapped me in a hug, "Don't worry about it, Warrior. Let's have some fun."

Draping an arm over my shoulder, he led me back into the waiting area. Mike then took us through the doors outside to the pool where the seals were.

There were five seals swimming in the water, along with another employee in a scuba suit. Mike got in before us, then Ryker followed and helped me in. Mike then introduced us to the other trainer, Sarah, before giving us more information about what we were going to be doing.

"During your interaction, you can feed and touch the seals. You'll probably get wet, but this is definitely an experience you'll never forget so have some fun with it."

Some of the seals had started swimming around us in circles, while the others jumped in and out of the water a short distance away. Reaching out to the one that was closest to me, I placed my hand on it as it glided by. I laughed as it turned around and stuck its flipper out of the water and waved as it came back toward me.

"It wants to shake your hand," Sarah commented.

I looked at Ryker, who nodded. Focusing back on the seal, I tentatively stretched my hand toward its flipper and grasped it. It wiggled in my hold as I shook it and giggled. When I pulled away, it sat up in the water and swam to me before kissing me on the cheek and diving back under the water.

"Did you see that?" I exclaimed with a huge smile as I turned toward Ryker.

He laughed, "Yeah. I think he likes you. Should I be jealous?"

"I don't know, he was pretty cute," I joked.

"Maybe I need to show him that you're my girl," he replied before moving toward me and kissing me deeply. "Think he gets the picture?"

"I don't know, I think you need to show him again," I teased before smiling up at him.

Ryker pressed his lips against mine again as he pulled me into him, framing my face in his hands. As usual, his kiss left me slightly breathless when we broke apart, and I hoped that never changed.

We spent another twenty minutes playing with the seals before we fed them and exited the tank. Before we left, Mike stopped us and said, "We took some pictures of your interaction. Would you like to see them?"

"Sure," I replied enthusiastically. I definitely wanted some mementos to remind me of our experience, even though I knew that I'd never forget it.

Mike led us to a computer before pulling up our photos on the screen. I wasn't great with photos, but I was able to deal with them better than mirrors. There were some great candid shots, but the one that caught my eye was of when Ryker kissed me.

The shot was of right before our lips met. Ryker's hands cupped my face and my arms were wrapped around his waist. Both of our eyes were closed as we anticipated the kiss, and the look on our faces… well, it reminded me of two people in love. I was no expert, but I'd seen couples in love before. They had that stupid, enamored look that I'd always envied because I thought I'd never have it. And there I was, on that screen, with it plastered all over my face. And so was Ryker.

There was a sign on the wall behind the desk where the computer was that listed the prices of the photos. I pulled my wallet out of my purse as I told Mike, "I want to buy some, please."

"I'll get them, baby," Ryker offered.

"It's okay, I can pay for them—you've spent enough today."

Ryker scoffed and firmly stated, "You're not paying."

As I was about to argue more, Mike interrupted, "Write down the numbers of the ones you want and I'll get them processed while you two figure out the payment."

"I'm paying," Ryker repeated as I started to write down the numbers of the ones I wanted. I wanted them all, but it would've cost way too much, so I chose the five that I liked best before sliding the paper to Ryker. He wrote down only three, including the one of us right before we kissed.

He handed the sheet to Mike, who began typing on the keyboard. Once he finished, he stood and said, "I'll be right back with your pictures."

When he returned, he held two photo envelopes and a disc. "These are on the house."

"No, Mike, you've done enough today. I—"

Mike interrupted Ryker's statement, "I insist. It's the least I can do after everything."

"I was just doing my job—you really don't have to do this."

Mike looked at me. "Is he always this persistent?"

"You mean stubborn?" I replied, laughing.

Ryker glared at me as Mike insisted, "Seriously, man, it's on me."

"Thank you," Ryker conceded, shaking Mike's hand. "I'll give you some free training sessions for all this."

"I can't say no to that. I'll text you to set them up, okay? I have to get back to work."

We said our goodbyes and thanked Mike again, then went back into the main aquarium. We toured the rest of the floors before heading back to Ryker's truck.

When we got in, my phone started ringing. The screen showed that Bryce was calling me again. I declined it and stuffed the phone back in my purse.

"Who was that?" Ryker asked as he started the truck.

"Bryce."

"Bryce? You still talk to him?" Ryker questioned defensively, his tone becoming harsh as his face hardened slightly.

"I've been ignoring him, but I finally told him that I couldn't see him anymore, but that I still wanted to be friends. He's called me a few times after I sent the message, but I haven't answered."

His features relaxed some, but I could tell he was still pissed off. "Maybe he needs to be talked to personally."

I shook my head. "I don't think seeing him will help—he'll probably try to convince me to change my mind."

"I meant me," he replied gruffly.

That wouldn't end well. "You don't have to do that—I'm sure he'll get the picture."

"He better," he grumbled.

His irrational jealousy caused a smile to take over my lips. I tried to hide it, but it was almost impossible when he looked so adorable scowling over the whole thing when he had nothing to be worried about. "There's no reason for you to be mad, baby."

"I'm not mad at you. I'm just pissed that he wants what's mine, and doesn't seem to be taking the hint."

"I didn't know I had become property all of a sudden," I replied, slightly offended, even though Ryker referring to me as his caused a little spark of pride within me. Not to mention lust.

"You know what I mean, Ky."

"No, I don't. I don't even know what to call this," I gestured back and forth between us.

"It doesn't matter what this," he mimicked my movement, "is called—together, dating, whatever. All that matters is that you're mine, and I'm yours."

We had locked eyes during the exchange, and his softened once he finished speaking. "I just don't want him to think he has any chance with you when he doesn't. He doesn't, right?"

In that moment, Ryker looked… vulnerable. I'd never seen him look that way—he was always so confident and cocky. "No, he doesn't," I smiled reassuringly.

The left corner of Ryker's lip curved into his trademark grin that I loved so much. "Ready to go home?"

"Yours or mine?"

His smile morphed to a devious, lustful smirk. "Mine."

Chapter Twenty

Ryker

Everything had been going so well with Kaiya over the past few weeks that I was afraid something bad was going to happen to balance it all out. Things just couldn't possibly stay this good; they never did.

We had been spending every other Saturday working on self-defense routines one-on-one. Kaiya had been wanting more practice ever since she started coming back to class after her hiatus. The meeting she had about her abuser had really shaken her up, but at the same time, it had made her more determined. She had begun to ask more questions and wanted to try new techniques to improve her form and skills, in addition to wanting the extra classes.

One Saturday morning, Kaiya and I were working on rear hold escape techniques when *he* walked in. At first, I thought I was dreaming, possibly hallucinating, because there was no fucking way that he would really be there. The last time we spoke, I threatened to bash his face in if I ever saw him again.

Stepping away from Kaiya, I clenched my fists in anger. "What the fuck are you doing here, Ethan?" I growled.

Ethan held his chin up confidently, but I could see the

apprehension in his eyes. His Adam's apple bobbed as he swallowed nervously. "Good to see you, too, Ryker. Tristan's birthday is coming up. I thou—"

"You thought what? That I'd forget what you and that whore did to me?" I seethed.

A muscle in Ethan's jaw ticked as he gritted, "She's not a whore. She's my wife and the mother of my child—your nephew."

"I don't have a brother, so how can I have a nephew?" I asked condescendingly as I crossed my arms over my chest.

"I don't know why I thought you would've changed. Everyone told me you wouldn't have, but I hoped that you would've matured after this long," he spat.

"This has nothing to do with maturity. This," I emphasized as I gestured between us, "is because my own brother betrayed me. I don't know if you forgot, but I told you that I never wanted to see you again. So, get the fuck out!" I roared angrily.

Ethan's furious expression faded somewhat as sadness took over his features. *Good—I hope he hurts as bad as he hurt me.* Wordlessly, he turned and exited the room, glancing back only once before he walked out of my sight.

I don't know how long I stood there before Kaiya tenderly placed her hand on my bicep. "You okay?"

I was far from okay—seeing him had ripped open my scars and threw acid in the open wounds. But I lied, not wanting to burden her with my issues since she had enough to deal with on her own. "I'm fine, baby."

She gave me a knowing look as she moved in front of me. "You can tell me, Ryker. I'm here for you." She linked our hands together.

Kaiya's words thawed some of the ice that had started to freeze within my chest from seeing Ethan. She smiled warmly at me when I looked down at her. She'd already trusted me with so much, opened up to me more than she had with anyone else besides Kamden and Nori. I owed it to her to open up, as well. Sighing, I replied, "That was my brother, Ethan. We haven't spoken in over four years."

"Why?"

"Right after high school, I met this girl, Molly. We dated through college, and she ended up getting pregnant during our senior year. At first, I was scared, shocked actually, but then I was so happy. I loved her and was excited to be starting a family together. I proposed to her a few months after we found out, and she said yes."

"What happened?" Her eyes held a look of concern as they searched my face.

I released another heavy breath. "When Molly was around eight months pregnant, she told me that the baby wasn't mine—it was Ethan's."

Kaiya's hand flew to her mouth as her eyes watered. "Oh my God! Ryker, I'm so sorry!"

"Don't be—it's not your fault. I blamed myself for the longest time, wondering what I did wrong." *Wow, I'm really opening myself up here.*

"You did nothing wrong! They're the ones who were wrong! I can't believe that your own broth—" She abruptly stopped, her eyes widening as if she realized something.

"What?" I asked as she shook her head and hugged herself.

"Nothing," she quickly responded. Avoiding my gaze, she began to tense up. Most people wouldn't have even noticed it, but I did. I had learned so much about her over the past few months that I knew that she was holding something in.

Pulling her to me, I wrapped her in my arms. Even though she probably thought I was only trying to comfort her, in reality, I also needed to hold her, to feel her against me. Seeing Ethan had resurfaced so many bad feelings that I wanted her to wash away, like she always was able to do. I pressed a kiss to the top of her head. "You can trust me, Warrior."

She buried her face in my chest. "I know, it's just hard for me to talk about." Her voice was muffled against my shirt. "I… I don't want you to be disgusted by me."

Framing her face in my hands, I forced her to look up at me, "I could never be disgusted by you. Ever."

Her lips trembled as tears began to rain down her cheeks. "I… I have another brother. His name is Kaleb. He… he was the one who abused me when I was little."

Holy shit. I had no clue what to say, what to do to make it better, but I wanted to do anything to take the pain from her. "Oh, baby, no wonder you fight so much. I'm so sorry."

"I didn't fight hard enough—I should have made him stop, but I was too weak. I'm still weak," she sobbed, burying her face in my chest again.

I tilted her chin up to look at me again. "Hey, you're not weak. You know how strong you are to survive something like that?"

"I survived, but I'm… damaged—completely damaged. Everything he did to me slowly broke me, leaving nothing but fragments for me to try and put back together."

Looking deep into her eyes, I caressed her cheeks with my thumbs. "I'll help you pick up the pieces if you let me, Warrior. I want to be the one to make you whole again."

More tears flowed freely down her rosy cheeks as she clasped my face in her hands, bringing my mouth to hers. Her lips claimed mine with desperation as she pressed our bodies together, showing me how much my words meant to her. So much was said in that kiss, more than we could have expressed in words at that point—it spoke of hope, faith, and trust, helping both of us in the right direction to becoming whole again.

My arms had wrapped around her waist, lifting her to where her toes barely touched the ground. My hands began to roam lower, and I knew if we didn't stop that I was going to end up taking her right there on the mat like our first time. The problem was that there were still people in the gym, unlike before when we were the only two there.

Breaking away, I set my forehead against hers. "If we don't stop, I'm going to take you right here, right now."

Reconnecting our lips, she whimpered with desire. "I need you."

Fuck me. There was no way I could say no to that. Picking her up, her legs wrapped around my waist as our mouths collided. I walked to the door before fumbling with the handle and locking it, then headed to the closet.

Once inside, I kicked the door closed. I maneuvered around most of the boxes and equipment before positioning us against one of the bags that lined the walls. No one should find us, unless one of the other employees happened to come in for some reason, but I really didn't give a fuck at the moment—I had to have her.

As I moved her shorts and panties to the side, she grabbed my cock and pulled it out, eager for me to enter her. Guiding me to her, her hands placed my tip at her opening, which was already wet.

Slowly, I pushed myself inside her, gradually filling her until her pussy surrounded my length. We groaned in unison as I began to pound her against the bag, grasping her hips for deeper penetration.

My mouth found Kaiya's neck as she continuously moaned, her cries of pleasure becoming louder and louder with each of my thrusts. Savoring her skin, I began to push her shirt up, needing to feel her flesh against mine. Kaiya maneuvered to help me take off her top before removing her sports bra, letting it fall to floor.

My shirt was added to the pile as Kaiya eagerly pulled it off. Her hands roamed over my shoulders and arms as my mouth claimed her breast, my tongue ring flicking over her hardened nipple. She arched against me as I moved to her other tit, sucking it deep into my mouth.

Wrapping her legs tighter around me, she forced my dick deeper inside her sex. Growling my approval, I thrust harder as her nails dug into my biceps and her head tipped back against the bag.

"Ryker?" a voice called out from outside the door. *Shit.*

I stilled, my cock still inside Kaiya. Her eyes widened as she looked from me to the door and back again. Putting my finger to my lips, I gently set her down and slid myself out of her. I motioned for her to hide behind the bag as I put my dick back in my shorts and went toward the door.

Glancing over my shoulder, I made sure Kaiya was hidden from view then turned back around and exited.

One of the other trainers was in the middle of the studio, searching for me. "You need something?" I asked as I shut the door.

He turned around. "Where were you?" he asked suspiciously, looking over my shoulder.

"Doing inventory in the supply closet. What's up?"

"I just wanted to tell you that Mark can't make it to class tomorrow night, so he asked me to fill in for him. Is that cool?"

Really, you came in here and interrupted my sex session for that? "Yeah, that's fine. Be here at seven."

"All right, see you tomorrow," he replied as he walked to the door.

Once he left, I waited a minute or so before going back into the supply room. "The coast is clear," I called out.

Kaiya peeked her head out from behind the bag before coming out of her hiding spot. Her face reddened in embarrassment. "That was a close one," she said, straightening her sports bra and brushing her hair behind her ears with her fingers.

Chuckling, I made my way to her. "Yeah, it was. You want to pick up where we left off?"

"Ryker, we almost got caught," she chided, even though a smile lined her lips.

"So?" I teased, but she gave me a disapproving look. "Fine, but we're finishing this tonight."

Grinning seductively at me, she agreed, "Deal."

We spent another hour or so working on more techniques before I had a personal training session with another one of my clients. Kaiya planned to come over to my place after my shift ended, and I was looking forward to finishing what we had started.

When Kaiya arrived at my place, I had already set another plan into motion. I had been working on breaking another one of her rules, the one about staying over. I routinely broke the other two rules, almost nightly, so I was determined to break them all. *Two down, two to go.*

Whenever she came over, I always asked her to spend the night, but she resisted me. I hadn't stayed the night with a girl after that whore and I broke up, and I'd never wanted to until Kaiya. Everything was different with her, from the way she was able to make me smile so easily to the way she set a fire inside me with just one look. I loved every minute I spent with her.

We were hanging out on the couch watching T.V. when Kaiya mentioned, "I feel like dancing."

I played with her hair, twirling it around my fingers. "Yeah?" I replied in surprise. We hadn't been out to a club since the night that she'd been attacked.

"Can we go tonight?" She asked hopefully as she looked up at me.

I didn't really see the point in going to a club when the main reason that I had gone to them before was to pick up girls. I didn't need to do that anymore now that we were together. But I knew that Kaiya loved to dance, so I gave in. "Sure, baby. Where?"

"How about that new one that just opened up? I think it's called," she paused, looking up to the side and pursing her lips as she thought. "Tunnel."

"Yeah, I've heard of it. We can go if you want."

"Yay!" She hopped up off the couch excitedly. "I'll call Nori. Maybe you should text Drew to meet us—they seemed to have fun together the last time." She giggled as she tromped toward my bedroom.

I loved seeing her laugh—her smiles and laughs had become regular occurrences, replacing the scowls and sorrow that I had thought were permanently etched on her face. Some of the sadness still lingered at times when she thought I wasn't looking, but I was able to chase it away for a while. My goal was to totally eradicate it one day. That would be my biggest challenge yet.

I got off the couch to get my phone from the counter. I sent a text to Drew, who was down with the idea since he had fun with Nori the last time. He hadn't been able to close the deal with her, so I knew he'd be planning to tonight. If she was anything like Kaiya, he'd need all the luck he could get.

Kaiya came back into the room before grabbing her purse. A smile lit up her face. "Nori's in. I need to go home and get ready, then we'll meet you there, okay?"

"Yeah. Text me when you're on your way."

She stood on her toes to kiss me. "Okay, baby. See you later."

Once she left, I decided to head over to Drew's to wait until they were ready. We drank some beers to pass the time and when Kaiya finally text me, it was quarter till midnight. I didn't know what took women so long to get ready, but the end result was usually worth it.

This time was no exception. When Kaiya walked up to us outside the club, my pulse raced as the blood rushed to my cock.

She was wearing a tight, black one-shoulder dress that stopped right above her mid-thigh. She bit her lip as our eyes locked, her cheeks flooding with color as I admired her. I doubted I would ever get tired of looking at her; everything else paled in comparison to her stunning beauty.

Peering up at me with those captivating eyes, she smiled shyly. "Hey."

I leaned down to kiss her. "Can I just take you home now? I don't think I can wait with you looking like that."

Her grin spread as she laughed. "Then, all my hard work to look this way would be wasted."

"Oh, it won't go to waste. I'll make sure of it."

She rolled her eyes playfully then slid her hand into mine. As we walked to the entrance, Drew draped his arm around Nori, who was already giggling flirtatiously. *Yeah, he should be getting some tonight.*

We had to wait a few minutes in line before we were let into the club—the place was packed wall to wall, and the heavy bass of the music vibrated the air as we squeezed through the throng of people to get to the bar.

Decorated in various shades of gray with splashes of reds, the club was long and narrow, like its namesake. Rows of lights ran overhead, and they pulsed to the music as the colors fluctuated, taking on every hue of the rainbow. Couches lined the walls of the VIP area, but there was only standing room everywhere else, so we chose a spot close to the dance floor after taking a shot and ordering our drinks.

Kaiya sipped her cocktail as her eyes scanned through the crowd before settling on mine. A shy, yet seductive smile came over her lips as she glanced away.

Nori started pulling Drew towards the dance floor, but he resisted. "I'm not drunk enough for that yet." He chuckled.

Nori pouted. "Please. I promise I'll make it up to you later."

Drew conceded, letting Nori pull him out to the floor. They soon were lost in the sea of bodies as I directed my attention back to Kaiya. "You wanna dance, baby?"

Eagerly nodding, she threaded her free hand with mine and pulled me into the dancing crowd. Swaying to the beat, Kaiya pressed her ass into my cock, and my hands automatically went to her lithe hips as she moved against me.

Leaning into me, her body undulated rhythmically against mine, making me want to take her home early even more. My dick began to stiffen from her sensual movements as my mouth found her neck. Tilting it, she allowed me better access to taste her as my tongue traced along the slender flesh.

Pushing my erection against her, I caused her to bite back a moan as she turned her head to connect her lips with mine. Our tongues tangled along with our bodies, the sensual movements making our skin heat from a combination of body heat and arousal. I was on the verge of hiking up that dress and slipping inside her right in the middle of everyone—that's how crazy she made me, making me want her unlike anything before.

"Kaiya?" someone shouted over the music, interrupting us.

Kaiya broke away from me, her fair skin flushed and those full lips slightly swollen. My head followed hers as it turned in the direction of the voice, and anger began to simmer under my skin once I saw the source—Bryce.

Kaiya stiffened nervously as she uncomfortably said, "Hey, Bryce."

He stepped towards us, causing me to instinctively move in front of Kaiya. His eyes hardened as they met mine, and I knew he was pissed about her being with me. *Too fucking bad. She's mine.*

He looked around me, focusing back on Kaiya. His eyes softened some as he spoke to her, "You haven't returned my calls—I wanted to talk about what you said. I—"

"She obviously doesn't want to talk to you about it, or she would have answered your calls. Why don't you take a hint and leave her alone?"

Bryce moved toward me, coming right up in my face. *Brave, but stupid.* "I don't remember asking your opinion."

Clenching my fists, I snarled, "Back the fuck off before you get hurt."

"Guys, stop," Kaiya pleaded as she squeezed between us, pushing Bryce away from me. She put her back against me as she faced Bryce, keeping her hands on his chest. I growled low as I put my arms around her waist and pulled her away from him.

Kaiya gave me a look over her shoulder, but didn't say anything until she redirected her attention to Bryce. "Look, Bryce, I'm… Ryker and I… we're together now. Like I said in the text, I can't see you like that anymore, but I still want to be friends."

Glaring between me and her, he patronizingly remarked, "Really? After everything we've been through, you're just going to drop me for some… some… meathead that you just met?"

Meathead? Did he really just call me a meathead? What are we, in middle school? "This meathead will beat your ass if—"

"Stop!" Kaiya yelled, gaining both of our attentions, as well as some of the people's around us. "Look, Bryce, I'm sorry, but I can't help the way I feel. Ryker and I just connected, and—"

"Save it, Ky. I'm glad to finally see where I stand," Bryce spat before pivoting and disappearing into the crowd.

Shoulders slumping, Kaiya gazed sadly in the direction he went and sighed. "I didn't mean to hurt him."

"I know, Warrior. Try not to worry about it," I said as I rubbed my hands up and down her arms, hoping to comfort her. I knew from some of our talks about him that Bryce had provided stability for her when she needed it, and that she cared for him. I could tell that Bryce felt the same for Kaiya, too, maybe even loved her. How could he not? I was falling hard for her myself, and there was nothing I could do to stop it, even if I wanted to. I should've wanted to, should've been more concerned with protecting myself from being hurt again, but Kaiya had found a way to slip past my defenses, making me let my guard down.

Turning around, she wrapped her arms around me, hugging me tightly. I returned her embrace, enjoying the warmth it stirred in my stomach. I'd only felt this way once before, but it was already becoming stronger than it was back then. *Holy shit, I think I love her.*

Being the coward that I was, I pushed the thoughts away. Neither of us was ready for that, and I couldn't bring myself to say the words yet. I wasn't prepared for the repercussions of speaking them, especially if Kaiya didn't feel the same way, even though I was pretty sure she did. When she thought I wasn't looking, I caught the way she stared at me sometimes, that look of love—the one that was so evident on both of our faces in that picture we took at the aquarium.

Even still, I couldn't voice my feelings, too afraid of her rejection. I didn't want to push her away, unsure of how I would deal with not being with her anymore. The idea twisted my stomach uncomfortably, and I quickly pushed it away and focused on something else.

"Ready to go, baby?"

"Yeah." She scanned the dance floor. "Where's Nori and Drew?"

Looking around the club, I searched for them, finding them making out on the dance floor. Pointing them out to Kaiya, I joked, "I don't think they're ready to leave yet."

"I need to tell her we're leaving—she gets pissed when I leave without telling her," she replied before walking toward them.

When she came back, I linked our hands and led her through the crowd to get to the exit. The fresh breeze that hit us once we stepped outside was a welcome change from the hot air inside the club.

Once we got to my apartment, I was on Kaiya as soon as we walked through the door. Our mouths collided as I lifted her, my hands gripping her exposed thighs as she hooked her legs around me. I slipped her dress up further as I headed for the couch, unable to wait any longer. I had been waiting all day to have her, and now that we were finally alone, I was taking full advantage.

Kaiya straddled me once I sat down. Her hands immediately found my jeans and she hastily unbuttoned them, as eager as I was for me to sink inside her.

As she pulled my cock out, I moved her panties to the side, and then she was lowering herself down on me. Filling her inch by inch, I groaned as she cried out in pleasure until she took all of me.

Slowly, she moved her hips into me as I removed her dress. Pulling her flush against me, my mouth found her tits as she continued to ride me. I teased her nipple with my tongue before nipping and sucking it lightly, causing her to moan over and over again.

Kaiya's pace increased as my hands caressed her silken skin and my mouth consumed her. I traced my teeth and tongue along her collarbone to her neck, then brought her lips to meet mine, needing to taste her sweetness. Our tongues threaded together as her hands knotted in my hair and pulled tightly as she rocked harder on my dick, bringing us both closer to ecstasy.

Grasping Kaiya's ass, I began to thrust upward, meeting her movements stroke for stroke. I could feel myself nearing release, so I broke my mouth away from Kaiya's, breathing heavily as I spoke against her lips, "I'm gonna come."

She didn't stop as she replied, her voice full of desire, "Come inside me."

Fuck me. "Are you sure?" I asked before biting her bottom lip.

"Yes," she moaned. "I'm on the shot."

I didn't know what that was, but I figured it was some form of birth control. I didn't really care, plus I was sure that Kaiya wouldn't let me come inside her if she wasn't on some type of contraceptive.

Rolling her hips, Kaiya's snug walls continued to perfectly caress my cock. I pounded up into her, jetting my cum inside her after only a few more strokes. Her pussy pulsated around my dick as her body shuddered her orgasm against me.

We stayed like that until our breathing evened. Then, Kaiya reluctantly sighed, "I better get going home. It's late."

I brushed her hair out of her face, then caressed her cheek with my thumb as our gazes met. *Here goes nothing.* "Stay with me."

Her eyes searched mine. Framing her face with my hands, I pulled her to me, pressing a tender kiss on her lips before softly saying, "Please."

Silently, she lay her forehead against mine as she exhaled a deep breath. She remained quiet, and the longer time passed, the more I was sure she would say no. My pulse pounded as I waited for her response, and after what seemed like hours, she finally whispered, "Okay."

Abruptly pulling back, I looked at her in surprise. "You'll stay?"

She smiled softly at me. "I'll stay."

Grinning back, I stood and carried her to the bedroom. After getting ready for bed, I slid under the covers as Kaiya stood nervously on the other side. "This is the part where you get in with me," I teased with a grin.

Toying with the hem of the shirt I let her borrow to sleep in, she bit her bottom lip nervously as she looked at me. "I've never spent the night with a guy before."

"Never?"

"Never," she repeated.

Sitting up, I scooted to the edge of the bed where she stood, framing her between my legs. I linked both of my hands with hers as I pressed a kiss to her stomach, then tilted my head up to look at her. "Are you afraid of me, Warrior?"

Her brows furrowed as she firmly responded, "No."

"Do you trust me?" That was the million dollar question.

We stared at one another as she contemplated her answer. My heart pounded in my chest waiting for her response, wanting so badly for her to trust me, needing her to. "Yes," she finally replied, barely above a whisper.

The tension in my chest faded away from her answer. I moved back on the bed, pulling her with me as I lay down. Facing each other, I brought her into me as I covered us with the blanket. Pushing some hair behind her ear, I gently kissed her lips, then her forehead before wrapping my arms around her. "Goodnight, Warrior."

Sighing, she rested her head on my bicep as her arms draped over my bare side. Her stiff body relaxed as I rubbed her back, and she snuggled closer to me. Burying my face in her neck, I inhaled deeply, enjoying my smell still lingering on her skin. Closing my eyes, I loved the feel of her warm, delicate frame against my much larger one. Even though our bodies were so different, hers was perfect for mine in every way.

Tangled with the girl of my dreams, it didn't take long for me to surrender to sleep.

Chapter Twenty-One

Kaiya

My eyes fluttered open to Ryker's sleeping face. Once the fog of sleep lifted, realization sank in. *Holy shit, I spent the night.* Anxiety attempted to trap me in its clutches, my heartbeat and breathing starting to speed up as panic tried to set in.

Focusing on Ryker's handsome face, I took deep breaths as I studied his features. *You're with Ryker. You're safe. He won't hurt you.* That warm, fuzzy feeling that he gave me so often began to set in as I stared at him, melting away the anxiousness building inside me.

My eyes moved down, scanning over the beautiful artwork inked on his chest and arms. I wanted to trace over them with my fingers, commit them to memory, but I didn't want to wake him when he was so peaceful.

After several minutes, he began to stir before stretching lazily like a cat as he opened his eyes. When they met mine, a sleepy smile spread over that sexy mouth. "Good morning, beautiful," he said, his voice still thick with sleep.

"Morning," I murmured back.

He leaned forward, eyes on my lips, but I pulled away. He gave me a questioning look, to which I replied, "I haven't brushed my teeth."

Laughing, he threaded his fingers through my hair as he said, "I don't care about your breath, baby. Before I do anything else, the first thing I want to do is kiss my girl."

Damn, he just gets better and better. I smiled before conceding, "Okay, but closed lips until I brush my teeth."

He chuckled again, the sound vibrant and full of life. "Whatever you say, Warrior."

Leaning toward me again, he pressed his lips to mine. Even just that small kiss sent tingles throughout my body.

When he pulled away, he rubbed my back. "How'd you sleep?"

"Surprisingly well."

"You didn't think you would?"

"Honestly no. I have nightmares, and I don't sleep well, even at home. I definitely didn't think that I'd get any here, but that was the best sleep I've had in a while."

"Maybe you should stay over more often," He raised his eyebrows suggestively.

"Maybe I will," I replied teasingly. "If you're lucky."

Ryker gave me a playful grin before he pounced on me. Pinning my body beneath his, I squealed as he tickled me. Our laughter filled the room as I squirmed under him, trying to free myself from his grasp.

"I'm going to pee if you don't stop," I warned, still laughing.

Relenting, he propped himself on his elbows, framing my face between his arms as he gazed down at me. His lips parted to say something, but he closed them and stayed silent as he brushed some hair back that had fallen across my face and kissed me again. *I wonder what he was going to say.*

My internal thought was forgotten as the kiss deepened, the feel of his almost naked body atop mine so alluring that I didn't care whether I brushed my teeth or not. When his tongue parted my lips, I eagerly reciprocated, twining mine with his as he pressed his morning erection into me.

Ryker's hands pushed the shirt I was wearing up until it came off. I slipped down his boxer-briefs as he moved my panties to the side, just like last night. His hard shaft pressed against my slick entrance, slowly pushing in as he stretched me. His mouth captured a moan that escaped me as he cupped my face in his hands, passionately kissing me.

Ryker slowly pumped his hips into me, gently thrusting in and out of my sex. The delicate way he was touching and fucking me was so different from the way we normally had sex, but it was just as amazing. The emotion he was creating within me was unlike anything I'd ever felt before, connecting us in a way I'd never experienced with anyone else. In that moment, I knew no one would ever compare to Ryker—my body was made for his, and his for mine. He completed me in every sense of the word.

Pleasure swarmed every nerve from his touch, filling me with molten fire. Electricity began to build in my core, radiating through my body as my orgasm approached. *How does he do this to me?*

My hands knotted in his hair as he continued to rock into me, possessing all of me with his sinful mouth, inked hands, and divine cock.

Arching against him, he sank further inside me, my walls molding to him as he caressed them.

"Fuck, baby, I love your pussy," Ryker growled against my lips before slipping his tongue back in my mouth. *Fuck, so good.*

I could only moan in response, my mind already lost in oblivion from Ryker pleasuring my every cell. *Almost there, almost there.*

Pushing deeper each time, Ryker repeatedly thrust into me. After a few more strokes, my orgasm found me, trickling through every limb and drowning me in bliss. One hand tangled in my hair, softly pulling the long tresses as the other stroked every curve of my body. He stilled above me as warmth coated my core and his cock throbbed inside me.

Panting breathlessly, Ryker hovered over me as he stared down at me. Sweat glinted over his golden skin and dampened his messy hair as he smirked at me. *I could get used to this every morning.*

He gave me one last kiss before we disentangled ourselves. As I made my way to the bathroom, my phone rang. I went back to grab it, and saw Kamden's face and number on the screen. *Shit.*

I answered the phone to hear Kamden's enraged voice, "Where

the fuck are you, Ky?"

"Good morning to you, too, Kamden," I greeted sarcastically.

"Morning? It's almost one in the afternoon, Kaiya. Where are you?" he gritted through the phone.

"I'm at Ryker's," I snapped back, immediately regretting it. *Fuck, I shouldn't have told him that.*

"What? You stayed the night at Ryker's?" he exclaimed angrily.

"Yeah, I did. I'm a grown woman for fuck's sake."

"You could've at least called me—I've been worried sick." His voice was strained, but it was more with concern than anger. He was still upset, but I could tell that he was relieved that he was hearing from me.

I sighed, feeling like shit. "I'm sorry. I didn't mean to worry you. I'll be home soon, okay?" I said, softening my tone, as well. I should have been more considerate—I'd only spent the night at Nori's before, and I called him beforehand to let him know. I felt like such a jerk for worrying him over something that could have easily been avoided.

After we said our goodbyes, I hung up the phone and turned around to go to the bathroom.

Ryker stood against the door, looking concerned as he asked, "Everything okay?"

"Yeah. Kamden was just upset that I didn't let him know I was staying here."

"He's protective over you," Ryker commented.

"He's been like that since the whole thing with Kaleb." I still couldn't believe that I had told him that Kaleb was my brother the day before.

"I would be, too if something like that happened to my sister."

Reaching him in the doorway, he blocked my path before tugging me in his arms. He must have sensed my unease about talking about Kaleb because he stated, "He's never going to hurt you again, Ky. I'll kill him if he tries."

Our eyes had locked as he spoke, and the warmth normally present when he looked at me was gone—he was completely serious. I knew without a doubt that he meant what he said, and that both comforted and scared me. If Kaleb ever did get released, he'd come after me. And that meant Ryker would protect me, and possibly get hurt. Kaleb always hurt people I got involved with, and I didn't want that for Ryker.

I didn't know how he found me—I hadn't told anyone at home about the party. They all thought I was spending the night at Nori's house.

One of the varsity football players, Liam, and I were upstairs. It was his best friend's party, so he let us use his bedroom to hook up.

We were both pretty drunk, and had been all over each other the whole night. By the time we made it to the bed, lust had gripped us in full force, and most of our clothes were off.

Liam ripped a condom open with his teeth and fumbled to slip it on. I needed him to be faster, wanted him to rid me of Kaleb's touch and replace it with his; anything to make me forget, at least for a little while.

Finally, he entered me, flushing out my thoughts and filling me with sensation. I couldn't focus on anything else except the intimate tangling of our bodies, and that was exactly what I wanted; to lose myself, if only for a short time.

Noise filled my ears, like a door slamming, but it didn't completely register, my mind lost in sexual oblivion as it closed off the outside world.

Only when I felt the loss of Liam against me did I start to comprehend what was happening. Kaleb was atop Liam on the floor, repeatedly punching him. Shit.

"Kaleb, stop!" I screamed as I pulled the blanket to cover my naked body.

Hand raised in the air, ready to throw another punch, he stilled before turning to look at me. He had that look in his eyes, the one that I had come to fear, the one that there was no reasoning with. Fuck.

I clutched the comforter tighter to me as he approached. Sitting next to me on the bed, he pried the covers from my hands and pulled them away, exposing my bare flesh to him. I cringed as he began to trace his fingers down my skin, trembling in fear for what he might do to me, how he would punish me.

"Kaleb, don't," I whimpered.

His fingers dug into my thigh as he snarled, "So, he can touch you, but I can't?"

Flinching, I cried out, "You're not supposed to touch me like that, Kaleb. You're my brother!"

His other hand came up to roughly grab my jaw, squeezing it painfully. "Yes, and that means that you're mine! No one else's! You let him fuck you, gave him what was mine," he accused angrily.

There has to be something wrong with him. He shouldn't be this way with me. Or maybe there's something wrong with me. Maybe I'm crazy. No one else makes their brother act this way.

"Look at me, Kaiya!" he yelled as he gripped my jaw harder.

My eyes snapped open to meet his, which were identical to mine. Same unique shade of blue, but I hated them. Tears trickled down my cheeks as he let go of me and roamed his hands over my breasts down to my sex.

I pushed his hands away and prepared for the backlash, clenching my eyes shut. Noise of footsteps and talking from outside the door caused them to snap back open. Kaleb stood up and backed away. Thank God.

Kaleb made his way for the door, glancing over his shoulder as he said, "This isn't over. I will take back what's mine."

I zoned out after that, pretending that I didn't hear his words, and wishing that my life was different.

"Ky? You with me, baby?" Ryker asked, cupping my cheek, bringing me back to the present. His eyes were brimmed with concern as he searched my face.

"Yeah, I'm fine. I get lost in my head sometimes." I smiled weakly. *Too much.*

"Don't get too lost up there. I want to be able to find you," he said as he grazed his thumb softly over my skin.

I couldn't stop myself from speaking what I felt in my heart. I'd always been strangely drawn to Ryker, like iron to a magnet, unable to stay away from him, even from the beginning. There was no way I'd be able to now. "I'll always find my way back to you."

Ryker brought my body into his as our lips joined in a tender, passion-filled kiss that made my knees feel like quicksand. When we finally separated, I wavered a little as I braced myself against him. He grinned cockily as he steadied me before smacking me lightly on the butt and letting me pass him to go into the bathroom.

After I finished getting ready, Ryker drove me home. He walked me up to the door, but I didn't want him to come in, afraid that he and

Kamden would get into a fight because of last night. I really couldn't deal with that right now. I was trying to hold myself together after my flashback of Kaleb.

"See you at class tonight?" I asked as I tiptoed to kiss him; kissing him always chased away the darkness that threatened to swallow me.

Wrapping his arms around my waist, he placed his hands on my lower back, deepening the kiss before pulling away seconds later, way too soon. My lips tingled and I immediately missed the warmth of his mouth on mine. "Yeah. See you later, Warrior."

His smirk tightened my stomach, making me think about the morning and night before. My hand clumsily fumbled for the doorknob, and I slipped slightly as I missed it. Blushing profusely, I gave him an embarrassed smile as I found the handle and turned it. "Bye."

"Bye, baby," he replied, still wearing that grin. Turning, I entered my apartment and shut the door before leaning against it and letting out a breath. *The things he does to me.*

"Have fun?" Kamden questioned, notes of anger still lingering in his voice from earlier.

Really? Is he still mad? I thought we worked things out over the phone.

I pushed off the door. "I did, actually. Thanks for asking," I replied as I walked past him down the hallway.

"Kaiya, we need to talk."

"About what?" I asked as I stopped.

He approached me with his arms folded over his chest. "You and Ryker. Since you didn't take my advice and stay away from him, we need to talk about things."

"What things? Our relationship is none of your business, Kamden." I didn't understand why I was being so abrasive—I knew he was only concerned about me, but I hated that he was so adamant that Ryker and I not be together.

"Why are you acting like this? I'm just worried about you."

Sighing, I replied, "I know, but I'm not a kid anymore. I don't need you to protect me."

Kamden looked pained as he responded, "I didn't protect you when you needed me. It eats at me every day, Ky. Every. Single. Day. I just don't want you to get hurt again."

My eyes watered. I hated that he felt responsible when it wasn't his fault. If anything, it was our parents' fault for not paying more attention to their children. I set my hand over his crossed arms. "It wasn't your fault, Kam. We were just kids."

His mouth set in a hard frown as he inhaled deeply and shook his head. "You're my baby sister—I was supposed to protect you from anything like that ever happening."

I'd never be able to convince him otherwise, no matter what I said. We were both stubborn in that way. Once we got something in our head, there was no changing our minds. "You've more than made up for it by taking care of me and supporting me. I would've never made it without you," I replied sincerely.

He gave me a weak smile. "Yes, you would've. You're stronger than you know."

I rolled my eyes—I was the weakest person I knew. Having breakdowns and being afraid of your own reflection didn't equate to being a strong person in my book.

"Look, I know you're just worried about me, but don't. I haven't been this happy since… well, ever. Ryker may seem like an asshole, but he's… he's amazing. If anything, you should worry about me hurting him. My kind of crazy isn't good for people," I joked, or at least attempted to.

Kamden didn't laugh, but his smile broadened a tiny bit.

"You're not crazy, *sorella.*"

"Whatever you say. Seriously, don't worry about me. Ryker treats me very well." *Huge understatement.*

"If that changes—"

"You'll be the first to know," I interrupted, finishing his sentence.

Continuing my way down the hall, I headed to my room and stripped off my clothes before jumping in the shower. Once I emerged, fully refreshed, I made my way to my office, wanting to check my calendar to see the upcoming projects for the next few weeks and possibly get some work done on them. Ryker occupied a lot of my time, so I tried to squeeze in work whenever possible so I wouldn't get behind.

After I scanned over my desk calendar for the rest of August, I flipped up the page to look at September, my eyes zeroing in on a date circled in red. My body stiffened as fear began to root itself in my stomach, the darkness attempting to creep back in. *Kaleb's release. Holy shit, it's only a month away. Fuck, fuck, fuck.*

My leg bounced nervously as I stared at the date, unable to tear my gaze away from it. My pulse pounded in my ears as a thin sheen of sweat started to cling to my skin, making me uncomfortably hot. The blackness began to suffocate me, trying to blanket it me with its poison and send me spiraling into a breakdown. *Fight it, fight it. Focus on something else.*

I knew exactly what the perfect something was—Ryker. He always saved me, and breaking me from the tainted darkness was no exception. His face came into my mind, chasing away the inky mass threatening to crush me.

I broke free of the trance I was in as I threw the calendar, sending it flying off my desk. Pens and other office supplies joined it as they scattered over the floor.*Breathe, breathe, breathe.* Needing to escape, I rushed to my room as I repeated the phrase over and over in my head. Grabbing my phone, I immediately dialed Ryker, but it went to his voicemail. *Fuck, he's probably already at work.*

I paced nervously back and forth in my room, gnawing on my bottom lip. *Calm down. You're safe. Ryker and Kamden will protect you. Breathe, breathe, breathe.*

My hands shook with nerves as I sat on my bed. Pulling my knees up, I wrapped my arms around them and began to softly rock back and worth, attempting to soothe myself. Wet warmth coated my cheeks, my fight to contain my tears lost. *So weak.*

My phone rang, startling me. Glancing down at it next to me, Ryker's face filled the screen. I instantly grabbed it and answered. "Hello?" My voice was strained, thick with emotion.

He must've heard the panicked sadness in my voice because his response was quick and full of concern. "What's wrong, baby?"

I thought about lying, but I couldn't lie to Ryker. I was so good at it with everyone else but not him. Taking a deep breath, I tried to steady my voice. "Kaleb's release is a little over a month away. I just saw it on my calendar."

"Are you okay? Do I need to come over?"

My knight in shining armor. My lips curved up slightly from the gesture, warmth filling my body and ridding me of the cold that the darkness left snaking through my veins. I wiped my cheeks, which were tight from my dried tears. "No, I'm okay. I just wanted to hear your voice."

"Are you sure, Ky? I can leave work if you need me."

He didn't even understand how much I needed him. He had become the glue that held me together, the stitches that were slowly repairing the scars on my heart.

"No, I'm fine. I'll see you at class in a little bit."

"Call me if you need me, okay? I'll keep my phone on me." His voice was still edged with worry.

"Okay."

"Bye, baby."

"Bye."

When we hung up, I exhaled another breath before getting off the bed. Grabbing my laptop, I decided to do some work on it instead of facing the mess that I left in the office. Anything to keep my mind occupied.

I thought about going to Kamden, but I had been selfish with him our entire lives. I needed to learn to cope on my own, no matter how difficult it was. And now I had Ryker to help me through until I could handle everything on my own. Kamden deserved a break.

By the time I made it to the gym, I was like a balloon that was inflated to the point of bursting. I needed to see Ryker, to have him calm me down like only he could.

I arrived thirty minutes early so I could talk to him before the other students showed up. If not, I'd probably lose it and have a meltdown during class.

When I walked into our training room, Ryker immediately came over to me. His eyes searched mine. "Are you okay?"

"Yeah. Better now that I'm with you," I said as I forced a smile. It wasn't a lie, but I was still being plagued by the impending date looming over me, overshadowing the happiness Ryker brought me.

Slowly rubbing both of my arms up and down, the concern in his voice increased, "Maybe you should skip class tonight."

My brows furrowed as I frowned. "No. If anything, I need to get this out. Bottling it in only makes it worse—trust me, I know."

His mouth set in a tight line. He knew he wouldn't win this argument. "Fine, just take it easy."

Yeah, right. Me, take things easy? Nothing is ever easy when it comes to me. "I'll try. I really need to kick the shit out of something, though."

Ryker's lips quirked up to one side in a lopsided grin. "Always fighting."

Before I could respond, another student came in with David and an unfamiliar employee, not the normal instructor Mark. Ryker followed my gaze and said, "Mark couldn't make it tonight. Another one of the staff is filling in for him—I need to go brief him on class."

"Go ahead, I'll get my gear on."

Ryker walked away as I dropped my stuff by the bag I always used. I wrapped my hands with athletic tape, which I started using upon Ryker's insistence since I bruised so easily, then slipped on my gloves.

When class finally started, my pent-up frustration and stress still coursed through my body, making my muscles ache from the tension. I couldn't completely push the thought of Kaleb being released from my head, probably because of how soon it was. If I didn't expel everything soon, I was going to spontaneously combust. *What better way to release it all than to take it out on the bag?*

I began with simple jabs and punches, but after my fists connected with the vinyl, my moves intensified as fury took over my body. The bag morphed into Kaleb, and I completely lost it. Control was no longer mine as I cascaded into that abyss inside me, the source where all my demons lay.

My arms and legs flew as I pummeled Kaleb with elbows, kicks, and punches, making him hurt as he had hurt me all those years. Sweat drenched my face as I continued, unable to stop; if I stopped, he would only hurt me back, punish me for fighting him.

My chest burned as I struggled to breath, but I couldn't stop. I had to keep going, had to protect myself. Dizziness settled over my body like a heavy weight as my vision blurred, and I felt my knees meet the ground. *No.*

Ringing filled my ears from the piercing scream of someone, and I covered them to drown out all the noise. I clenched my eyes shut as I folded into myself, wanting to conceal as much of my body as possible from Kaleb's backlash.

Rough hands gripped my shoulders, causing me to strike outward. The hit was weak, but I still connected before slumping forward in exhaustion. I heard a familiar voice, but it didn't sound like it normally did; it was frantic and laced with fear. "Look at me, Ky! Come back to me, baby."

Trying to concentrate on the sound, I lifted my head slightly, but it caused everything to spin around me so I put it back down. My heart thudded as the voice urged, "Breathe, baby, breathe."

Closing my eyes again, I focused on taking deep breaths, trying to claw my way out of the dark chasm I was buried in. That voice kept talking to me, saying soothing things that helped bring me back towards reality, helped me regain some control.

Some of the pressure constricting me lifted, enough so that I opened my eyes to try and focus on my surroundings. The first thing I saw was a pair of warm, brown eyes that were creased in worry. *Ryker.*

Some of the tension eased from his strained face as he forced a smile. "There's my Warrior. I knew you'd fight your way back."

I blinked a few times to combat my blurred vision and dispel the rest of the disequilibrium clinging to me.

Ryker pushed my sweaty hair out of my face before handing me an open water bottle. "Drink."

Sipping the cool liquid, what had happened started to sink in. Embarrassment heated my already fevered face as tears stung my eyes. I glanced around the room, expecting to find a bunch of scared faces staring back at me, but there were none. The room was empty except for Ryker and me.

I gave him a confused look, and he answered my unspoken question. "I made everyone leave."

Completely humiliated didn't even come close to how I felt. I doubted that I'd be able to come to class ever again; Ryker would have to give me private lessons. If he still wanted to be with me.

"I'm sorry," I whispered as a tear rolled down my cheek..

"Sorry? For what?" His eyes held a look of confusion.

"That I flipped out and totally lost it, that you had to stop class because of me, that I embarrassed you," I bitterly replied as I looked down, angry for my lack of control.

Ryker gripped my chin and tilted my face to look at him. "I'm not embarrassed by you. Concerned, yes, but not embarrassed. And I don't give a fuck about stopping class—you are all I care about."

There's that amazing feeling stirring. "Thank you. I think I'm okay now."

"What happened?" He brushed his knuckles down the side of my face as his eyes met mine.

"I'm not exactly sure. I was trying to let my anger over Kaleb out on the bag, but I lost control. All I could see was him, and then I got lightheaded and disoriented. I can't really remember too much after that."

"You went crazy on the bag. You probably felt that way because you were holding your breath. When you fell, you scared the shit out of me—you were screaming so loud, and I had no idea what was wrong."

I was the one screaming? This just gets better and better. "I'm sorry. That happens sometimes. I thought I had better control over it now, but getting closer to his possible release is starting to get to me."

"That's understandable, baby. Don't stress yourself out about it." He rubbed his hands up and down my arms before threading our fingers together. "You know you're not alone in this—you have me. You don't have to fight by yourself, Warrior."

There was that feeling in my chest again—that one that made my heart beat faster and wrapped me in happiness. He was borderline perfect, knew exactly what I needed and the right words to say. I had no clue what the hell he saw in me—I was a hot mess.

"It's not easy to talk about. It's bad enough that I can't escape him since I see him whenever I look in the mirror."

"You look a lot alike? You and Kamden don't," Ryker commented.

Shit. I really didn't want to go there, but Ryker had become my rock, my anchor when I needed security and strength. I'd already realized if things didn't work out between us, there'd never be anyone that could take his place. He was it for me. If anyone deserved my trust, it was him. "He… he's my twin."

Ryker's face hardened, his beautiful mouth being dragged down in an angry frown as he seethed, "What?"

I didn't say anything. His rage was palpable, and even though I knew he wasn't angry at me, I didn't want to set him off. He abruptly stood before slamming his fist into the punching bag a few feet away from me. Roaring angrily, he threw it like it weighed almost nothing towards the center of the room.

His outburst didn't scare me. In fact, it made me feel good; it showed me that he truly cared. Never trusting anyone besides Kamden and Nori made it hard for me to judge whether someone's intentions or feelings were genuine, but there was no denying Ryker's. There was no doubt that he cared about me, maybe even loved me. *Could he possibly love me?* The thought was almost laughable since I was certain that I was completely crazy. Even if I wasn't, Ryker was still too good for me. Girls like me didn't get guys that looked like models. Not to mention that Ryker had such a good heart. *Yeah, he's way too good for me.*

Pacing the room, he cursed furiously. His face was painted red with anger as he looked toward me, locking his eyes with mine.

"He's your twin?" he asked again in disbelief.

"Yeah. We look identical, which makes it harder for me. I see him staring back at me all the time when I look in the mirror, so I avoid them as much as possible."

He looked utterly confused, almost at a loss for words. "How? Why?" he stammered, seeking answers that I'd been searching for years, answers I still didn't really have.

My eyes glistened as my chest tightened, but not in the same way Ryker caused. The tightening I was experiencing was from pain, anger, and sadness because of everything my own twin did to me.

"I never really got an answer to that. Kaleb always said that I was made for him. I was his. The psychiatrists and doctors said he had several mental conditions that caused him to be the way that he was, that it wasn't his fault," I bitterly replied. Even though I knew it was true, that his disorders contaminated him, controlled him, I couldn't forgive him for everything he did to me, for scarring me so deeply.

"Fucking bullshit," he muttered angrily. Approaching me, he sat beside me on the floor before cradling me in his lap. The position made me feel vulnerable and safe at the same time. Ryker tucked some hair behind my ear, releasing a sigh before promising, "He'll never get his hands on you again. No one will *ever* mistreat you again."

His statement broke the dam holding my tears. "I don't know what I did to deserve what he did to me," I choked through the sorrow clenching my throat.

Ryker clasped my face in his hands, forcing me to look at him. "You didn't deserve *any* of what he did. You hear me, Ky? None of it. What you deserve… what you deserve is to have everything you ever wished for. You deserve happiness, not sadness, love, not pain. You deserve more than I could ever give you, but I'm damn well going to try to give you everything you deserve."

I wanted to tell him that he was everything I ever wanted, more than I deserved, but there was still that small part of me that cowered in fear, afraid to give myself completely to Ryker. So I didn't say anything, like the coward I'd always been.

His thumbs wiped away the tears on my face before he kissed me, ever so gently. "Let's get you home."

Ryker drove me home, despite my protesting that I was okay to drive. I usually took the underground transit to work so I wouldn't have to pay ridiculous amounts for parking. Kamden could take me to pick up my car the next day when we went to work out, so it wasn't a big deal.

When we got to my apartment, I asked Ryker to come up. I was still fighting the feelings brought on by the events of the day and really needed him. Enough so that I was willing to deal with whatever Kamden had to say about it.

I walked up to the door, worried that Kamden would be on the other side and give me a hard time about Ryker. But as I opened it and stepped in, our apartment was dark except for a small light shining from the kitchen.

"Kam, I'm home," I called out, but there was no response. Ryker followed behind me to the kitchen and laid down the bag from the Chinese takeout we had picked up. When I went to the refrigerator to get plates and drinks, I found the note Kamden left, letting me know he had gone out with some friends. *Good for him.*

Ryker's arms wrapped around my waist and I leaned back against him. "He's not here. Went out with friends," I said, feeling a sense of relief. Kamden spent so much time taking care of me that he seldom did anything for himself.

"That's great. I get you all to myself," he whispered in my hair before pressing a kiss to my temple.

I brought my hands over his, smiling. "That sounds really nice." I took in another deep breath, inhaling his masculine scent before I pulled out of his hold. "We better eat."

Grabbing some dishes, Ryker helped me set the table. I glanced up at him periodically as we fell into a comfortable domestic routine, and I couldn't keep the smile off my face, thinking about how normal we seemed.

After finishing dinner, I started cleaning up the to-go boxes and plates when Ryker disappeared from the kitchen. I was slightly irritated that he wasn't helping me, but I wasn't going to say anything about it, not wanting to cause any tension between us. I'd had enough drama for one day.

As I was putting the last of everything in the trash, Ryker called from down the hall, "Hey, babe, can you come here for a second?"

I wiped my hands on a dish towel and threw it on the counter. I went to my room, but when I entered, he wasn't in there. *What is he up to?*

"In here," Ryker said, his voice coming from my bathroom. *What's he doing in there?* The door was slightly ajar, so I slowly pushed it open before stepping into the room. My eyes widened in surprise as a smile spread over my lips.

The room was dimly lit by candles that I had along the rim of my garden tub. Bubbles crested the top of the bath water that Ryker must have drawn for me while I cleaned up our dinner.

"I thought you needed to relax after today, so I got a bath ready for you. I hope you don't mind."

Walking over to him, I slipped my arms around his neck. "No, I don't mind. This is just what I needed. Thank you so much, baby."

"I'll let you relax," Ryker said as he leaned down. He pressed a kiss to my lips, then grinned and stepped around me and out of the bathroom.

The bath was exactly what I had needed, and I felt so much better after getting out. My muscles felt relaxed and most of the negativity still plaguing me had washed down the drain with the bathwater.

Wrapping my towel around me, I walked into my bedroom, ready to thank Ryker again for being so considerate. As I opened my mouth to speak, I immediately closed it when my gaze landed on him. He was sleeping on top of the comforter of my bed.

My heart warmed at the sight of him sleeping so peacefully. He had said earlier that I deserved more than him, but he was wrong. He was perfect for me; if anything, I didn't deserve him.

Not wanting to wake him, I quietly grabbed clothes to change into for bed and went back in the bathroom. He was still asleep when I came out, and I gnawed on my bottom lip as my thoughts attempted to ruin everything. *I've never had a guy spend the night in my bed before. I don't know if I can do this. Sleeping over at his house was one thing, but at mine is another. This is more personal, more intimate.*

Sitting cautiously on my bed, careful not to wake Ryker, I studied him as my mind warred. *Ryker won't hurt you. Look at everything he's done for you. You already broke your rule anyway.*

My decision made, I slipped under the covers. The movement caused Ryker's eyes to open. He blinked several times before his gaze met mine. "I didn't realize how tired I was," he yawned. "I better get going."

"You wanna stay?" My tone was hopeful, yet nervous.

"Isn't that against the rules?" he asked with a teasing grin.

Rolling my eyes, I smiled. "You're right. I guess you should go, then." I started pushing him off the bed for emphasis.

Grabbing my arms, he pulled me into him. "You know I like breaking rules, especially yours. I'll stay."

Letting go of me, he stood and kicked off his shoes. I was entranced by the rippling of his muscles as he removed his shirt and stripped his shorts off, leaving him in only his boxer-briefs. *Dear lord, thank you for this man.*

Joining me under the covers, he wrapped me in his embrace, spooning me. I felt his hot breath on my neck right before he placed a kiss there and whispered, "Night, Warrior."

Laying my arms over his, I snuggled back into him. The smile was still on my face as I drifted into sleep.

Chapter Twenty-Two

Ryker

Kaiya's screams woke me in the middle of the night. Gasping for air, she sat up and clutched her throat as tears ran down her face. I tried to rub her back once I sat up, but she jerked away as soon as I touched her.

"Hey, it's just me, Warrior. You're safe," I murmured softly, trying to soothe her.

Her eyes were wide with fear as she looked at me, examining every inch of my face, making sure it was really me. Finally, she leaned into my body and sighed before starting to sob again. *Fuck, I hate when she cries.* Pulling her into my lap, I attempted to comfort her, just like earlier that day. "Shh, baby. Don't cry. I'm not going to let him hurt you ever again."

Heavy footsteps pounded outside the door, getting louder with every step. Bursting into the room, Kamden flipped on the light, and his eyes darted from Kaiya in my arms to my face. "What did you do to her?" he seethed, his teeth gritted and fists clenched as he approached the bed.

"Nothing—she had a nightmare," I defended. Kaiya had her face buried in my chest. Her tears dripped down my skin as she continued to cry uncontrollably.

"Let me have her," he demanded, motioning with his hands for me to hand her to him.

I felt like I was having deja vu from the night she was attacked. I shook my head. "Nah, I'm good. I've got her."

Kamden's nostrils flared as we stared each other. "You and me," he gestured stiffly, the anger evident in his tone and body. "We need to have a talk."

"Not right now we don't," I countered, not backing down.

He stuck his jaw out defiantly. "In the morning."

"Fine," I clipped. *Leave already.*

He angrily stalked out of the room without another word, leaving me alone with Kaiya. *Finally.* Softly stroking her hair, I whispered words of comfort and rocked her gently. I didn't know how long we sat there like that, but I didn't care. She needed me, and I was going to do everything I could to be there for her.

Once she finally pulled away, her face was splotchy and her eyes were red. Moisture streaked her cheeks as she gazed up at me, still loosely holding her throat.

"Wanna talk about it, baby?"

She scanned over my face again as she bit her bottom lip, deciding whether or not to tell me. I expected her to say no, but she shocked me by nodding and letting out a heavy breath.

"We were seventeen. Kaleb had been more aggressive than normal for a few weeks, so I'd been avoiding him as much as possible, staying late at school, hanging out at Nori's, partying, going anywhere but home. That really pissed him off, and…" She paused as a sob broke through. I rubbed her back while she took some deep breaths to calm herself. Her voice was still shaky when she spoke again. "He… he took it out on me one afternoon when no one else was home. He took off my clothes, and started touching me, which I was used to already, but then… then he started taking off his clothes, too," she softly cried, choking back another sob.

My body was a volcano ready to erupt with rage. *How could her brother, her twin no less, do that to her?*

"He'd never done that before, and I put two and two together, knowing what he planned to do. Usually he just took my clothes off, but he'd caught me having sex with a guy from our school, found out that I'd given something away that was supposedly his, so he wanted to take it back. I mean, it wasn't the first time that I'd had sex, but it was the first time Kaleb had found out about it."

One hand squeezed mine as the other fingered the scar on her throat. "I fought against him, but then he pulled a knife to my throat. He touched me more before stopping to take off his shirt. I tried to get away then, but he caught me before I got to the door. He pinned me and pressed the knife into my neck." She took a deep breath, and her lip quivered as a few more tears trickled down her face. She composed herself some before continuing, barely above a whisper, "Kamden came home early and busted through my door. He pulled Kaleb off me, but I ended up getting cut in the process. Kamden beat Kaleb unconscious, and then called 911."

Wow. "What happened after that?"

"I had to tell the police everything, which was so much. Things had been going on for as long as I could remember, even when we were really young. I didn't know it at the time, but he was overly affectionate and touched me inappropriately. It progressed over time, and he started becoming aggressive and possessive, touching me regularly when we started middle school. Everyone questioned me, asking me why I didn't say anything sooner, but it was all I ever knew. I thought it was normal until high school, but even then, I was too scared of him. He always said he'd kill me if I told anyone, and I believed him. I didn't think anyone would believe me anyway. I mean, Kaleb was my twin. Who would think that my own—" she sobbed, unable to speak anymore.

"I'm so sorry, Warrior," I murmured as I placed a soft kiss on her forehead.

Tilting her head, she looked up at me as I cradled her in my arms, her hand covering her throat. Gazing down at the beautiful, broken woman in my arms, all I could think about was how I could save her from her darkness, the darkness created by someone who should have never been the cause of it.

Reaching my hand up, I lay it on top of hers. I wanted her to feel less self-conscious about her scar, to let go of the fear and negativity associated with it. Slowly pulling her hand away, I kept our eyes locked. She slightly stiffened but didn't pull away or object to my actions.

I ran my fingers through her hair as I gently tipped her head back. Bringing her closer to me, I leaned down to her neck and pressed light kisses along the scar on her throat. Her body trembled as she cried beneath my lips before she grasped my face in her hands.

Moving my head away from her neck, she brought my mouth up to meet hers. Connecting our lips, she wrapped her arms around my neck and molded against me. I felt her tears on my face before she pulled away and brought our foreheads together. "Thank you," she whispered.

I wiped the tears from her cheeks before laying us back down. Positioning our bodies together, I enveloped her in my arms as my body fit to hers. Kissing the back of her neck, I murmured, "Go back to sleep, baby. I got you."

Moving closer to me, she relaxed in my embrace. A short while later, her breathing deepened as sleep found her again, and I hoped that I could keep her nightmares away.

The blaring of Kaiya's alarm clock woke us. She withdrew from my arms and slid to the edge of the bed to turn the stupid thing off.

"Come back to bed. It's still dark out," I grumbled as I reached for her.

"I have to go to work," she replied as she rubbed her face, her voice heavy with sleep.

"Call in sick or something. We can play doctor," I said as I raised my eyebrows suggestively with my eyes barely open. She laughed, but still rose up off the bed.

"I'd like that, but Mondays are busy for me at the office. There's no way I could miss."

Throwing the sheets off me, I sat up before stretching and yawning. "I'll drive you."

"It's okay, you can sleep. I'll take the T," she called from her closet.

I scoffed. Like I'd really let her take the transit. "You're not taking the T. I'll drop you off."

We went back and forth a few times before she finally conceded. I got dressed before Kaiya made Kamden and me breakfast. Then, she went back to her room to finish getting ready, leaving us alone.

"So, about that talk," Kamden started as he stirred his coffee.

It's too early for this shit.

"Yeah?" My voice was gruff and irritated. I was so not in the mood to talk to him.

He turned in his seat to face me, crossing his arms over his chest. "What are your intentions with my sister?"

I laughed dryly, "None of your business."

"Kaiya is my business!" he roared as he slammed a fist on the counter. He craned his neck to look down the hall toward Kaiya's room before directing his attention back to me. He lowered his voice, but the anger in it was still obvious, "If you hurt her, I swear to God, I will-"

"Look, I lo-" I paused for a split second, catching myself, "care about Kaiya. I'm not going to hurt her."

We glared daggers at each other until Kaiya walked back into the room. Tension radiated from both of us as she looked from Kamden to me. "Everything okay?" she asked.

"Everything's fine, *sorella,*" Kamden answered with a forced smile, his voice still strained with lingering anger.

Kaiya met my eyes, seeking my agreement with her brother's statement. "Yeah, everything's great, baby."

I could tell by the wary look on her face that she didn't completely believe us, but she didn't press the issue further. "Ready to go?" she asked as she came up to me.

Nodding, I followed her to the front door. She said goodbye to Kamden before we walked out. As we went down the stairs, she questioned, "What was that all about?"

"Just Kamden being protective, that's all. Don't worry about it." I shrugged nonchalantly.

Rolling her eyes, she responded in irritation, "He acts like I'm a child."

Chuckling, I replied, "He's just worried about you—he loves you."

"I know," she sighed as a small smile took over her face. "He can be a little much sometimes, but he really is a great big brother."

"Great for you; me, not so much," I joked.

"Yeah, I'd hate to be in your shoes. He doesn't like you very much," she admitted with a light laugh.

"His opinion doesn't matter to me—only yours does."

We reached my truck, and I walked Kaiya to the passenger side. She turned to face me, placing her back against the door. "I guess you're lucky that I like you," she teased with a playful grin.

Tugging on one of her curls, I twisted it around my finger and leaned in to kiss her. As I pulled away, I looked into her eyes, letting go of her hair as I ran my knuckles down her cheek. "Yeah, I'm pretty lucky."

Kaiya's cheeks flushed as I opened the door. I helped her step into the raised cab before getting in on my side and starting the engine.

Kaiya rested her hand on my knee the whole drive to her work. She leaned over to kiss me when we reached her office and groaned when we broke apart. "I really don't want to go to work."

Pulling her back to me, I gave her another kiss. "I told you to call in sick, but you insisted that you had to come."

She glanced up at the tall building before looking back at me. "Fine," she moaned. Gripping the handle of the door, she cracked the door open. "See you later?"

"Yeah, baby. Have a good day."

She smiled as she hopped out of my truck and shut the door. Blowing me a kiss goodbye, she waved and walked toward the building.

After I dropped her off, I went back to my house to sleep before I had to go to work. I had a busy schedule filled with training sessions and classes to look forward to, so I needed to have as much energy as possible to get me through the day. I couldn't imagine having to get up early every morning like Kaiya did to go to work.

I woke up a little before lunch time, and I didn't have to go in until a couple hours later. I decided to see if Kaiya had gone on her lunch break yet.

Me: Have you had lunch yet

Warrior: No

Me: Can I pick you up

Warrior: Sure :) my break is in twenty

Me: See you soon

Kaiya met me outside her office building twenty minutes later, and we decided to go to a deli around the corner to save time. After we were seated, I asked, "How's your day been?"

She groaned unhappily, "Grueling. Mondays are the worst. We have so many meetings. How about you?"

"Good. I went home and slept for a couple of hours."

"Must be nice," she replied sarcastically.

"Eh, it was okay." I shrugged. "I'd much rather have stayed in bed with you." I wiggled my eyebrows suggestively.

"Me too, but I don't have the luxury of working after lunch time like some people." She gave me a playful glare.

The waitress, a cute blonde with a heavy Boston accent, came to take our drink order. Once she left, we talked about one of Kaiya's meetings until the server brought us our waters and wrote down our meals.

When she walked away, Kaiya asked, "Do you have a busy day today?"

"I have a few classes and personal training sessions. They should keep me busy."

Kaiya swallowed nervously before saying, "Speaking of classes, I don't know if I should go to self-defense anymore."

"What? Why?" My face scrunched in confusion.

Sighing, she looked away at the wall. "I totally embarrassed myself last night. How am I going to be able to look those people in the eye after they saw me freak out like that?"

"Hey, look at me." I grabbed her hand across the table and rubbed it until she met my eyes. "No one will judge you. Hell, some of them have been in abusive relationships, and probably can relate to feeling out of control. Don't worry about what everyone else will think."

She exhaled a breath. "Can't you just give me private lessons?"

"Although I would love to," I paused, smirking as I thought about all the things we could do if I gave her private lessons. I put the thoughts to the side, saving them to act out later. "I'm not going to. I know you can do this, Ky."

Pouting, she reluctantly gave in. "Fine. I'll keep going."

"That's my girl," I stated proudly as I squeezed her hand. She was used to running when things made her scared or uncomfortable, but she had become much stronger than she was when we first met, even if she didn't believe it. I knew she could do anything she set her mind to as long as she fought her fear.

After we finished our lunch, I took Kaiya back to her office, then went back to my apartment to get ready for work.

As I drove to the gym, I thought about the conversation Kaiya and I had at lunch, about how much Kaiya and I had changed since that first day we met. I was glad I had decided to go after her, even though she fought me and made me work to finally have her. She was so worth it, and I couldn't imagine my life without her now. *Things would be so different.*

I headed straight for my office when I entered the gym, needing to look over my schedule one more time to make sure I was prepared for all my sessions and classes.

The day went by pretty quickly, and it seemed like only a couple of hours had passed when Kaiya and Kamden arrived at their usual time. Both of their faces were lit up in smiles when they walked in. *I wonder what's going on.*

I had to wait until I finished with a client before I was able to talk to Kaiya. Dragging me into my office, she shut the door, threw herself into my arms, and kissed me.

"Well, hello to you, too," I mumbled against her lips.

"I have great news. Kaleb's release was denied!" she exclaimed excitedly after pulling back from me.

"That's amazing, baby!" I hugged her and gave her another kiss.

"I feel like a huge weight has been lifted off me. I still can't believe it." Her eyes were bright with happiness and a huge smile spread from ear to ear.

I loved seeing her so happy. Maybe she would be able to get rid of all the negativity dragging her down since Kaleb wasn't getting out now.

"We need to celebrate. Anything you want to do this weekend, consider it done."

Squealing giddily, she bounced up and down. "I can't wait. Thank you for being so wonderful throughout this whole mess. Most guys would have turned and run once they got a glimpse at my issues."

I wouldn't have been able to stay away from her—I had tried and failed miserably. Kaiya had captivated me from the very beginning, and although we had some rough times, she brought so much good into my life, changing me for the better.

"I'm not most guys. You know I like the challenges you give me," I said with a playful wink. Pausing, I debated saying more, wary of going deeper into how I felt about her. I wasn't ready to tell her everything, but I wanted her to know that she meant something to me. "My life wouldn't have been the same without you, Ky."

Giving me a sweet smile, she laughed lightly. "I know that I wouldn't be the same if I didn't have you, but I doubt it goes both ways."

"Oh, it does, Warrior. I definitely wouldn't be this… alive if you didn't come fighting into my life," I replied sincerely as I cupped her cheek, grazing over it with my thumb.

Standing on her tiptoes, Kaiya pressed her lips to mine and slipped her tongue in my mouth.

Suppressing a groan, I snaked my hand around to the back of her head, cradling it as I deepened the kiss, my fingers tangling in her soft hair. Her hands traveled up my chest to around my neck as she pulled herself against me, moaning softly in my mouth. *Fuck, I don't think anyone will ever taste as good as she does.*

Pushing her back against my desk, I propped her up on it as her legs wrapped around my waist. Our hands roamed over each other's bodies, eagerly exploring as they sought more.

A knock on the door jarred us apart, leaving us both panting for air. Kaiya slid off the desk, keeping her distance from me as she stared at the door.

I cleared my throat from the lust clogging it. "Come in."

One of the other trainers walked in, holding a stack of papers in his hands. "Oh, I'm sorry, I didn't know you were with a client. Can you come to my office when you're finished?"

"Sure thing," I replied, irritated at the interruption. We shouldn't have been doing anything in the first place, but that wasn't the point. I wanted as much of Kaiya as I could get. It didn't matter where we were, even my work.

Once he left, my eyes ran over her, appraising her hungrily. "Now, where were we?"

Chapter Twenty-Three

Kaiya

There was no word to describe the elation I felt when I heard that Kaleb wasn't going to be released. Joy, relief, and excitement all combined within me to form some amazing emotion I hoped I felt more of in the future. Everything was finally falling into place for me, and I was ready to move on with my life without Kaleb looming over me.

I was really nervous about going back to class on Tuesday following my meltdown, even after my talk with Ryker. Although I was afraid of facing everyone, I didn't want to be ruled by my fear anymore. There was nothing I feared more than Kaleb, and now that he was out of the picture, I wanted to try and face any challenge presented to me.

Sitting in my car outside the gym, I took some deep breaths before getting out. The entire walk to the kickboxing room, I silently chanted, *you can do this, you can do this.* The whole situation might not have been a big deal to anyone else, but it made me so self-conscious that other people had a glimpse at my personal demons. I worked so hard to keep them private, and now everyone in class knew there was something wrong with me.

Stopping outside the door, I reached for the handle, but stilled before grabbing it. I noticed that my hand was shaking. I balled it into a fist to stop the trembling.*What if they make fun of me?* I laughed at myself. *What am I in high school? Who cares if they make fun of me? It's not like their opinions matter. Suck it up and quit being afraid.* I took another deep breath, repeated my mantra again, and opened the door.

Avoiding eye contact, I searched for Ryker, needing his support if I was going to make it through class. If he wasn't the instructor, I doubted I would have come back at all.

Our eyes met from across the room. His sexy smile sent warm tingles through my body, and my stomach flip-flopped, making me forget my apprehension about class.

He wore that grin as he approached me, wrapping his arms around me once he reached where I stood. Placing a kiss below my ear, he murmured in that deep, husky voice that I loved, "I missed you."

Ryker hadn't been hiding his affections for me for the past few weeks at class, so most of the students, if not all, knew that we had something going on. That was another reason I worried about returning—I didn't want them to judge Ryker because of my actions. I was sure they already questioned why he was with me in the first place; hell, I asked myself that question daily. After witnessing my breakdown, they probably thought he was just as crazy to be with me.

"I missed you, too," I softly replied, feeling my cheeks heat. Ryker still affected me the same way after almost six months, and I prayed that it never changed.

When he pulled away, I could feel the stares on us. I'd always hated that feeling, the one that made the hair stand up on the back of my neck. But with the way Ryker was looking at me, I didn't care about what anyone was thinking as they watched us. All that mattered was that look in his eyes, the one I first saw in the picture we took at the aquarium, the one I'd glimpsed on several occasions since; the one I was sure was evident on my face every single day.

I'd never been in love before, but I was never more certain of anything in my life than I was at that moment. I loved Ryker. But was I going to tell him? No. I was scared. My number one fear had gone from Kaleb being released to losing Ryker.

Telling him I loved him might chase him away. I knew that many guys ran when a girl said those three words, and that was the last thing I wanted to do. Not willing to chance it, I decided to wait until he said it first. If he ever did. *I hope he does.*

Another student had started talking to Ryker, so I headed for my bag to get ready for class to start. I avoided making eye contact with anyone as I stretched out and slipped on my gloves.

As soon as my fists and legs hit the bag when we started the first combo, I was happy that Ryker convinced me to come back. I didn't know why I thought I could give it up—kickboxing had become a part of me, just like Ryker had. Both made me feel stronger, more empowered… capable of anything. Even though I started taking the class to protect myself for when Kaleb was released, I couldn't see myself giving it up now that he wasn't.

Ryker came over as I was working on the second combo that he demonstrated. Those full lips of his tipped up playfully as he teased, "And you didn't want to come back."

Stopping, I rolled my eyes. "You were right. Thank you for making me come back."

"I couldn't let you give it up. Plus, I'd miss watching you work that amazing body of yours." His voice had deepened, taking on the tone that meant he was getting turned on.

I let out a laugh before I pushed him away. "Stop distracting me."

Backing up, he gave me a sexy pout, then headed to another student. I fought the butterflies he caused in my lower abdomen as I focused back on the bag.

Once the first part of class was over, we gathered as a group like always. When Ryker asked if anyone had requests for the next portion of class, I surprised everyone, including myself, when I raised my hand. Ryker gave me an inquisitive look, his eyebrows raising in surprise as he called on me. "Kaiya?"

I lowered my hand. "Can we learn how to defend against knife attacks?"

He smiled proudly at me, causing more butterflies to somersault in my stomach. "We can. Knives are easier for criminals to get their hands on than a gun, so many attacks involve a knife. Get with your partners."

As Ryker walked toward me, he had a look of admiration on his face.

"What?" I asked with a shy smile as our eyes met.

"Just proud of you," he grinned widely. "Are you sure you want to do this?"

"I'm sure. I want to know what to do if it happens again. I might not be so lucky the next time around."

Ryker's eyes hardened, and his jaw tensed as his lips set in a frown. "There won't be a next time, that's for damn sure," he practically growled.

I waited for his expression to soften, but it didn't. He was actually upset at the thought.

"Hey, it's just a precaution, right? No reason to get upset," I said calmly as I placed my hand on his bicep.

His stiff body relaxed some as he gave me a small smile. "Yeah, you're right. I just don't like the thought of you getting hurt."

His words warmed my insides like coffee on a cold day. *He really cares about me, doesn't he?*

He walked over to one of his supply tubs and brought out a prop knife. Stiffening slightly from the reminder of my attack, my hand instinctively went for my throat. Ryker noticed my apprehension as he came back to me. "We don't have to do this if you're not ready, Ky. Kaleb isn't getting released anymore."

Our eyes met again, and I remembered how his loving touch the other night had made me realize that I couldn't let my attack have the kind of power it had over me; I couldn't let Kaleb have that kind of power over me anymore. I was done being afraid.

"No, I'm ready." I said after taking a deep breath.

Ryker paused, searching my face briefly. "Okay. First, I'm going to show you what to do if someone is coming at you with a knife. Then, we can work on defense from behind."

Ryker took up his fighting stance, holding the knife in his right hand. "Typically, an attacker is going to try to stab you in the stomach, thrusting directly forward like this," he demonstrated, slowly moving the knife towards the center of my abdomen. "And, most will repeatedly stab you, so you need to disable them, not just block their initial attack because they'll come at you again."

Handing me the knife, he instructed, "Pretend that you're going to stab me." When I did as he said, he shifted his hips back, moving his torso out of the way as he threw his arms out to trap mine. The back of his right arm was on top of mine while the back of his left sat under, sandwiching it in place. "When they thrust at you, you need to block their arm, prevent it from getting near you while moving your body back. Your dominant hand needs to be on top, right above their elbow, and your opposite arm needs to be under their forearm. So, for you, your right arm will be on top. I basically made my arms into an X, trapping yours in between and securing it from going further."

Nodding, I asked, "Then what?"

"Then, you're going to turn your top hand over, gripping the bottom of the tricep. Once you have a secure grip, move your other hand to their elbow and pull their arm into your chest, trapping it there. Act like you're sawing their tricep with your right hand until your wrist is digging into it and then clasp your hands together. Now, you have them in a simple arm bar."

He had executed the moves as he spoke, so I was bent over with my arm pulled back and trapped between his two, huge, muscular ones. For me, I wasn't in any pain, just uncomfortable, because I was pretty flexible, but Ryker could easily snap my arm from the position I was in.

"Now, you're going to want to take a step back to protect yourself from getting hit. Most people will reflexively put their other hand down on the ground to stabilize themselves. If they do, you can stomp on their fingers, which will almost guarantee breakage. Or you could just do some knees to the face, which will knock them out after a few solid hits."

Ryker loosened his hold on me, then helped me stand upright. He rubbed my arm. "You okay?"

"I'm fine. You know I'm flexible." I gave him a playful smile.

"That I do." He winked, and his dark, seductive eyes gleamed with mischief. "Let's go through it again."

We repeated the maneuver twice more before we switched roles.

Ryker had to talk me through the moves as I completed them at a snail's pace the first two times, but they were becoming more fluid after my third try. By the fifth time, I had a pretty good grasp on the concept, but I knew I would need to practice again to really get it. Something to do at our next Saturday session.

"Now, I want to practice if someone comes up behind you and puts a knife to your throat. You think you can handle that?"

My stomach contorted uncomfortably at the thought. *It's not a real knife and it's only Ryker. You can do this. You wanted this.* Swallowing the knot of fear in my throat, I nodded. "I can do it."

Ryker didn't look convinced as his eyes perused my face. "If it gets too much for you at any point, just tell me and we'll stop, okay?"

"Okay," I meekly replied, my voice sounded frail and gauzy as I tried to hide my nerves and push down the fear trying to take over.

"Baby, I don't like seeing you like this. Maybe this isn't a good idea." His eyes filled with concern, and his voice was heavy with doubt.

I was about to take the easy way out and agree, to tell him that I couldn't do it, but I wanted to be stronger, wanted to make him proud. "I'm okay. I can do this," I replied, hoping I sounded stronger than I felt.

Ryker didn't say anything for a few seconds before he conceded, sighing. "Fine. I'll talk you through the whole thing."

As usual, Ryker had me act as the attacker first, walking me through the steps of how to defend. That was the easy part. After demonstrating several times, he asked, "Ready to try?"

I nodded, afraid to speak and betray the fact that I was borderline terrified of having that thing pressed against my throat, scared that it would cause another panic attack in the middle of class.

Ryker's familiar body pressed up against my back. Leaning into him, I reveled in the feel of his large body and strong frame, needing it to get me through the maneuver. *You can do this. Conquer your fears. Overcome your weakness.*

Closing my eyes, I waited for the pressure of the knife against my scar. Instead, Ryker's hands grazed my bare arms, trailing down until he linked our fingers together. I felt the warmth of his breath on the side of my neck before his lips met my skin. His mouth lingered there several seconds, causing a shiver to run up my spine as he whispered, "You can do this, Warrior. You're one of the strongest people I've ever met. I believe in you."'

My heart stuttered in my chest, my breath catching at the tenderness of his words. *What would I do without him?*

His hands left mine, but he continued to talk to me. "I'm going to put the prop to your throat now. Remember, it's not real, and I would never hurt you."

One of his hands came up to grip my shoulder as he brought the fake knife to my neck. Stiffening as I felt it push against my scar, my heart started to beat erratically. *It's not real. Don't freak out over nothing.*

"It's just me, baby. Relax. You can do this."

I eased against him, focusing on his words.

"Good, now grab my arm with both hands, one hand on the outside, one on the inside, pulling it away as you throw your head back."

Doing as he instructed, I fit my hands around his bulky, inked forearm, near his wrist, and threw my head back. Ryker angled to the side so that he wouldn't get hit, expecting my move.

"Good, now after you connect, step to the side opposite of the knife, lean forward, and push that sweet ass into me."

A laugh burst from deep in my belly because of his words. Feeling the tension leaving me over the whole situation, I followed his directions, rubbing my ass against his growing erection as I leaned over. A low, strangled groan came from him as he buried his head in the middle of my back.

"You okay back there?" I asked in a teasing tone, loving the reaction I had caused.

"Great," he replied before clearing his throat. "Now, use your left hand to throw a hammer-fist to my groin. If I were using my other hand to hold the knife, you would use your right hand instead. After you connect, use that same arm to elbow me in the stomach and or face."

I performed all the moves lightly, so that I wouldn't hurt him. Ryker continued his instructions, moving on to the next step, "Keep your hands securely around my wrist as you rotate your body outward, away from me, twisting my arm around. You should end up facing me with my arm upside down in front of you, between us. From here, kick the groin and then keep twisting my arm in the opposite way from its natural bend until I fall."

Believe it or not, I made Ryker fall flat on his ass when I did that, but he probably fell for my benefit.

"Now, you can either kick me in the ribs a few times, pry the knife from me and run, or both; your choice. I would do both just to be safe because you don't want them to chase after you, especially if they still have the weapon."

Opting to do both like he suggested, I completed the maneuver. Ryker stood and came over to me, wrapping me in his arms and praising in my ear, "You did it, baby. You did it."

Squeezing him back, I held back the tears that were trying to escape. They were happy tears, but I still didn't want to cry in the middle of class again. *I did it, I really did it.*

Ryker pulled back, smiling proudly at me. "You wanna practice it again?"

"Yeah. Let's do it again." I smiled back.

"That's my girl. I knew you had it in you, Warrior."

As we continued to practice the routine, I couldn't keep the smile off my face.

The following Saturday morning, loud banging on my front door woke Ryker and me. The sun was barely creeping in my window, so I could tell that it was still early.

"Who the fuck is that?" Ryker muttered groggily.

I started to get out of bed, but Ryker pulled me back into him, wrapping his arms around me and burying his face in my messy hair. "Let Kamden get it."

Kamden's footsteps sounded a few seconds later, so I snuggled into Ryker and closed my eyes to go back to sleep. The sound of yelling caused them to snap back open again moments later. *I know that voice.*

Outraged and shocked, I threw the covers off me and flung open my door. I could hear Ryker calling after to me, but I stormed down the hallway towards Kamden and the person he was arguing with. My mother.

When she saw me, her face reddened in anger as every feature tightened. Pointing her finger at me, she screamed, "You! This is all your fault."'

My fault? Is she fucking serious? "None of this is my fault. Kaleb did this to himself!" I shouted.

"Mom, you need to leave," Kamden replied stiffly.

Our mother ignored him, and instead of doing as he requested, she lunged for me. Ryker stepped in front of me as Kamden grabbed our mom around the waist and pulled her out the front door.

"No! This is all her fault. My baby is stuck in there because of her! He's devastated!" she wailed before Kamden slammed the door.

I could still hear them arguing outside the apartment as my face burned with a combination of rage and sadness. *How can my own mother blame me for what Kaleb did to me? How is it my fault?*

Hot tears ran down my cheeks as a small sob burst through my throat. Ryker turned around, abandoning his defensive stance to cradle me to his chest. "Don't cry, baby. She doesn't know what the fuck she's talking about."

The feel of his smooth, bare skin against me was soothing, helping calm my ragged emotions. My mom and I were never that close. Kaleb had always been her favorite, but her words still stung regardless.

"She hates me," I cried into his chest.

"She doesn't hate you. And if she does, then it's her loss." He rubbed my back softly. "For her to choose that monster over you is ridiculous. You're a beautiful, amazing woman."

Hearing the door open and shut, I peeked under Ryker's arm to see Kamden walking towards us. I pulled back and wiped my face when he reached us.

"You okay?" he asked with concern.

I sniffled as I nodded. "Yeah, hurt and confused, but I'll be fine."

Ryker continued to rub my back as Kamden said, "I'm not condoning her actions or anything, but she's just having a hard time dealing with all this. I don't know how I'd cope if my son had molested his twin sister for most of their lives, especially when I hadn't known."

"But it's not Kaiya's fault. There's no reason for your mom to blame her, especially after everything Ky's been through," Ryker defended with a scowl.

Kamden gave him a death glare before focusing his attention back to me. "I'm not trying to justify her actions, I'm just trying to help you understand why she's acting the way she is."

"I know," I sighed. I couldn't help but feel a little pang of pain in my chest because it did seem like he was defending her. I knew it must have been difficult for her to deal with the issues within our family. My dad had left after Kaleb was committed, making it worse, but there was no reason for her to start pointing fingers, especially when they were being directed at the wrong person. It was too early for me to try to make sense of what had just happened, so I opted for escape. "I'm going back to sleep."

Ryker followed me back to my room, where we cocooned back in the warmth of my bed. Facing him, I placed a kiss on his collarbone as his arms came around me. His lips pressed against my forehead as he draped my leg over his thigh, fitting the lower half of our bodies together. He pulled the blanket over us, and as we lay there, entangled in my bed, I never felt safer.

Chapter Twenty-Four

Ryker

After Kaiya's confrontation with her bitch of a mom, she stayed in bed, pretending to sleep, long after I knew she was awake. I lay there with her, faking sleep, too, until I figured out a plan I thought would cheer her up. Then, I got out of bed and headed for the kitchen.

Kamden was sitting at the breakfast bar drinking coffee when I walked in. Remaining silent, I walked to the refrigerator and opened it, pulling out a few items and setting them on the counter.

"How is she?" Kamden asked. I could feel his eyes on my back as I began making Kaiya breakfast.

I didn't turn around. "Not good. She's laying in bed, pretending to sleep."

"I'm going to go talk to her," he stated. The sound of his chair pushing against the tile followed his words, and then I heard his footsteps leaving the room.

Kaiya loved French toast. Luckily, it was one of my favorites too, especially since it was a cheat day only meal, so I knew how to make it.

After I fixed a plate for Kaiya, I poured her a small glass of milk, grabbed the syrup, and put it all on a tray before carrying it down the hall toward her room. Kamden exited, leaving the door slightly cracked. He didn't say anything as he walked past me, but I caught the smile that crept over his face when he saw the tray in my hands.

I gently kicked the door open and walked in. Kaiya was still in bed, facing the window. When I rounded the bed, her puffy, red eyes locked on mine, and I wanted to punch something because of the pain in them. I never wanted her to feel pain again now that her bastard of a brother wasn't getting released.

Her gaze traveled down to the tray in my hands. Those pretty lips curved slightly as I sat down beside her, placing the tray over her lap. "I made you breakfast," I said, hoping the gesture would brighten her mood.

As she focused on the plate, her smile widened and her eyes lightened as she looked back at me. "Baby, you didn't have to do this."

Leaning toward her, I kissed her temple. "I wanted to cheer you up. I know how much you love French toast."

"I do. Thank you," she replied genuinely, her voice losing most of the sadness present earlier. Picking up the fork and knife, she started cutting the bread into small squares before pouring syrup on top.

As she ate, I stole bites from her plate, getting my fingers sticky with syrup. After I took my fifth piece, Kaiya smacked my hand and playfully scolded, "Stop taking my food. Get your own."

Chuckling, I slowly sucked the syrup from my fingers, making sure she was watching me. Those beautiful blue eyes heated with desire as she focused on my mouth, her lips parting slightly as she swallowed deeply. *Fuck me.*

As I moved toward her, I heard her breath stutter right before our lips met. Her mouth was slightly sticky and sweet from the syrup as my tongue parted her lips, meeting hers and tangling languidly.

I nibbled on her bottom lip before pulling away. Her cheeks were flushed as she peeked up at me from beneath her dark lashes. I loved when she looked at me that way, so innocent and seductive at the same time.

"French toast is definitely my favorite," I joked as I licked my lips.

Kaiya burst into a laugh from my words. "Mine too."

After Kaiya finished eating, she seemed to be in a much better mood. Her face was no longer weighed down with sorrow as a smile replaced the frown from earlier. Her eyes returned to their normal, vibrant hue instead of being tainted with redness and tears, but I could still see a trace of unhappiness in them, no doubt from her mother's harsh words. I hoped she'd be able to get over it soon—there was no reason for her to be upset over her mom or Kaleb ever again.

We took the dirty dishes back to the kitchen, where Kaiya insisted she make me my own plate of French toast.

I sat at the breakfast bar as she cooked, inhaling the smell of cinnamon and vanilla as it wafted through the kitchen. "You excited about tonight?" I asked as I watched her.

She nodded as she flipped a piece of bread in the pan. "I can't wait! I've never been to the opening of a club before."

A new club was opening in downtown Boston, and I planned to take Kaiya out to a late dinner at an upscale restaurant before heading there. I hadn't told her where we were going, and the anticipation was eating her up.

"Why don't you just tell me where you're taking me for dinner?"

"Nope. That would ruin the surprise."

Letting out a frustrated groan, she flipped the bread again. A few minutes later, she brought my plate, and pressed a kiss to my cheek. I couldn't help but smile, thinking about how I could get used to being this way with her. Sleeping in before making breakfast together on the weekends. Waking up to that gorgeous face every morning. Going to bed with her wrapped in my arms each night.

"What?" Kaiya asked as she sat next to me.

I wanted to tell her how I felt, but the words were stuck, caught in my throat. Clearing it, I replied, "Nothing, babe. Thank you." *Pussy.*

She smiled sweetly back at me, kicking my heart rate up. Just her smiles made me crazy. "You're welcome."

After I ate, I helped Kaiya clean up the kitchen. Then, I got dressed, and went back to my apartment to get ready for work. I planned to pick Kaiya up after my shift ended, and the day passed by sluggishly since I was excited about our date, thoughts playing in my head of what I wanted to do to her once we were alone afterward.

When she opened the door to greet me, I knew I wasn't going to be able to wait until after the date. The dress she was wearing—fuck, it was so hot on her, but the only thing I wanted to do was rip it off, revealing that creamy, soft skin underneath. I needed her right there and then.

Her expression told me that she felt the same. Nibbling that full, bottom lip, it basically looked like she was fucking me with her eyes as they traveled down my body.

"You want to come in?" she asked seductively. "Kamden's not home. He should be gone for a while."

Fuck yes. "Yeah," I answered, my voice already thick with lust as my eyes greedily devoured her body, taking all of her in.

When she turned around, leading me into her apartment, my eyes focused on that sweet ass swaying back and forth as she walked. I wanted to bend her over the bed, lift that dress up and sink into her from behind. And that's exactly what I planned to do.

"Like what you see?" Kaiya asked, interrupting my thoughts, a sinful gleam in her eyes as she glanced over her shoulder at me.

Reaching her bedroom, I smirked. *Hell yeah I do.* "Yeah, baby, just wait till I show you how much."

Then, I was on her. Our hands were everywhere as our mouths crashed together, nipping and sucking as we consumed each other.

Backing her up toward the bed, I turned her around when I felt her legs hit the mattress. Bending her over, I roughly pressed my dick against her ass, causing her to moan.

Kaiya pushed against me, rubbing that perfect ass on my cock, which was straining through my jeans.

"Yeah, baby, lift that sweet ass for me."

My hands slowly inched the bottom of her dress up over her hips, revealing her lacy thong. Unbuttoning my jeans, I pulled my dick out before rubbing it over the soft skin of her ass.

Reaching between her thighs, I moved her panties to the side as my fingers found her pussy, which was soaked. "Fuck, baby, you're so wet for me. So fucking wet."

I continued to play with her clit as my cock neared her entrance. Teasing her, I rubbed it back and forth along her pussy, causing strangled cries of pleasure to sound from her.

"You like that, baby? You want my dick inside you?"

"God, yes," she groaned.

In one, hard thrust, I sank myself into her until she was completely full of me. Her pussy clenched me tighter from our position as I gripped her hips, pumping in and out of her.

Our skin slapped together as I pounded into her. She fisted the sheets in her hands, moaning loudly as I fucked her. My pace increased as I felt her pulsing around me, knowing that she was close to coming. One of my hands reached around, my fingers finding her drenched clit before rapidly stroking it, causing her to tremble beneath me.

Seconds later, Kaiya came, her pussy throbbing around my cock as she gutturally cried out my name. I loved how it sounded coming from her lips, loved that I made her as out of control as she made me.

Gripping her hips tighter, I thrust roughly into her, shooting my cum inside her. Fuck, I loved coming inside her, claiming her pussy as mine. And she was mine—my drug, my addiction, my high. Kaiya was my everything.

Rolling to the side, I pulled her with me, keeping my dick inside her. I nuzzled her neck before kissing her, murmuring against her skin, "You like that, baby?"

"Mmm, hmm," she mumbled in pleasure as she lazily traced her fingertips along my arm.

Pulling out, I got off the bed to grab a towel. Once we were all cleaned up, Kaiya straightened her dress before fixing her hair and make-up.

"Ready to go?" she asked when she came out of the bathroom.

I couldn't help but notice the rosy flush on her cheeks from our sex. Smirking, I nodded and grazed my knuckles over one of her cheekbones before taking her hand in mine and walking down the hall.

I had made reservations at a fondue restaurant. Neither of us had ever been to one, but I had heard that the experience and the food were one of a kind.

When we entered, the room was dimly lit, each table had a trio of candles, and soft, romantic music played in the background. Kaiya smiled widely as she took in the environment, squeezing my hand in excitement.

Once we were seated, a waiter came to take our drink order. We decided to get a bottle of wine for the special occasion, and after our server left, Kaiya was beaming with happiness. I loved seeing her like that, especially when I was the cause.

"You excited, baby?" I asked as I rubbed her thigh softly.

"Yes! I've heard amazing things about this place. I can't wait!" Her voice came out as a squeal as she smiled giddily.

When the waiter came back with our wine, he poured both of us a glass before asking, "Have you ever dined with us before?"

"No, this is our first time," I answered.

"Okay, well thank you for choosing us to spend your evening with. Let me explain your options. If you want the full experience, I suggest all four courses, which is cheese, salad, entree, and dessert." His tone was formal and polite as he continued to discuss our choices. Once he finished, he questioned, "Which option would you like go with?

I glanced at Kaiya, who still had a huge smile on her face. "I think we'll go for the four courses so we can get the full experience."

"Excellent choice, sir."

After we made our selections for cheese and salad, the server left to put our order in. When he returned, he had the ingredients to make our first course and prepared it tableside. Kaiya watch with enthusiasm, her eyes wide and the same huge smile still overtaking her whole face, as the waiter crafted our cheese fondue. Just the sight of her so happy made everything right in the world.

Once dessert came, we were both already getting full, even though the portions in each course were small. We had chosen a white chocolate Crème Brulee, and it came with sliced strawberries, bananas, cheesecake squares, marshmallows and other small cake and dessert bites. The spread looked too good to pass up.

When Kaiya dipped a strawberry in the melted chocolate, I suddenly wished we were at home. Grabbing the elongated fondue fork from her, I guided it to her mouth before feeding her.

Our eyes met as it slipped into her mouth. Some of the chocolate dribbled on her lip, and I used my thumb to wipe it before bringing it to my mouth. She licked her lips when I pulled the utensil away, keeping our gazes locked.

"I wish we had this at home. I know so many places I would love to lick chocolate off of, all of them on your body," I said huskily.

Kaiya flushed, pinker than the Moscato in her glass. "Then, we'll have to buy one. Like tomorrow."

She giggled as she mimicked my action, feeding me a piece of banana dipped in chocolate.

The rest of the course continued that way, with us taking turns feeding each other, giving seductive glances, and basically fucking with our eyes.

After the waiter cleared the table of everything but the wine that we had left, I reached in my pocket and grabbed the small box I had brought with me. "I have something for you."

Kaiya's lips curved and her face lit up. "Baby, you didn't have to do that. This amazing dinner was enough."

Taking out the box, I handed it to her. "I wanted to. Go ahead, open it," I urged. Sweat began to line my forehead as I waited for her to open it. *I hope she likes it.*

Her gaze left mine to look at the box. Slowly, she took off the top before taking out the small, velvet pouch inside. She carefully removed the bracelet from the bag before examining the piece of jewelry with both hands.

"I hope you like it. It took me so long to decide what charms to get for it."

Her eyes watered as she darted them back and forth between me and the bracelet. "It's perfect," she whispered. Even though her voice was soft, it was still full of emotion. "I love it."

She looked at it a few seconds longer before asking me to put it on her. After I clasped it around her slender wrist, I admired how it looked on her. The charms I had chosen all signified something, showcasing our relationship since it began.

The one closest to the clasp was a martini glass. I ran my finger over it as explained, "I got this one to symbolize our first kiss and first date since alcohol was involved in both."

She chuckled and shook her head. "Almost all of our dates involve alcohol." She pointed to the charm a few links away, a seal. "And this one?"

"This one is for our trip to the aquarium. My favorite of all our dates."

She sniffled and smiled up at me. "Mine too."

The third was an open book. "I know you love to read, that it helps you escape sometimes." She had told me that when thoughts of Kaleb overwhelmed her, sometimes she read to help get her mind off him.

Her voice was choked by emotion as tears began to rim her eyes. "This one."

She was pointing to the charm on the opposite end, a pair of boxing gloves. "Ah, this one… this one is my favorite. I picked it because we got closer once you started taking self-defense." I tucked a loose curl behind her ear as I looked into her eyes. "I don't know where I'd be if you hadn't walked into my class."

"I'm glad I did," she whispered.

My fingers moved to the script letter K for her name. "This one explains itself."

The last charm was in the center, a heart that I had engraved with the word "Warrior." I gripped it as I spoke, "This one signifies that you'll always have my heart. I'll never be the same without you, Warrior."

My eyes traveled up to hers, and I wiped the tears off her cheeks. "I'm not going to buy you presents if you're going to cry. I hate to see you cry."

Kaiya laughed softly as she leaned into me. "They're happy tears. I really do love it. Thank you."

Pressing her lips to mine, she softly kissed me. My hand glided around to cup the back of her head as my tongue parted her lips. Chocolate and wine still lingered in her mouth as I massaged her tongue with mine.

"The check whenever you're ready, sir," our server interrupted.

Neither one of us pulled away, too wrapped up in one another to care. I almost waved him off, but I was too focused on Kaiya, enjoying the feel and taste of her. When we finally parted, her lips were swollen and her cheeks were even more flushed.

"Ready to go?" I asked, pulling out my wallet.

Kaiya nodded as she scooted out of our booth. I left cash on the table, not wanting to wait to get my card back. I was already ready to take Kaiya home, and we hadn't even gone to the club yet.

After we left, we drove to a parking garage near the club. As we got out of the truck, Kaiya commented, "Dinner was amazing. Everything was perfect—the music, the wine, the food, your gift." She looked down at her bracelet before looking back up at me. "Thank you so much."

"You don't have to thank me, baby. I enjoy spoiling you." I threaded our fingers together and guided Kaiya to the elevator. The club was about four blocks up from the garage, and by the time we got there, the line was around the side of the building.

Kaiya sighed in disappointment. "We're never going to get in if we have to wait in that line."

Smiling reassuringly, I stroked the back of her hand with my thumb. Passing the line, I gave the bulky bouncer my name, and after looking at his list, he ushered us in. I heard several people cursing and shouting angrily as we walked through the doors.

Hip hop music greeted us as we entered the main room of the club. Leading Kaiya to the bar, pushing through masses of people, I ordered our usual drinks.

As we waited, Kaiya began moving her hips to the beat of the music. The only good part about taking her to a club was that I got to have that fine body rubbing against me.

"Hey, sexy. Wanna finish what we started the last time we were together?" The annoying voice was sort of familiar, but I didn't place who it was until I turned to look at her. *Shit.*

The chick that I'd hooked up with when Kaiya had stopped talking to me sidled up next to me, ignoring the fact that my arm was draped around Kaiya on my other side.

Trailing her fingers down my chest, she spoke again, "I know I do. I still remember how good your dick tasted in my mouth."

"Ryker, who the fuck is this," Kaiya asked accusingly, her eyes narrowed and lips curved in a snarl. I could feel the anger wafting off her in waves.

Before I could diffuse the situation, the stupid blonde retorted, "Who the fuck are you?"

Fuck, this is about to get bad. "Baby, let's—"

Kaiya moved in between us, getting in Blondie's face as she interrupted me, seething. "I'm his girlfriend, bitch. Fuck off."

My warrior was so fucking hot when she was pissed and jealous, but I couldn't focus on that, not when shit was about to hit the fan.

The other woman smugly replied, "Oh, you must be new. I don't remember him having a girlfriend when we hooked up."

Kaiya was fuming as she pushed the blonde bimbo, snapping, "Well, he does now, so go find someone else to open your legs for."

Blondie's eyes narrowed as she lunged at Kaiya. Big mistake. With her training, Kaiya could seriously hurt the unsuspecting girl. And by the look in her eyes, she planned to beat the crap out of her.

Stepping in between them, I moved Kaiya backward before leading her outside. She snatched her arm out of my grasp and stormed away from me, drawing the attention of people still waiting to get inside the club.

"Babe, stop. Let me explain," I said as I followed after her. In the past, I would've never chased after a woman who walked away from me; I would've just moved on to the next one.

"Who the fuck was that?" she spat as she whirled around to face me.

"Nobody. Some chick that I almost hooked up with."

"What do you mean almost? She seems to think that you two hooked up. And when did this happen? Before or after we started having sex?"

I really didn't want to discuss all that, but I wasn't going to lie to her. She meant more to me than that. She deserved honesty.

"When you stopped talking to me, I went out with Drew and got drunk. That chick was there, and I was trying to forget about you, so we went back to her place. But we didn't have sex. I couldn't go through with it."

Tears blurred her eyes, making them shine in the light of the streetlamp overhead. "What did you do?" she gritted through clenched teeth.

Sighing, I ran my hand roughly through my hair. *Here goes nothing.* "She started sucking my dick, but I made her stop. Then, I left."

The look of betrayal on her face tore up my insides. "But, she still sucked it. You still hooked up with her."

"We weren't even together, Ky. It doesn't matter," I defended. I knew that I'd said the wrong thing as soon as the words left my mouth. *Fuck.*

Her eyebrows rose incredulously. "It doesn't matter?"

"You wouldn't even talk to me. I thought we were through," I replied, trying to justify my actions.

"So, I don't talk to you for a week or two after we get involved, and you try to find the next pair of legs to get between?" She crossed her arms over her chest and glared at me.

"Ky, you're overreacting. I—"

"Overreacting? I'm overreacting? Do you know how hard it is to trust someone after everything I've been through?" She thrust her arms toward me. "How can I trust you not to do something like that again?" she screamed as tears ran down her face.

"Baby, I'm sorry. Don't cry," I pleaded, opening my arms to embrace her.

Moving away from me, she threw out her hand to stop me. The gesture felt like a punch to my gut.

"Don't. I can't do this right now. I need time to think." Her words were pained, her expression torn between anger and sadness.

"What are you saying, Ky?" *Shit. No, no, no.*

Ignoring me, she walked to the edge of the street, sticking her hand out as she waved at an oncoming taxi.

"Warrior, talk to me. Don't do this." My heart beat frantically as my pulse pounded. *I can't lose her.*

The taxi slowed as it pulled over to the curb and came to a stop. Kaiya looked at me as she opened the door, that sadness that I was so close to erasing back in full force all over her beautiful face. "I just need some space right now. I need to figure out what this means for us."

"It means nothing. She meant nothing. Don't do this, baby. I lo-"

She shut the door before I could finish. Tears burned my eyes as I thought about losing her, of not being with her ever again. Inhaling deeply, I pushed them back as I watched her drive away. *What the fuck just happened? The night was perfect until a few minutes ago.*

Stalking angrily back to my truck, my mind was all over the place. *Do I go after her? Give her space? I didn't even do anything wrong. What the fuck do I do?*

Once I sat inside my Chevy, I furiously pounded the steering wheel with my fists and roared my frustration. *She's so fucking stubborn. Well, two can play that game.*

Making my decision, I started the engine and peeled out of the parking garage.

Chapter Twenty-Five

Kaiya

"Kam, I'm home," I announced as I kicked my shoes off by the front door, trying to sound like everything was okay, even though it really wasn't. I was upset with Ryker, and I didn't know where things were going to end up between us after our fight. *I knew things were too good to be true.*

Kamden didn't answer—usually he replied back to me, even if it was just a grunt or single word. His door was closed, so he might have already been asleep, but I decided to check after changing out of my constricting dress.

After slipping into my sleep shorts and a comfy muscle shirt, I walked to Kamden's bedroom. As I knocked, the door crept open, and I caught a glimpse of him unmoving on the floor. "Oh my God, Kamden!"

He was so still—*no, no, no. What happened?* Pushing open the door, I rushed to his side, laying my head on his chest, searching for a sign of life. *Please don't be dead.* I heard nothing; just overwhelming silence so ironically loud that it deafened my ears.

My cheeks were soaked with moisture as I wrapped my arms around Kamden. Pressing my head against his chest, I sobbed into him.

Then, I heard it—one of the most beautiful sounds I'd ever heard. It was faint, but it was there—his heartbeat. *Thank God.*

I noticed the small amount of blood pooling under his head as I was yanked away and trapped against a larger body.

"Miss me, love?" The words brushed against my ear, causing me to instinctively cringe. I hadn't heard that voice in so long, but I'd never be able to forget it. It haunted my dreams and tainted my memories. Kaleb. Pure and utter fear seized my body, choking the air from my lungs and clenching my muscles. *No.*

I couldn't move, couldn't do anything as Kaleb dragged his nose across my neck, inhaling my skin before repeating the path with his tongue. "God, I've missed you. You know how much I've thought about you over the years? About touching your skin? Tasting your sweetness? I haven't been able to think about anything else."

"How'd you get out?" My voice shook weakly as I spoke, my body petrified with fear.

A sinister chuckle vibrated against my neck. "Do you really think I could stay away from you?" He nipped my neck as he ran his hands along my arms. The familiar touch made bile build in the back of my throat. One hand traveled up my arm and wrapped around my neck, squeezing firmly before his fingers laced in my hair and tugged my head back. "You're mine," he growled.

He kept one hand in my hair as the other released my throat, venturing down my breasts and stomach to the juncture of my thighs. The violating action snapped me out of my fear-induced paralysis. Using what Ryker had taught me, I stomped on Kaleb's instep before slamming my elbow directly into his stomach, freeing myself from his grasp.

As he stumbled back, I threw a side-kick to his groin before taking up a defensive stance. I didn't fully connect, but I could tell the impact still hurt him because he hunched over and grunted in pain. "You've learned to fight back, huh? This is going to be fun."

I should've run the second I was free, like Ryker always told us, but I couldn't leave Kamden. I didn't know what Kaleb would do to him without me there to focus on. Kaleb charged at me, but I ducked and threw a back-fist into his shoulder. Each time I connected with his body empowered me, making me feel less weak and helpless. I was not a frail, little girl anymore. I was a strong, powerful woman.

Kaleb angrily whirled around with a snarl before coming at me again. I landed a roundhouse to his ribs, but he caught my leg, caging it against him as he backed me toward Kamden's bed. *I can't let him get me on the bed.* My training flew out the window, suddenly forgotten as panic took hold. I swung my arms wildly, trying to hit Kaleb anywhere to get him to let me go.

I made the biggest mistake—I left my face open. Kaleb took advantage, backhanding me in the jaw. The hit stunned me, sending me falling onto the bed. Kaleb had me pinned instantly, crushing me with his weight as his legs opened my thighs. My sense of power began to fade as Kaleb turned the tables. *Keep fighting. Don't give up.*

Struggling against him, I pounded against his arms as he tugged at my clothing. My shirt tore from the shoulder down across my chest, exposing my bra. I started to scream, hoping someone would hear me and call the cops, but Kaleb slapped me across the face, silencing me as the sound of the smack echoed in Kamden's bedroom.

Bringing my arms up to cover my face, I blocked his next hit, but I didn't expect the punch to my ribs. The air was sucked from my lungs as pain assaulted my body, the intensity of it making my eyes blur.

Kaleb pushed my arms out of the way, the movement causing more pain to slice up my side. He pulled down my bra, revealing my breasts before grabbing one in each hand and slowly kneading them with his fingers.

Don't let him do this to you. You have to fight! Don't be weak! Kaleb was focused on my breasts, the vacant look in his eyes telling me he was lost to his darker side. Shoving my arms forward, breaking his loose hold on me, I braced my hands against his shoulders as I readied to execute the rest of the first technique Ryker had ever taught me.

One foot pressed against his hip, then two, as I fluidly performed the move. My hands slid down to his wrists as he pulled back, just as Ryker said an attacker would. Immediately, I began kicking upwards, landing a few kicks to Kaleb's face before he fell off of me, landing on the floor with a thud.

Springing off the bed, I headed for the door as a hand wrapped around my ankle. Losing my balance, I fell to the floor, breaking my fall with my forearms. I struggled to free myself, but Kaleb was much stronger than me, always had been.

Kaleb climbed up my body, grasping at my shorts and pulling at them. *No!* I repeatedly began kicking him in the face, causing more blood to surface from the wounds I was inflicting. *Take that, asshole. I hope it hurts as much as you hurt me.*

Instead of slowing him down, everything seemed to amp up his rage and power as he yanked my bottoms off with ease. I tried to crawl away, but Kaleb latched his hand around my ankle and dragged me back to him.

My body went into survival mode, ignoring the pain spiraling outward from my ribs through me as my arms and legs struck out, hoping to hit anything and stop him.

Then, he was on me again, in between my legs despite my efforts. My chest heaved raggedly for breath as exhaustion began to weigh me down. I forced my thighs shut, but he pried them apart, digging his nails into my flesh and drawing blood as he opened them again.

As he reached for my underwear, wanting to remove the last barrier I had protecting me from him, I thrust a palm strike right to his nose, causing him to grab it instinctively as blood began to stream from it.

Squirming out from under him, I flipped over and pushed up on my knees in preparation to run for the front door. Kaleb swept my legs out from under me just as I stood, sending me back to the hardwood floor. Reacting too late, my face slammed into the unyielding ground before I could brace myself. Stars shot into my vision as the iron tang of my blood filled my mouth.

Kaleb rolled me over and mounted me. I weakly tried to push him off me, but he reared back and slapped me with so much force that my ears rang. My eyes began to shut on their own accord as he pulled his shirt off. I just lay there, practically defeated, unable to find the strength to fight back anymore as pain smothered everything else. *I'm not strong enough.*

"I finally get to finish what I started all those years ago," he mumbled in a lust-laden voice.

Never give up, Warrior. Always fight back. Ryker's voice played in my mind.

I weakly brought my knee up, connecting with his crotch, but it barely affected him. *I have no fight left. He always wins.* Tears began to trickle down my face before I began to numb myself, hoping to withdraw internally enough so I wouldn't feel anything that Kaleb was going to do to me.

Then, pounding on the door startled both Kaleb and me. He stilled with his hands on the button of his jeans, then snapped his gaze up to mine. His eyes gave a silent threat, but I opened my mouth to scream anyway before his hand slammed down and muffled my cries.

A dull voice yelled through the door. "Kaiya, it's me. Please come talk to me, baby."

Ryker! Oh, thank God! My brief happiness was extinguished as Kaleb leaned over me, whispering in my ear. "Don't make a sound."

As I was about to ignore him and scream for Ryker, I felt cold, hard metal digging into my side. *Where did he get a gun? Oh my God, did he shoot Kamden?*

Fear penetrated my being, instantly silencing any form of protest as I froze in place.

Ryker continued to bang on the door. "I know you're in there. I'm not leaving until you come talk to me—I'll stand out here all night if I have to."

Tears watered in my eyes at the thought of Kaleb hurting Ryker. *Please leave.*

"I mean it, Ky. I'm not going anywhere," Ryker yelled as he knocked harder.

Kaleb cursed under his breath as he stood, pulling me up with him as he kept the gun pressed to my side. He walked us to the door as he quietly threatened, "Make him leave or I'll kill him."

My heart clenched at the thought of Ryker dying, especially

because of me. I never should've gotten involved with him, never should've entangled him in my web of issues.

When we reached the door, Kaleb dug the gun deeper into my injured side. A small yelp of pain burst from me, but I smashed my lips together to stop it so Ryker wouldn't hear. I wasn't sure if Kaleb would kill me, at least not until he had raped me, but I knew without a doubt he would kill Ryker. I needed to protect him, even if it meant breaking my heart by pushing him away.

"What do you want, Ryker?" I asked, trying to keep my voice even.

"Baby, let me in. I want to talk to you," he pleaded. The pain in his voice tightened my chest.

"That's not a good idea. You should just leave," I snapped as I fought back tears.

"I'm not leaving until you talk to me." His tone was firm, the one he used when his mind was made up.

Damn it, he's so stubborn.

"I'm talking to you, now go!" I yelled as my tears broke through. *Please just leave.*

"Why are you acting like this, Warrior?"

I set my forehead against the door, wondering if Ryker was doing the same on the other side. Kaleb twisted the gun, reminding me of my task. I hissed loudly in pain as I gritted the lie. "I don't want to see you anymore."

"Don't do this, Warrior. I can't lose you. Tell me what to do to fix this."

Tears rolled down my cheeks. My vision blurred from a combination of the moisture in my eyes and pain from the barrel digging into my ribs. "I can't be fixed. Some demons just don't leave you alone. They haunt you forever," I eluded, hoping Ryker would understand what I meant and get help once he left. But even if he did, they probably wouldn't make it in time.

He didn't respond for several seconds, and I thought he had left. Then the silence broke when he said, "I understand. I'll give you some space tonight, but I'm coming back over here tomorrow to straighten everything out. We can face those demons together."

I heard his footsteps going down the stairs as Kaleb pulled me away from the door, leading me to my bedroom instead of Kamden's. He tucked the gun in the back of his pants as he tightened his hold on my arm, driving his nails into my skin.

Then, chaos erupted as Ryker burst through the front door. Kaleb reached for his gun, but I threw my weight into him, sending both of us crashing into the wall as Ryker neared us.

"He has a gun!" I warned.

The impact caused Kaleb to lose his grip on me, but also made me lose my balance, sending me stumbling back into the opposite wall. Ryker slammed into Kaleb, tackling him to the ground. They rolled on the floor several times before Ryker finally pinned him, and started elbowing him in the face.

The gun flew backwards from Kaleb's hand and went off as it hit the floor. Ryker stilled, then snapped his eyes to me, making sure I hadn't been shot, which gave Kaleb the opportunity to punch him square in the jaw.

Stunned, Ryker wobbled slightly before Kaleb hit him twice more, causing him to fall to the floor. Kaleb darted for the gun on the ground a few feet away from me, but Ryker grabbed his leg, making him stumble and crash to the floor. Kaleb used his other foot to kick Ryker in the face several times. Blood streamed down his face as he let go and lay dazed against the floor. *No.*

Kaleb rushed for the gun again, and I knew I couldn't let him get a hold of it. I couldn't let him shoot Ryker. I threw myself at the weapon, causing it to skid away from me when I hit it. Frantically crawling, I stretched my arm out to grab the handle, but Kaleb's foot came stomping down, crushing my hand beneath his boot.

Yelping, I pulled my hand back, clutching it to my chest as I watched Kaleb reach the gun. *Shit.* I scooted back, desperate to get to Ryker, to protect him.

Ryker groaned when my hand brushed against him. Tugging on his bicep, I helped him sit up as Kaleb picked up the gun. I draped his arm around my shoulder before struggling to pull him to his feet.

Kaleb pointed the gun at Ryker, so I stepped in front of him, blocking as much of Ryker's bulky body with my much smaller one. All I cared about was him—Kaleb could do whatever he wanted to me if it meant that Ryker would be safe.

Kaleb's eyes blazed in anger at my action, obviously pissed that I was protecting Ryker. "Move, Kaiya," he growled.

I silently shook my head, fearing my voice would waver if I spoke. Kaleb cursed and threatened, "Don't make me do this."

I didn't respond—inside I was screaming, the frail, weak part of me begging me to move out of the way. But, something else was keeping me there, something stronger than fear—love.

Tears burned my eyes—we were probably going to die and Ryker didn't know how I felt, that I loved him. *Oh my God, I love him.* There was no doubt or question anymore. The reality of it had finally sunk in. I knew with every fiber of my being that I was in love with Ryker.

The click of the gun snapped me from my thoughts. Everything happened so fast after that—Ryker pushed me out of the way as Kamden stumbled out of his bedroom and threw himself at Kaleb.

The gun was pointed straight at me when it went off from my brothers fighting over it. My body froze at the sound, the only movement being my eyes shutting tight in fear.

I expected excruciating agony, but the burning that I felt in my chest was not what I anticipated. My eyes snapped open to Ryker's bloody face; his eyes were scrunched in pain as sweat trailed down his skin. His arms were tightly wrapped around me, his chest pressed against mine.

Looking down, I was utterly unprepared for what I saw. A bullet was sticking out of my blood-splattered chest, right over my heart. But that wasn't even the worst part.

My breath caught in my throat as I focused on the bloody bullet hole in Ryker's chest in front of me. Realization clicked at what just occurred. "You saved me," I whispered in shock.

Wincing, he forced a smile. The pained expression didn't look right on his beautiful face. "I told you that I always would," he croaked.

Tears trickled down my cheeks as he slumped against me, forcing me to bear his weight. My legs gave out, unable to hold the both of us up as I fell to my knees.

Shifting Ryker to cradle him in my lap, I pulled off my ripped shirt, balling it up and pressing it against Ryker's wound. He clenched his eyes shut as he hissed in pain.

"I'm sorry, baby. I have to stop the bleeding," I choked, my tears now falling like a torrential downpour.

Sounds of a scuffle reached my ears, causing my head to jerk up. Kamden and Kaleb still wrestled over the gun about ten feet away from me. Then, Kamden finally ripped it from Kaleb's hands before pointing it at him.

Sirens sounded in the distance, probably from a neighbor calling to report the yelling and gunshots. *I hope an ambulance is coming with them.*

Kaleb stepped closer to Kamden, who threatened, "Don't come any closer."

Kaleb curled his lip up before spitting blood on the floor. "We both know you won't shoot me, brother. You're too weak, just like you were too weak to protect Kaiya from me all those years."

Then, Kaleb threw himself at Kamden. Struggling over the gun once again, it fired, the sound making my stomach clench. Both my brothers fell to the floor, and I couldn't tell who had been shot. *Please don't be Kamden. Please don't be Kamden.*

Neither one moved as my heart pounded wildly in my chest, my adrenaline lacing my veins and making me feel like a charged up live wire. Kamden finally groaned before starting to get up, and I exhaled a huge sigh of relief. *He's alive. He's okay.*

Kaleb didn't move. Even though he had tormented me for so long, a little piece of my heart still hurt at the thought of him being dead—he was my twin, after all. Even after everything he did to me, I still felt a small part of that special bond that only twins have, which had made all his abuse so emotionally damaging.

Ryker moaned softly, drawing my attention back to him. His hand clutched mine, which was still holding my shirt against his chest. Tears fell from my face onto him as he stared up at me through half-lidded eyes.

His hand reached up to swipe the tears from my face before he rested it there, cupping my cheek. I leaned into his palm as I brought my free hand to rest atop his. *Tell him.*

Just as I was about to speak, he mumbled, "Kaiya, I—"

His hand went limp, falling from my face as his eyes shut.

No. "Ryker! Ryker, wake up!" I shrieked as I lightly smacked his face, trying to wake him. "Don't leave me!"

The stomping of multiple pairs of feet sounded behind me, but all I could focus on was waking Ryker up.

"Open your eyes! Damn it, look at me, baby! Please!" I desperately screamed.

I heard voices, but I couldn't make out what they were saying. Hands grabbed me and pulled me away from Ryker as two people took my place next to him, sending me into a fit of crazed panic.

"No! Ryker! I need to be with him! Please! Don't take him away from me!"

Thrashing wildly against whoever was holding me, I screamed until my throat was raw. I didn't know how I was able to move due to all my injuries, but the only pain I felt was my heart ripping apart as I thought about Ryker being dead.

More hands gripped onto me as another person came into my view, but my eyes were so blurred with tears that I couldn't see who they were. Despair sucked the air from lungs, suffocating me as I continued to struggle. Other sets of hands grabbed me, holding me still as I felt a sharp sting in my arm.

Still fighting, I kicked and flailed until my body began to feel boneless, my vision swimming as my eyes suddenly became heavy and dizziness swarmed me. I slumped against someone right before blackness blanketed me.

Annoying beeping woke me. I groaned as pain assaulted me everywhere, making me wish I'd stayed in the black void I'd been in. *Where am I?*

"*Sorella*?" a tired voice spoke. "Are you awake?"

"Ugh, why are you yelling?" I mumbled groggily.

A sigh of relief followed by a strained chuckle met my ears as a hand squeezed mine. I struggled to open my eyes, which felt like they had been sealed with superglue. I managed to open one as I turned my head toward where I heard the voice.

Kamden gave me a small smile as he stood and kissed my forehead. "Are you thirsty?"

My mouth felt like someone had stuffed it with cotton after buffing my throat with sandpaper. "Yes," my voice cracked hoarsely.

Kamden handed me a cup with ice chips. When I finished, he set the cup back on the bedside table, I took in my surroundings—I was in a hospital room, which explained the annoying beeping of the machine hooked up to me. Memories of what happened with Kaleb rushed back, and I gripped Kamden's hand tighter. "Where's Ryker? Is he okay?" I asked as I fought back tears. *Please be alive.*

"He's fine. He's in the room right next door. They had to sedate him because he kept fighting to get to you—he ripped open his stitches."

I exhaled a huge sigh of relief. *He's alive. Thank God.* "When can I see him?"

"I don't know. We'll have to ask your doctor. You have some fractured ribs, as well as some small fractures in your right hand and face. He said your gunshot wound wasn't that extensive; the bullet came out fairly easily. You were very lucky— Ryker took the brunt of the impact and slowed the trajectory, otherwise, it would've…"

Kamden choked, unable to finish his sentence. The tears I'd been holding broke free then, the severity of what happened almost strangling me. "He saved me."

"He loves you," Kamden said softly with a knowing smile.

My head snapped up to his, and I winced from the sharp throb that resulted. "He said that?"

"No, but no one takes a bullet for someone unless they love them.

I saw how you protected him—you love him, too, don't you?"

"Yeah, I think I do," I replied softly.

"You do. I can see it on your face."

I changed the subject, not completely comfortable with discussing how I felt about Ryker with Kamden yet. I needed to talk to Ryker first, see if what Kamden was saying was true. "How about you?"

"I suffered a small concussion and some bruises, but nothing major like you."

"Kaleb?" I hesitantly asked.

Kamden's face tensed as his eyes watered. He shook his head, unable to voice what happened. I couldn't imagine what he was feeling, but I knew it wasn't good. My heart became heavy for him. He had to kill our brother for something that should've never been an issue between the three of us.

"I'm sorry." I squeezed his hand.

His eyes met mine as he nodded, sorrow etched into every feature. I wanted to comfort him, to take away his pain, but I knew that look; he wasn't ready to talk about it yet. I would be there for him when he was, just as he had always been for me.

The door opened, and a man who looked to be in his forties walked in wearing the traditional doctor's coat, holding an iPad.

"Ah, good, you're awake. I'm Dr. Wright," he introduced as he walked to the side of my bed, opposite of Kamden.

I gave him a polite smile, then impatiently asked, "When can I see Ryker Campbell? He's the patient next door to me."

The doctor laughed softly. "First things first. Let's get you checked out before we move on to anything else."

After he checked my vitals and all the other routine crap they have to do, he lifted the gauze covering my wound to examine it. "No sign of infection, and your stitches look good. But, I still want you to stay a week or so just to be safe."

"Can I get up and walk around?"

He responded with a knowing smile. "Yes, just don't exert yourself too much. You just got shot, plus you have multiple fractures and bruising all over your body—you need to take it easy. Give your body time to recuperate."

"I will." *After I see Ryker.*

Dr. Wright nodded as he typed something on his tablet. "I'll be back to check on you tomorrow."

Kamden and I both thanked the doctor before he left. "Help me up," I requested as soon as the door shut. I wasn't wasting any more time. Being away from Ryker was eating me up inside. I needed to make sure he was okay. I didn't care how much it would hurt.

Kamden gave me his disapproving big brother look. "Ky, you heard the doctor—you need to take it easy."

Narrowing my eyes, I threatened, "Help me up, or I'm going to get up without you, and I'll probably further injure myself."

Kamden sighed in defeat. "Fine. You're such a brat."

In true brat-like fashion, I stuck my tongue out at him. He pulled me up by my arms since one of my hands was in a splint and helped me scoot to the side of the bed. I winced in pain from the movement, and the side where my fractured ribs were seared me in agony, making me squeeze my eyes shut and grit my teeth.

Kamden stopped and let me go. "Ky, this isn't—"

"I'm fine, now help me stand," I demanded, my voice leaving no room for argument.

He mumbled something indiscernible under his breath, but I was able to hear a few choice words as he complied with my request. My whole body hurt as I strained to stand, but I fought through the pain, needing to see Ryker.

I hobbled like a ninety year old grandma with arthritis as we made our way from my room to Ryker's. Kamden used one hand to brace my arm the entire way, keeping me from losing my balance and falling while he pulled my IV stand with us.

It felt like it took hours to get to Ryker's room. I was about to bust out of my skin when Kamden opened the door and slowly led me in. I had to stop myself from pulling away and running to Ryker's bed.

"Hurry, Kam," I urged when Ryker came into view.

He was sleeping when I finally reached him. Kamden steadied me before pulling up a chair behind me for me to sit in, but I stayed standing as I threaded my uninjured hand with his. Tears trailed down my face as I assessed him—he had a black eye, his lip was busted, and multiple bruises and cuts marred his beautiful face.

I squeezed his hand before bringing it up to my lips and gently kissing it. I didn't know when he would wake up, but I wasn't leaving until he did.

Letting go of his hand, I awkwardly struggled to push the rail on the side of his bed down, planning to climb in next to him. I needed to be as close to him as possible, to feel his chest rise with breath, hear his heartbeat, and feel the warmth of life in his skin. I didn't have enough strength to lift myself in, and tears started to rim my eyes.

"Kamden, help me," I cried softly.

"Kaiya, I—"

Interrupting him, I begged, "Please, Kam. I need to be near him right now."

Kamden never did well resisting when it came to me. He gingerly helped me get into the small bed with Ryker. All of my efforts had exhausted me so much that as soon as I rested my head against Ryker's chest, right over his heart, sleep took me away.

Ryker

I'd lost count of how many times I'd driven around the block of Kaiya's apartment before I finally parked outside her building.

What are you doing? She told you she needed time to think, and you show up like some stalker at her place.

I looked up through my windshield at her apartment. She'd said she needed space, but I was worried she was trying to run again, and I didn't want to let her slip away because we were both being stubborn.

I hopped out of my truck, shut the door, then started walking toward the stairs. After a few steps, I stopped, turned around, and went back to my truck.

Fuck! What do I do?

I stared at my reflection in the window of the driver's side door, debating what to do.

Should I leave and give her the space she asked for, or resolve the issue now before she overthinks everything and runs again?

I exhaled a breath, and turned back around, deciding to put everything on the table, then let Kaiya have her space if she still wanted it. She needed to know how I felt about her before making any decisions about us.

As I jogged up the stairs, nerves balled up my stomach. I was afraid she would slam the door in my face, maybe not even open it at all, but I hoped that her feelings for me would convince her to hear me out at least.

When I reached her door, I paused and took a deep breath. I didn't want our relationship to end, and I was unsure whether or not my actions would dig myself deeper into the hole I'd made, or help me out of it.

I knocked on the door, then waited. After several seconds with no response, I knocked harder. "Kaiya, it's me. Please come talk to me, baby."

When she didn't respond again, my gut tightened.

She must be really pissed if she's not even answering me.

I pounded on the door again, not caring if I sounded like a crazy person. I wasn't going to let Kaiya go without a fight. "I know you're in there. I'm not leaving until you come talk to me—I'll stand out here all night if I have to."

No response again. Worry began to eat at me because something didn't seem right. Even if Kaiya didn't want to talk to me, I expected Kamden to answer the door and tell me to fuck off or something.

I knocked harder, raising my voice to make sure she heard me. "I mean it, Ky. I'm not going anywhere."

I finally heard footsteps coming from inside; it sounded like there was more than just one set, but I figured Kamden might have been hovering over her like his normal over-protective self, not wanting her to let me in.

Several seconds passed before Kaiya replied, "What do you want, Ryker?" Her voice shook with fear and was strained with emotion.

My eyebrows furrowed. *Why did she sound like that?* "Baby, let me in. I want to talk to you."

"That's not a good idea. You should just leave," Kaiya snapped back. I could tell that she was trying not to cry, and the sense I had that something wasn't right grew stronger. I wasn't sure exactly what was going on, but I wasn't going anywhere until I found out.

"I'm not leaving until you talk to me," I replied firmly.

"I am talking to you, now go!" she yelled before starting to cry.

I balled my fists and placed them against the door, wishing I could hold her instead of talking through the stupid barrier separating us. "Why are you acting like this, Warrior?"

A few moments passed before she answered, "I don't want to see you anymore." She sounded like she was in pain, words gritted through clenched teeth.

I felt like the wind had been knocked out of me.

This can't be happening.

My heart started racing in panic. "Don't do this, Warrior. I can't lose you. Tell me what to do to fix this."

She was sobbing when she spoke again. "I can't be fixed. Some demons just don't leave you alone. They haunt you forever."

Demons? What does she mean demons?

Then, everything clicked. The multiple sets of footsteps, the fear in her voice, why she sounded like she was in pain.

Kaleb.

Fear snaked inside my chest and wrapped around my heart. I didn't want to tip Kaleb off that I knew he was in there, but I couldn't just stand outside formulating a plan. Every second counted, and the decisions I made from that point on were crucial.

As calmly as I could, I replied, "I understand. I'll give you some space tonight, but I'm coming back over here tomorrow to straighten everything out. We can face those demons together."

I started walking down the stairs so that they would think I left, then paused. After a few seconds, I went back up, then put as much distance between myself and Kaiya's apartment, wanting as much momentum as I could get to bust through the door.

I didn't even think twice about my decision. Kaiya was in danger, and I would risk my life saving her from her asshole of a twin. That's how much I loved her.

I broke into a run, heading straight for Kaiya's apartment. Leaning down, I prepared my shoulder for the brunt of the impact, then barreled through the door.

Fuck, that hurt.

My shoulder pulsed with pain as I took in the scene. Kaiya was being held by her brother, who reached behind his back. I charged toward Kaleb as my warrior threw herself into him. "He has a gun!" she shouted.

Kaleb lost his grip on Kaiya, sending her into the wall. Tackling her brother to the floor, we rolled a few times before I finally pinned him. I started elbowing him in the face as I heard the gunshot.

Oh God. Please, no.

I stopped and jerked my head up, searching for Kaiya to see if she'd been hit by the bullet. As we made eye contact, Kaleb punched me in the jaw.

Cheap shot.

The impact stunned me, and Kaleb capitalized on the opportunity, hitting me a couple more times. I fell back, dazed from the multiple blows. Kaleb scrambled out from under me, heading for the gun a few feet away from us.

Spots dotted my vision, but I knew I needed to focus. I grabbed Kaleb's leg, making him trip and fall back to the floor. Enraged, he kicked me in the face several times, dazing me. I let go and fell back, floating in and out of consciousness. I fought to stay awake, knowing that Kaiya needed me.

Get up, you pussy. Kaiya's life is on the line.

I felt a hand brush up against me. I blinked several times, looking for the source, and finally made out Kaiya's form.

Draping my arm over her shoulder, she struggled to lift me. I was slowly getting my bearings back, and was able to stand once she helped me up.

Stepping in front of me, Kaiya blocked my body.

"Move, Kaiya," her brother snarled in anger.

What is she doing?

One of my eyes had started swelling shut, so my vision was limited, but I could see the gun pointed at us.

"Don't make me do this," Kaleb threatened.

Fuck, he's going to shoot.

I had to get Kaiya out of danger. I had promised her that I wouldn't let Kaleb hurt her, and I'd already failed by not being here earlier to protect her. I was going to make good on my promise.

I heard the click of the gun as I pushed Kaiya out of the way. Kamden burst into the hall from his room and attacked his brother, fighting over the weapon.

The gun went off again, and it was pointed straight at Kaiya. She clenched her eyes in anticipation of the impact, but I jumped in front of her, wrapping my arms around her as the bullet hit me.

Fuck.

I gritted my teeth to combat the excruciating pain, but it didn't help. My chest felt like it has been ripped open and set on fire.

Kaiya's eyes snapped open, shock evident in her face. She looked from me, down at her chest, then back up at me. "You saved me," she whispered.

Dizziness clouded me as I forced a smile. "I told you I always would."

Tears streamed down Kaiya's face as I slumped against her, the energy draining out of me like water gushing from a busted faucet.

My poor Warrior couldn't hold us up, and we fell to the ground. She cradled me in her lap and then pressed something against my wound, sending a sharp stab through my chest. I hissed in pain.

"I'm sorry, baby. I have to stop the bleeding." Kaiya sobbed.

I was so tired; all I wanted to do was sleep.

You have to stay awake and protect Kaiya.

Sounds of a scuffle and yelling came from across the room, and I hoped that Kamden had been able to stop Kaleb. I was pretty much fucked, and there was nothing else I could do.

There is one more thing.

Reaching up to cup her cheek, I groaned. My chest and shoulder screamed in agony, but I had to tell Kaiya how I felt just in case I didn't make it. I knew I'd lost a lot of blood—we were both covered in it.

I squeezed her other hand with mine and wiped the tears from her face. I could barely keep my eyes open as I faded in and out of consciousness. "Kaiya, I— "

My hand fell from her face, and my eyes closed as the darkness pulled me under. The last thing I remember was Kaiya's desperate screams.

Electronic beeping woke me from my sleep.

Kaiya.

"Kaiya?" I struggled to open my eyes as I fought through the haze of anesthesia. "Kaiya?" I shouted.

A face with a surgical mask appeared over me. "Sir, please calm down. You've suffered a great deal of trauma."

Fuck, I hate hospitals.

I tried to sit up, but the doctor eased me back down. "I have to get to Kaiya. I need to see her."

"Sir, you've just had major surgery. You need to calm down or you're going to rip your stitches." He looked up at someone and nodded.

I didn't give a fuck if I'd had both legs amputated—I needed to make sure Kaiya was okay. "Get off me—I have to see my girlfriend!" I yelled, straining against the two sets of hands holding me down.

"Sir, please."

I growled in anger, wrenching my arm from a nurse who'd come to assist the doctor. I felt my chest rip open, but my adrenaline and anger numbed the pain. I didn't care about anything except Kaiya. "Let me go!"

A needle pricked my forearm, and I felt the cold of medicine being injected into me.

Fuck. Goddamn assholes.

My eyes became heavy, and my arms went limp. Cursing, I fell back, and I was out within seconds.

Chapter Twenty-Six

Ryker

When I awoke, the faint smell of strawberries and vanilla filled my nose as I inhaled deeply, causing a smile to spread on my face. *Kaiya.*

My eyes snapped open before my gaze traveled down, focusing on hair the color of dark chocolate, porcelain skin, and a small, familiar body—Kaiya. *How did she get here?*

"As soon as she woke up, she made me bring her to you," a voice answered my unspoken question.

My eyes met Kamden's, who sat in a chair next to my bed. He looked like he had aged years since I saw him last, and exhaustion laced his face. Deep, purple bags rimmed his eyes, and his skin looked pallid. "Sounds like her. She's so stubborn," I chuckled, then winced from the resulting pain in my chest.

"You okay? Do you need me to get a nurse?"

I looked down at Kaiya's head on my chest, and smiled. "Nah, I'm good now."

"You love her?" Kamden abruptly questioned.

I looked up at him. After what we had gone through, after what

I'd done for her, I didn't have to even think about my answer. "Yes, I love her."

He gave me a small, but genuine smile. "Thank you for…" He cleared his throat as his eyes watered. "For saving Kaiya. I don't know how I can ever repay you, but I'll find a way."

"You don't have to do anything. I have everything I need right here." I gestured to Kaiya in my arms.

His smile widened as he wordlessly stood and walked to the door. When he grabbed the handle, he looked over his shoulder. "I'll be outside if she needs me."

Focusing back on the amazing woman next to me, I softly ran my fingers through her hair as I quietly spoke, "Wake up, my Warrior."

She began to stir as I continued to run my fingers through her long locks. I probably should've let her sleep, but I needed to see her, needed to make sure she was really okay, especially since I hadn't completely stopped the bullet. I didn't know if I'd ever be able to forget the image of it embedded in her skin.

Her head shifted as she looked up at me. Those gorgeous eyes captivated me as they met mine, making me lose myself in her as I sank into them.

"Hi," she murmured as her lips tipped up in a soft smile.

"Hi. How are you feeling?"

"Sore, but better now that I'm here."

"I heard you fought your way over here."

"Me? What about you? I heard you ripped your stitches open trying to get to me," she countered as her mouth quirked up playfully.

"They told you that, huh?" I glanced away, slightly embarrassed by my behavior.

"Yep," she replied, putting extra emphasis on the P as she gave me a teasing grin. "Now, why would you do something crazy like that?"

"When I want something, I have to have it. You know that."

She scooted up a little, bringing our faces closer together, maybe only inches apart. "So did you get what you wanted?"

Closing the distance between us, I tenderly pressed my lips to hers, ignoring the light pain it caused in mine. "Now, I did." I set my forehead against hers.

"Don't ever do something like that again," Kaiya scolded as she gripped onto my hospital gown, her playfulness from moments before gone. The tone in her voice told me that she was crying, so I pulled back to cradle her face in my hands. The sight of all the cuts and bruises, along with her tears broke my heart—I hated to see her hurt.

"I'd do it again if I had to." I grazed my thumbs over her cheeks. I'd take a bullet for her no questions asked.

Her watery eyes locked on mine. "Why?"

We'd never talked about love before, both of us afraid of what it signified. Our pasts had made us scared to love, but after almost losing her, I wasn't going to take what we had for granted anymore. "Because I love you."

Her lip trembled as more tears flowed from her eyes. "I love you, too," she sobbed before bringing our mouths back together again. Our lips caressed each other, embracing softly as our tongues lightly laced together. Passion was evident in every movement, present in every breath as we demonstrated the love that we had just spoke.

When we finally broke apart, Kaiya's lips were swollen and her skin flushed beneath the bruising. Her cheeks were stained with tears as she looked at me.

"So, all I had to do was take a bullet for you to get you to tell me that you love me? Why didn't I do that sooner?" I joked.

She rolled her eyes at me as she lightheartedly retorted, "I've never been in love before—how was I supposed to know what it felt like?" She poked a finger into the uninjured side of my chest. "You, on the other hand, have loved someone before, so why didn't you tell me?"

"That's exactly why—I've been in love before, and I got hurt because of it. The way I feel for you is so much stronger than I ever felt for her, even when I thought she was pregnant with my kid. So you could hurt me way more than she did—I'd never recover from you."

More tears trickled down her face as our eyes locked. "Me neither. I'm trusting you with those tiny, broken pieces of my heart, everything that's left of me. There'd be no way to put them back together after you—you're the only one who knows how."

I smiled at her; I'd been waiting for this moment, waiting for Kaiya to fully trust me. I couldn't even explain how it felt to have the woman I loved love me back, to trust me after everything she'd been through. Spectacular didn't even come close.

As she settled on her side next to me, I leaned my forehead against hers. From that angle, I could see the gauze covering her injury through the opening in her hospital gown. I slowly pulled it back, wanting to see the damage done by the bullet.

A small, jagged circle sat right over her heart. I couldn't believe how close I'd come to losing her. *Thank God I stopped it.* Her skin was bruised around the injury, which was puffy and red, but it wasn't that deep.

She did the same with mine, pulling the gauze back to look at my wound, which mirrored hers the way we were facing one another. Mine was bigger and more inflamed, probably from ripping out my stitches and the severity of the trauma, but it was almost exactly in the same spot as hers, just on the opposite side.

More tears dripped from her eyes as she looked over my injury. I brought my hands up to wipe them away before lifting her face to look at mine.

"Stop crying, Warrior. We're both still alive."

"I don't like seeing you hurt, especially because of me." She traced the tattoos around the injury softly, careful not to get to close. "It's going to scar—it'll mess up your beautiful tattoos."

"I'll bear any scar for you, Ky. Plus, scars are sexy," I said with a smirk, trying to lighten the mood.

Kaiya wasn't amused, her face still marred by a frown. "Not on women they're not."

"Yours will be incredibly sexy because it matches mine. Both will always remind me of the moment I realized I couldn't live without you, that I was completely in love with you."

My words turned her lips up into the beautiful smile that I loved, but also caused more tears to flow. "You're kinda perfect, you know that," Kaiya said as she looked at me, her voice full of emotion.

"So are you, baby. Absolutely perfect for me." I kissed her

forehead, letting my lips linger as I breathed in her scent.

When I pulled back, Kaiya settled next to me, laying her head on the uninjured side of my chest. We lay there in peaceful silence, both of us emotionally and physically exhausted. I drifted off to sleep, content with the love of my life in my arms.

Epilogue

Kaiya

People say that time heals all wounds. I still call bullshit. I've learned that even the deepest scars can be healed by the right person but not because of time.

The saying should be rephrased to say that love heals all wounds because that's what's been healing me over the past few months. I'm not completely healed, but I'm getting there—I make progress every day.

I had to stay in the hospital for a little over a week, but Ryker had to stay almost three because of his injuries. The bullet had gone clean through him before it hit me, so his surgery and recovery were more extensive. I stayed by his side every day until visiting hours ended, and came back first thing the next morning when they opened again.

I took a leave of absence from work to deal with the aftermath. After everything that happened, I changed; we all did. Even though Kaleb is gone, the pain and scars from what he did to me still remain, but Ryker heals them more and more every day.

Kamden has his own scars to deal with following the shooting. Killing Kaleb haunts him, even though it was in self-defense. He's seeing a therapist regularly to cope with the backlash of the incident. Therapy is definitely not my thing, but it's working for him, and I hope it helps his healing process.

Ryker started physical therapy because some of the nerves in his chest that connected to his shoulder were damaged by the bullet. I worried that he would never be able to train or work out again, but he's determined to make a full recovery. And he will—he always loves a challenge.

I don't know what I'd do without Ryker. It's amazing how someone can just come into your life, completely flip it upside down, and make you wonder how you ever lived without them before.

Ryker insisted I move in with him, but that was too much, too soon for me. Even though I love him, being in a committed relationship is definitely an adjustment for me. Plus, I couldn't leave Kamden alone, especially since he's been having trouble dealing with the repercussions of that night.

We compromised—Kamden and I moved into Ryker's apartment complex, only one building away. There's no way we could stay in ours after what had happened there.

I alternate between sleeping at Ryker's place and mine, but Ryker usually ends up at my apartment on nights that I don't stay with him. We were both used to sleeping alone, but now I wouldn't be able to sleep without him.

We've been suffering from nightmares for the past several months, waking up in cold sweats and struggling to breathe. But we're there to pull each other through each one, saving the other from the suffocating darkness. I have no idea how long they'll last, or if they'll ever go away, but we'll get through it. We'll always save each other.

Every night before we go to sleep, Ryker presses a kiss to the scar on my chest, showing me that not all scars are bad. Some are beautiful despite their ugly appearance, the meaning underneath what's important. I've learned that all my scars, even the ones left by Kaleb, have made me who I am, have taught me valuable lessons. But that one, the one that Ryker and I share, means the most to me. It symbolizes love, a love I'd never thought I would have, a constant reminder to never take it for granted. And I never plan to.

the End

Playlist

~ Gotten – Slash ft. Adam Levine
~ Poison and Wine – The Civil Wars
~ This Woman's Work – Maxwell
~ Undone – Haley Reinhart
~ Demons – Imagine Dragons
~ Better Than Me – Hinder
~ Words – Skylar Grey
~ Broken – Seether ft. Amy Lee
~ Fix You – Coldplay
~ Distance – Christina Perri
~ Warrior – Demi Lovato
~ Just Save Me – Like A Storm

Acknowledgements

First off, I would like to thank my family for their support in this next step of my journey. They've never discouraged me from following this amazing dream of mine, and their support means so much to me.

Thank you to my beta readers, Vanessa, Natasha, Ena, Nicki, and Stephanie for their invaluable feedback. They helped make *The Scars of Us* what it is, and I'm so grateful for their input.

To my editor, Ana Zaun, for pushing me and helping me take my writing to the next level.

To Kari at Cover to Cover Designs, thank you for putting up with my OCD demands when it came to my cover—it came out gorgeous and I love it.

To my muse, Andrew England. Thank you for being the perfect inspiration for Ryker, and for being so easy to work with. I look forward to working with you on my upcoming projects in the future.

To Simon Barnes for the amazing photo used for the cover. I loved working with you and Andrew, and can't wait to see what we come up with for my other books.

I want to give a huge thanks to my self-defense instructor, Master Philip Lobo at Wolfpack Fighting and Fitness Academy. I really wanted the self-defense maneuvers that I used in the book to be actual, effective techniques, and he answered all my questions and demonstrated each and every one for me. His teachings were priceless, and I'm so thankful to have learned so much from him.

And most importantly, to the readers. Thank you for reading *The Scars of Us*. Time is precious, and I'm beyond grateful that you spent some of your time to read my work. I hope that you fell in love with Kaiya and Ryker, just like I did when I wrote their story.

Mending Scars

NIKKI SPARXX

Prologue

Kaiya

It's amazing how scars can still affect you long after they're inflicted. Even though Kaleb's gone, the scars he left continued to resound in the depths of my soul, tormenting me and overshadowing the happiness that Ryker has brought me.

After everything Kaleb had put me through, I still hurt because of his death. I couldn't explain why, but the pang of pain, although small, was undeniable; so was the hollow sliver in my heart for him.

I knew Kamden was hurting, too. I could see the guilt and remorse eating at him every day as he tried to wash them away with liquor, and that made me feel so much worse. I hated that he had to carry such a burden because of me.

Everything was always my fault.

The shooting still haunted me, adding to the nightmares that relentlessly plagued me. Ryker was the only thing that got me through, especially since Kamden was slowly sinking into an all-too-familiar hole of despair. I needed to save him, to salvage and mend the fragments that were left of him, but how could I when I couldn't even save myself?

I didn't think anything else could flip my life upside down again, but I was wrong. So very, very wrong.

Chapter One

Kaiya

I sat up in bed, waking from a nightmare. The air was sucked from my lungs, and sobs racked my body as images of Ryker being shot and the feel of his blood all over my chest and arms assaulted me. My heart pounded furiously against my chest as I screamed through choking tears. "No! Ryker! No!"

"Ky, look at me, baby," a voice heavy with sleep urged. Firm, callused hands cupped my face and forced me to look into mocha-colored eyes filled with worry. *Ryker.*

Sighing in relief, tears trickled down my fevered cheeks as I clasped my hands over his. His thumbs moved beneath my palms as he stroked my skin. "Just another nightmare, Warrior. I'm right here. I'm not going anywhere."

My grip tightened on his inked hands as my eyes ran over his face. My voice was weak and hoarse when I spoke. "It always feels so real."

He brought his lips to my forehead and pressed a soft kiss there. My eyes closed as I enjoyed the tingle he still sent through me. I felt his breath against my face as he sighed, his voice softening with his reply, "I know, baby. I know."

Even though a couple of months had passed, we both still had nightmares about the shooting. When we stayed the night in my own apartment, Kamden often woke us with his or vice versa. I didn't know when or if they would ever stop, but I hoped they eventually would. I didn't want to have nightmares for the rest of my life.

"Same one?" Ryker asked, brushing his lips across my skin again. His hands moved from my face down to my shoulders. My eyes opened and locked on his as he began to softly rub up and down my arms.

I swallowed deeply and cleared my throat. My voice was clogged with ragged emotion. "Yeah."

An exact replay of the events of that night had become my worst nightmare—worse than the ones of Kaleb molesting me over the years, worse than the ones of the *incident.* Seeing Ryker get shot was unbearable, and having to relive it over and over again was agonizing.

My eyes fell to his chest. Bringing my hands up, I placed one over his heart and delicately traced over his scar with my fingers.

I still can't believe how close I was to losing him.

Another flood of tears burned my eyes, but I forced them back.

There's no reason to cry. Ryker's still here. He's still with you. Stop being weak.

Leaning in, I pressed my lips to his scar, letting them linger on his skin before pulling back and looking up at him.

Ryker cupped the back of my head and gently pulled my face to his.

My eyes fluttered shut, my stomach tightening as his mouth met mine. Every touch filled me with bliss, bringing me a happiness I still couldn't believe I had. Ryker was my remedy, the only one capable of washing away the taint from my nightmares, the only one able to take away the pain.

When our lips parted, he lay his forehead against mine. "I love you, Warrior."

My heart warmed, chasing away the ugly, biting cold that crept in from the nightmare.

I don't think I'll ever get tired of hearing him say that.

My response was automatic, instinctive because of how much I felt for him, how real it was. "I love you, too."

Ryker lay us back down and enveloped me in his arms. Draping my leg over his, I nestled into him and released a sigh of contentment. Being like that, warm in his embrace in bed, was my favorite place to be—my own personal heaven from the hell in my mind, keeping my demons at bay.

I yawned as my eyes became heavy. Ryker's fingers softly ran through my hair, and it didn't take long for him to lull me back to sleep.

I loved waking up in Ryker's arms. Even though I absolutely loathed mornings, seeing his handsome face the moment I woke up always made me smile.

He stirred, opening one eye as he gruffly murmured, "Mornin', beautiful."

The grin I had spread wider, making my cheeks feel tight. "Morning, baby."

Pulling me to him, he pressed his lips to mine. I had stopped trying to fight him on that, even though I was mortified by my morning breath. I thought it was sweet that kissing me was still the first thing he wanted to do when he woke up.

We had spent the night at his apartment, where we usually stayed on the weekends. I couldn't be at mine when Kamden drowned himself in alcohol, which was how he spent his Friday and Saturday nights. I had tried to stop him multiple times, but it only escalated things, especially with Ryker being so protective over me. I didn't want to watch the two men that I loved fight, so I let Kamden be—at least for the time being.

I hated watching Kamden burrow himself deeper into his hole. Even though therapy had helped in the beginning, he was slowly sinking into an all-consuming depression. I prayed I could bring him out of it, but I wasn't sure if I'd be able to. I'd still be buried in mine if it wasn't for Ryker.

The brush of his knuckles down my cheek brought me out of my thoughts. "Ready for breakfast?"

"Yeah. I want to check on Kamden first, though." Turning away from him, I reached for my phone on the nightstand. I quickly dialed Kamden's number, but his phone went straight to voicemail.

Damn it.

I pulled the phone away from my ear before getting out of bed. "Went straight to his voicemail. I'm going to go over there and make sure he's okay."

Ryker threw the covers off and slid to the edge of the mattress. "I'll go pick something up." He stood and walked toward me, then wrapped his muscular arms around my waist. My hands wound around his neck as he dipped his head to kiss me again. When he pulled away, I was left in a haze from his kiss, as usual.

God, those lips.

Ryker smirked knowingly when our eyes met. He made me feel like a giddy school girl, even after being together for so many months, which may not have been long for most, but was sort of a record for us. Neither of us were relationship people, and I definitely never thought I would have a love like the one Ryker and I shared. Some things still took some getting used to at times.

I stepped around him, my face heating as I headed for the bathroom. I could hear him chuckling softly as he followed behind me, apparently amused by his effect on me.

When we finished getting ready, Ryker and I left his apartment together. My place was only the next building over, so I walked there while he hopped in his truck and drove out of the parking lot.

I thought moving out of our old complex would help, but it didn't seem like it was. Kamden was still having trouble coping with killing Kaleb, no matter what I said or did. He had even started skipping his therapy sessions.

When I reached my apartment, I slid my key into the lock and twisted the knob. Anxiety knotted my stomach when I entered, worry for Kamden eating at me since he hadn't answered my phone call. "Kam?"

He didn't answer.

Probably passed out, wasted.

I made my way to his room, and the door was wide open. Kamden lay face down, wearing a muscle shirt and a pair of gym shorts. A half-empty bottle of Jack was tipped over on the floor beside the bed. Kamden's arm dangled over the side of the mattress next to it. "Kam?" I slowly crept toward him before sitting beside him.

No response again.

His mouth was wide open and drool dampened the pillowcase.

I gently shook him on the shoulder, but he didn't stir. I jostled him more forcefully, making his upper body shake. He grumbled obscenities and moved slightly, but didn't wake up. I continued to shake him, and he finally jerked awake, sitting up and roughly grabbing me by the forearm.

"Kam! It's just me—it's Kaiya!" My heart pounded as I attempted to pry my arm from his grasp, pulling at his fingers with my own. He squeezed my arm so tightly that I knew I was going to have bruises.

His glazed, bloodshot eyes darted over me before he let go. "Sorry," he muttered, rubbing his hands over his face. I couldn't help but notice his stubble—it looked like he hadn't shaved in days.

I pulled my arm to my chest protectively and rubbed it with my other hand. Glancing down, I could see bruises from Kamden's fingertips already forming.

Shit. Ryker's going to be pissed.

When I looked back up at Kamden, he had his elbows on his knees, cradling his head in his hands. His eyes were closed, and his face was scrunched in discomfort.

"Let me get you some water," I said as I stood. I walked to the kitchen and grabbed a water bottle out of the refrigerator before returning back to Kamden, who was still in the same position.

Sitting back down next to him, I nudged his arm with the water bottle and handed it to him. He took several slow sips before laying back on the bed and groaning.

"You need to stop drinking so much, Kam. I'm worried about you."

"Don't worry about me. I'm fine," he mumbled, draping his arm over his eyes.

I scoffed. "You are not fine. Look at you!" I gestured at him with my hands, even though he couldn't see me.

"Don't fucking start, Ky," he growled in a combination of anger and irritation.

We'd had this conversation before, and I usually let it go because one, I was a coward, and two, I didn't want to fight with him. He had always been there for me, and I wanted to give him his space and let him cope in his own way like he had let me. But this was getting out of hand. "Kam, please talk to me. Don't shut me out."

"Oh, so you can do it to me, but I can't do it to you?" He sat up abruptly and glared at me before pointing his finger in my face. "You're such a fucking hypocrite, Ky."

I flinched, hating the way his words cut through me and impaled my heart. My eyes watered as I meekly replied, "Kam, I-"

He looked away from me, avoiding my gaze. "I think you should go."

I was about to do as he said, but the stubborn side of me said fuck that. I swiped the few tears that had fallen down my cheeks and crossed my arms over my chest. "No."

Kamden's head snapped to me, and his nostrils flared. "Get out, Kaiya."

He may not have been yelling, but there was no mistaking the ire in his low tone. He was pissed off—really pissed off.

I swallowed the lump in my throat, and held my ground, maintaining eye contact as I repeated, "No."

We stared at each other for what felt like forever until he finally sighed and dropped his head, grumbling under his breath.

Uncrossing my arms, I reached one hand toward him and linked our fingers together. "I'm here for you, Kam."

After several seconds, he finally squeezed my hand back, but remained silent, almost as if internally debating whether or not to confide in me.

"Talk to me." My tone was pleading, practically begging him to open up.

"I'm tired of talking—that's all the therapist wants me to do is talk, talk, talk. And for what?" He thrust our joined hands and his other arm forward as he spoke, the volume of his voice increasing with every word. "She doesn't understand shit. She doesn't know our family. She doesn't know what we went through, what you went through, so what's the fucking point?"

He was right—that's why I never went to therapy. A psychiatrist would never understand what I had experienced. But Kam and I had endured everything together and understood what the other had gone through.

"What if I go with you? Would that help?" I spontaneously spoke, then immediately regretted it.

Shit, why did I say that?

He brought his eyes up to mine, and the hope that lay beneath the drunken haze in them tightened my chest. I knew I'd do anything to help him if that glimmer meant I was getting my brother back.

"You'd do that for me?" Even his tone was brighter, optimistic.

Yeah, I'm fucked.

I smiled softly. "Yeah, I would." I squeezed his hand tighter.

"You hate therapists," he remarked with a chuckle.

"I do," I admitted with a shrug. "But I love you. And I'd do anything to help you."

My words caused something amazing to happen—Kamden smiled. The first real one I'd seen since the shooting. Months had gone by since I'd seen his beautiful smile, the one that had gotten me through so many rough times. The one I missed seeing every day.

"I love you too, *sorella."* Pulling me to him, he embraced me in a hug. I scooted closer on the bed and wrapped my arms around his waist. He smelt like liquor and sweat, but I didn't care. I was taking another step to getting my brother back.

"We'll get through this," I promised.

I wasn't going to fail Kamden, just like he'd never failed me over the years.

Chapter Two

Ryker

Push through the pain—don't be a pussy!

My chest felt as though it was going to rip apart from the aching tension in the muscles around my scar and up into my shoulder. Even though I went to physical therapy for months following the shooting, I still had pain when I did certain exercises—like the one I was doing.

Grunting through it, I did a couple more reps before pushing the bar up and racking it. Sweat coated my skin as I sat up and reached for my water. I chugged back what was left in the bottle as I got up and headed for the water fountain.

After refilling my bottle, I headed back to my bench and grabbed the dumbbells next to my gym bag. I should've picked a lighter weight for my right arm, but that stubborn side of me couldn't swallow his pride. Fifties weren't that heavy anyway.

Settling back on the bench, I planted my feet, then extended my arms out in front of me. Keeping them straight, I brought them out to the sides before bringing them back to their starting position.

I completed a few reps before I cramped up. I dropped both weights, sending them clanging to the floor before sitting up and reaching for my chest.

Fuck, fuck, fuck!

Hissing in pain, I stretched out my right arm and rubbed the muscle above my scar with my other hand. I clenched and unclenched my fist as I waited for the pain to subside.

Once it finally did, I rotated my shoulder several times to try and alleviate the lingering ache and tightness. Grabbing my towel, I wiped the sweat from my face and angrily stood. Frustration flooded me as I snatched my bag off the ground and headed for the kickboxing room.

You're stronger than this. What the fuck is your problem?

I dropped my shit on the floor once I entered the studio. I didn't even bother getting gloves; I still had wraps around my hands from that lame excuse for a workout.

I chose one of the heavier bags and started doing combinations, ignoring the tension in the right side of my chest and shoulder. I put most of my power into my punches with my left arm and my kicks.

I didn't stop until my lungs screamed for air. Both my arms burned as I walked to grab the water bottle I'd dropped next to my bag. I chugged the liquid back, drinking until nothing was left.

Most of my anger had been taken out on the bag, but there was still some lingering frustration as I caught my breath. I needed to compose myself before my next training session, which was in fifteen minutes.

My phone sounded with a text. I swiped my password and the message from Kaiya automatically popped up. My lips curved into a smile as I read her text:

Warrior: Miss you <3

As I typed back my response, I felt the majority of my anger lifting from just thinking about Kaiya.

Me: Miss you too baby

After sending the text, I went back to my office to ice down my injury—or handicap—as I thought of it. The physical therapists said those muscles might never be the same again, but I was determined to prove them wrong.

I was still a little irritated for the rest of the day until Kaiya walked into the kickboxing studio for class. The remaining frustration weighing me down evaporated when I saw her beautiful face and bright, blue eyes.

My Warrior.

She was the first one there, as usual. It had become a routine for Kaiya to get there early so we could talk about our day and have some time to ourselves before class started. When we reached each other, I wrapped my arms around her waist, lifting her feet off the ground as I kissed her.

"How was your day?" I asked when I set her back down.

"Swamped—we have three new projects that we just started working on this week. How about you?"

I shrugged. "It was okay."

She gave me a knowing look, quirking up one eyebrow and crossing her arms over her chest. "Okay?"

I chuckled and shook my head. "Nothing gets past you, huh?"

"Nope, now tell me," she demanded, trying to keep a stern, straight face as a smile fought its way through.

"Nothing big—I just cramped up during my workout. Bothered me for most of the day."

Her eyes went to my chest where my scar was, and her forehead creased in concern. "Are you sure you're okay? Maybe you should go back to the physical therapist."

I definitely did not want to go back to therapy. They'd limit my workouts, and I was already going easy to begin with. Well, for me, at least. "I'm fine. It was more annoying than anything."

That was a lie—my chest and shoulder hurt from earlier; they always did. The bullet had ripped through muscles around my shoulder blade in the back, as well as nerves in my chest that connected up to the top of my shoulder. There was always a dull, constant pain that never went away.

She brought her worried eyes up to mine and linked our fingers together. "Please be careful, baby."

The look she was giving me, combined with the pleading tone of her voice, made me feel terrible. Kaiya was my weakness.

Maybe I should take it easy.

Gently squeezing her hands, I stroked her smooth skin with my thumbs. "I will."

It had only been a couple of weeks since physical therapy had ended and I'd started working out again. Kaiya was apprehensive about the idea, afraid I would injure myself more. I told her not to worry, but that was like telling her not to breathe.

Kaiya's lips curved up slightly, and that small smile twisted up my insides.

Damn, the things she does to me.

I smiled back before leaning down and pressing a kiss to her forehead. My nose brushed her silky hair, and I breathed in her scent before pulling away. She always smelt so good. Students began coming in then, so Ky and I got ready for class. I liked that she still came, even though Kaleb wasn't a threat to her anymore. I wanted her to be able to defend herself in case something happened and I wasn't around. Anything could happen, especially with all the fucked up people in the world. Plus, getting to touch her during the techniques was an added bonus; I couldn't get enough of her.

Once we finished the kickboxing segment, we went straight into self-defense techniques. The students had mentioned in the previous class that they wanted to practice defending against forward punch attacks. "Sometimes, attackers don't try to grab you or subdue you first. Instead they come out swinging. Today, we're going to focus on counters to this type of assault."

After modeling with one of the other instructors, Mark, I had the class split up into their pairs. Kaiya and I went to our usual spot on the mat to get started. She got in her defensive stance and gave me a playful grin as she awaited my instructions. I smiled as I thought of how much progress she'd made since that very first class, when she'd been so tense and nervous. My warrior had come so far. "Ready, baby?"

Her grin spread. "You know it."

I laughed. "Okay, throw a straight punch while coming toward me." Once she did as I instructed, I moved closer to her while simultaneously shifting to face the arm she used to punch with, blocking the incoming hit with both of my arms. "Instinct tells us to back away from an attack, but the best thing to do in this situation is to get in close."

Kaiya's eyebrows furrowed in confusion. She looked so cute when she made that face. "Why?"

"An attacker isn't going to throw just one punch—they'll keep throwing them as they advance on you, and eventually, they will hit you. So you need to disable them before they land one."

She nodded. "Okay. What do you do from here?"

"Grip their forearm with your outside hand, keeping them close to you. Then using your other arm, throw a back elbow to their face and follow it with a forward elbow on the opposite cheek."

I softly modeled each move, careful not to hurt Kaiya. "Grip their shoulder and knee them in the groin before throwing a side kick to the knee closest to you. If the groin hit didn't put them down for the count, the side kick definitely will."

After releasing her, I walked Kaiya through the steps and had her practice a few times before moving on to a slight variation for if she was backed into a wall or car.

"Many attacks happen in parking lots at night. If someone ever pins you to a car and rears back to punch you, you can still use this same technique."

Kaiya quirked up a brow in intrigue. "Really?"

I smiled at her. "Really. I actually think it's more effective. A car can help you do more damage to the asshole attacking you."

I led her to the padded side of the room we used for wall defense techniques. I gently backed her against it as I explained, "Typically, an attacker will push you into a car or wall if one is around, wanting to trap you." Caging her face between my forearms, I leaned in closer to her. "As in every attack, you can't panic, which is what most people do when cornered like this."

Kaiya wasn't afraid of me, but I knew my proximity would kick her heart rate up, just like it did mine. Her eyes focused on my lips, which curved up as I closed the distance between us and kissed her.

Even though I wanted to do more—much more—I broke the kiss and moved back slightly. Kaiya's face reddened as she glanced around, checking if anyone saw us before she met my eyes and gave me a shy smile. I loved that I made her get flustered like that.

"Aren't you supposed to be teaching me something?" she questioned playfully, looking up at me coyly and batting her eyelashes.

"Yeah, but I can't when you keep distracting me," I teased.

Her eyebrows shot up. "Me? I'm not even doing anything."

"Yeah, you are." My eyes ran up and down her body.

Damn, she's so hot. Especially in those tight shorts.

I leaned to the side and craned my head to get a glimpse of her ass.

Fuck, that ass.

Kaiya cleared her throat and stifled a laugh. "Excuse me, but we don't have all night. I'd really like to learn this routine."

This girl.

I straightened and chuckled. "Fine—let's get back to business. After the attacker pushes you against the car, they'll probably hold you there by choking you, pressing down on your chest, or gripping onto your clothes. And they're going to be all up in your space. Remember, you can't panic."

Flattening my hand over her chest, I softly pushed her back into the wall. Then, I brought my other arm back, readying to punch. "When I throw the punch, do the same thing I taught you earlier—block it with both arms."

I slowly threw the punch, and Kaiya turned to block it with her arms. "Good, now grip my forearm and throw the back elbow. I want you to use the momentum of the strike to force me into the wall, pinning me there with your forearm on my throat."

Once Kaiya had me in that position, I continued. My voice was garbled by her arm on my throat. "Now you can throw some elbows, get some knees to the groin, or grab their head and slam it into the car."

We practiced a few more times before I brought the group back together. "I hoped you learned something that will be able to help you if you're ever put in a situation like this. There are several techniques for a straight punch attack, but I felt this was the easiest and most effective. We'll learn others in the future. Any questions?"

I scanned over the class—everyone's faces had a sheen of sweat but held that look of fulfillment from having a good workout. No one raised their hand or commented, so I dismissed the class.

After Kaiya helped me lock up, we headed back to my apartment. I had gotten stuck at a light on the way, so Kaiya's car was parked in her normal spot when I pulled in. We both had keys to the other's apartment, so she was probably already inside.

When I walked in, I threw my keys on the table and shut the door. "Ky?" I called out as I kicked off my shoes.

She didn't answer, but as I went down the hallway towards my room, I could hear water running. A smirk curved over my lips as I thought of Kaiya naked and wet in my shower.

As I entered the bathroom, my eyes went straight to her. Her back was to me as she rinsed her long, dark hair, and water dripped off every inch of her flawless skin. My gaze roamed lower to her sweet ass as I pulled off my muscle shirt and gym shorts.

When I opened the shower door, she turned and gasped, placing a hand over her heart. "Oh my God, Ryker! You scared me!"

Grabbing her hand, I chuckled. "Sorry, baby." I kissed her palm before pulling her into me, immersing myself in the stream of water and pressing our naked bodies together.

Her hands glided up to my shoulders as I nuzzled into the curve of her neck. Gripping her ass, I nipped at her collarbone while lifting her up. Her legs wrapped around me automatically as I backed her into the tile wall.

Kaiya's fingers knotted in my hair as our mouths crashed together. Her lips parted against mine as my tongue slipped inside, finding hers instantly and tangling together. "Fuck, you taste so good. I've wanted to taste you all night."

Kaiya moaned in my mouth as my hands roamed over her wet skin before finding her tits. I played with one of her nipples, squeezing and pulling it, making her whimper louder. "You like that, baby?" I bit her bottom lip before sucking it into my mouth.

"God, yes." Her legs tightened around my hips, and she ground herself against me.

I pushed my cock harder against her clit, making her cry out again. "You want my dick inside you?"

"Yes! Fuck me now, Ryker." Her tone was desperate with lust.

I trailed one of my hands down her stomach between us before grabbing my cock and guiding it to her pussy.

Fuck, she's so wet already.

Teasing her, I rubbed against her and slipped the tip of my dick inside her sweetness before pulling it out.

Kaiya bit my lip when I put just the head of my cock in again. I circled the rim of her pussy, causing her to bite down harder and moan. "Ryker," she breathlessly pleaded as she pulled me closer to her.

I couldn't help myself when she sounded like that—her need and want for me evident in every noise she made. I thrust myself inside, filling her completely as we both groaned out in pleasure.

The water rained down on us as I hammered Kaiya against the tile. My mouth found her nipple, and I toyed with it with my tongue ring as I continued to pound into her. She gripped my hair as I savored her, sucking her tit as her sweet pussy hugged my dick.

She feels so good… fucking perfect.

Kaiya's nails dug into my head as she arched into me. My hands caressed her soft flesh as I drove deeper inside her. I was close to coming, and by the look on her face, she was too.

Her eyes were closed as she bit down on that full, bottom lip.

Fuck, she's so sexy.

Our wet skin slapped together as I increased my pace, thrusting harder into her, bringing us both to the brink.

I wanted to taste her as I made her come, capture the sounds of bliss she made because of me. I grabbed her face and crushed her lips with mine, opening her mouth with my tongue and slipping it inside.

Fuck, so good.

After a few more thrusts, Kaiya cried out, and her pussy tightened around me. I followed, coming inside her as she trembled against me.

Holding Kaiya up, I pressed kisses along her neck as we caught our breath. "I love you," I murmured against her skin.

Turning her head, she grazed her lips against mine. "I love you, too."

Some of her hair clung to her face as she leaned her head against the wall. I pushed the drenched strands back before kissing her again.

Kaiya's legs had loosened, but as our kiss deepened, she tightened them around me again. My dick started to harden inside her.

Damn, she drives me fucking crazy.

I slowly pumped my cock in and out of her, growling against her lips. "You want more, baby? You want me to fuck you again?"

She sucked my tongue into her mouth. Hard. "Yes, please fuck me," she loudly moaned.

I smirked and roughly thrust into her, eliciting a gasp of pleasure from her swollen lips. We stayed there in the shower until long after the water ran cold.

Chapter Three

Kaiya

I awoke with a satisfied smile on my face, even though the annoying blaring of my phone's alarm assaulted my eardrums. Last night in the shower with Ryker was pure heaven. As I reached for my phone, Ryker shifted behind me and captured me in his arms. I barely grabbed my cell before he pulled me back into him and tented the covers around us.

I turned off the alarm and shifted to face him. He gave me a sleepy smile, and his eyes were still half-lidded in sleep. "Mornin, beautiful."

He leaned in and pressed his full lips against mine. After a few seconds, I groaned, "I need to get ready for work." If we didn't stop now, I'd definitely be late.

He grunted but didn't protest. If it were up to him, we would have stayed in bed until noon every day. I would much rather do that, but I'd already taken enough time off work after the shooting.

I gave Ryker another quick kiss and scooted to the edge. He reached for me, then dragged me back into him. I giggled, able to easily fall back into his loving embrace. "I have to get ready," I said, giving him my best responsible stare down.

"Fine, babe. I'll lay back here and watch your sweet ass wiggle its way to the bathroom." He propped his head on his arm and watched me. I couldn't help but smile the entire way.

I turned into the bathroom and my smile vanished as my head darted away from the mirror. Although Kaleb was gone, I saw him whenever I looked at myself. His face haunted me, and I feared it always would. How could I forget it when it was a replica of mine?

After getting ready, I went to say goodbye to Ryker, who had fallen back asleep. His arms were wrapped around my pillow, and his face was buried in it. Butterflies fluttered in my stomach at the endearing sight, and I smiled as I leaned down and kissed his cheek. "I love you," I whispered, not wanting to wake him.

"Love you, too," he murmured in his sleep, not opening his eyes. I quietly walked out of the room, grabbing my purse and keys from the table before exiting the apartment and heading to work.

Work dragged on and on every day since I'd returned about a month ago. I'd gotten spoiled, spending most of the day with Ryker, sleeping in late every morning, and having sex for most of the day in each room of both of our apartments. My phone vibrated next to my keyboard. I expected a text from Ryker when I entered my password, but instead, there was a message from a unknown number. *Weird.*

Unknown: I'd be careful if I were you bitch

I stared at my phone in shock, my eyes glued to the screen for several seconds before warily glancing around. My heart pounded as a million thoughts ran through my head.

What the fuck? Is this some sort of joke? Who would've sent this?

My instincts told me to call Ryker, but I didn't want him to overreact. It was probably some prank. I was about to delete the text, but decided to keep it just in case I got another one.

It's probably nothing, though.

I placed my phone back on my desk and tried to refocus on work, but now I felt like I was being watched.

Stop being paranoid, Ky. Someone is just fucking around with you.

After a few minutes of inputting figures into a spreadsheet, my phone buzzed again. My eyes darted to my phone, and I hesitantly reached for it before stilling my hand over it.

Oh God, get a grip, Kaiya.

I snatched my phone from the desk and swiped the screen. Another text message popped up on the screen, and thankfully it was from Kamden.

Kam: Therapy at 4 today

Shit! I totally forgot!

I normally got off work at four, so I'd have to leave about half an hour earlier to make it to the appointment on time. I typed a quick email to my boss to let him know, then replied back to Kamden.

Me: K see you there :)

Although I was dreading the appointment, I was also somewhat excited. I'd been watching Kamden sink deeper and deeper into the quicksand of depression for months, helpless to stop it. I was ready to stop being weak and help my brother in whatever way possible, and I prayed that going to therapy with him would do just that.

My stomach was jumbled in thick, tight knots as Kamden and I sat in the waiting room of the psychiatrist's office. Paintings of the Boston Harbor, boats, and sunsets hung on the cream-colored walls and a cliché potted fern sat in the corner of the room.

My leg shook nervously as I bit my nails. Just thinking about discussing Kaleb and my past made me sick.

I can't do this. I can't do this.

My phone chimed, interrupting my anxious thoughts, and I dug in my purse looking for it. When I swiped the screen, a text from Ryker popped up.

Ryker: Proud of you :) don't be nervous you'll be fine I love you Warrior

My stomach tightened for a different reason, and a small smile tugged at my lips. I glanced over at Kamden, who had his head leaned back against the wall. Bags laced his closed eyes, making them look sunken in. Stubble dusted the pale skin of his jaw, and I could tell that he'd lost some weight from his cheeks and neck.

My heart clenched as I appraised him—still the familiar face of my brother, yet so different. Aged. Sadder. Dulled. The vibrancy that his smile normally brought was gone.

Looking back at my phone, I took a deep breath and typed back my reply to Ryker.

Me: Thank you I needed that :) I love you too <3

The door next to the receptionist's window opened, causing Kamden to abruptly sit up. The woman who had checked us in stood in the doorway, smiling politely at us. "Kamden Marlow?"

We both got up and walked toward her. She led us to another room with a huge bookshelf, brown leather couch and matching armchair. More paintings of the harbor, boats, and seaside adorned the walls, continuing the ocean theme from the waiting room. Blue and tan pillows decorated the sofa, adding some color to the neutral decor of the office.

"Dr. Lowell will be with you shortly," the receptionist stated as she exited the room and shut the door.

I rounded the couch and sat down. Kamden sat on my right side and picked up a magazine from the coffee table in front of us.

He flipped through it aimlessly as I played a word scramble game on my phone, trying not to focus on where I was sitting at that very moment. I couldn't let my anxiety consume me, not when Kam was depending on me.

About five minutes passed when the psychiatrist walked in, but it felt like hours to me. I was ready to bust out of my skin—I hated therapists

Dr. Lowell looked to be in her forties, with dirty blonde hair pulled back in a low bun. She wore a basic, black business suit with coordinating pumps. Carrying a large legal pad, she smiled as she approached us.

We both stood as she stuck her hand out toward me. "Nice to meet you—you must be Kaiya. Kamden has told me so much about you," she said warmly.

Great.

I looked at my brother out of the corner of my eye. I could have sworn I saw him smirk, but it vanished as quickly as it had appeared.

Dr. Lowell turned her attention to Kam. "Good to see you again, Kamden. Please sit." She gestured to the couch and waited for us to sit before she turned and sat in the armchair directly across from us. "How have you been?"

I waited for my brother to answer, hoping he would be honest and tell the doctor how he'd been struggling. But I couldn't blame him if he didn't—it would be hard for me to address my issues, also.

Kamden leaned forward and rubbed the back of his neck. He exhaled a heavy breath before speaking. "Some days are worse than others."

Dr. Lowell began writing on her note pad as she asked, "Could you elaborate on that?" "Honestly?" Kamden snorted and ran his hands over his dark, buzzed hair before slapping them down on his thighs. "I don't want to."

He was internally shutting down. I did the same thing all the time so I recognized what he was doing. I needed to be stronger for him, for both of us—to help get through the mess we were in.

I placed my hand over his and stroked over it with my thumb. "Kam," I softly urged.

He balled his hand into a fist under mine and sighed deeply. After a few seconds, he turned his palm over and linked our fingers together. Our eyes met, and I gave him an encouraging smile as I squeezed his hand.

He looked away when he spoke. "For so long, I… I wanted to kill

Kaleb for what he did to Ky. Guess I got what I wanted," he said dejectedly as he hung his head.

The room was soundless except for the scribbling of Dr. Lowell's pen on the paper. The silence constricted my chest, making it hard to breathe as I struggled to hold it together. My eyes burned from tears I knew I wouldn't be able to contain much longer. I hated that Kamden was experiencing all these horrible emotions because of me.

"At least I saved her from more abuse from him, right?" His eyes watered, and he swallowed deeply. "I wasn't able to protect her before, but I took care of that. He won't hurt her again."

"Kam." His name sounded disjointed when I spoke as tears dripped down my face. I cleared my throat, hoping my voice would be steady. "Don't blame yourself for what Kaleb did to me—it was never your fault."

He scoffed. "I was supposed to protect you, Ky—that's what big brothers do. I'm a fucking failure. And a murderer."

Rage rushed through my veins at his self-accusation. I jerked his hand, making him look up at me. "You're neither of those things. It wasn't your responsibility to protect me from Kaleb—that was Mom and Dad's job. They're the fucking failures! And you're not a murderer—you killed Kaleb in self-defense to protect us."

He held my gaze as a single tear fell from each eye down his cheeks. "Doesn't matter—I killed my own brother."

He looked away again, hanging his head in shame. No matter what I said, he never believed me. He still blamed himself. I looked to Dr. Lowell, hoping she would chime in and agree with me.

Setting her pen down, she clasped her hands together on top of the legal pad. "Kamden, you can't keep blaming yourself for this. In order to move on, you have to make peace with yourself. You can't dwell on the past."

Easier said than done, lady.

Kamden abruptly wrenched his hand away from mine and threw his arms out in front of him. "How?" he screamed. His voice boomed and was riddled with emotion. "Can you teach me? Because I've been trying to do that, and the only way I get the pain to go away is to drown myself in alcohol." His face was reddened with fury as more tears fell from his eyes. It ripped my heart apart to see him like that, to know I was one of the causes of his suffering. "What kind of person kills their own brother?"

My heart thumped wildly as my own anger took over again. Shaking my head in disagreement, I interrupted his rant to start one of my own. "Stop it, Kam! You wanna know what kind of person you are?" I moved my face to meet his eyes, but he avoided me. I raised my voice to get his attention. "Look at me!"

It took a few moments before he finally brought his gaze to mine. My hardened eyes relaxed some as I held his stare. "You're the kind of person that holds his grown sister when she has a nightmare. You're the kind of person who has held her hand through every bad time, who has never let her give up, who saved her from the hell she lived in. You're the kind of person who has sacrificed everything for her. You—" I choked through a sob before taking a deep breath and softening my voice. "You're the best kind of person there is."

Our eyes met, and his face reflected the emotions that were swarming me: hurt, fear, guilt, sorrow. All I wanted was for him to go back to the way he was before—to be my strong, stable big brother again. Even though I had Ryker, I still needed Kamden—more than he would ever understand.

Kamden silently stared at me as if knowing I had more to say. I took a shaky breath and continued pouring my heart out to him, hoping my words would bring him back from the ledge he was teetering on. "There aren't words to describe what you mean to me, Kam." I gripped both his hands in mine. "I can never repay you for saving me—from Kaleb and myself. You were there every time I needed you, and I still need you. I need my brother back."

Kamden remained silent for several seconds, then spoke so low that I could barely hear him. "I don't think I can be him again."

His words slammed into my heart, splintering some pieces of it. I squeezed Kamden's hands tighter, hoping to hold on to him in more ways than one, to tether him to me. A steady stream of tears flowed down my face as my voice cracked. "Please try, Kam. Don't give up."

He shook his head before looking up at me, scanning over my face. Pulling his hands from mine, he brought them up and wiped the tears from my cheeks with his thumbs. He gave me a small, forced smile. "I'll try, *sorella.* For you."

My lips slowly spread in a full grin as I threw my arms around Kamden's neck and hugged him tightly to me. My voice was soft but threaded with emotion. "We'll get through this, Kam. Together."

He hugged me back. "I hope so."

I knew he didn't completely believe my words, but I would prove them. I wouldn't give up until I saved Kamden from the darkness that had plagued me for so long.

As I was about to leave the psychiatrist's office, I called Nori, wanting to talk to her about the text message and everything going on with Kam. With traffic, I'd have anywhere from thirty to forty minutes until I would get home, so I had time to talk to her.

Nori's cheery voice greeted me, "Hey, girlie."

"Hey. Are you busy?" I chewed my lower lip as I sat in my car in the parking garage.

"Nah, just got home. What's up?"

I sighed and started driving. "I just got done with my first therapy session with Kamden."

Her tone peaked with curiosity and excitement. "How did that go?"

"Better than I'd expected, but we didn't talk about Kaleb much so that's probably why."

"What did you talk about then?"

Pulling out of the garage, I merged into traffic. "Kamden's issues. He blames himself for everything. He thinks he's a terrible person for killing Kaleb. He called himself a failure and a murderer."

"What?" Her voice raised with anger. "How can he think that? It was in self-defense!"

"That's what I said. But he refuses to listen—he's so stubborn," I said in irritation.

"Coming from the queen of stubbornness herself," Nori joked.

"Ha ha, very funny."

Traffic slowed to a crawl.

Ugh, it's going to take me forever to get home.

"There's something else I wanted to talk to you about."

"Oh, really? I hope it's about sex with that hot man of yours."

I laughed. "Sorry to burst your bubble but no. I got this weird text from an unknown number today."

"Weird how?"

"Hold on, I'll forward it to you real quick."

Traffic was stopped at a light, so I was able to pull up the message and send it to Nori. I put the phone back to my ear. "Just sent it."

"Okay, lemme check." She paused for a few seconds. "Creepy. Did you tell Ryker?"

I blew out a frustrated breath. "No—I don't want him to overreact. It's probably nothing, right?"

Nori didn't reply for several seconds. "Yeah, it's probably some punk teenagers or something."

"You don't sound so sure." I said as the cars in front of me moved past the intersection.

"I was just thinking about who would send something like that to you. But I think it was a onetime thing, maybe even a wrong number."

I hope so.

"Yeah, you're probably right. I just wanted to talk to someone about it."

"Well, you picked the right person. If you get another one, let me know, okay? I'm here for you."

"I know. Thank you."

We chatted for a little longer, then made plans for lunch later that week, making the drive a little bearable for a while. As I continued to fight traffic on the way home, I thought about the events of the day, hoping that everything would turn out all right.

Chapter Four

Ryker

Kaiya felt lifeless in my arms.

Please, God no.

I slumped to my knees, cradling her to me as the warmth of her blood soaked through my shirt and coated my arms. My fingers smeared blood over her fair skin as I framed her face in my hands. "Open your eyes, Warrior! Damn it, open your eyes!"

My entire world crumbled down on me as my life lay, dying in my arms, slowly slipping away from me. "Kaiya! Don't do this to me, baby! Come back to me!" My voice was hoarse and full of desperation—desperation I'd never experienced before.

Nothing. No movement, no sound. Was my heart even beating anymore? How could it when it was lying dead in my arms?

The hollow pain inside me seeped into the depths of my soul, searing me with its agony. I buried my face in Kaiya's neck and sobbed. "No! Not her! Take me instead!"

"Kaiya!" I yelled as I sat up in bed. I was covered in sweat as I fought to regain my breath. My heart pounded furiously as I turned my head and glanced over at a sleeping Kaiya.

Just another dream. Thank God.

Laying back down, I propped myself on my elbow and watched Kaiya sleep. Her cheek was on her bicep as she slept facing me. Some hair had fallen into her face, and her lips were slightly parted. *My beautiful Warrior.*

Watching her sleep helped calm me down when I had nightmares. I needed to see her chest rise with breath, see that her heart was beating. Just like hers, my nightmares felt so real; too real.

I brushed the hair back out of Kaiya's face and kissed her forehead softly. She mumbled a sound of contentment and stirred slightly, but didn't wake up. I watched her for a few more minutes before getting out of bed.

Needing air, I went out on the balcony and leaned against the railing. I took a deep breath, enjoying the feel of the crisp, fall air against my heated skin. Images of the nightmare played in my head, and I couldn't believe how much fear a dream could make me feel.

I shook the thoughts from my head, not wanting to think about Kaiya dying. I tried to focus on something else, and my mind veered to Ethan, yet another thing tormenting me.

Normally, I would get pissed off that I even thought of him, but after seeing Kaiya trying to help Kamden over the past few months, I wondered if I should try to make amends with my own brother. Technically, he was the only family I had left.

Before our parents had died, Ethan and I had been close. He was two years older than me, and we both had been on the football, lacrosse, and wrestling teams together throughout junior high and high school.

After the accident, everything had changed. Ethan and I had trouble coping with the loss of Mom and Dad, and when Ethan had turned eighteen a few months after, he left for college and all but disappeared.

I thought I reminded him too much of what he lost. I resembled my dad, who had been our role model since we were little. He would do anything and everything to help us succeed, and had always been there when we'd needed him. Both of our parents had been. Their death left a hole neither of us knew how to fill.

I thought that had changed when I'd left for college. I'd followed Ethan to Boston University, where we both had received scholarships for lacrosse. Our parents' life insurance had helped with the rest of the costs, and Ethan and I were able to get an apartment off campus. Everything seemed to be going back to the way things had been between us, but I'd been wrong.

I had met Molly in my Biology class. She had blonde hair and green eyes, and half the male population at our school was after her. So naturally, I'd wanted her. I'd made it my mission to make her mine.

It had only taken a few weeks before I succeeded—she hadn't given me a challenge like Kaiya had when I pursued her. Looking back, I doubted that she was ever mine to begin with. She wouldn't have cheated with my brother if she had been.

I'd been stupid for not seeing it. Maybe I'd wanted so badly to fill the void from my parents that I'd ignored the signs—the way they snuck glances at each other, how I'd come home sometimes and Molly was already there, how I wasn't able to get a hold of them at times. Plus, I never thought that Ethan would do something like that to me.

After their betrayal, I'd sworn that I'd never let another person in. But Kaiya changed that—she made me feel things I'd never felt before, and showed me what love really was. But deep down, I sometimes wondered— if my own brother was able to hurt me like that, would Kaiya do the same one day?

The sound of the sliding glass door interrupted my thoughts. I looked over my shoulder to see Kaiya, half-asleep trudging toward me. She had her arms wrapped around herself and rubbed her hands up and down her skin. "What are you doing out here, baby?" she mumbled. I turned to face her. Even with her hair all messy from sleeping and no makeup, she was the most gorgeous thing I'd ever seen. I smiled warmly and leaned back against the railing as she pressed against me.

Laying her head on my chest, she wound her arms around me and exhaled.

I pushed a strand of hair behind her ear and kissed the top of her head. Inhaling the sweet smell of her hair, I closed my eyes. "Just needed some air—had a nightmare."

"You should've woken me up. You're always there for me with mine. I wanna be there for yours, too." She propped her chin on my chest to look up at me.

"Okay, Warrior, next time I'll wake you." I chuckled as I looked down at her. I loved holding her, feeling her body warmth with life, not cold with death like in my nightmare.

"Is something else bothering you? You seemed to be deep in thought when I came outside."

I debated for a few seconds before sighing. "I was thinking about Ethan."

Kaiya lifted her head off my chest and pulled back to look at me better. Her face became lined with concern. "What about? Did he call again?"

I shook my head. "No, he didn't call. I was just thinking about you and Kamden, and that maybe I should try to make things right with Ethan."

"Is that what you want?"

"I don't know." I shrugged. "He's the only family I have left, but I'm not sure if I can forgive him for what he did. Even though I have you, and don't care about Molly anymore, he still betrayed me."

Kaiya nodded in understanding. "Whatever you choose to do, I'll support you."

Smiling, I leaned down to kiss her. "Thank you."

A cold breeze blew past us, and Kaiya's skin raised with goose bumps as she shivered. "Let's go back inside. Warm you back up," I said, backing her toward the open sliding door.

Once we were back in bed, I pulled Kaiya into me, bringing her leg over mine and leaving little space between our bodies. I lowered my head to her chest before kissing her scar, just like I did every night. I never wanted to forget its importance or what it signified. I never wanted to take for granted the gift I'd been given. "I love you, Warrior," I whispered against the marred, yet still beautiful skin.

She brought my face up to hers and brushed her lips over mine. "I love you, too."

Kaiya snuggled into me, laying her head on the inside of my bicep and keeping her leg draped over mine. She fell back asleep almost instantly, but thoughts of the shooting and Ethan kept me awake. My mind wouldn't turn off.

I closed my eyes, and lay my head against Kaiya's, trying to shut my brain down. I focused on the sound of her breathing next to me, the smell of her hair, and the feel of her body tangled up with mine, blocking out everything else.

I felt my body relax and my eyes become heavier. Kaiya was my drug, giving me exactly what I needed when I needed it. Sleep finally found me, pulling me under its dark veil.

Chapter Five

Kaiya

A couple weeks had passed before I received another text from an unknown number. I had just arrived at work when my phone buzzed in my purse—I hadn't even had the chance to take it out yet.

Unknown: I'm coming for you

The familiar feeling of fear lacing my veins rushed over me.

Was this text from the same person as last time? Who is it? What should I do?

All the questions ran through my head and combined with my fear and anxiety, making me nauseous. I sped out of my office to the bathroom down the hall, hoping I would make it in time before I threw up.

Bursting through the door of the women's restroom, I darted into the nearest stall and proceeded to vomit my breakfast into the toilet.

Gross. I hate throwing up.

I rinsed my mouth out and splashed some water on my face. Catching a glimpse of myself in the mirror, I thought of Kaleb. I felt sick again as my heart pounded, my anxiety increasing the longer he lingered in my mind.

Closing my eyes, I took a few deep breaths to dispel the queasiness assaulting my stomach and calm my nerves.

Kaleb's gone. Those texts are just some prank. You're safe.

When I composed myself, I headed back to my office. I grabbed some gum from my purse so I wouldn't be stuck with vomit breath for the rest of the day.

As I sat in my office chair, my hands trembled slightly. I clenched them tightly to stop the shaking, but my nerves were shot. There was no denying that I was starting to get scared. I grabbed my phone and forwarded the text to Nori.

Me: FWD: I'm coming for you

Me: Got this a few minutes ago

A few seconds later, she messaged me back.

Nori: WTF Who do you think it's from?

I bit my bottom lip and typed my response.

Me: Idk do you think I should tell Ryker?

Nori: I would do you think it's your mom?

I furrowed my brow.

Could it be her? Would she really sink this low?

I hoped the answer was no—that deep down, my mom still loved me, even if it was just a tiny bit.

I was so excited. I'd just gotten my grade for a huge science project that took me weeks to work on, and I couldn't wait to show Mom and Dad.

At dinner that night, I waited until everyone had plated their food before I brought it up. "You know that project I've been working on? For my biology class?""

What about it, sweetheart?" Dad responded as he picked at his food. He always seemed to be somewhere else, not really with us.

A smile spread over my face as I excitedly replied, "Well, we got our grades, and I got an A! I was so—"

"That's nice, Kaiya," Mom interrupted. Her tone was dismissive and

uninterested. "How was your day, Kaleb?" She asked brightly, turning her attention to him.

My head hung as I focused on my plate, trying not to cry. Mom never cared about me. She was only concerned about Kaleb and Kamden.

I always tried to sit between Kamden and Dad so I wouldn't have to be near Kaleb. Kamden nudged me and leaned in closer, giving me a beaming grin. "Proud of you, sorella. *Great job."*

A small smile tugged at my lips.

At least someone cares.

Kamden asked me more questions about my day, and I ignored Kaleb and Mom for the rest of dinner.

Maybe she never loved me—she never seemed to care. I sighed and focused back on my phone, dispelling the memory of my mom to type my reply.

Me: Idk maybe

My head hurt thinking about the whole situation. I put my phone down on my desk and pinched the bridge of my nose.

Who would want to do this to me?

I thought about my mom again. We'd never been close, but I was still her daughter. Plus, she didn't have my number, and I knew Kam wouldn't give it to her, so it wasn't likely that it was her.

But then who could it be?

I had a presentation to finish for a new client that afternoon, so I blocked out everything else to focus on it. I had way too much to do that day to spend time worrying about something I had no control over.

Ryker will know what to do… I hope.

Therapy with Kam was not what I wanted to do after the day I'd had. My head had been throbbing since the morning, and it was hard to concentrate on anything other than that stupid text message.

We had just sat down on the couch in Dr. Lowell's office when she opened with her usual question. "How have you been feeling?"

Kamden sighed and rubbed his hands together. "This week's been hard."

"And why is that?" she asked.

He didn't answer for several seconds. "My mom's been calling and leaving me harassing messages."

My head jerked toward him. "What?" I questioned angrily, my voice shrill. "Why didn't you tell me?"

"I didn't want you to worry. You worry about me enough as it is."

My head throbbed more from what Kamden had just told me.

Maybe my mom is sending those texts—trying to harass both of us for what happened with Kaleb.

Dr. Lowell interrupted my thoughts when she asked Kamden, "How do you feel about that?"

Kamden balled his fists. "Upset. Angry. Guilty."

"Don't listen to Mom's bullshit, Kam. She doesn't know what the fuck she's talking about. You have no reason to feel guilty." I blurted out, pissed off about the whole situation.

I am so done with this day.

Kamden didn't reply. He just sat there silently, staring at floor and wringing his hands together.

"Tell me about your mother," Dr. Lowell said, breaking the silence.

Is she fucking serious? This day keeps getting worse and worse.

Kamden's jaw clenched and his hands stilled. I didn't think he was going to speak, but he swallowed deeply, then answered, "My mom has always been different. Definitely not your loving, affectionate type of mom. Well, except with Kaleb. She treated him differently than me and Kaiya." I swallowed the lump that had formed in my throat. Listening to Kamden talk about my mom and Kaleb made my stomach turn—they both had made my life a living hell.

"He'd always been her favorite. Kaleb could do no wrong in her eyes. After I'd stopped Kaleb from… from raping Kaiya, she'd been angry with me for hurting him. She didn't even care about what he'd done to Kaiya, or that he'd been abusing her for years. Hell, she even blamed Kaiya for Kaleb's actions."

My face burned with anger and hurt. Tears blurred my vision as I looked down at my joined hands. I hated being reminded about my past, about everything I had to endure my whole life.

Dr. Lowell quickly scribbled on her paper. "Why do you think she was like that?"

I had to give Kamden credit—if she was asking me all those questions, I would've lost my shit or completely shut down by now.

Kamden shrugged. "I don't know. I'm starting to believe that she might have some type of mental illness like Kaleb—it's the only explanation I can think of to justify her actions. What kind of mother would she be otherwise?"

I'd never considered that before, but I wouldn't know what normal was even if it smacked me in the face. Mental illness sometimes ran in families, so it could be possible that my mom had some type of condition similar to Kaleb.

I could see her having some type of personality disorder, or a combination of different disorders. It wouldn't surprise me. My mother acted bat shit crazy sometimes.

"Kaiya!" my mother yelled from downstairs.

Shit.

Kamden and Kaleb were both at football practice, and I was upstairs doing homework. I stood from my desk and headed out my bedroom door. "What?" I called out as I trudged down the stairs.

She didn't answer, and when I reached the bottom of the stairs, I didn't see her in the living room. "Mom?"

Still no response, so I headed into the kitchen. She was standing in front of the counter, and the overhead cabinet above her was open. As I approached her, I could see her tightly gripping the edge of the counter. "You called me, Mom?"

Her head jerked toward me. "Yes, come take a look at this, Kaiya," she gritted through clenched teeth.

I hesitantly inched toward her, unsure what she was angry about. She grabbed my arm and roughly pulled me next to her in front of the open cabinet. "You put the plates up wrong!"

I looked up at the cabinet—everything looked fine. I'd made sure to neatly stack the plates and keep them from touching the other glasses and dinnerware.

"You don't even see your mistake, do you?" she scoffed in irritation. She squeezed my arm tighter.

"No, I thought that's how they're supposed to be." I replied, trying, but failing to keep my voice steady.

She flung my arm away from her in disgust. "You put the salad plates where the dinner plates go. Dinner plates go on the bottom shelf and salad plates go directly above them on the middle shelf."

"I'm sorry. I'll fix th—"

"Don't bother," she spat. "I'll do it since you couldn't do it right the first time."

She turned away, dismissing me as she set to work, fixing my mistake. I forced back the tears as I walked back to the stairs and up to my room.

"How do you feel about that, Kaiya?" Dr. Lowell's voice broke through my stumble down memory lane.

"About what?" I replied, avoiding her gaze.

I really don't want to talk about this.

"How your mother treated you." She quickly jotted down something on her pad.

I sat back on the couch and crossed my arms over my chest. "She was a bitch." I shrugged. "Still is. If her and my dad had been better parents, things might have been different… better."

Dr. Lowell wrote something else before looking up at me. "Could you elaborate on that?"

Glancing uneasily at Kamden, I rubbed my sweaty palms against my pants. He gave me a small, yet reassuring smile.

You're doing this for him—to help him heal. Suck it up.

I took a deep breath, but my lungs felt constricted. I blew it out shakily. "Yeah, um, maybe my twin wouldn't have molested me for most of my life. He might have gotten the help he needed, and none of this would've happened. He wouldn't be dead right now. Kamden and I wouldn't be sitting here dealing with this bullshit, and I wouldn't be a fucked up mess."

I hadn't noticed I had balled my fists until my palms hurt from my nails digging into them. When I loosened my grip, my hands trembled and my head pulsed again. I felt like the room was closing in on me.

Shit, don't panic. Calm down. Breathe, breathe, breathe.

I shut my eyes as a wave of nausea washed over me.

Don't throw up, don't throw up.

Kamden grabbed my hand. His tone was laced with worry as he questioned, "Ky, are you okay? What's wrong?"

I gripped his hand back as I took several slow breaths to quell my anxiety. My voice cracked as I spoke, "I'm fine."

That was reassuring.

When I opened my eyes, his stormy blue ones scanned over my face with concern. "Are you sure?"

My eyes stung as I battled the tears that wanted to form. I wanted to tell Kamden about the texts, tell him that I hated this and make him take me away from here and never bring me back. But I didn't. Instead, I lied, "Yeah, I'm fine."

Kamden looked unconvinced, but he didn't press me further. Dr. Lowell didn't either. Maybe she knew I wasn't going to talk anymore. And I didn't—I stayed silent for the rest of the therapy session, fighting an impending breakdown.

Chapter Six

Ryker

I knew something was wrong with Kaiya as soon as she walked into the studio. Her body was tense and her face wasn't lit up by that beautiful smile like when she normally saw me.

She forced a smile when our eyes met, but I knew my Warrior—something was off. I walked toward her, and we met in the middle of the room. "What's wrong?"

She didn't answer. Instead, she dropped her bag and fell into me, wrapping her arms around my waist and pressing her head against my chest. Her hands gripped the back of my muscle shirt as she hugged me tightly.

I cupped her face in my hands and forced her to look up at me. "Baby, what's wrong? What happened?"

Her eyes were puffy and red—she'd been crying. Anger and worry built up inside me, and I wanted to punch something, preferably whoever was the cause.

"I had a bad day." Her voice was strained, like she wanted to cry again, but was holding back.

I stroked her cheeks. "Tell me what happened."

Kaiya sighed and proceeded to tell me about therapy with Kamden and the text she'd gotten. My anger amped up at the thought of someone threatening her, especially when there was nothing I could do about it. "Let me see your phone," I seethed, clenching my fists as I tried to remain calm.

Kaiya pulled back to dig through her purse before taking out her phone. After she handed it to me, I clicked the text icon and pulled up the messages from the unknown number.

After reading the messages several times, I gave Kaiya back her cell.

"What should we do?" she asked.

Blowing out a breath of frustration, I roughly ran a hand through my hair.

Fuck.

I didn't know what to do, and Kaiya needed me.

Some fucking boyfriend you are.

When I didn't answer, she continued, "What about the police?"

I scoffed. "They probably wouldn't give us the time of day."

Her voice took on a higher, anxious pitch. "Well, what are we going to do, Ryker?"

Shit.

She sounded so vulnerable and afraid, like when she used to talk about Kaleb. I never wanted her to feel like that again—I was supposed to make her feel safe, protect her. And I was failing.

I pulled her into me and kissed the top of her head. My breath rustled her hair as I spoke. "We'll figure something out. I'm not going to let anything happen to you."

She buried her face in my chest and let out a heavy sigh. Then, the door opened, causing Kaiya to lift her head and turn to look at it.

Some of the students walked in, and Kaiya stepped away from me. She gave me a small smile and hefted her bag over her shoulder before walking toward her usual punching bag.

Once class started, I couldn't get my mind off the texts. Thoughts were running through my head non-stop as I watched Kaiya hit the bag.

Who is it? What do they want? What should I do?

I walked around the room, monitoring the students as I tried to think of a solution for our problem. The police would probably be a dead end—they'd make us fill out a police report that would get forgotten at the bottom of a stack of other reports.

Maybe Kaiya can call her cell phone carrier and see if they can trace the number. That's probably the best option we have right now.

Kaiya seemed to feel better after hitting the bag—her body wasn't as tense and some of the worry lining her face was gone. But once we moved on to the self-defense part of class, I saw it come back when I announced what we would be working on.

"Today, we'll be practicing techniques to get out of a choke that comes from behind. This is a very common M.O. for rapists and muggers."

Kaiya still wasn't comfortable when we did choke maneuvers, but I was concerned that whoever was texting her would come after her at some point. She needed to be prepared in case I wasn't around.

After demonstrating the first technique with Mark and David, I met Kaiya at our usual spot. "I know you hate chokes, but I want you to be ready for any situation, especially since someone is threatening you."

"I know. Let's get this over with." She exhaled heavily.

"Come behind me." When I felt her at my back, I continued, "Now, put your dominant arm around my neck and squeeze my throat with your bicep. Use your other hand to secure the choke by grasping right below your wrist."

I squatted some so she could reach my neck. When she had the choke in place, I instructed, "When put in this position, the escape is actually pretty simple. First, you're going to move your inside leg around and behind your attacker like this." Kaiya had me in the hold with her right arm, so I moved my left leg around her right one, shifting my body to face her as I planted my foot behind her. My dick pressed against her hips. I had to shake the dirty thoughts that formed in my head so I could concentrate on the move.

Focus. She's yours—you can have her later.

"Feel how my body's fitted to yours? My elbow is right against your stomach, so I'm going to use that to my advantage. Throw an elbow strike to the stomach, then follow through using your body to push them over."

I lightly elbowed her, then pushed against her, turning my body into her and using my momentum to knock her over my thigh to the ground.

I helped Kaiya up, then pretended to brush some non-existent dust off her ass, trying to get her to loosen up. She giggled and swatted my hand away, giving me a look of amused disapproval.

"What? You had something on your ass." I laughed.

She rolled her eyes. "Sure." She was trying so hard not to smile, but it broke through after several seconds.

"Ready to try, Warrior?"

Her smile faded some as she stiffened slightly and nodded.

"I'm going to come up behind you and put you in the choke, okay?" I made sure to meet her eyes and get her approval before walking behind her. I hated how tense she was, especially considering that it was me—I felt like she didn't trust me.

Rubbing her shoulders, I attempted to help her loosen up. "Easy, baby, it's only me. You know I would never hurt you."

She relaxed some and shook out her arms. "I know, I know. It's not you—it's me. Some habits are hard to break."

I knew it would take her time to get over her trust issues, but it still made me feel like shit that after everything we'd been through, she still didn't trust me. I told myself that it would take longer to reverse all those years of fear and trust issues, and I was determined to break through every wall by earning her trust.

I let go of her shoulders. "I'm going to put you in the choke now." I slipped my arm around her neck and secured the hold with my other hand. "Bring your left leg around behind my right one, squatting slightly into a horse stance."

Once she was in the correct position, I continued, "Now elbow me and continue to push while turning your body into mine. Use as much force as possible to knock me backward over your knee."

It took Kaiya a few times to knock me over, so we practiced until she became more comfortable with executing the move before I ended class.

Everyone joined together on the mats. "I hope that learning this technique will be helpful to you if you ever need it. Remember to practice at home so that the movements become reflexive and automatic. Have a good night, everyone."

After I locked up, Kaiya and I picked up some Chinese takeout for dinner, then headed back to her place. When she opened the door, she called out, "Kam? We're home."

Kaiya slipped off her shoes and threw her keys and purse on the table as I shut the door. "Kam?" Kaiya repeated louder.

I set the bag of takeout on the table while Kaiya searched the apartment for Kamden. She entered the dining room with a perplexed look on her face. "He's not here. He's usually home by now."

She went to her purse and pulled her phone out. After dialing his number, she put the phone to her ear and paced back and forth between the living and dining room. She chewed on her bottom lip as she waited for Kamden to answer.

Her face fell as she lowered the phone. "No answer. I hope he's okay. I wonder why he didn't call or text me."

I took out the various boxes of food and placed them on the table. "I'm sure he's fine. Kamden can take care of himself."

"Yeah, you're right," she halfheartedly agreed as she stared down at her phone in her hands. "I'm going to send him a text, anyway."

Her thumbs quickly swiped over her screen as she typed her message. Once she was finished, she went into the kitchen to grab some plates before coming back and setting the table.

Throughout dinner, Kaiya barely touched her food or spoke. I could tell she was still preoccupied about Kamden. "Don't worry, babe. He's probably out drinking or something."

Her eyes snapped up to mine, then narrowed in anger. "That doesn't make me feel any better. He's an alcoholic."

I reached across the table and placed my hand over hers. "I didn't mean to upset you, I'm just saying that he's probably at a bar, and can't hear his phone because of the loud music."

Ignoring my comment, she grabbed her phone off the table and angrily swiped the screen. She put the phone to her ear and stood from the table before storming into the living room.

After several seconds, she pulled the phone away from her ear and cursed, "Damn it, where is he?"

I stood from the table and walked over to her. I rubbed my hands up and down her arms. "Don't worry, baby. I'm sure he'll be home soon."

She sighed in frustration, then changed the subject. "Let's clean up this mess." She gestured to the dining room table.

After we put the dishes in the dishwasher and packed up the leftover food, we headed to Kaiya's room to get ready for bed.

Once we showered and changed, Kaiya insisted that she wait up until Kamden came home. We went back out to the living room and curled up on the couch with one of her extra blankets.

Kaiya was laying with her back on me in between my legs. She leaned her head back against my chest and let out another deep sigh.

I tried to keep her mind occupied by asking, "Tell me more about therapy today."

Shit, this probably isn't the best topic.

She turned over, propping her chin on her hands atop my abdomen as she looked up at me. I expected her to get upset and not want to talk about it, but she didn't. She seemed relieved to have the chance to get it off her chest. "We talked about my mom."

"What about her?" Kaiya's mom was a crazy bitch, and I didn't see how talking about her would help Ky or Kamden.

"Kamden said she'd been leaving him messages and harassing him. Then, Dr. Lowell asked him how he felt about that and wanted to hear both of our opinions about her."

No wonder she was so stressed when she walked into class—Kaiya's mom was a tough subject for both of them. Add in the threatening text message and her day seemed pretty shitty. "I'm sorry—sounds like you had a bad day."

She chortled. "Bad is an understatement. To top it off, I've had a fucking headache all day. This therapy shit sucks."

I laughed and rubbed her back. "I think it's great that you're doing it for Kamden. I'm really proud of you."

She smiled warmly and pushed up to kiss me. My hands moved down to grip her ass as I slipped my tongue in her mouth. I pressed her down into my hardening cock, making her gasp and break the kiss. "We can't—what if Kamden comes in?"

I smirked and squeezed her ass. "So?"

She smacked me on the shoulder and scoffed. "Ryker!"

I laughed. "Okay, okay. I'll behave."

Kaiya scooted down and lay her head back in the center of my chest. We talked a little longer before we both drifted off to sleep.

Loud, drunken laughter and the door hitting the wall woke both Kaiya and me. Kamden and some girl stumbled into the living room—both of them were wasted. They could barely stand, and their eyes were bloodshot and red.

Kaiya got up and furiously strode toward Kamden, who was oblivious to us. She placed her hands on her hips and stared up at him when she reached the drunken couple. His glazed eyes focused on her as he directed his attention away from the blonde that was all over him.

"Where have you been, Kam? I've been worried sick about you!" Kaiya's voice was clouded by sleep, but there was no masking the anger in it.

Kamden's eyes narrowed as he slurred, "None of your fucking business."

Kaiya was about to speak again as Kamden walked around her with the girl in tow. "You are my fucking business, Kamden! I just want to help you!" Kaiya yelled as she followed him. She grabbed his arm. "Talk to me, Kam."

"I don't want to fucking talk anymore!" Kamden roared as he wrenched his arm from Kaiya's grasp. "Leave me alone, Kaiya!"

Rage lit up my veins, sending my heart pummeling against my chest as I watched him push her away into the wall.

Fucking bastard!

Shock and hurt filled Kaiya's face as I rushed over to them. I reared back to punch Kamden in his fucking jaw for touching my girl. I didn't give a fuck that he was her brother.

Kaiya's voice was barely above a whisper as she stopped me, gripping my forearm with both hands. "Don't. Just let him be."

Kamden's face morphed from anger to sadness as realization sank in. He let go of the blonde, who almost fell from the loss of his support, and approached Kaiya with open arms. "Ky, I'm so sorry. I didn't me—"

Kaiya turned away from him, burying her face in my chest. I wrapped my arms around her and shook my head at Kamden. He had another thing coming if he thought I was going to let him near her after what he just did.

Kamden backed away as he apologized again, "I'm sorry, *sorella.* So sorry."

Kaiya softly cried into my bare chest, and I clenched my fists to temper my anger. Kamden was so fucking lucky that Kaiya was in between us, or I would've beat the shit out of him.

Kamden turned and went into his room. He slammed the door, leaving the drunk girl leaning against the wall in the hallway. I lifted Kaiya into my arms and carried her to her bedroom, only concerned about her well-being. I couldn't care less about Kamden's booty call.

Once I shut the door, I heard banging. The girl yelled, "What the fuck, Kamden? You said you'd show me a good time."

Ignoring her, I lay Kaiya in bed before climbing in next to her. I covered us with her comforter and wiped the tears from her face. "Don't cry, baby. He didn't mean it."

Her bottom lip quivered. "I know. I just feel like I'm losing him. How can I save him?"

"You can't save someone who doesn't want to be saved."

She closed her eyes. "I can't lose him—he's the only family I have left."

I caressed her cheek. "You have me, too, Warrior. Always."

Her vibrant blue eyes opened and locked on mine. "I love you."

I brushed my lips over hers before leaning down to her chest. I gently kissed her scar, then moved back up to her lips again. "I love you," I murmured against them.

Enclosing Kaiya in my arms, it didn't take long for us to fall back asleep, exhausted from the events of the night.

Chapter Seven

Kaiya

My eyes burned as I stared at the computer screen at work. They were still puffy and swollen from crying the night b ore. Kamden pushing me had been replaying in my mind since I woke up. Plus, I still had the same fucking headache, and I'd thrown up again this morning when I'd gotten out of bed.

I rubbed my eyes as I swiveled away from the screen. My phone buzzed on my desk, and I thought about ignoring it, not wanting to deal with another text from the unknown number.

Don't live in fear—you wasted most of your life doing that.

I grabbed the phone and keyed in my password. A message from Kamden popped up on the screen.

Thank God.

Kamden: I'm sorry sorella

My stomach tightened uncomfortably thinking about what happened. Kamden had never laid a hand on me before, and it was like a piece of my heart broke when he pushed me into the wall.

I gnawed on my bottom lip as I thought about what to text back. I was hurt and upset, but not to the point where I didn't want to talk to him and resolve everything.

Me: It's ok I know you didn't mean it

I set my phone down and tried to concentrate on my projects, but with everything on my mind, it was virtually impossible. I was lucky that I hadn't been fired for my lack of work since I'd returned from my leave of absence, but my boss had been understanding of my situation, which I was extremely grateful for.

I had just typed some figures into one of my new account's spreadsheet when my phone vibrated again. A new text popped up on my screen, and fear strangled the air from my lungs.

Unknown: Soon you will pay for what you did

My heart thundered in my chest as I stared down at my phone. I exited out of the message and went through my phone log to call Ryker. I clicked on his name and was about to press call when I stopped.

Ryker was already worked up about the texts, especially since he couldn't do anything about them. I didn't want to worry him when there was nothing he could do—that would only frustrate and upset him more. And I didn't want both of us stressed out over the situation. Plus, I still needed to call my phone company and see if there was anything they could do on their end, and I wanted to be able to give Ryker answers.

I went back to my home screen and opened my texts. I tapped Nori's name and started typing a message.

Me: Wanna grab some lunch today

It only took a few seconds for her to respond back with her answer. Nori worked about ten minutes away from my office, so we decided to meet at a small cafe about halfway between our buildings.

I took a cab to the cafe to save time, and Nori was already there, waiting for me outside.

We rushed in, clutching our coats around us as a gust of wind attacked us. The door practically slammed behind us from the force of the wind blowing outside.

I unbuttoned my coat. "Why didn't you wait inside for me? It's freezing outside."

Nori shrugged. "I don't mind the wind, unlike you. You freeze when its fifty degrees outside and a small breeze brushes past you."

I rolled my eyes. "I'm not that bad." I really was.

Nori gave me a seriously look, arching an eyebrow with a playful smirk. We both laughed after I failed to fight a smile. Nori and I always had a good time together, and it was nice to forget about everything that relentlessly weighed down on me, if only for a brief time.

Once we were seated, I took off my jacket and set it beside me in the booth. Nori did the same as she asked, "So, what's new?"

I groaned and Nori chuckled. "That bad, huh?"

Exhaling a heavy breath, I nodded. I proceed to ramble about the therapy sessions with Kamden, the confrontation the night before, and the text I had received this morning.

Nori sat in stunned silence, both her eyes and mouth wide open as she took everything in. "Wow, I, uh-"

Just then, the waitress walked up, interrupting our conversation. "Hi, my name is Amy and I'll be your server today. What can I get you to drink?"

Once she left with our orders, I urged Nori, "Well?"

She looked at a loss for words, which was definitely unusual for her. After a few seconds, she finally spoke. "Damn, girl—I don't know what to say."

I snorted. "That's a fucking first."

Nori flipped me the finger and laughed. "Hey, you threw a lot at me at once. Give me some time to process."

"Yeah, its some heavy shit. I've been so stressed out that I've been throwing up every morning and have never-ending headaches."

"Wait, what? You've been throwing up every morning? For how long?" Nori asked with her eyebrows raised.

"Um…" I thought back to when I got the first text. "A few weeks maybe. Why?"

"Do you think you might be pregnant?" Nori blurted out.

I laughed loudly. "Are you joking?" When she didn't join in my laughter, I stopped and met her gaze. "Wait, you're serious."

It wasn't a question. The look on Nori's face told me she wasn't joking—she was dead serious. "I can't be pregnant. I'm on the…"

Oh shit. When was the last time I went for my shot? The last I remember was before the shooting. Fuck.

Nori smiled sympathetically. "Would it be that bad if you were?"

Would it?

I never planned to have kids because I didn't think I was in the right emotional state to be able to raise any that weren't totally fucked up. I rubbed my palms on my pants. "No, but I'm sure it's just stress."

Nori gave me a knowing look. "Maybe you should take a pregnancy test—just to be safe."

I sighed. "Fine, I will. But I really think it's only stress."

The waitress came back with our drinks and wrote down our lunch order. When she left, Nori said in disbelief, "I can't believe Kamden pushed you."

I sadly shook my head, then stared down at my hands in my lap. "Me neither. He's gotten really bad. I don't know what to do to help him."

"Just keep doing what you're doing. Don't give up on him."

I looked up and made eye contact. "I won't." I could never give up on Kamden after everything he'd done for me.

Nori changed the subject. "So, what does Ryker think about the text messages?"

I took a drink of my water. "He's beyond pissed. Especially since he can't do anything about it."

"What about the police? Have you thought about going to them?"

"Yeah, but Ryker said they won't do anything." I stirred the straw around in my drink before taking another sip.

Nori shrugged. "Maybe, maybe not. I think it's worth a shot. What if they could help?"

She had a point. Ryker didn't know for sure whether or not the police would be able to help, and the messages weren't stopping like I wanted. "You're right. I'll look into it."

Amy came with our food, and we started eating. In between bites,

Nori said, "Tell me something good. I'm tired of all this negative bullshit."

"Tell me about it." I laughed. "I don't have much to tell you, except that everything with Ryker is amazing. I keep waiting to wake up from this dream."

"Aww, that's so sweet," she crooned with a smile. "I'm so happy that you finally found someone that treats you how you're supposed to be treated."

My lips curved up. "Yeah, I'm pretty lucky."

Nori took another bite of her sandwich. "At least you have him to help you through all this."

I nodded as I swirled my spoon in my soup. "Yeah, I'd definitely go crazy with all this if I didn't have him."

That's an understatement.

Ryker was my anchor, keeping me from drifting out and getting lost in the sea of despair that still tried to tow me under constantly.

Once Nori and I finished eating, we paid our bill and left. We both gave each other a hurried hug goodbye as we hailed down taxis, and I promised to keep Nori updated on everything.

As I reluctantly trudged up to my office, I thought about what Nori had said about going to the police. Ryker worked today, so I could head down to the station on my way home without him knowing. I didn't want him to worry more than he already was.

The rest of the day was uneventful—I got absolutely nothing done at work. My mind was consumed with thoughts of Kamden, the text messages, and, of course, me being pregnant.

You're not pregnant. It's just stress.

I told myself that if I kept throwing up over the next few days, that I would take a pregnancy test.

But I'm not pregnant.

Yeah, keep telling yourself that.

I took the elevator to the parking garage, then got in my car and drove to the police station. I was so nervous that they'd laugh in my face and tell me to grow up, but Nori was right—I'd regret not going to them.

Taking a deep breath, I got out of my car and walked to the entrance. Another man was walking up at the same time as me and opened the door. "Thank you," I said as I hurried inside and to the front desk.

The cop barely acknowledged me, not even glancing up from his computer. "Can I help you?" he asked, the irritation apparent in his tone.

Maybe this isn't such a good idea.

"Hi, I, um, wanted to speak to someone about some threatening text messages I've been getting from a blocked number."

He looked at me like I was stupid as he handed me a clipboard with a paper. "Fill out this police report, and we'll look into it."

I'm sure you'll get right on it.

"Okay, thank you."

Even though I doubted that they were going to do anything to help me, I filled out the form. When I finished, I took it back to the desk and handed it to the police officer. He gave me a fake smile as he said, "We'll be in touch."

Yeah, sure you will, asshole.

"Thank you so much." I smiled sweetly, returning his fakeness tenfold.

Dick.

As I drove home, my mind warred as I debated whether or not to tell Ryker. With the police seeming to be of no help like he said, and no other options, I didn't really see the point in worrying Ryker when nothing could be done.

I'll just deal with it myself. No sense in both of us stressing out.

When I got home, Kamden was sitting on the couch. He stood and came toward me as he asked, "Hey, can we talk?"

I set my purse down. "Yeah, sure." I slipped off my heels and padded over to the couch before sitting down. I patted the cushion next to me as I looked up at him.

Kamden sat down and rubbed his hands anxiously on his jeans as he avoided eye contact with me. "Look, I'm… I'm really sorry for last night. I wasn't thinking straight."

I placed my hand over his on his thigh and smiled softly. "I know."

He met my eyes. "I would never hurt you—that's the last thing I'd want to do. I don't want to be anything like *him.*"

That last word was laced with so much disgust. I squeezed his hand. "You're not, Kam. Nothing like him."

"How could I do that to you?" he angrily asked. I knew he was more asking himself than me, so I didn't answer. He looked away. "What's happened to me?"

I happened. This was all because of me and Kaleb. Kam would have been so much better off without us.

"We're all having trouble dealing with the shooting, Kam. It's o—"

He abruptly stood and narrowed his eyes at me. "Don't tell me it's okay, Kaiya. You have no idea what I'm feeling. No fucking idea." He took a deep breath as his eyes watered. "You didn't pull the trigger—you didn't take your brother's life."

Rising off the couch, I reached my hand out to touch his shoulder. "Kam, I—"

"Don't," he growled as he whipped away from me and stalked down the hall toward his room. I heard the door slam a few seconds later.

Damn it.

I flopped back on the couch and clutched my head in my hands.

What the fuck am I going to do?

Chapter Eight

Ryker

Kaiya hadn't been acting like herself since the whole incident with Kamden a couple of weeks ago. She tried to pretend like everything was okay, but I knew her well enough to know when she was putting on her armor.

My stubborn Warrior.

Even though she hadn't gotten any more texts, I wanted to be on the safe side and continue to teach techniques that would be helpful in case something happened. Plus, the phone company had told her that the number couldn't be traced because it was from one of those disposable burner phones, so there really wasn't anything they could do. At least I was doing something by teaching her what I could.

"Today, we're going to work on rear hair pull defense. Having long hair is a disadvantage in a fight scenario since it can be used against you. But there are some easy techniques to turn the tables."

After explaining the move a few times with Mark and David, everyone split up and got to work. I paired up with Kaiya and turned around as I instructed, "Grab my hair."

"Where? You barely have any." She chuckled.

"Run your hand up my head until you can grip something."

Her fingers went up the back of my head and almost to the top when she finally grabbed a good chunk and tugged lightly. "Good, now pull harder."

As she jerked my head back, I put my hands on top of hers and secured them in place. "First thing you want to do is grab their hand and trap it on your head—it may seem like the opposite of what you should be doing, but this keeps you from having your neck snapped and makes it harder for them to jerk you around."

"Next, bring your elbows to shield your face in case your attacker tries to slam you into something." I pivoted into her. "Then, turn into your attacker and duck under their arm." I squatted under her arm and went to the outside, forcing Kaiya to bend over as her arm twisted unnaturally. "Now, you have them in an arm lock. If they haven't let go by now, then you can throw a side kick to the ribs, a roundhouse to the stomach, or if you really want to do damage, throw a sidekick to the knee. I guarantee that'll put them out."

I let go of her arm. "Pretty simple, right?"

She rubbed her elbow. "Almost seems too good to be true. I can't believe it's that easy."

I laughed. "Well you just felt how much it hurt. Sometimes it doesn't take that much effort to inflict pain." I stepped behind Kaiya as I spoke. "Your turn."

I grabbed Kaiya's ponytail and wrapped my hand around it once before tugging. "Bring your hands up."

She clasped her hands over mine and pushed down against her head. "Now get in a horse stance and pivot inward as you duck under my arm."

Kaiya wrenched my arm around, bringing it up as my body was forced to bend over. "Good, throw a sidekick into my ribs."

I let go as she kicked my side. I shrugged the shoulder of the arm that was just twisted and shook it out.

Good thing it wasn't my other arm—I'd be in some serious pain.

"Great job, Warrior. Let's practice again, a little faster this time."

Kaiya turned around, and I gripped her ponytail and pulled. She made a noise that sounded like a gasp and a low moan put together.

My dick twitched.

Holy shit, did she just moan?

I snaked my other hand around her waist and brought her against me, pressing that ass into my growing cock. I leaned next to her ear and murmured, "You like that, baby?"

She nodded and cleared her throat. Her voice was throaty with arousal when she responded, "Yeah, I do. Maybe we can practice more at home."

Fuck me.

I pulled her hair tighter and fought the urge to suck on her earlobe. She moaned again as I rubbed my erection against her. "Ryker."

Focus—your students are still in here.

I looked around to make sure no one was paying attention to us before yanking her ponytail one more time and growling in her ear. "I want to fuck you so bad right now. Just slip those shorts over and slide into you from behind."

I could see her biting her lip as she stifled a whimper.

Fuck, so hot… damn it, concentrate! Hair pull defense.

My voice cracked as I put some distance between us and asked, "What are you supposed to do now?"

Kaiya didn't answer or move. "Ky?"

"Huh? What?" Her voice was still coated with lust.

I chuckled and pulled her hair again. "What do you do now?"

"Oh, um, this?" She brought her hands up to cover mine and secured them in place.

"Good, and then?"

She ducked under my arm and twisted it, forcing me to bend over as she kicked me in the stomach with a roundhouse.

"Great job, baby," I praised when she let go. We practiced one more time before I dismissed class.

After everyone left, I asked Kaiya if she wanted to stay and practice sparring. Those text messages were still in the back of my mind, and the thought of her being attacked made me sick to my stomach. I needed to do whatever I could since I wasn't able to prevent another text or track down whoever was sending them.

I wanted her to be as prepared as possible for any attack, and that meant conditioning her body and developing her muscle memory. Doing combos on the bag helped with that, but sparring was the best way to get comfortable with fighting and defending yourself.

I locked up the gym before meeting back up with Kaiya in the kickboxing room. She had already started putting on her gear when I walked in. "Ready, Warrior?"

"Born ready, baby," she said, bouncing up and down on the balls of her feet.

I chuckled as I grabbed a helmet from the equipment bin and strapped it on. I stood across from Kaiya on the mat and got in my defensive stance. "I'm going to go a little hard on you because I want you to be ready for anything."

She brought her gloves up in front of her face. "Let's do this."

I smiled—Kaiya loved sparring, and had gotten really good over the past few months. She was becoming more natural and fluid when she fought and executed more combos than in the beginning.

She was a better defensive fighter than offensive, so I advanced toward her and threw a jab, which she easily blocked.

That's my girl.

She countered with a ridge hand, one of her favorite moves, but I knocked her hand away. She followed up with a roundhouse to my thigh. "Good leg check, babe."

We exchanged several hits and kicks before I decided to up the ante. Grabbing Kaiya by the arms, I backed her into the padded wall and pinned her against it.

She tried to wriggle out of my grasp, forgetting her basic defense maneuvers she should've been using, like knees and elbows. Most people tended to forget their training when put in a high stress situation like the one I was subjecting Kaiya to. Mix that with adrenaline, and panic resulted. That was why it was so important to train your body to automatically react. And the only way to do that was to practice those specific scenarios.

Kaiya was breathing heavily, and her tits quickly rose and fell against my chest. Feeling her sweaty skin and body on mine combined with our sexual tension leftover from class made my cock harden.

Adrenaline rushed through my veins from sparring, making my heart rate increase. I forgot about the exercise. All I could think about was being inside Kaiya and filling her with my cock. I ripped my gloves and helmet off before trailing my hands down her arms to her hips. Leaning into her, I gruffly spoke, "I know I should be concentrating on training you, but feeling you against me like this makes me fucking crazy, baby."

I pressed my dick against her and was rewarded with a moan from that sexy mouth.

Fuck, I have to have her. Now.

She rushed to take her gloves off as I slipped her helmet off. Hooking my arm under Kaiya's thigh, I lifted her leg up as I pulled my dick out with my other hand. After moving her shorts and panties over, I rubbed my cock against her wet clit and sucked on her bottom lip.

I roughly thrust into her pussy, making her gasp in pleasure. Then, I lifted her other leg and picked her up. She wrapped her legs around me as I pressed her against the wall and slammed myself deeper into her.

Grasping her wrists with my hands, I brought her arms up and pinned them above her head. My mouth greedily claimed hers as I drove harder into her.

I loved the sounds Kaiya made when I fucked her. Those needy whimpers and moans were like the perfect soundtrack when we had sex—a masterpiece only I was capable of creating with her. Just for us.

Slowing my pace, I dragged my cock out of her before inching myself back in, stretching her pussy as I filled her. Her walls perfectly hugged my dick as I continued to stroke in and out of her.

Kaiya's head fell back against the padding as she cried out it pleasure. Her legs quivered around me as I sped up, hammering my cock further inside her.

My grip tightened on Kaiya's wrists when I came, filling her sweet pussy with my cum. Letting go, I wrapped my arms around her and held her to me as we caught our breath.

Kaiya's lips curved up when I set her down. "So, is that the proper technique for how to escape being pinned against a wall? Because I don't think it's very effective."

"Ha ha, very funny." I smacked her ass. "I can't help myself with you sometimes."

Grabbing me by the straps on my muscle shirt, she pulled me to her. She stood on her tiptoes to kiss me. "Maybe we should practice it again. I don't think I have all the steps down right."

I smirked as I gripped the undersides of her thighs and lifted her. She wrapped her legs around my waist again as I pinned her against the wall. "Sure, baby, I can show you again. I can show you over and over again until you get it." I guided my dick to her pussy and rubbed the tip against her wetness.

She tugged on my bottom lip with her teeth before making a sound between a growl and a moan. "Yes, show me again."

And I did. I sank my cock inside her and showed her over and over again.

Chapter Nine

Kaiya

I stared down at the sink of my office's restroom while I brushed my teeth. I had been consistently throwing up in the mornings at work, so much so that I had to bring a toothbrush to combat my vomit mouth.

I was still getting texts from the unknown number, and things with Kamden were rocky at best, so I continued to contribute my nausea to that. But it was getting harder and harder to deny what Nori had suggested at lunch two weeks ago.

I rinsed my mouth before staring at myself in the mirror.

Maybe you're pregnant.

Shit.

I decided I would pick up a pregnancy test from the store on my way home from work, just to be safe. If I was pregnant, I wanted to get the proper medical care, and if I wasn't, I needed to get back on the shot.

Begrudgingly, I dragged myself back to my office and slumped in my chair. I was so exhausted lately, and still had to suffer through constant headaches on top of everything else.

My office phone beeped. I groaned before picking up the receiver and putting it up to my ear. "Yes?"

Our receptionist, Amanda, answered, "Miss Marlow, there's someone on the phone for you."

Great.

I was definitely not in the talking mood. "Can you take a message, please? I'm not feeling well."

"Sure, Miss Marlow. I'll leave it in your box."

"Thank you, Amanda." I hung up and sighed, then directed my attention to my computer screen. Opening a spreadsheet from my files, I began inputting numbers, trying to take my mind off everything hanging over me.

A few minutes later, my cell phone vibrated on the desk.

Unknown: Too busy to take my call?

My heart felt like it stopped beating as fear hooked itself deep in my stomach.

They know where I work? Holy shit.

Darting my hand out to grab my office phone, I knocked it off the receiver, then scrambled to pick it up. I pushed the button for the receptionist's desk and Amanda answered, "Yes, Miss Marlow?"

I tried to keep my voice steady. "Amanda, who just called for me?"

"I don't know, ma'am. When I tried to take a message, they said that they'd call back and hung up."

Fuck.

"Was it a man or a woman?"

"It was a man. Why? Is something wrong?"

I swallowed the lump in my throat. "No, everything's fine, Amanda. Thank you."

I hung up before she could respond. Panic clawed at me, constricting my chest like it used to when I thought about Kaleb. My head throbbed, and I struggled to breathe. Clenching my eyes shut, I tried to pull myself free of the demons inside me.

Breathe, breathe, breathe.

Inhaling and exhaling deeply, I blanked my mind, then refilled it with thoughts of Ryker—my light in all the darkness that always tried to smother me.

I played his voice in my head.

I love you, Warrior. I'll never let anything happen to you.

The tightness in my chest faded.

Ryker will keep you safe.

Opening my eyes, I stared at my phone.

Maybe I should get a new number.

That would stop the texts, but the person knew where I worked and could call my office incessantly to harass me that way.

Fuck.

I decided I was going to tell Ryker everything—this phone call took things to a more serious level that I wasn't capable of handling by myself. I needed him.

I sent him a text asking to meet me on my lunch break at the police station so that we could follow up on my report. He didn't see the point until I'd told him about the strange call I'd just received.

Ryker was there when I pulled into the lot of the station. When I parked next to his truck, he got out and came around to my driver's side to meet me. "Hey." He leaned down and kissed me.

I linked our fingers together. "Hey."

He gave me a forced smile before leading me inside and up to the front desk. He cleared his throat to get the attention of the officer behind the desk, who had his back to us.

The officer swiveled around in his chair. It was the same asshole that had taken my report. "Can I help you?"

Ryker released my hand and placed them on top of the counter. "Yeah, my girlfriend said she filed a report a couple of weeks ago and we wanted to check the status. She's been getting threatening text messages and calls."

The officer stood. "Have you received a call from the station?"

"No." I moved to stand next to Ryker. "But—"

He rudely interrupted me. "Then, we're still working on it."

Ryker's body tensed as he tightly gripped the counter. "Well, it doesn't look like you're doing anything but sitting here on your fat ass eating donuts."

The officer's lip curled up. "Sir, I'm going to have to ask you to leave."

Ryker raised his voice. "My girlfriend is being harassed by some lunatic, and something needs to be done about it!"

Two other officers came from the hallway to our left. They eyed Ryker warily, then directed their attention to the asshole behind the desk. "Rick, you okay out here?"

Rick gave us a smug smirk and crossed his arms over his chest. "I asked this guy to leave, but he's refusing."

The two officers loosely placed their hands on their gun holsters, giving Ryker an unspoken warning.

"Ryker, let's go." I grabbed his forearm and tugged him toward the exit.

His muscles tensed beneath my hand. "I'm not leaving until I get some answers," he gritted out.

"If you don't leave right now, I'll be forced to arrest you for failure to obey a police order." Rick threatened.

I pulled on his arm again. "Ryker."

He wrenched his arm away. "Fine. Let's go."

I rushed to keep up with him as he stormed out. When we got to where we were parked, he punched the door of his truck and roared angrily. "God, that was such fucking bullshit!"

He paced back and forth beside our vehicles. "If you get anymore threats, I'm going to come back up here and force them to do something. I don't care if I get arrested."

Fear slithered through me. That was exactly what I was afraid of.

Ryker stopped and our eyes met. "Don't worry. I'll take care of everything from now on. Next time you get a call or text, you let me know immediately, okay?"

I swallowed the lump in my throat. "Okay," I lied. There was no way I was going to tell him anything else and risk him getting arrested. I decided to keep everything to myself like I'd originally planned. Ryker was too hot-headed when it came to me. I was going to have to deal with it myself.

When I returned to work, my head painfully throbbed throughout the remainder of the day, making me feel like my skull was going to explode. Knots formed in my stomach, elevating my nausea, and I did the best I could to block everything out by immersing myself in all the presentations and documents I was so behind on.

When it was time for me to clock out, I was caught up on my work. I was exhausted, but also relieved to have been able to zone out for a while without worrying about Kamden, the man harassing me, or my possible pregnancy. Not to mention the new worry of Ryker getting arrested.

As I hopped in my car, my next destination caused me to think about how Ryker might react if I was pregnant.

Will he be angry? Happy? Disappointed?

Closing my eyes, I rubbed my temples as I sat in my car. There was so much shit going on that I couldn't even began to analyze how Ryker would feel. I couldn't even decipher my feelings because my mind and emotions were so jumbled.

Taking a deep breath, I started my car. I told myself not to worry when I wasn't sure yet. I had enough to stress over without adding something on top that might not even be an issue. I'd deal with it once I was positive.

I stopped at a drug store on the way home from work to pick up a pregnancy test. Standing in the aisle, I stared at the shelves of all the various pregnancy tests and started to get a little overwhelmed.

Which one do I choose?

I dug my phone out of the bottom of my purse and called Nori. "Hey girl, what's up?"

"Guess where I am," I said as I scanned over the boxes.

She chuckled a little. "Alaska."

I snorted. "I'm staring at the million pregnancy tests they have available. How the fuck am I supposed to choose one when there's so many different options?"

Nori's laughter echoed through the phone. "Just pick one, Ky. They're all the same."

"But I want to pick the best one. Not some cheap one that might not be accurate."

"Well, then you're going to have to read the boxes and see which one is the most accurate."

I groaned before sarcastically replying, "Thanks for the help."

"Sorry, babe. Call me as soon as you find out. I want to know whether or not I'm going to be an auntie!" Nori squealed.

Her enthusiasm brightened my mood, getting a small laugh out of me. "I will. Bye."

I put my phone back in my purse and grabbed one of the tests off the shelf. I read the back, then did the same with a different box. I went through about five or six before I finally decided on the one that I thought was the best.

Looking down at it, I sighed before walking to the register. "Here goes nothing."

I stared at the pink pregnancy test in my hands.

Just open it and pee on the damn thing, Kaiya.

Blowing out a long breath, I ripped open the box and took out one of the tests. I had read the directions about a hundred times—one more time wouldn't hurt.

I sat on the toilet and positioned the stick as indicated.

Great, now I can't pee.

My leg bounced nervously as I tried to get myself to go to the bathroom.

Waterfalls. Showers. Oceans. Rivers.

I still couldn't go, so I got up with a huff and turned on the sink, then sat back on the toilet. I closed my eyes and concentrated on the sound of the water as I repositioned the pregnancy test under me.

After several seconds, I finally started peeing.

Thank God.

When I finished, I put the test on the counter and washed my hands. Then, I set the timer on my phone and waited.

And waited.

And waited.

I paced the bathroom and chewed on my bottom lip as I waited for the designated amount of time. The minutes seemed to last a lifetime as I waited for the answer that would change my life.

The timer went off, and I froze. My heart pounded, ready to burst from my chest as I slowly inched toward the sink. My mouth went dry as I approached, and my stomach twisted in anticipation.

What if it's positive? I can't be a mother.

But what if it's negative?

My heart sank into my stomach as I considered that I might not be pregnant.

Do I really want to be? Am I ready?

Is Ryker ready?

I rested my hands on my flat belly and rubbed it. A smile formed on my face as I thought about having a little Ryker inside me.

I grabbed the test off the counter and looked at the result window. Two pink lines.

Two pink lines.

I'm pregnant. Holy shit, I'm pregnant!

My mind ran a mile a minute as I stared at myself in the mirror.

I can't be a mom. I'm too fucked up.

Kaleb's face took over my reflection. I shut my eyes and gripped the edge of the sink as my heart began to pound.

He ruined you. You can barely take care of yourself let alone a baby.

My face felt flushed, and my breathing quickened as anxiety crept in.

Calm down, Kaiya. Breathe, breathe, breathe.

I slowly inhaled and exhaled, attempting to push Kaleb out of my mind as I thought about the life growing inside me—something I never pictured having because of my past and the scars inflicted from the abuse I endured.

You can do this.

Kaleb's voice played in my head. "You're too weak to raise a baby. It's going to end up fucked up like you."

No!

"You're a failure. You destroy the lives of everyone around you. You'll do the same with your baby."

Closing my eyes, I covered my ears with my hands. "No! No! No!"

"Maybe they'll look like me." His sinister laughter echoed in my head. "Then, you'll have to deal with my face for the rest of your life."

Tears leaked from my closed eyes as I tried to fight from the abyss Kaleb always pulled me in. "No!" I screamed, on the brink of losing control.

Calm down. Let go of the past and embrace the future. You've been given a gift—don't take it for granted.

I opened my eyes and released another deep breath, facing the source of all my demons in the mirror.

"My child will be nothing like you." I stated resolutely. "You hear me? Nothing like you!"

My face came back into focus as Kaleb's slipped away. Easing my grip off the counter, I stepped back and stood taller.

Time to move on.. You have to take care of your baby—give them a better life than you had.

Tears filled my eyes as I stared down at my stomach and placed my hands over my belly. "Hi, little one. I'm your mommy."

Mommy—I'm going to be a mommy.

Thoughts about how Ryker would react filled my head again. After everything that had happened with Molly, I doubted that he wanted to have a baby. We'd been together for less than a year, and having a baby together would be the ultimate commitment. There was no denying the love we had for each other, but I wasn't sure that either one of us were ready to be parents.

I looked down at the test on the counter again, and my stomach flip-flopped. In a matter of minutes, my life had been changed. I was left feeling more conflicted than I'd ever been before. Feelings of joy and excitement combated with worry and uncertainty. I had no idea what Ryker would think, but I prayed that he would be happy—I needed him now more than ever. And so did our child.

Chapter Ten

Ryker

When I got home from work, the apartment was filled with the smell of steak and spices. I threw my keys on the table and made my way to the kitchen, where Kaiya was pulling a tray of roasted vegetables out of the oven. "Hey, baby."

Kaiya set the pan on the stove as she turned to look at me. She gave me a nervous smile. "Hey. How was the rest of your day?"

I was still irritated from what had happened at the police station earlier that day, but working out had let me relieve some of the tension and aggression. "Better."

"Good. I don't want you to worry about that anymore. I have a relaxing evening planned for us."

I loved coming home on days like this. We didn't always have time to have a home-cooked meal, and I always felt special when Kaiya made me dinner.

I walked over and pulled her into my arms. "Whatever you say, baby. How was the rest of your day?"

She ran her hands up my chest and around my neck. "Interesting." Bringing my head down, she pressed her soft lips to mine.

Mmmmm.

The timer on the oven beeped, interrupting our kiss. Kaiya stepped back from me and slipped on her oven mitt as she said, "Dinner's almost ready. I made your favorite—Filet Mignon with roasted veggies and baked sweet potatoes."

I quirked my eyebrow curiously. "What's the occasion?"

She gave me a mischievous smile. "It's a surprise."

Bending over, she opened the oven and grabbed another cookie sheet with sweet potatoes on it. I lightly smacked her on the ass as I moved past her. "Guess I'll go get cleaned up for this surprise."

I took a quick shower and threw on some clothes before going back into the kitchen

Kaiya was in the adjoining dining room, setting the table with our plates of food and silverware. "Need any help?" I asked as I leaned against the door-frame.

"No, I think I have everything," she replied as she bunched her lips to the side.

I went to the table and pulled her chair out for her. Once she sat down, I kissed her cheek. "Thank you."

I rounded the table and sat down across from her. "This looks amazing, babe."

"Thanks." She smiled brightly.

"How was work?" I asked as I started cutting my steak.

Kaiya frowned. "Exhausting. I finally caught up on everything, though. I've been so behind. How was yours?"

"Pretty good. Every client met their goals for the week, and all my classes went well."

Kaiya took a bite of her sweet potato. "That's great. Has your shoulder been bothering you?"

"I've been taking it easy like you wanted so it's been fine." I ate a piece of my steak. "This is delicious, babe. You cooked it perfectly."

Kaiya blushed and a smile curved her lips. "Thank you."

We continued talking as we ate, but once I had finished my food, I noticed Kaiya had barely eaten anything. "You okay, Warrior? You didn't eat very much."

She gave me a small smile. "Yeah, I've just been feeling a little sick lately."

My eyebrows furrowed in concern. That was news to me. "Really? Sick how?"

"I've been throwing up and having bad headaches for the past month or so."

That didn't sound good at all. A lump formed in my throat that I quickly swallowed.

Don't freak out. It's probably just the flu or something.

"Maybe you should go to the doctor."

"Yeah, I'm going to call and make an appointment tomorrow. I'm going to have to make several appointments."

Now I was getting really worried. "Why? What's wrong?" My chest constricted as I thought about Kaiya having some serious illness that she hadn't told me about.

Her lips curved up in a wide smile. "I'm pregnant."

My stomach clenched as my heart pounded wildly.

Did she just say what I think she said?

I cleared the huge lump that formed in my throat. "What?" I finally managed to croak.

Her eyes watered even though her face was beaming with happiness. "I'm pregnant. We're going to have a baby, Ryker!"

We're going to have a baby.

I couldn't stop the huge smile that spread over my face as I rushed over to Kaiya.

She stood once I reached her and threw her arms around my neck. I picked her up and spun her around before setting her back down again. I cupped her face in my hands and looked in her eyes. "You're pregnant?"

She nodded excitedly. "I took a test when I got home. I've been throwing up at work in the mornings, but I thought it was from stress. Nori asked if I could be pregnant, and I remembered that the last time I got my shot was before the shooting. It completely slipped my mind."

I was letting everything sink in as a million thoughts raced through my mind.

Is it a boy or a girl? Will I be a good dad? Are we ready for this?

"Are you upset?" Kaiya nervously asked. She bit her bottom lip as she stared up at me.

I stroked her cheeks with my thumbs. "Upset? Why would I be upset, baby?"

Tears filled her eyes again. "Well, we've never talked about kids before. I don't even know if you want a baby with me, and you thought I was on birth control, and—"

I pressed a finger to her lips, cutting her off. "Stop. I'm not upset." I looked down at her stomach, then back up to meet her eyes. "I love you, Ky. We've never talked about kids before, but that doesn't mean that I don't want to have them with you."

She brought her hands up to cover mine and gripped them tightly. "Really?"

"Really, baby. You've made me so happy with what you just told me."

Letting go of her face, I knelt down and lifted her shirt to look at her stomach. I thought about the baby growing inside her and my smile stretched wider.

My baby.

I leaned forward and softly kissed her belly. Ky rested her hands on my head as I pressed more kisses all over her abdomen.

I'm going to be a dad.

I scooped her up and cradled her in my arms. "This calls for a celebration!" I started walking down the hall to my room.

Kaiya giggled and wrapped her hands around my neck. She raised an eyebrow and gave me a flirty smile. "What did you have in mind?"

I smirked. "It's a surprise."

Chapter Eleven

Kaiya

Ryker gently laid me down on the bed and straddled me. As his eyes met mine, the amount of love I saw in them caused my heart to swell and my stomach to knot. Tears pooled on the rims of my eyelids as he leaned down, propping himself on his forearms on each side of my head. Cupping my face in his hands, he softly feathered his lips over mine before murmuring against them, "I love you, Warrior."

My response came out in a breathless whisper. "I love you, too."

Ryker pressed another kiss on my lips before moving down my body. He lifted my shirt and stared down at my stomach in admiration. A sweet smile curved his full lips as he brought his face down to my belly and tenderly kissed it.

His hands framed my stomach as he ran his thumbs over my skin. "Hey, kid. I'm your dad."

Tears trickled down my cheeks even though happiness streamed through me. My adoration for him must have been apparent all over my face because I felt it deep in the darkest recesses of my soul, bringing new life to the pieces of me that had long been dead inside.

Ryker kept looking at my abdomen as he talked to our baby. "I'm going to do my best to take care of you and your mom. I love both of you so much." He glanced up at me and softly grinned. "I don't know if I'll be a good dad, but I do know that you're getting the perfect mom."

Those warm chocolate eyes captured mine as more of his sweet words poured out. "She's the most beautiful, caring, and selfless person I know. I don't deserve her, but I'm so lucky that she's mine."

He lowered his head back down and pressed his lips on my belly again, then trailed his mouth up to my breasts, searing my skin with heat and kindling a blazing fire in my core.

Ryker inched my shirt up as his lips continued their journey along my skin. They brushed over my collarbone and up my neck as he tugged my shirt over my head and tossed it to the floor.

His mouth barely grazed mine as his hands caressed my bare skin, fueling the inferno overtaking me. A shaky breath shuddered through my body as Ryker sparked every nerve alive with his touch.

He unhooked my bra and tossed it aside before pulling off his shirt. The rest of our clothes came off in a blur, and then his warm, inked skin finally met mine.

The way he felt on top of me, fitted between my legs, was absolutely perfect. Ryker had gradually been able to erase my insecurities and trepidations about sex, helping me heal from the abuse I'd sustained. And now, because of him, I truly understood how beautiful sex was; how it was one of the best ways to express your love for someone, giving every part of yourself to them in the most intimate way possible.

I could feel Ryker's love for me in every caress of his skin, every press of his lips, and it was the most incredible feeling I'd ever experienced.

Ryker laced his tongue with mine, flooding my mouth with his intoxicating taste. Passion was evident in every brush of our lips as we slowly savored one another.

His cock nudged my entrance as he rocked against me. I couldn't help but moan as he repeatedly stroked my clit with his thick, hardened shaft.

As he slowly inched inside me, a gasp escaped my lips. I loved how he completely filled me, molding our bodies together flawlessly as we made love.

Clasping my face in his hands, Ryker leisurely pumped his hips against me, prolonging every sensation with each deliberate thrust as he brought me closer to ecstasy. He whispered huskily against my lips, "I love you."

"I love you," I responded in a throaty moan as I threaded my hands in his hair.

He nipped my jaw as he drove deeper into me. His rough hands left my face to caress my skin as he trailed them down my body, sending a shiver through me. I arched against him, so close to unraveling from his divine touch.

"So perfect, baby. So fucking perfect," Ryker growled against my neck.

Our lips met again, and after a few more deep thrusts, I cried out in bliss as Ryker brought me to heaven; the only heaven I had ever known.

My body quivered as Ryker continued his strokes, intensifying my orgasm as it spread through my limbs. He stilled and groaned in my mouth as he followed me into euphoria.

He rested his sweaty forehead against mine as we regained our breath. Pressing another sweet kiss to my lips, he rolled off me and pulled me into him. He traced circles on my stomach as he propped himself up on his elbow. "So, we're having a baby, huh?"

I giggled and stared up at him. "Yeah, we are."

Our eyes met, and he smiled. He brought his lips to mine, and soon, we were lost in the beautiful haze our bodies created once again.

I called my gynecologist's office as soon as they opened the next morning to make an appointment. They were able to fit me in that afternoon, so I sent a text to Ryker to let him know.

Me: The dr can see us today at 430 :)

Ryker: Great baby I'll pick you up

Me: Ok :) I love you

Ryker: Love you too Warrior

Ryker had the day off, so he had dropped me off at work. I had meetings all day, along with a couple of presentations that were interspersed in between. I was so eager to find out more about the baby that I knew work was going to drag on and on until the appointment. My head kept snapping back and forth to the clock on the wall throughout the day as I waited and waited until four o'clock finally came around.

When Ryker picked me up, I could see the excitement all over his face, especially in his huge smile and shining eyes. Once I got in the truck, he asked. "How was your day, babe?"

"Long," I groaned in displeasure. "I've been so anxious all day for the appointment."

"Me too," he replied as he put the truck in drive and merged onto the street. "Where's this place at?"

I gave Ryker directions to my doctor's office, which was only a few blocks away from my work. We parked in the parking garage across the street before heading to the elevator. Ryker threaded our fingers together. "You nervous?"

I looked up at him. "A little. I have no clue what I'm doing. I know nothing about being a mom."

He stroked the back of my hand with his thumb and gave me a reassuring smile. "We'll figure it out together, Warrior."

Some of the tension and unease filling me were alleviated with Ryker's words. He always knew exactly what to say when I needed it most.

Once we checked in and I filled out the extensive paperwork, Ryker and I waited in the waiting room to be called back. Thankfully, it only took a few minutes for the nurse to come for me. "Kaiya Marlow?"

Ryker and I both stood, but the nurse stopped him. "We only need Kaiya for this part." She smiled politely. "I promise I'll bring her right back."

Ryker glanced at me reluctantly. "Okay."

I gave him a reassuring smile and squeezed his hand before following the nurse to the nurse's station. She handed me a plastic cup and lid that had a label with my name on it. "We need a urine sample. When you're done, please place it on the shelf above the toilet."

She directed me to the bathroom, and I went in and did my business. I left the sample where indicated on the shelf and washed my hands before exiting.

The nurse, who was wearing a name tag that read 'Sophie', took my blood pressure, height, and weight before walking me back to the waiting room. "We'll call you back for the rest of the exam shortly."

I sat back down next to Ryker, who was flipping through a fitness magazine. He glanced up at me. "Everything okay?"

"Yeah, they just did some routine stuff—height, weight, blood pressure."

We waited another fifteen minutes when Sophie came back out to get us. She led us to a room, and handed me one of those exam gowns that barely covered anything. "I'll give you a few minutes to change, then I'll be back to take your blood sample."

I quickly changed into the unattractive paper gown and hopped on the exam table. Ryker sat in a chair next to me right as a knock sounded on the door.

"Ready?" Sophie asked.

That was fast.

"Yes," I replied.

Sophie opened the door and came in with some small vials and a huge needle. I gulped.

Fuck.

Sophie laid out all the equipment on the counter before sterilizing my arm with an alcohol-soaked cotton ball. I began to feel hot, and my heart pounded as she tightly secured a band around my bicep and prepped the needle.

Ryker linked our fingers together and tugged on my hand. I looked toward him and squeezed tightly. He brought my hand up to his mouth and kissed the back of it. "Did I ever tell you about the time I got my first tattoo?"

I tried to remember if he had mentioned it. "No… I don't think so."

"Well, I had just turned eighteen. Tribal tattoos were popular, and almost everyone had one, so naturally, I wanted to get one, too." He paused and looked at his right arm, which had a huge tribal that wrapped from his shoulder down to below his elbow. My eyes followed his gaze to the ink on his arm as he continued talking. "My boys and I went together to this tattoo shop in downtown Boston to each get a different tribal piece."

My eyes went back to his as he continued speaking. "When I sat on the table, my heart was pounding and adrenaline surged through my veins. Once that needle pierced my skin, I was hooked."

"Doesn't it hurt?"

What a dumb question. Of course it hurts, genius.

He chuckled. "Yeah, it hurts, but the rush you get from it is awesome. Everything about it is addicting, even the pain."

"I've always been too scared to get one. I hate needles," I replied.

"All done."

I looked away from Ryker to Sophie, who was cleaning up the counter. I glanced down and saw a Band-Aid already applied to my inner elbow. "I didn't even feel it."

"You had a good distraction." She chuckled as she motioned to Ryker before opening the door. "Dr. Wallace will be with you shortly."

My eyes went to Ryker, who had an adorable, lopsided grin on his face. He shrugged. "I didn't want you to panic."

My insides somersaulted and a smile spread over my lips.

He is so sweet sometimes.

"Thank you, babe."

After a few minutes, my doctor knocked and entered. "Hi, Kaiya. How have you been?"

"I've been good. Busy, but good."

"Great," she replied as she looked at the iPad in her hands. After several seconds, she looked up and smiled. "I have your results."

Ryker stood next to me and squeezed my hand. My heart thudded wildly and my stomach twisted in anticipation as we waited for the answer that would change our lives.

Dr. Wallace's smile stretched wider. "Congratulations! You're having a baby!"

Tears welled in my eyes as I looked up at Ryker. He wrapped his arms around me and hugged me tightly to him as he kissed the top of my head.

Hearing the confirmation from Dr. Wallace was so much more fulfilling than seeing it on a plastic stick. I couldn't remember a time when I felt so happy. "We're having a baby, Ryker." I softly murmured into his neck.

Pulling back, Ryker cradled my face in his hands and softly kissed me. He stroked my cheeks with his thumbs and looked deep into my eyes.

He didn't need any words to express how he felt. I wasn't sure there were even words to describe the emotions we were experiencing at that moment. Pure love and joy reflected in those beautiful brown eyes that always captured me. I would never get tired of seeing him look at me like that.

Dr. Wallace cleared her throat, gaining both of our attentions. She gave us an apologetic smile. "I'm sorry to interrupt, but we have a lot to discuss."

She came and sat down in an office chair across from the exam table and wheeled it closer to us. "Let's go over your medical history, then we'll get to your exam and hear your baby's heartbeat."

Your baby.

The grin I had on my face widened.

She used a stylus to tap the screen of her iPad several times, quickly scanning over it with her eyes. "It says here that you're a twin, which means that you have a higher chance of having twins yourself."

And just like that, my stomach sank.

No.

"We can check that during your first sonogram."

Ryker rubbed my back and gave me a sympathetic look. It wasn't that I wouldn't be happy with two babies, but just the thought of having twins after what I went through with Kaleb gave me anxiety.

They wouldn't be like Kaleb and me—don't worry over nothing.

Easier said than done. My mind was preoccupied as we went through the rest of my medical history. After answering several questions, Dr. Wallace asked one that I didn't have the answer to. "When was the date of your last period?"

I swallowed nervously. "Well, my periods have never been regular. I was on the shot, but I can't even remember when I came in for it the last time, or my last period."

Dr. Wallace peered back down at the tablet in her hands. "According to our records, the last time you received your contraceptive was in June."

Shit, that's over six months ago. I can't believe it slipped my mind for that long.

Dr. Wallace continued. "We'll need to do an ultrasound to determine how far along you are. Let me see if there's an ultrasound tech still here."

She swiveled in her chair and placed the iPad on the counter before reaching for the phone. "Rachel, can you please check if there's an ultrasound tech available."

A few moments later, she spoke into the phone again. "Thank you. Please send them to room nine."

Turning back to face us, she stated, "Let's get you all checked out. Lay back, please."

Ugh, I hate this part.

A few seconds after she finished with my exam, a knock sounded on the door.

"Just in time," Dr. Wallace said as she took off her gloves and washed her hands. "Come in."

A woman opened the door and entered with a large cart. "Hi, I'm Jen. I'll be your ultrasound tech today." She smiled at us. "Ready to see your baby?"

"Yes," Ryker and I said simultaneously.

"Great! Lay back down and lift the top part of your gown up."

Jen wheeled the cart next to me and grabbed a tube. "This is going to be cold, okay?"

I nodded. Jen squirted the gel on my stomach before placing the ultrasound wand on it. Immediately, the computer screen on the cart came to life, but it took a few seconds before she found the right spot. "There's your baby," she practically cooed.

Both Ryker and I stared in awe at the screen with our tiny baby on it.

Our baby.

Looking up at him, I briefly wondered if he had done all this with Molly, and if he felt the same way with her as he did with me. I quickly pushed the thoughts aside, not wanting to ruin the moment of seeing my future child for the first time.

Dr. Wallace studied the screen. Jen glanced at her before stating, "I'd say she's about twelve or thirteen weeks along."

Dr. Wallace nodded. "I think so, too." She directed her attention to me. "Only one fetus—no twins."

Thank God.

"Would you like a picture?" Jen asked.

I nodded enthusiastically. "Yes, please."

After she pressed a few buttons on the computer, a small sonogram picture printed out. She took the wand off my stomach and cleaned me up before handing me the photo. "Here you go—the first picture of your baby."

I glanced down at the sonogram in my hands, then up at Ryker. He was staring at the image with so much love all over his face that it made my heart skip a beat.

He darted his eyes to mine and gave me a sweet smile. I couldn't stop my own from forming over my lips because of his. I handed the picture to him as Jen said, "It was nice meeting you. Good luck with your pregnancy."

My head turned to see her wheeling the cart out the door. "It was nice to meet you, too. Thank you so much!"

Dr. Wallace sat back down in her chair. "Do you have any questions for me?"

I looked up at Ryker, then back at my doctor. "This is all so new and overwhelming, but my mind is blank right now."

Dr. Wallace laughed warmly. "That's understandable. This is your first child, and not everyone knows what to ask. That's why we have a packet with everything you need to know to take home. We can go over it before you leave."

Some tension left me, and I sighed in relief. "Thank you. I feel so much better."

Dr. Wallace's eyes lit up as her eyebrows rose. "Oh, I almost forgot! Let's listen to your baby's heartbeat." She stood and grabbed a handheld machine and another tube of gel from one of the cabinets. It had a wand similar to the ultrasound machine at the end, only smaller. "This is a fetal doppler."

Dr. Wallace squeezed more gel on my belly and placed the wand on my stomach. Static and swooshing filled the room as she moved the sensor around my stomach. "Where are you, little one?"

She traced my lower abdomen before a noise that sounded like a horse galloping mixed with the other sounds. "There you are."

I looked from my stomach to Dr. Wallace. "That's the heartbeat? It's so fast."

"That's perfectly normal. The heartbeat of a fetus ranges anywhere between one hundred twenty and one hundred eighty beats per minute."

I continued listening to the beautiful sound. Ryker squeezed my hand and gave me a huge grin. It was amazing hearing something that he and I created together, something so pure and perfect.

Dr. Wallace left the wand there a little longer before pulling it off, and I immediately missed the sound once it stopped. I could've listened to it all day if she let me.

Before we left, Dr. Wallace went over some of the packet of with us, answered what questions we had, and scheduled my next appointment for four weeks later.

As we walked out, Ryker held the door for me and asked, "Crazy, huh? We're having a baby."

I laughed. "Yeah. Who would've thought?"

He linked our hands as we walked to the elevator. "Not me. You turned my life upside-down." He pressed the down button with one of his free fingers then poked my stomach.

I feigned offense. "Hey, you're the one who wouldn't leave me alone." I playfully yanked my hand from him, but he pulled me into him and closed his huge arms around me, trapping my body against his.

"I'm glad I didn't." Our eyes met as he looked down at me. He reached his hand up and brushed his knuckles down my cheek, making my knees weak and causing my face to instantly heat.

Ryker's proximity always made my heart race. My voice was unsteady as I spoke. "Oh, yeah? Why?"

The right corner of his mouth curved up in a sexy grin as he leaned, barely brushing those heavenly lips against mine. "Because I wouldn't have found my family if I hadn't."

My heart fluttered from his words. *Family.* The only family I'd ever truly had was Kamden, and to hear Ryker say that I was his family made me feel… amazing.

His hand pressed against my stomach as he closed the sliver of a gap between our mouths and kissed me. The elevator sounded, and Ryker pushed me through the doors and against the wall.

I didn't know if anyone was in there, and frankly, I didn't care. When Ryker's lips were on mine, all I was concerned about was consuming as much of him as I possibly could. The building could catch on fire and I'd be oblivious to it.

My hands framed his face as his tongue slipped past my lips. His fingers threaded through my hair until he reached the back of my head and gripped tightly, devouring me right there in the elevator. And I loved every second of it.

When the elevator sounded again, Ryker broke away from me, leaving me breathless and flushed. My lips tingled when I gave him a flirty smile as we exited.

I called Nori as soon as we got in the truck. The excitement was evident in her voice as she answered the phone. "So? What's the verdict?"

I paused for dramatic effect. "They said I'm about twelve weeks pregnant. I'm due August 2."

Nori squealed like a five year old into the phone, "Shut up! Oh my God, I'm so happy for you, Ky!"

Ryker started driving, then placed his hand on my leg and rubbed it affectionately. "Thank you. I think I'm still in shock."

"How did Ryker take it? Is he excited?"

I grinned as I looked over at him. "Very. The smile still hasn't come off his face."

"Aww, that's so sweet." She paused before squealing again. "I'm going to be an auntie!"

We chatted for a few minutes about my appointment hanging up.

"She's excited, huh?" Ryker asked as he turned at a stoplight.

"Yeah, she is. Already planning a baby shower and everything." I chuckled.

"How do you think Kamden will react?"

Shit.

I hadn't thought about that. Given his current state, I couldn't even speculate what his response to the news would be. "I don't know. I think he'll be happy, but I'm not positive."

Ryker squeezed my thigh. "I'm sure he will be. Don't worry about it, Warrior."

I looked out the window and sighed. I hoped that he was right.

Ryker

As Kaiya and I waited to see her doctor, a flurry of thoughts rushed through my mind. I'd been in this situation before with Molly, and I was trying not to let that ruin my experience with Kaiya; it was hard not to compare the two when it was a memorable event in both cases.

The nurse, who was named Sophie, finally called us back and led us to a room, then handed Kaiya a paper gown. "I'll give you a few minutes to change, then I'll be back to take your blood sample."

Kaiya changed into the gown and hopped on the exam table. I sat in the chair next to her, then a knock sounded.

"Ready?" Sophie asked, her voice muffled by the door.

"Yes," Kaiya replied shakily. I could tell she was nervous by her stiff demeanor and worried expression.

The nurse opened the door and came in with some tubes and one of the largest needles I'd ever seen. Kaiya gulped, fear evident on her face.

My poor Warrior.

Sophie set all the equipment on the counter before sterilizing Kaiya's arm with a cotton ball. Kaiya looked like she was about to pass out as the nurse tightly secured a band around her bicep and prepped the needle.

Grabbing her hand, I joined our fingers together and tugged it toward me to get her attention.

She looked at me and squeezed tightly, her eyes strained with nervousness. I brought her hand up to my lips and kissed the back of it. "Did I ever tell you about the time I got my first tattoo?"

Her eyebrows pursed together in thought. "No … I don't think so."

"Well, I had just turned eighteen. Tribal tattoos were popular, and almost everyone had one, so naturally, I wanted to get one, too." I paused and looked at my right arm, remembering the rush I'd had the whole day from when I woke up to when the tattoo artist wrapped my arm. "My boys and I went together to this tattoo shop in downtown Boston to each get a different tribal piece."

Her gaze went from my tattoo to my eyes. Smirking, I con-tinued speaking as the nurse stuck the syringe in Kaiya's arm. "When I sat on the table, my heart was pounding and adrenaline surged through my veins. Once that needle pierced my skin, I was hooked."

"Doesn't it hurt?"

I laughed. "Yeah, it hurts, but the rush you get from it is awesome. Everything about it is addicting, even the pain."

"I've always been too scared to get one. I hate needles," Kaiya replied, frowning.

"All done," Sophie said, setting the needle and filled vials on the medical cart.

Kaiya looked away from me to the nurse, who was cleaning up the counter. She glanced down at the Band-Aid applied to her inner elbow. "I didn't even feel it."

"You had a good distraction." Sophie chuckled as she motioned to me before opening the door. "Dr. Wallace will be with you shortly."

Kaiya's eyes came back to me. Grinning innocently, I shrugged. "I didn't want you to panic."

A smile spread over those beautiful lips of hers. "Thank you, babe."

I love making her smile.

After a few minutes, the doctor knocked, then entered. "Hi, Kaiya. How have you been?"

Kaiya sat up straighter. "I've been good. Busy, but good."

"Great," her doctor replied as she looked at the iPad in her hands. After several seconds, she looked up and smiled. "I have your results."

My heart thumped wildly as I stood up next to Kaiya and squeezed her hand. My gut twisted in anticipation as I waited to hear whether or not Kaiya was pregnant.

Dr. Wallace's smile stretched wider. "Congratulations! You're having a baby!"

Tears pooled in Kaiya's eyes as she looked up at me. I wrapped my arms around me and hugged her tightly, then kissed the top of her head.

"We're having a baby, Ryker." Kaiya softly murmured into my neck.

I'd never been so happy in all my life, even when I'd thought I was having a baby with Molly. With Kaiya it was different, more special because of how in love with her I was. I cradled her face in my hands and gently kissed her. Stroking her cheeks with my thumbs, I looked into her eyes.

There weren't words to express how I felt, but I could see the same emotion reflected back at me in Kaiya's gaze. Even though the pregnancy was unplanned, there was no denying we both wanted a baby together.

Dr. Wallace cleared her throat. "I'm sorry to interrupt, but we have a lot to discuss." She sat down in an office chair across from the exam table and wheeled it closer to us. "Let's go over your medical history, then we'll get to your exam and hear your baby's heartbeat."

Your baby.

After asking Kaiya a bunch of medical questions, Dr. Wallace continued, "We'll need to do an ultrasound to deter-mine how far along you are. Let me see if there's an ultrasound tech still here."

She swiveled in her chair and placed the iPad on the coun-ter, then reached for the phone. "Rachel, can you please check if there's an ultrasound tech available?"

A few moments later, she spoke into the phone again. "Thank you. Please send them to room nine."

Turning back to face us, she stated, "Let's get you all checked out. Lay back, please."

I turned my head, trying to give Kaiya some privacy, even though I was very familiar with that part of her anatomy. A few seconds after the doctor finished with the exam, a knock sounded on the door.

"Just in time," Dr. Wallace said as she washed her hands. "Come in."

A woman opened the door and entered with a large cart. "Hi, I'm

Jen. I'll be your ultrasound tech today." She smiled at us. "Ready to see your baby?"

"Yes," we said simultaneously. The sonogram had been my favorite part of the whole experience with Molly.

"Great! Lay back down and lift the top part of your gown up."

Jen wheeled the cart next to Kaiya and grabbed a tube. "This is going to be cold, okay?"

Kaiya nodded. Jen squirted the gel on her stomach before placing the ultrasound wand on it. Within seconds, the computer screen on the cart came on, but it took a few seconds for her to find the right spot. "There's your baby."

Both Kaiya and I stared in awe at the screen with our tiny baby on it. I couldn't take my eyes off of the little bean shape.

Dr. Wallace studied the screen. Jen glanced at her before stating, "I'd say she's about twelve or thirteen weeks along."

Dr. Wallace nodded. "I think so, too." She directed her attention to Kaiya. "Only one fetus—no twins."

The relief on Kaiya's face was instantaneous. I knew she was worried about having twins, and them ending up like her and Kaleb had.

"Would you like a picture?" Jen asked.

Kaiya nodded enthusiastically. "Yes, please."

After she pressed a few buttons on the computer, a small sonogram picture printed out. After getting Kaiya cleaned up, she handed her the photo. "Here you go—the first picture of your baby."

Kaiya glanced down at the sonogram in her hands, then up at me. She handed me the picture as Jen said, "It was nice meeting you. Good luck with your pregnancy."

Kaiya called out after her. "It was nice to meet you, too. Thank you so much!"

Dr. Wallace sat back down in her chair. "Do you have any questions for me?"

Kaiya looked up at me, then back at her doctor. "This is all so new and overwhelming, but my mind is blank right now."

I was right there with her. Even though I'd done this before, I couldn't think about anything but the sonogram in my hands.

My baby.

When I'd found out that Molly's baby hadn't been mine, I was devastated. I felt like I'd been given a second chance with Kaiya, a blessing I could never be thankful enough for.

Dr. Wallace laughed. "That's understandable. This is your first child, and not everyone knows what to ask. That's why we have a packet with everything you need to know to take home. We can go over it before you leave."

Kaiya sighed in relief. "Thank you. I feel so much better."

Dr. Wallace's eyes lit up as her eyebrows rose. "Oh, I almost forgot! Let's listen to your baby's heartbeat." She stood and grabbed a handheld machine and another tube of gel from one of the cabinets. It had a wand similar to the ultrasound machine at the end, only smaller. "This is a fetal doppler."

Dr. Wallace squeezed more gel on Kaiya's belly and placed the wand on her stomach. Static and swooshing filled the room as she moved the sensor around. "Where are you, little one?"

She traced Kaiya's lower abdomen before a noise that sounded like a horse galloping mixed with the other sounds. "There you are."

Kaiya glanced from her stomach to Dr. Wallace. "That's the heartbeat? It's so fast."

"That's perfectly normal. The heartbeat of a fetus ranges anywhere between one hundred twenty and one hundred eighty beats per minute."

I squeezed Kaiya's hand and grinned widely. It was amazing hearing our baby's heartbeat, and going through the experience together. The only downfall was that everything that had happened with Molly was looming in the back of my mind, making me have doubts.

I kept reassuring myself that Kaiya and Molly were two different people. Kaiya wouldn't lie to me about something as monumental as a baby, especially since she knew about how bad Molly had hurt me.

At least I hoped she wouldn't.

Chapter Twelve

Ryker

Kaiya was nervous about telling Kamden about the baby the whole drive home. She was worried he would blow up at her for being irresponsible, and to be honest, I was concerned about how he would react, too. He had become pretty hot-headed since the shooting.

When we walked in, the smell of fresh, baked bread greeted us. Kaiya gave me a confused look as she tossed her keys on the table and took off her coat. "Kam?"

"In here," he yelled back.

I followed Kaiya into the kitchen, where Kamden was cooking. He turned his head toward us and smiled as he stirred a pot on the stove. "Hey."

"Hey, yourself," Kaiya replied as she quirked up an eyebrow. "What are you doing?"

He set the spoon he was stirring with on the counter before facing us. "I know I haven't been the easiest person to deal with lately." He rubbed the back of his neck sheepishly as he looked at Ky. "I wanted to start making up for how I've been acting. I shouldn't have taken my issues out on you, and I'm sorry."

Kaiya didn't say anything in response. Instead, she rushed to Kamden and threw her arms around his waist. A loving smile spread over his lips as he wrapped his arms around her and hugged her tightly. "I'm going to try and stop drinking, too. Haven't had a drink since Saturday."

"That's amazing, Kam. I'm so proud of you."

My mouth curved up involuntarily as I watched them. Kaiya loved Kamden so much, and watching him sink into a downward spiral had been tearing her apart inside.

The timer on the stove went off, and Kamden let go of Kaiya. "Don't want the bread to burn."

He grabbed an oven mitt and opened the oven before pulling out a tray with French bread on it. He set the tray on the stove and said, "It's nothing elaborate, but I did make the meatballs from scratch."

"It's perfect, Kam. You really didn't have to do this," Kaiya said.

"I wanted to, *sorella.* Now go sit down. It's almost ready."

Kaiya walked to the cabinets. "Let me set the table at least."

Kamden blocked her path and gave her a stern look. "Out," he ordered as he fought a smile.

"Fine." Kaiya laughed. She grabbed my hand as she walked by me and tugged me into the dining room.

Kamden came with plates a minute or so after we sat down. He set one down in front of each of us, then went back into the kitchen.

When he came back and set everything on the table, he sat down across from us and gestured to the food. "Go ahead. Dig in."

Kaiya and I served ourselves, then waited for Kamden to do the same before we started eating.

Kamden stopped and rose from his seat. "Forgot drinks."

He came back with three water bottles and handed us each one. He unscrewed his bottle and took a drink as he sat back down. "How's everything with you guys?

Kaiya glanced over at me and smiled. "Well, uh, we have some exciting news."

Kamden took a bite of his spaghetti. "Oh, yeah? What?"

Kaiya joined our hands under the table, but directed her attention to her brother. "I'm pregnant." Her voice was shaky and unsure.

Kamden choked on the water he'd just drank and quickly cleared his throat. "What?"

She squeezed my hand. "I'm pregnant. We just found out today. Isn't that great?" Kaiya asked nervously.

His eyes darted back and forth between us before they settled on Kaiya. "Are you sure you're ready for this, Ky?"

Kaiya's face fell and her shoulders sagged. "Yes. Ryker and I love each other. Aren't you happy?"

His eyes softened. "I'm concerned, *sorella.* That's all. If you're happy, I'm happy."

"I am." She looked down at her stomach and smiled. "We got to hear the baby's heartbeat and everything. Wanna see the sonogram?"

"Of course—let me see my future niece or nephew," Kamden replied enthusiastically.

Kaiya started to stand, but I stopped her. "I'll get it, baby. You relax."

I went to Kaiya's purse and dug around for the sonogram. II found it in one of the inner pockets of her purse. A smile came over my face as I looked down at the little bean shaped image.

I'm going to be a dad.

A fullness in my chest filled me. I'd never felt anything like it before—I was in love with a little bean. And then I remembered, I had felt that way before. I closed my eyes as my stomach dropped.

What if he's not mine?

Doubt replaced the joy. I glanced over at Ky and Kamden, who were laughing at the table. Her eyes found mine from across the room, and they told me everything I needed to know.

Fuck all the doubts.

Molly had never looked at me that way, even at our best times. Kaiya's love for me was always written all over her face. There was no reason I should be doubting her.

Our eyes remained locked as I walked back to the dining room. I leaned down and kissed Kaiya before handing her the sonogram. She excitedly gave it to Kamden. He scanned over the picture as a grin tipped up his lips. "Is it a boy or a girl?"

"We won't find that out until between eighteen and twenty weeks. I'm only about twelve or thirteen weeks now," Kaiya answered.

Kaiya told Kamden about what we had learned at her appointment throughout dinner. Once we were finished, she started collecting the dishes from the table as Kamden asked, "What are you doing?"

"I'm cleaning up—you did enough tonight," Kaiya replied as she stacked the plates and began putting the dirty silverware on top of them.

"I don't think so—you need to rest." Kamden took the dishes from her.

Kaiya rolled her eyes. "I'm pregnant, not dying."

Kamden chuckled. "Enjoy it while it lasts. Once you pop out that baby, you'll get all your old chores back."

"Seriously, go rest, Warrior. You've been stressing yourself out too much." I stood and rubbed her arms. "It's not good for the baby."

She sighed. "Fine. I'm gonna go lay down. You coming?"

I kissed her on the forehead. "I'll be right there."

Kaiya turned and walked away. You could see the exhaustion in every weary step she took—she was so stubborn sometimes.

Kamden had taken most of the dishes off the table, but I grabbed the remaining bowls with the leftover spaghetti and salad in them and carried them into the kitchen.

I set the bowls on the counter as Kamden began loading the dishwasher. "Thanks."

"No problem." I leaned back against the counter. "I just wanted to say that I think it's great what you're doing. I know it means a lot to Kaiya."

"Yeah. I can't keep hurting her like I have been. That night I pushed her" —he shook his head and scowled— "was an eye-opener. I hadn't realized how bad I was."

Before I could comment, Kamden looked up at me and changed the subject by asking, "You're going to take care of my sister and the baby, right?"

I could hear the warning in his tone. I stood tall and crossed my arms over my chest. "Of course. I love her." And I wasn't a punk bitch who ran away from their responsibilities.

Kamden looked me up and down. "You better."

I never understood why Kamden and I'd never gotten along. Maybe older brothers were always assholes to their sister's boyfriends, or felt they had some kind of territory to mark, but he had another thing coming if he thought I was going to let him intimidate me.

I stepped up to him. "Look, let's get this straight. I don't give a fuck what you think. Kaiya and our baby are the only things that matter to me. Get your own shit together and let me worry about Kaiya."

His jaw clenched as we stared each other down.

"Ryker?" Kaiya called out from her room.

I kept my eyes locked on Kamden's as I replied, "Coming, babe." I held his stare and said, "I'm going to take care of Kaiya and the baby. You handle your business and I'll handle mine."

I brushed past him to go down the hall. I heard dishes roughly clanging together as I entered Kaiya's room and shut the door.

She was lying down on the bed, propped up with pillows under her back as she read a book. She glanced up at me and smiled as she closed it and set it on the nightstand. "Hey."

"Hey." I flopped onto the bed and scooted next to her. I pulled her body into mine, and she curved up against me and rested her head on my chest. "Big day today, huh?" I asked.

I played with her hair as she traced my abs through my shirt. "Yeah, I was just thinking about what we're going to do when the baby comes."

"Like what?" She moved so that she could look up at me. "Like whose apartment we're going to live in, everything we need to get for him or her, stuff like that."

I hadn't thought about where we were going to live once the baby was born—I was still processing the fact that we we're even having one. "Definitely not here." I was not living with Kamden.

Kaiya chuckled. "Well, your apartment is too small—we need a nursery for the baby."

"We can get a bigger apartment or maybe even a house."

Her eyes lit up. "Really?"

I ran my fingers through her hair. "Yeah." I smiled. "Get our own place, start a family."

Kaiya smiled sweetly and looked at me dreamily. "That sounds perfect."

I had to admit that it did. Settling down hadn't ever appealed to me, but Kaiya always found a way to change my mind about things.

"Yeah, it does." I kissed the top of her head. "So are you happy about Kamden?"

The sigh she made was full of relief. "Yes. I hope he can pull through this. I want him to be a part of the baby's life, but not if he's going to be angry and drunk all the time."

That's not going to happen. I wouldn't let Kamden near our baby if he didn't get his shit together, Kaiya's brother or not. "I'm sure he will. He's stubborn like you, so I don't think he'll give up."

She smacked my chest and scoffed. "I'm not stubborn."

My chest rumbled with laughter. "Sure, baby, whatever you say."

Kaiya softly giggled, then suddenly stopped and became serious. "Do you think I'll be a good mom?"

I looked in her eyes and cupped her cheek. "The best. I couldn't have asked for a better woman to have my kids."

She placed her hand over my mine and her eyes watered. "I'm just worried that because I'm so fucked up that I'll screw their life up, too." She hung her head and avoided my eyes.

I framed her face in my hands, forcing her to look at me again. "Hey. You're not fucked up, Warrior. You may be scarred, but you're not broken. You're the most incredible person I've ever met. You've changed my whole life, made me better." I paused and stroked her cheeks softly. "You're going to be an amazing mother, Ky."

A few tears slipped down her face. I wiped them away as she leaned up and softly kissed my lips. She pulled back, and the corner of her mouth slightly lifted. "I think you're biased but thank you."

I lightly chuckled. "No, I'm not—you are. You think what Kaleb did to you made you weak, but in reality, it did the opposite. He tried to break you, but he didn't. He only made you stronger."

"He didn't make me stronger." Her eyes held mine. "You did."

I smiled and caressed her cheeks. "I only built on what was already there. You may have had some splinters and cracks, but your foundation was still strong."

She turned into one of my hands and kissed my palm. "I don't know where I'd be without you. Thank you for everything you've done for me." She looked down at her stomach and placed her hands on it. "Especially blessing me with this."

Leaning my forehead against hers, I followed her gaze. "You're the one blessing me, Warrior. You carrying my baby is just…" I put my hands over hers. "Amazing."

We stayed like that for several seconds before Kaiya spoke. "Did you say kids?"

I pulled my head back from hers. "Huh?"

She grinned playfully. "A minute ago—you said that you couldn't have asked for a better woman to have your kids."

I raised an eyebrow. "Yeah?"

"Plural, meaning more than one?"

I chuckled. "Yes. I want you to have my kids, plural."

She tucked some of her hair behind her ear. "You know, I never planned to have kids."

"Well, sorry to have ruined your plans," I teased.

She stared into my eyes. "You didn't ruin anything. I wasn't living before. I always blocked out the world and the ugliness it contained." She gave me a shy smile. "You changed that—you showed me how beautiful life can be."

My eyes ran over her face. "Same here. After my parents died, life wasn't the same. And then, everything that happened with Ethan and Molly solidified what I thought—life's a bitch, and then you die. But then I met you, and you reminded me that life is a gift." I brushed my knuckles down her cheek. "You are my gift."

Leaning in, I gently kissed her lips and pulled her against me. My heart raced every time that sweet mouth of hers met mine. Kaiya was my high, the addiction I couldn't satisfy. No matter how much I had of her, it wasn't enough; I still wanted more.

My hands went to her ass as I pushed my hardening cock against her. She softly moaned in my mouth and threaded her fingers through my hair.

A knock on the door broke us apart. I buried my face in one of Kaiya's pillows and let out a groan of frustration.

Damn it, we should have stayed at my place.

I peeked up at Kaiya to see her lips twitching as she fought a smile. She mouthed sorry before saying, "Come in."

Kamden stuck his head in the room. "Hey, I rented a couple of movies for us to watch. I was just about to put the first one in." He raised his eyebrows expectantly, like a kid asking for ice cream.

I knew Kaiya would say yes before she even spoke. The endearing look on her face said it all. "Okay, we'll be right there."

"Awesome, I'll make some popcorn," Kamden replied before turning around and going back down the hallway.

Kaiya yawned as she sat up on the edge of the bed. "I don't know if I'll even make it through the first movie. I'm so tired."

She came around to my side as I stood up. "Are you sure you want to stay up? Maybe you should get some sleep—it's been a long day."

"No, it's okay. I want to spend some time with Kam, especially since he's trying to work through his issues."

I draped my arm around her and kissed her temple. "Okay, Warrior. Whatever you want."

We headed out the door toward the living room. Even though I would much rather be in bed alone with Kaiya, I still enjoyed doing homey stuff with her.

We sat down as the sound of popping and the smell of popcorn filled the air. Kaiya snuggled close to me and leaned her head on my shoulder, then yawned again.

Yeah, she'll be asleep in half an hour, tops.

I put my arm around her as Kamden brought the popcorn in two bowls and handed us one. Kaiya started munching on the snack as Kamden started the movie.

Kaiya made it about twenty minutes before she started dozing off. Her head would slip off my shoulder and she would jolt awake and start fighting sleep again.

Kamden laughed. "Tired, *sorella?*"

"No," Kaiya lied. "I was just resting my eyes."

I snorted, causing Kaiya to glare at me as she sat up.

So stubborn.

She finally gave in to sleep halfway through the movie. I gently cradled her in my lap before rising off the couch. "I'm gonna take her to bed. It's been a long day."

I heard the movie turn off as I walked down the hall to Kaiya's room. I shut the door with my foot and laid her down on the bed. She didn't move an inch, even when I covered her and kissed her lips—she was completely out.

I took off my jeans and shirt, then slid into bed next to her. Wrapping my arms around her waist, I placed one of my hands on her stomach and smiled.

My baby.

The smile was still on my face when I fell asleep.

At work the following day, my mind was still swarming with thoughts about the baby. Most were good, but every now and then, a negative one slipped in there.

What if the baby's not mine?

I pushed the thought away, not wanting to ruin the happiness I felt. I hated that what had happened in my past was making me question Kaiya, but I couldn't help having doubts given my experience with Molly.

I wasn't upset over Molly and Ethan anymore, but what they did had left a mark on me, a scar I would never forget. But now that I was going to be a dad and start a family of my own with Kaiya, I was starting to see that there were more important things than holding grudges.

Ethan had also been in and out of my mind all morning. Seeing Kamden trying to make an effort to rebuild his relationship with Kaiya made me think more about doing the same. Ethan was my blood, and I didn't think my parents would want us to be the way we were.

I still had his number in my phone; I could never bring myself to delete it. I'd told myself it was so I would know not to answer his calls or texts, but I think deep down, I didn't want to completely let him go.

I scrolled through my contacts until I came to Ethan's. I pressed the text message icon, and began typing my message to him.

Me: You free for lunch today? Wanted to talk

I set my phone on my desk and looked over my client invoices for the month. A few minutes later, my phone buzzed, and I was surprised by how nervous I was. I hadn't spoken to my brother since before the shooting, and the times before that weren't on the best of terms.

Grabbing my phone, I clicked on the text icon and pulled up Ethan's message.

Ethan: R u serious or is this a joke?

The corner of my lip curved up. I couldn't blame him for not trusting me, especially with how hostile I'd been every time he'd tried to contact me.

Me: I'm serious do u want to meet up or not?

Ethan: When and where?

I told Ethan to meet me at one o'clock at a deli not too far from the gym. Once sending the text, my nerves skyrocketed. The meeting could either completely destroy what little remained of our relationship or get us on the path to mending it. I tried to tell myself that I didn't care either way, but deep down, I was hoping we could make amends.

I was a few minutes early, but Ethan was already seated at a table. When he saw me, he stiffly waved his hand and gave me a tight-lipped smile.

I walked toward him, disliking the unease settling in my gut. I was starting to second-guess my decision.

Why am I doing this? What are we going to talk about? How can I ever trust him again?

When I reached the table, I sat down.

"Hey," Ethan nervously greeted.

This is awkward already.

"Hey."

Ethan anxiously tapped his finger on the table. "So, how have you been?"

"Fine," I clipped. I wasn't ready to share personal details about my life just yet—baby steps. "How about you?"

"Good. Everything's good. Tristan is getting big." He smiled broadly.

Thinking about Tristan used to piss me off so much. He used to remind me of what I had lost and the betrayal committed against me by my own brother. It still irked me a little, only because there was still animosity between Ethan and me, but I didn't have anything against the kid.

I visualized having my own son, and a small grin tipped my lips. "That's good."

Ethan leaned back in his seat and scanned over my face. "Why did you invite me here, Ryker?"

The million dollar question. I cleared my throat. "A lot has happened since I last saw you, and they've made me realize some things." I paused and rubbed my hands together. "Life is-"

A tiny brunette interrupted me. "Hi, my name is Brooke, and I'll be your waitress today. Can I get you something to drink?"

After she left to get our drinks, Ethan's eyes met mine. "You were saying?"

I sighed. "Life's too short to hold grudges and take things for granted. You're my only brother, and I wanted to try and make amends. Mom and Dad would've wanted that."

We silently stared at one another until our waitress came back with our drinks. "Are you ready to order?"

"We need a few minutes," Ethan responded without breaking eye contact. Brooke said something I didn't make out and walked away, leaving us alone again.

After a minute or so, Ethan smiled. "I'd like that. Believe it or not, I miss your arrogant ass."

I snorted as our waitress came back up to our table. She raised her eyebrows at us. "Ready?"

We scanned the lunch specials, and settled on sandwiches. When she walked away, Ethan asked, "Does this change of heart have anything to do with the woman you were with when I came to the gym?"

I smiled as I thought about Kaiya. "Yeah. She's made a big difference in my life."

"Tell me about her," Ethan urged.

I took a drink of my water. "Kaiya is… something else." I chuckled. "I've never met anyone like her. She's shown me what real love is."

"Sounds pretty serious." Ethan raised his eyebrows.

"Yeah, we are. We just found out she's pregnant." The grin on my face spread wider.

"That's great! Having a child is one of the most fulfilling things you'll ever experience. Tristan is the best thing that's ever happened to me."

As if realizing he said something wrong, Ethan's smile fell. "Look, I'm really sorry about what I did to you. Neither one of us planned to. We just fell in love. I don't regret it, but I do regret hurting you in the process."

A year ago, what Ethan had just said would've sent me into a furious rage. What they did had disrespected my relationship with my brother. It still annoyed me, but didn't piss me off like it used to. "I know. Let's just try to move on—put the past behind us."

Ethan nodded. "Sounds like a plan."

Once our food came, we started talking about our lives—work, daily life, likes and dislikes, basically trying to get reacquainted. So much had changed since college.

While we waited for our tab, Ethan suggested, "Maybe we should all go out to dinner—me, you, Molly, Kaiya, and Tristan. Get to know each other better."

I was not ready for that. Reconciling with Ethan was one thing, but Molly was a different story. "I'm not sure about that just yet. Let me think about it."

"Too much, too fast, huh? I understand. Let me know when you're ready."

I nodded. "This was good. Maybe we can do it again next week—start off with that."

Ethan stuck his hand out across the table. "Deal."

I looked at it hesitantly before grabbing his hand with my own. "Deal."

Ethan shook my hand firmly and smiled. He reminded me so much of my mom with his green eyes and light brown hair.

Maybe this'll work out.

Our waitress came with our tab, and I took my wallet from my back pocket. Ethan protested as he placed his card on the table. "Let me."

"It's cool. I got it." I slipped a ten on the on the receipt for my part of the lunch. I wasn't ready to take anything from him.

Ethan chuckled and shrugged. "Suit yourself."

We made plans to get together for lunch the following week—same time, same place. As I drove back to work, I felt like some weight had been lifted off me from trying to work things out with Ethan. I just hoped that he didn't end up screwing me over again.

Chapter Thirteen

Kaiya

The day following our appointment, Ryker texted me questions he wanted me to ask my doctor about attending class. He'd read some of the packets Dr. Wallace had given us before going to work and had thought of a few questions when he got to the section on exercise. The fact that he took the time to read any of it warmed my heart—I didn't think most guys would even bother.

I'd found out that I could continue kickboxing until I was about seven or eight months along, but I wouldn't be able to keep doing the self-defense techniques the same. I wasn't allowed to throw anyone or be thrown, spar, or take any type of hits to the stomach whatsoever.

I wasn't surprised when Dr. Wallace informed me of my limitations. I'd already assumed that I would just have to watch class if I wanted to continue learning the various self-defense maneuvers before she confirmed it.

I was disappointed, especially since I was still receiving the harassing texts from the blocked number. I wanted to keep practicing, but I knew I had to think about the health of my baby first.

When I walked into the studio, Ryker smiled broadly as he strode toward me. "I have some good news."

"Oh yeah? What?" I replied, tiptoeing up to kiss him.

He rubbed his hands up and down my sides. "I did some research and found some self-defense maneuvers you can do."

A hopeful grin teased my lips. "Really?" My voice brightened from the dull tone I'd had after talking to my doctor.

"Yeah." He nodded. "The techniques come from jujitsu martial arts. They're referred to as small circle hapkido techniques."

My eyebrows furrowed. "What makes the moves different from the ones you usually teach in class?"

Ryker gripped my hands in his and held them in between us. "Small circle hapkido focuses primarily on wrist and hand locks and maneuvers, which disable your attacker with just simple, fluid movements focusing on various pressure points in the hands and wrist."

He took my right hand in both of his and massaged it. "There are so many vulnerable spots that take just a little force to cause substantial pain." He squeezed the area between my thumb and index finger, right next to the base of my thumb. "Like here. It was interesting to read about."

I was still skeptical. "Hmm, are you sure? I don't want anything happening to the baby."

The corner of his lip curved up in a small smirk. "I called your doctor and described the techniques. She said they were fine."

I quirked my eyebrow up in surprise. "You called Dr. Wallace?"

He nodded. "I didn't want to do anything that would endanger you or the baby."

My heart melted. "That was sweet of you, baby. Thank you."

Ryker reached out his hand and placed it on my stomach. "Anything for you, Warrior."

I stood on my tiptoes to kiss him. His hands traveled around my sides to my back, pulling me against him. I broke the kiss and smiled. "I love you."

He brushed his fingertips down my cheek. "I love you, too."

The other instructors walked in, so I went to my bag and put my gear on as Ryker approached them to discuss the class.

Once we finished working on the bags, Ryker gathered us on the mats. "Today, we're going to start a series of self-defense techniques that are different from what we normally practice, but just as effective, if not more."

He motioned for Mark to come to him and grabbed his hand. "We're going to focus on maneuvers that concentrate on the hands and wrists to disable your attacker." He gripped two of Mark's fingers and pushed them back, causing Mark to wince in pain and squirm in discomfort. "As you can see, I'm putting very little effort into causing Mark pain already."

Ryker twisted Mark's hand while keeping his fingers bent back. Mark fell to his knees and tapped out almost instantly. Ryker let go and addressed the class. "Simple, but extremely effective. Even those that don't know any punches, kicks, or other self-defense maneuvers could still defend themselves using these techniques."

"Looks easy—too easy," one of the students voiced.

Ryker smirked. "Looks can be deceiving. Let me show you the first technique before you make your mind up."

After Ryker demonstrated, he came over and stuck his arm out. "Grab my wrist."

I gripped his thick wrist like he instructed. "Most of the small circle techniques defend against some type of grab." Using his other hand, he reached over and grabbed my hand, right at the base of my fingers. "So if someone grabs your wrist, there are various ways to get out of it without exerting too much force."

He squeezed and started prying my hand off his wrist. "Secure your hand over the top of theirs and apply pressure. Then, pull their hand off and turn it as you bring it up to your chest. Their palm should face away from you." The side of my hand was twisted uncomfortably as Ryker held it against his collarbone. "From here, bring your other hand up and grasp the inside of their elbow." He pressed his fingers against my inner elbow and pulled it back. "Then, apply pressure while pulling and pushing down on the joint."

Ryker had forced me to bend over to compensate for the pain and unnatural position he'd put me in. "Once you have them in this position, you can easily snap their arm, get some kicks to their stomach or groin, or even some knees to the face."

He loosened his grip but held onto my arm. Moving his hands up my forearm to my elbow, he started massaging the strained joint. "You okay?"

"Yeah, I'm good." I pulled my arm away and started bending and moving my elbow to get rid of the remaining tension. "My turn?"

One side of Ryker's mouth lifted. "Yeah, Warrior." He grabbed my slender wrist with one of his large, inked hands. "Go ahead."

The move was pretty simple to execute, so I didn't need much guidance from Ryker. Like some of the other students, I was skeptical about how easy the small circle techniques seemed and wondered if the moves were as effective as Ryker said.

But as soon as I brought Ryker's hand up to my chest and saw his face straining from the pain, my doubts faded. While the move was uncomfortable for me, it didn't hurt too much because I was flexible. However, Ryker, and most men for that matter, weren't typically limber. At all.

Ryker tapped out as soon once I started pulling back on his elbow. I let him go and giggled. "I can't believe it's that easy."

Ryker rotated his shoulder and bent his elbow several times. "I told you. Simple, but effective."

"But what if the person tries to hit you while you're attempting the move?"

Ryker stepped toward me. "That's a good question. With any technique that I teach you, there's always that possibility. You have to stay aware of what your attacker is doing and counter if needed. How an attack will progress can't be predicted, and that's why I teach so many different maneuvers so that you're as prepared as possible for whatever is thrown at you."

I nodded. "That makes sense. It sucks not knowing what they're going to do, though."

"I know, baby. What's good is that most attackers aren't trained like you are, so you have that advantage. Plus, when someone is in pain, that's typically all they focus on. They don't even think about anything else like fighting back. All that's on their mind is how to stop the pain."

Ryker had me practice a few more times and threw in some punches for me to block as I tried to execute the move. While it was more difficult, I instinctively reacted and countered. The move took longer, but I was still able to complete it.

Once class ended, many of the students gave Ryker a lot of positive feedback on the new technique. They were excited to learn more, which thrilled him. He'd been worried about how small circle hapkido would be received by the class.

As we walked into the parking lot, my phone started ringing. I grabbed it out of my purse and automatically answered it without looking at the screen. "Hello?"

There was no response, so I repeated myself. "Hello?"

Heavy breathing sounded through the phone. My stomach tightened as I pulled the phone away and looked at the caller ID on my screen. It was an unknown number.

I immediately hung up and shoved my phone back into my purse.

"Who was it?" Ryker asked as we reached my car.

I swallowed the lump that had formed in my throat. "Wrong number."

"Weird." He leaned in to kiss me. "I'll see you at home."

I hugged him tightly for a few seconds after our kiss before letting go. "Okay."

"Drive safe." He smiled as he backed away in the direction his truck.

I quickly opened the door and got in the car. My hands trembled as I locked the doors and fumbled to get the keys in the ignition.

I dropped my keys on the floorboard. "Shit."

Breathe, Kaiya. Calm down.

I rested my head against the steering wheel and took deep breaths before reaching down for my keys. My hands were still shaking as I put the key in and started the engine.

I told myself that everything would be fine, but I knew better. Things were always too good to be true, and I wondered when this would come crashing down on me, just like everything else always did.

Kamden bounced his leg anxiously as we sat waiting for Dr. Lowell to come in for his weekly session. He was opening up more during therapy, which seemed to be helping with his drinking since he wasn't looking for a way out anymore. He was facing his issues and not trying to wash them away with alcohol.

Even though Kamden had been sober for about two weeks, he was more irritable than ever. He was strung so tight that I was afraid he would snap at any moment, but thankfully he hadn't yet. I hoped that it would start becoming easier for him soon so that he could stop his self-loathing and finally start healing. I could only imagine what he was going through.

Once Dr. Lowell came in and got settled, she opened with her standard greeting of asking us how we were doing. Kamden drummed his thumbs against his knees as he answered, "Still sober—going on two weeks now."

"That's great, Kamden." Dr. Lowell replied proudly. "How do you feel about that?"

Kamden looked down at the floor and rubbed his palms together. "I want to drink so bad. I want to get rid of this guilt eating at me; take away the pain. I've come so close to giving in."

Dr. Lowell scribbled on her notepad. "What's stopped you?"

Kamden sat up and fixed his gaze on the window. "I deserve it—the pain, the guilt. I deserve to feel every bit of it, not be a coward and hide from it."

His words stung my heart—I hated that he felt that way. He didn't deserve any of what he was experiencing, especially when it was because he had been protecting me.

Dr. Lowell set her pen down. "I know it's hard right now, and things will probably get worse before they get better. But, they will get better. Time heals all wounds."

Did she really just say that?

I hated that stupid saying. "Is that what they tell you to say to everyone? That's such generic bullshit. I can be the first to tell you that it doesn't. Time just allows scars to form over your wounds that you never forget." I crossed my arms over my chest and huffed in frustration. I didn't care if I looked like a bratty child.

I hate therapists.

Out of the corner of my eye, I saw a smirk tilt Kamden's lips. "Kaiya is an expert on wounds."

Dr. Lowell directed her attention to me. "It's not just time that heals your wounds. It's a combination of various things. Support from your loved ones is a big part of it, too. You being here with Kamden is an example of that. Believe or not, you are helping so much with his healing process just by being here."

I didn't believe that, but then Kamden looked at me and gave me a small, but genuine smile. "She's right, *sorella.* You're the main reason that I'm doing this."

I stared into his eyes—those familiar, stormy eyes that had kept me from completely losing it when my demons tried to pull me under. Reaching out, I placed my hand on his thigh. "I'm going to be there for you, Kam, just like you were for me. No one else ever has been."

Silence settled over the room as Kam placed his hand over mine. After several seconds, Dr. Lowell broke it by saying, "The bond you two have is very strong. The love between you is apparent. I want to know more about how your relationship developed into what it is today. Tell me more about your family life when you were younger."

I stiffened apprehensively and tightened my grip on Kamden's leg. My eyes widened as they locked on his, and his jaw tensed as he swallowed deeply and rubbed my hand.

I darted my gaze to Dr. Lowell. "How is that relevant?"

She held my stare. "No matter how much you hate your past and family, they're still a part of what made you who you are today. The source of most issues stems back to a specific part of someone's past. You need to face them in order to move on."

When neither one of us said anything, she directed her attention to Kamden and continued, "We've discussed your mother and brother extensively. Tell me more about your father."

Kamden stilled his hand over mine. "Our dad left shortly after Kaleb was committed. I think that broke the last thread he was tied to us by."

Dr. Lowell wrote on her notepad. "Was your father involved in your lives before that?"

Kamden shook his head and tightened his grip on my hand. "He was there, but not really there, you know? My mom didn't make life easy, and I can't imagine what he had to deal with being married to her. I think it was too much for him."

Thinking about my father, or lack thereof, made me angry. I pulled my hand away from Kamden and crossed my arms over my chest again. I felt that my dad should've protected me from my mom and Kaleb, prevented any of what they'd done to me from ever happening. He was a complete failure as a father in my eyes.

"Kaiya, do you have anything that you would like to add?" Dr. Lowell inquired.

My eyes watered. I shifted uncomfortably in my seat and avoided her gaze. I didn't want to have another meltdown like when we talked about my mother, and typically anything involving my past triggered my outbursts. "I agree with what Kamden said—he described our father pretty accurately."

"How does that make you feel?"

Damn it. This woman does not know when to quit. Fucking therapists.

Giving in, I sighed. "Angry. I think so much could've been prevented had he been more involved."

"Do you think this had any effect on your relationship with Kamden?"

I glanced at Kamden before meeting Dr. Lowell's eyes. "No. I kept everything to myself before everything happened with Kaleb. Our relationship didn't develop until after that." Looking over at my brother, I smiled softly. "He's kept me from falling apart ever since."

Kamden grinned and put his arm around my shoulders before pulling me into him. He kissed the top of my head and squeezed me tightly. He whispered softly against my hair, "Thank you for not giving up on me, *sorella*."

Winding my arms around him, I returned his embrace. "I could never give up on you, Kam. Ever."

Dr. Lowell spoke, "The support you give one another will be what pulls you through. I have no doubt in my mind that you will overcome this. Both of you."

I'd always thought that, but deep down, I was afraid that I wouldn't be enough to get Kamden through. I didn't consider myself to be the best person to lean on because of how unstable I was, so hearing Dr. Lowell say what she had just said was very reassuring.

I pulled away from Kamden and looked up at him.

We can do this. We will do this.

Ryker and I drove around one of the nicer, older neighborhoods in Cambridge, hoping to find a house to buy. We'd started looking the day after we found out about the baby, and a couple of weeks had passed without finding one that we really liked.

"Oh my God, Ryker. Look at that house!" I gasped in excitement as I pointed out my window.

Ryker slowed down and peered out toward where my finger was pointing. "Which one?"

"The white one with the big trees. It has a for sale sign out front."

Ryker pulled over and parked right in front of the beautiful home. A Victorian style house complete with a wraparound porch sat on a nicely manicured lawn with two huge magnolia trees in the front.

I stepped out of the car and stared in awe at the gorgeous home in front of me.

It's perfect.

Ryker came and draped his arm over my shoulder. "You like it, Warrior?"

I couldn't take my eyes off the house. "I love it."

He chuckled as he led me to the For Sale sign on the yard. Taking out my phone, I keyed in the number and called the realtor listed.

"Thank you for calling Cambridge Realty, this is Tanya, how may I help you?"

"Hi, I'm calling about one of your properties for sale. I'd like to set up an appointment to see it."

Her voice brightened. "Great! What's the address?"

I looked at the number on the house. "9603 Briarwood Lane."

"Oh, I love that property. It just went on the market last week." She paused for a few seconds. "I can show tomorrow at two. Will that work for you?"

"Hold on a second, please." I pulled the phone away from my ear and directed my attention to Ryker. "She can show us tomorrow at two."

He nodded. "Works for me."

I smiled and put the phone back to my ear. "We'll take it."

"Great! I have you down. Let me get some information from you before we hang up. I also want to get your email to send you the detailed listing for the house so you can look over everything before the showing."

I gave Tanya all of my contact information and thanked her before hanging up. I looked at Ryker. "She's going to send me the listing for the house tonight."

He reached out his hand toward me. "I bet it's expensive. It's a really nice place."

I took his outstretched hand, and he led me back to the car. "Yeah, I hope it's in our price range."

He opened the car for me. "Me too, Warrior."

After he shut the door, I stared out the window at what I hoped would be our new home. It reminded of the home I used to dream of having when I was little, a safe haven where I wouldn't have to deal with Kaleb or my mother.

Maybe my dreams are finally coming true.

A small smile formed over my lips as we drove away, and I couldn't wait for tomorrow to come.

Butterflies of excitement swarmed my stomach as we drove back to my dream house. I could barely contain my anticipation, fidgeting in my seat as I stared out the window.

"Excited?" Ryker chuckled, patting my thigh affectionately.

"You have no idea," I responded, still not taking my eyes off the passing scenery in the neighborhood. The landscaping of every house was like out of a movie scene, with beautiful trees, colorful gardens, and perfect grass.

I'd read over the listing several times last night before going to bed. The house was about fifteen thousand more than we had been pre-approved for through our lender, but we were hoping that the sellers would accept a counter offer.

I practically jumped out of the car when we pulled up. I felt like I was about to bust out of my skin because of the excitement coursing through me.

"Wait for me," Ryker laughed as he shut the door to car. He reached for my hand and led me up the walkway toward the house.

When we walked up the steps to the porch, I could see the front door open through the closed screen. A woman stood inside near the staircase to the second floor. She smiled broadly when she saw us. "Welcome!" She opened the screen door. "My name is Tanya. It's so great to meet you. Please, come on in."

I fell more in love with the house when we stepped inside. Hardwood floors spread beneath our feet. A fireplace crackled in the living room to our right, and the dining room sat to our left.

We introduced ourselves before Tanya started the tour. She gestured to the living room. "Let's start in here."

As Tanya led us through the house, she explained every intricate detail, from the crown molding to the vaulted ceilings. The home had been built in the late 1800s, but the interior had been completely remodeled within the last few years.

All of the bedrooms but the master were upstairs, along with a game room and two full bathrooms. In addition to the living room and dining room downstairs, there was also a half bathroom, a study, and the most amazing kitchen I'd ever seen. Perfect for us to build our life and start a family.

Tanya showed us the backyard last. Another magnolia tree sat in the back corner of the spacious lawn. A large deck led down to a stone-tiled patio and pool area. I pictured our children running around playing as Ryker and I chased them. I was completely in love.

Tanya turned toward us with a smile on her face. "So? What do you think?"

I looked up at Ryker hopefully. His eyes searched mine and he held my hands in his. "What's the verdict, Warrior?"

I squeezed his hands. "I love it. This is the one I want." I knew we should shop around and look at other houses, but my heart was set on this one. It was everything I'd ever dreamed of, and never thought I would have. This house was the setting of my happily ever after.

Ryker grinned before directing his attention to Tanya. "Where do we sign?

My joy faded when I remembered that we didn't have enough to cover the estimated costs. I directed my attention to Tanya. "We were only approved for fifteen thousand less than the list price."

"That's okay," she smiled. She took out her Blackberry and used a stylus to tap the screen several times. "I can give the owners your offer, then call you and let you know their answer."

My happiness started to return, but I didn't want to get my hopes up. "That would be great."

We went back inside the house and Tanya walked us to the front door. She shook Ryker's hand, then mine. "Thank you for coming. I'll call you as soon as I hear from the seller."

"I hope they accept the offer." I told Ryker as I fastened my seat belt when we got in the car.

"Me too, babe." He put the car in drive and made a U-turn. "We have to think positive."

My eyes ran over Ryker's face as he drove and my lips spread widely. I was still in slight disbelief over everything that had happened since Ryker and I met—he had definitely turned my life upside-down, but I'd never been happier.

The following Friday at work, I finally received a call from Tanya. I quickly swiped my phone off my desk and hurried to answer it. "Hello?"

"Kaiya? Hi, this is Tanya with Cambridge Realty."

"Hi, Tanya, how are you?"

"Good, thanks." She paused. "I heard back from the seller."

I felt like I had jumping beans in my stomach from the anticipation that had been building within me over the past week. "Good news, I hope."

"Well, I have good news and bad news. The seller rejected your offer, but did propose a counter offer. They're willing to drop the price five thousand, and cover the closing costs."

My heart sank into my stomach as I felt the sting of tears forming in my eyes. That was still ten thousand more than what we could afford.

"We can't afford that." My voice was meek, the sadness evident in every syllable.

"I'm sorry. Truly, I am. You and Ryker seem like great people." Her tone was genuine and sympathetic—she'd probably hug me if we were talking in person.

I took a deep breath to keep my tears at bay, not wanting to cry until I got off the phone. "Thank you. I really appreciate your time."

"No problem. Would you like me to look for other properties within your price range for you to consider?"

No, I want that house.

"Yes, please. That would be great." I sniffled.

"Great. I'll compile a list and email you next week."

"Thank you."

The tears started flowing as soon as I hung up.

I should have known things were too good to be true.

After several minutes of sobbing, I grabbed a few tissues from the box on my desk and wiped my wet cheeks and snotty nose. I needed to calm down so I didn't stress myself out more.

It's just a house. Your dream house, but still only a house. You'll find another one. Hopefully.

I was depressed for the remainder of the day, wearing a frown and slumping in my seat as a worked. I stayed in my office to eat my lunch, wanting to be alone. I'd done that a lot in the past before Ryker and I had met, but I'd been trying to be more social the past few months, so I ate in the break room.

A couple of my coworkers popped in from time to time to get documents signed or drop off reports, and I had to force a smile so they wouldn't pry. I couldn't wait to get off and go home, although I dreaded having to tell Ryker the news—I didn't want to relive the disappointment over again.

My stomach was jumbled with thick knots when I walked in the door to our apartment. Ryker was sitting on the couch on his laptop, but closed it when he saw me. "Hey, baby. How was your day?"

My voice trembled. "Not good."

Ryker set the laptop on the coffee table and stood up. "What's wrong? Did something happen at work?"

I shook my head as he approached, fighting tears. "No. Tanya called—the seller declined our offer."

Our eyes met. "I'm sorry, Warrior." Ryker's forehead creased, and his brows furrowed as he rubbed my arms.

I sadly smiled at him. "It's not your fault."

He wrapped me in his warm embrace. I buried my face in chest, unable to hold back the tears as I sobbed.

Damn pregnancy hormones.

After a few seconds, I pulled away and wiped my eyes. "I'm sorry. I think the baby is making me overemotional."

Ryker rubbed my back. "Don't be sorry. I know you loved that house."

"I did," I sniffled. "But there's no reason to be crying over it. There are other houses out there."

"That's true." His mouth curved up to one side. "We'll find one that's right for us."

My heart still weighed down my stomach.

But I want that one.

"Yeah, you're right." I forced a smile before laying my head against his chest and hugging him tightly. "We will."

Chapter Fourteen

Ryker

Ethan and I had been meeting weekly for lunch since the first time we'd met at the deli, and our relationship was slowly building back to how it used to be before our parents died—joking around, hanging out; normal shit brothers do.

After a month or so, I'd finally decided that it was time to take the next step and meet Tristan. I still wasn't comfortable seeing Molly, and I wasn't sure that I ever would be. She'd caused the rift between my brother and me, and we'd lost many years because of it. If I never saw her again it would be too soon.

We planned to catch a Red Sox game one Saturday. Ethan and I had never played baseball, but our dad had taken us to many games when we were kids, and Ethan wanted to continue the tradition with his own son.

They were already waiting at the gate when I walked up to the stadium entrance. As I approached them, Ethan waved me down. "I got the tickets already," he said when I reached him. He handed me one. "They're pretty good seats."

"Awesome." I looked at the ticket, then back up at Ethan. He picked up Tristan, who looked just like his dad when he was little.

Tristan looked me up and down. "My daddy told me you're his brother."

"Yep, that I am. Nice to meet you, little man."

"He says that you got mad at him, but now you're friends again."

I raised an eyebrow at Ethan, who looked away. "Yeah, I think we're friends again."

"Do you like hot dogs?" Tristan asked, changing the topic.

I laughed. "Yeah, with lots of ketchup."

"Good, then we can be friends, too." Tristan looked up at his dad. "Can we go inside now, Daddy?"

Thank God for a five-year-old's short attention span.

We definitely didn't need to be getting into the details of what had caused the problems between Ethan and me.

Ethan lightly chuckled. "Sure, buddy." He set Tristan down and grabbed his hand. "Let's go."

I followed behind them as we entered the stadium. Our seats were in the middle section, facing the stretch between third base and home plate. When we sat down, Tristan sat himself between his dad and me. Ethan smiled as his son looked up at me and said, "Did you know they call this place the Green Monster?"

A grin curved my lips. "Oh, yeah?"

He kicked his feet as he looked out at the field. "Yeah. But there's not really any monster. They just call it that because it's big and green."

My smile spread wider. "Good, because I'm afraid of monsters."

Tristan giggled. "Monsters aren't real, silly. Don't be scared."

I laughed and messed up his cap. Vendors were walking up and down the aisles as more people filled in the seats surrounding us. Ethan looked at me and asked, "Hey, you want a beer?"

"Yeah, thanks."

Ethan stood as he waved the vendor down and got two beers. He handed me one as he sat back down. I tipped the cup to him. "Thanks, bro."

Tristan tugged on Ethan's shirt sleeve. "Daddy, I want fries—the ones with all the stuff on them. And a hot dog, too."

"Don't forget the ketchup," I added.

Ethan took a drink and set it in the cup-holder. "Okay, buddy. Let's go." They both stood before Ethan looked at me. "You want anything?"

"Nah, I'm good, thanks." I took a sip from my beer.

Ethan picked up Tristan and nodded. "We'll be right back."

They pushed through the growing crowd of people toward the concession areas. I watched the players warm up on the field as I thought about how much my life had changed over the past couple of months. Six months ago, I never would've believed that I'd be at a Red Sox game with my brother and his kid, let alone be expecting one of my own.

If it's even mine.

Damn it, don't think like that.

I tried to push the thought away, but it always lingered in the back my mind. Every single time. There was no reason for me to question Kaiya, but I couldn't shake the doubt that hung over me. The scars from my past still affected me; I'd probably never forget the pain they resulted from.

When Ethan and Tristan came back and sat down with their huge order of chili cheese fries and a hot dog, Ethan gestured to the food. "Help yourself. We won't finish them all."

Tristan stabbed a clump of fries with his fork. "Yeah, Uncle Ryker, they're so good. Have some."

I laughed as he stuffed the food in his mouth, making his cheeks bulge out as he attempted to chew. Ethan's mouth twitched as he fought a smile while halfheartedly scolding, "Tristan, don't put so much food in your mouth. You could choke."

Tristan continued chewing his food before looking up at Ethan. "Sorry, Daddy." He rubbed his stomach in circles before patting it. "They're just so good."

A loving smile spread over Ethan's face. "I know. Just be careful, son."

Tristan continued eating as Ethan directed his attention to me.

"So, how's everything?"

"Pretty good—we've been looking for a house."

Ethan's eyebrows rose in interest. "Really? How's that going?"

"We found the perfect house, but we don't have enough—the seller denied our offer."

Ethan's face fell slightly. "I'm sorry, bro."

I shrugged. "It's okay—not your fault. They gave us a good counter, even offered to cover the closing costs, but it was still about ten thousand too much." I sighed, feeling defeated. "I just feel so bad that I can't give Kaiya the dream house that she deserves."

Ethan reached behind Tristan and patted me on the back. "You'll find something—don't worry about it."

I nodded. "Yeah." I took another drink from my beer before changing the subject. I hated thinking about the devastated look on Kaiya's face when we found out we couldn't afford the house. "How's everything with you?"

"Work has been great. I've been selling a ton of prime property above market value."

Ethan sold commercial real estate in and around Boston, which had proved to be a profitable career for him. He lived in a luxury condo in the Wellesley area of Boston and earned enough where Molly didn't have to work.

"And…" Ethan's eyes lit up as a wide grin spread over his lips. "Molly's pregnant."

"That's great, bro." I swallowed the lump that inexplicably formed in my throat. "Congratulations."

I didn't understand the uncomfortable twisting in my gut. I should've been happy for my brother, but I guess I wasn't completely over what had happened yet. Whenever Molly's name was mentioned, it caused anger to rush through my veins.

Ethan broke through my thoughts. "She's not as far along as Kaiya, though. Molly's only seven weeks. How many weeks is Kaiya now?"

I thought for a minute, trying to push aside the negative reaction I was having to Ethan's news. "She's about eighteen weeks. We find out the sex of the baby at her next appointment."

Ethan smiled knowingly. "You want a boy, right?"

I shrugged. "When we first found out, all I could think about was that I wanted it to be a boy." I chuckled and shook my head. "But lately, the thought of having a little Kaiya running around has been going through my mind a lot."

"That would probably be better than having another Ryker terrorizing everyone," he joked as he shoved my shoulder.

I bit my lip and clenched my eyes shut as a sharp pain shot up my neck and through my chest.

Ethan's humorous tone flipped to concern. "Hey, are you okay? I didn't think I hit you that hard."

I exhaled through my nose as I grit my teeth. "You didn't. I just have an injury that I haven't fully recovered from yet." I slowly rotated my shoulder and winced again. "You hit it in just the right spot."

"Injury? What injury?" Ethan asked in confusion.

I opened my eyes as the pain subsided. I could see Tristan out of the corner of my eye, oblivious to us as he munched on his hot dog. I sat up straight and moved my shoulder again to work out the remaining stiffness and lingering pain. I turned to meet my brother's perplexed eyes. "I was shot."

Ethan's eyebrows practically sprang up into his hairline. "What? When? And by who?" His voice rose angrily with each question.

"About six months ago. Kaiya had been shot at by her brother, and I blocked her and took most of the impact from the bullet." I rubbed my hands together anxiously as I remembered the shooting. The anguish of almost losing Kaiya felt fresh when I thought about that night. "But it still went through me and into her. I… I thought I'd lost her. The doctors said it was only inches from piercing her heart."

"Wow." Ethan's mouth hung open as he stared at me. "That's crazy," he said in disbelief.

I nodded and took a sip from my cup. "Yeah."

Our eyes locked. "Why didn't you call me?"

I held his gaze silently for several seconds before responding, "The only thing I was concerned about when I was in there was Kaiya. You didn't even cross my mind."

A flash of hurt crossed over Ethan's face before he forced half a smile and covered his heart. "Ouch, bro."

"Just being honest." I shrugged. "I learned to block out most of the pain and anger, but to do that I also had to block out the source."

He nodded in understanding before breaking eye contact. "How is it now?" He gestured to my shoulder with his head.

I followed his gaze. "Ripped some the muscles in my shoulder and chest and fucked up the nerves."

"It still hurts?"

"Always. The pain dulls, but never completely goes away."

His eyes came back to mine. "That sucks. I'm sorry."

I glanced away to look at Tristan, who was back to eating his fries. I quickly grabbed one and ate it before licking my thumb and index finger. I laughed as Tristan looked up at me and narrowed his eyes. "Hey!"

Darting my hand out, I snatched another fry from him and stuck it in my mouth. Tristan giggled as I looked up and away, pretending that I hadn't done anything.

"Daddy, Uncle Ryker keeps eating my fries," he tattled playfully.

My eyes widened in mock shock as I looked back at Tristan and tried to keep a straight face. "I didn't do anything."

"Tristan, you need to share," Ethan said in a parental tone.

"You sound just like Dad." I chuckled. I imitated my father. "Ryker, don't touch that. Get off your brother. Put that down. Go to time-out."

Ethan roared with laughter, and I did the same. Tristan stared at us like we were crazy as we continued laughing like hyenas.

"Daddy, are you okay?" Tristan asked in a confused voice.

Our laughter subsided. Ethan patted Tristan on the back. "Yeah, buddy, I'm fine."

More people began filling the seats around us. I took another drink of my beer and settled back into my chair. One of Boston's mascots started dancing around on the field, getting Tristan's attention. "Daddy, look!" He pointed enthusiastically in the direction of the oversized, cartoon red sock.

"I see it, buddy."

Tristan stood on his seat. "I can't see, Daddy. Lift me up."

Ethan picked up Tristan, then stood and set him on his shoulders. I smiled as I watched them laugh and talk about the performance on the field. My grin spread as I pictured myself one day doing the same with my own son.

Tristan crashed out about halfway through the sixth inning. How he was able to sleep through all the cheering and commotion was beyond me, but he stayed asleep until we left the stadium.

Once we got through the mob of fans celebrating the Red Sox victory, and made it to Ethan's SUV, I stopped and faced him. "This was great. We should do it again."

He disabled the car alarm and opened the door to the back seat. "Definitely." He carefully set Tristan in his car seat and strapped him in before quietly shutting the door. "Just let me know when."

We clasped hands and hugged. "Will do, brother. See ya later."

"Sure thing. Drive safe," Ethan called out as I walked away.

When I got home, Kaiya was sitting on the couch with her Kindle.

I tossed my keys on the table. "Hey, Warrior."

She closed her case and set the device on the end table next to the couch. "Hey. How was the game?"

I sat down next to her and pulled her legs into my lap. "It was good. Sox won nine to six."

"That's good. How was it meeting Tristan?"

I smiled. "He's a good kid. Looks just like Ethan."

She looked down and placed her hands on her stomach. Her belly was starting to look noticeable. "I hope our baby looks like you."

I followed her gaze and put my hands over hers. "I'd want our little girl to look just like her momma with gorgeous, blue eyes."

She scrunched her nose in displeasure. "I don't want them to look like me."

I didn't ask why because I already knew the answer. Kaiya had always battled with her appearance because of Kaleb. Having a kid that looked like her would remind her of him.

I tilted her chin up to look at me. "Our baby will be beautiful no matter who they look like."

She gave me a soft smile and nodded. After a few seconds of silence, she asked, "Speaking of babies, have you thought of any names you like?"

Honestly, I hadn't really thought about it. "No. Have you?"

"Of course. I've been thinking about names since we found out."

I chuckled. "Well, let me hear them."

Kaiya's smile spread over her face. "For a girl, I like the names Jocelyn, Harper, and Piper."

"And if we have a boy?"

"For a boy, I like the names Hayden, Asher, and Noah."

One name stuck out to me. "I like Hayden."

She brought her eyes to mine. "Yeah?"

I brushed my knuckles down her cheek. "Yeah, Warrior. I do."

"And if it's a girl?"

"Piper is cute. Harper is too. But we're having a boy so it doesn't matter," I joked.

Kaiya softly laughed. "Is that a fact?"

"Yep, boys run in my family."

Those full lips curved up at the corners. "A little Ryker wouldn't be so bad."

"Neither would a little Kaiya."

She shook her head. "You'd have your hands full with two of me. You wouldn't know what to do."

"Hey, I have a way with women. I'm sure I'd be fine." I smirked.

Kaiya rolled her eyes and changed the subject. "You hungry?"

"Yeah, baby. You want me to go grab something?" I asked as I rubbed her legs.

She bunched her lips together to one side. "Let's order in—take-out or pizza?"

I rubbed her stomach. "Whatever you and the baby want."

"I have a craving for Pad Thai. Extra spicy."

"Pad Thai it is." I pulled out my phone. "Which place?"

"Sugar and Spice. I like theirs the best."

I called the restaurant after Googling it. In the middle of placing our order, Kaiya tugged on my shirt sleeve and whispered. "Ooh, get some veggie dumplings, too."

I tickled her sides and she squirmed out of my grasp. "Can I also get an order of the veggie dumplings?" I paused as they confirmed my order. "That'll be it. Great, thanks."

I hung up the phone. "They said about thirty to forty-five minutes." I settled back onto the couch and started rubbing Kaiya's legs again. "How was your day, baby?"

She laid back on the couch. "Amazing. Nori and I went to this relaxing spa and got mani-pedis." She wiggled her toes and spread her fingers out in front of her. "You like the color?"

I looked down at her hot pink nails. "Yeah, babe." I could care less what color her nails were, but I complimented her choice anyway. "Looks great on you."

She gave me a shy smile as her cheeks turned a little red. "Thank you."

Kaiya's phone started ringing in front of me on the coffee table. She quickly swiped it and answered hesitantly after looking at the screen. "Hello?"

Her eyes darted to me, then quickly away as she repeated louder, "Hello?"

She tensed slightly before hanging up.

Strange. I wonder who that was.

I gave her a questioning look. "Who was that?"

She swallowed deeply and avoided my eyes. "Wrong number."

I couldn't stop the doubt that crept and settled in my stomach.

What if she's seeing someone else? This isn't the first time she's gotten a call from a "wrong number."

I shoved the thought away. "Everything okay?" I asked in concern.

"Yeah," she replied with a clipped nod. "Just tired."

Something seemed off to me, but I didn't want to prod her. Work and the pregnancy always wore her out. "Well, lay back and relax, baby."

Resting her hands on her little bulge, she laid back down and sighed. I couldn't help but repeatedly glance at her phone sitting right beside her, wondering who had just called her.

After a few seconds, the screen lit up. "You got a text," I said as I cocked my head toward it.

Her eyes went from me to her phone, then back again. "It's probably Nori. I'll check it later."

Something was definitely going on. My suspicions about her cheating seemed more valid with each passing second. So many calls from wrong numbers, her leaving the room or turning the phone away when she gets a text, not to mention that one time when I answered a call from an unknown number and they hung up.

Maybe she's still getting those texts from the unknown number. Would she really keep that from me?

"You're not still getting texts from the unknown number, are you? You'd tell me, right?"

She nodded stiffly. "Of course I would." She sounded unsure.

Well, then what is she hiding?

"You sure?"

Our eyes locked and she gave me that look that always knotted my stomach; the one that showed her love for me deep in those blue eyes. "Yeah, I'm sure." She grabbed my hand. "Can we drop this? You just got home. I haven't seen you all day, and I want to spend some time with you."

The distrust building within me started crumbling as Kaiya smiled her beautiful smile at me. She rubbed the back of my hand. "I missed you."

I looked at her for a second before turning my palm up and linking our fingers together. "Yeah, I missed you, too."

Kaiya pulled herself up and sat in my lap. She draped her free arm around my neck and placed our joined hands on her stomach.

Exhaling, she laid her head on my shoulder and snuggled into my neck. "I love you."

No, she doesn't. She's probably cheating just like Molly did.

Stop being paranoid.

I didn't have much proof to warrant my suspicions yet, and I hoped my past wasn't coming back to haunt me. I'd probably lose my shit completely if I was cheated on again.

Pushing the doubts from my mind, I leaned my head against hers and ignored the remaining knots in my gut. "I love you, too, Warrior."

Chapter Fifteen

Kaiya

Come on, fit!

I sucked in my stomach as I tried to button my jeans for the third time, and just like all my previous attempts, I had no such luck.

Letting go of the waist of my pants, I released a sigh.

No more skinny jeans for me.

I was almost twenty weeks, and had recently started showing. I hadn't gained much weight until a couple of weeks prior—the doctor said it was probably due to stress and all the morning sickness I'd had during my first trimester.

I'd been able to fit into all of my pants up until now. I frowned at my protruding belly.

I feel so fat.

I rubbed my baby bump. A smile replaced the frown as I thought about my son or daughter inside. The weight gain was more than worth it. Not to mention I had to get new clothes. Hello, shopping spree!

"Babe, have you seen my belt?" Ryker called from down the hall.

I could hear his footsteps approaching me as I answered, "I think it's in the closet."

His arms wrapped around my waist as he pressed against me from behind and placed his hands on my bare stomach. I was only wearing my bra and unbuttoned jeans. Leaning back into him, I tipped my head back on his chest. "My pants don't fit anymore." I pouted.

He chuckled before moving his hands down beneath the waist of my jeans. His fingers traced the delicate skin, slipping under my panties and sending a small shiver through me. "I guess you don't need them on anymore then," he whispered huskily in my ear.

My voice wavered slightly as desire began to wash over me. Ryker's touch always turned me into a sex-crazed fiend. "No, I guess I don't."

His fingers slipped into the loops of my jeans. Slowly, he shimmied them down my legs before his hands traveled back up and grasped my hips.

I pushed my ass back into him, wanting to feel his hardened erection against me. He gripped my hips tighter and growled as he pressed his cock into me.

I moaned as one of his hands slipped in the front of my panties and found my clit. He slowly rubbed his fingers against the sensitive bundle of nerves and nipped at my neck. "I love how wet I make you, baby."

Ryker moved us forward until my knees hit the edge of bed. He continued to expertly massage my clit as his other hand came up and gripped my ponytail.

He tugged my head back before his mouth claimed mine. His tongue parted my lips as his fingertips added fuel to the flames he was stoking inside my core. My body involuntarily quivered from his sinful touch, escalating closer to release with each stroke of his fingers.

Our lips broke apart as Ryker let go of my hair and bent me over the mattress. Climbing on, I knelt at the edge of the bed, eager for him to sink into me and ease the blissful ache he was building inside me.

I groaned in protest as his hand left my clit to pull off my panties. I heard him unzip his pants, then he grasped my hips and pressed his hard cock against my bare ass.

Oh, God, yes.

I felt the tip of his length nudge my opening, but he didn't enter me. Instead, he began to rub his thick shaft between my wet folds, continuing to blissfully torture me.

I shifted back against him, wanting, no, needing him to relieve the ache between my thighs. Gripping the sheets, my voice came out a strangled plea, "Ryker, please."

A shudder ran through me from the strokes of his cock against my sensitive flesh. "Please, what, baby? Fill your sweet pussy with my cock?"

I gasped as his length roughly pressed against my clit. I was too overwhelmed by the sensations taking hold of my body to respond intelligibly. A throaty moan escaped me, expressing my need loud and clear without words.

Ryker continued to torment me for what felt like an endless eternity before he slowly filled me. Pushing back, I sank myself on him, unable to wait any longer to feel him completely inside me.

He grasped my hips before pulling out and slamming back into me over and over again. I cried out in pleasure as Ryker grabbed my ponytail and tugged lightly, forcing my head to tip back. "I want you to come all over my cock, baby."

Fuck me.

That definitely wouldn't be a problem. I was already so close to coming, and Ryker knew exactly what to do to send me into that heavenly oblivion. Every. Single. Time.

He roughly thrust himself deep inside me before pumping his cock in and out of my pussy, stroking my walls and building up the orgasm that was on the cusp of overtaking me.

Ryker's hand trailed around my hip before I felt his fingers dancing along my clit again, causing me to cry out as my body trembled in anticipation of climax. I bit down on my lip as I fought against the sensations rushing through me, wanting to prolong the pleasure I was experiencing for as long as possible.

Ryker's ministrations intensified as he grunted huskily. "Come for me, baby. Come all over my cock."

I whimpered and slumped against the bed. My ass was up in the air as I buried my face in the mattress while Ryker relentlessly pounded into me. My whimpers morphed into moans as he hammered deeper into my sex and played with my clit. I writhed under him, struggling to maintain control over my body even though I knew I was fighting a losing battle—my body was Ryker's; always had been, always would be.

I cried out as my body shuddered and finally succumbed to the release I'd been resisting. I knotted my hands in the sheets as my orgasm ran through me while Ryker continued to thrust into my throbbing core. His grip tightened in my hair as he groaned and stilled behind me, coming inside my tight warmth.

He fell on the bed beside me a few seconds later. I relaxed against the mattress as Ryker draped his arm over me and pulled me closer to him. He kissed my sweaty forehead. "Better finish getting ready."

Smiling contently, I closed my eyes, still enjoying the waves of bliss streaming through me. I felt the mattress dip as Ryker got up, and then I heard the shower running a few seconds later.

I stretched lazily before getting out of bed and walking to the bathroom. I scrunched my face as I took in my disheveled appearance. Pulling out my ponytail holder, I ran my fingers through my hair to fix the flyaways and tangles from our tryst in the sheets.

"Wanna join me?" Ryker asked from behind me.

I met his eyes in the mirror as one side of his sexy mouth curved up in a lopsided grin.

"I think that would make us later than we already are." I smiled flirtatiously back at him. "Wouldn't want to keep your brother waiting."

Ryker chuckled. "He won't mind. Ethan is a very patient person."

Turning around, I leaned back against the counter as our gazes locked again. Steam from the hot water fogged up most of the shower, but I could still see those captivating eyes. Heat manifested between my thighs as Ryker's sinful stare penetrated me, rekindling my desire even though he had just sated it. "Get in here now, Warrior," he growled.

The dominating tone of his voice intensified my want. I quirked an eyebrow in challenge. "And if I don't?"

His eyes narrowed mischievously as his lips curved up in a sexy smirk. "I'll have to punish you."

Yes, please.

I couldn't fight the primal lust coursing through my body, drawing me to him as if he had some kind of gravitational pull. I stopped when I reached the glass door and looked up at him. "Now or later?"

I stepped back as he slowly pushed the shower open, revealing all of his naked perfection without the mask of fog clouding it. My eyes couldn't help but travel over every inch of his golden skin as he huskily replied, "Now."

Unable to resist his sexual magnetism, I entered the shower. Ryker closed the door and caged me between his muscular form and the glass. His mouth found my neck as he nipped the tender skin along the jawline.

Seconds later, his rough, inked hands were gripping my ass as he lifted me up and whirled me around. My back met the tile as he pressed me against the wall and roughly thrust into me. The water rained down on our entangled bodies until we both reached ecstasy again.

Needless to say, we were late because of our shower escapade. Ryker and I had planned to meet Ethan for brunch, but it was more like lunch by the time we got there.

I was already nervous about meeting Ryker's brother, and to top it off, I was now flustered about the reason we were so late. It was definitely not the first impression I wanted to make.

Hi, I'm Kaiya. Sorry we're late, but your brother and I got caught up having sex and lost track of time. Nice to meet you.

That would go over well.

I snorted at my inner ramblings, causing Ryker to glance over at me from the driver's seat of his truck. "Something funny?"

He turned his attention back to the road as I replied. "Just thinking about what reason we're going to give Ethan for being so late." I looked at my phone and shook my head. "We're almost thirty minutes late, Ryker."

He chuckled and turned right onto the street where the restaurant we were meeting Ethan at was located. "Don't worry, babe. I already texted him that we were running late when we left. He was fine with it."

"I'm so nervous," I said as I wiped my sweaty palms on my skirt. "And I'm making a terrible first impression by being so late."

Ryker placed his hand over mine on my lap. "No, you're not, Ky. Ethan's going to love you, just like I do." He rubbed his thumb over the back of my hand reassuringly and gave me a sweet smile.

Turning my hand over, I linked our fingers together and squeezed tightly. I darted my gaze out the window. "I hope so." Even though I had some animosity toward Ethan because of what he did to Ryker, he was the only family Ryker had left. I wanted to support Ryker's decision to make amends, and I didn't want to cause any more problems between them.

Once we parked and started walking to the restaurant, Ryker called Ethan. He talked to him on the phone as he navigated us to where Ethan was seated in a booth near the back.

Ethan stood once we reached him. "Finally. I'm starved," he greeted jokingly. Our eyes met and a huge smile curved over his lips. "You must be Kaiya."

Ethan looked a lot like Ryker, with a defined jaw, golden skin, and dark hair, but Ethan had green eyes instead of brown, and he wasn't built like Ryker was. Ryker was pure muscle, and while Ethan had a nice physique, he had nothing on his brother's immaculate body. Ethan also dressed totally different than Ryker and looked like he was ready to go to the country club with his pressed button-down, sweater vest, and khakis. Ryker was definitely more casual in his faded jeans and fitted Henley.

"I am." I nervously flung out my hand to shake his, but Ethan wrapped me in a hug instead, taking me by surprise. My widened eyes met Ryker's over Ethan's shoulders, and he grinned before patting his brother's back. "Don't scare her away now. You just met."

Ethan pulled back and turned his attention to Ryker. "If you haven't done that by now, I don't think there's anything I could do that would scare her off."

I smiled at their exchange. "Now, now, boys. It takes a lot more than that to scare me." I glanced down at my stomach before meeting Ryker's eyes. "I think you're stuck with me."

Ethan laughed, gesturing to the seat in the booth. "Please sit." He waited for me to scoot in before sitting on the opposite side and picking up a menu. "I think it's too late for brunch." His eyes darted back and forth between us knowingly, as if he knew the reason why we were late, before they settled on the menu in his hand. "But the lunch here is just as good, so no big deal."

My cheeks heated in embarrassment as I looked accusingly at Ryker, who shrugged his shoulders and picked up his own menu.

Ugh, men. Ryker probably text him all of the intimate details.

I rolled my eyes and picked up another menu, browsing over the lunch specials for that day for a few minutes. When I set my menu down, the brothers were already in a discussion about sports.

Kill me now.

Thankfully, the waitress saved me for a few seconds as she took our drink order, and I swiftly changed the topic of conversation once she left. "So, Ethan, Ryker told me that you're in commercial real estate."

Not exactly the most stimulating conversation topic, but it's better than sports.

"That I am. The market has been very good, but I don't want to bore you with the details. Tell me more about you—I want to learn more about the woman that changed my brother's life."

I stole a quick glance at Ryker, who smiled sheepishly and avoided my eyes. My mouth quirked up to one side as I thought about how rare it was to see Ryker embarrassed.

How sweet. I wonder what he told him about me.

Turning my attention back to Ethan, I stumbled for words as I tried to tell him more about me without divulging the crazy.

Yeah, good luck with that.

"Um, well, there's not that much to tell. I'm pretty boring. I'm a project coordinator for a marketing and public relations firm here in Boston. I live with my older brother Kamden in Cambridge, and I enjoy long walks on the beach."

Both Ryker and Ethan chuckled at my corniness as the waitress dropped off our drinks. I couldn't help but notice how she basically devoured Ryker with her eyes before walking away again.

You better think twice, bitch.

Ryker's eyes caught mine when I released my death stare from the waitress' back. His lips twitched as he stifled a laugh, but it broke through after a few seconds.

I smacked his arm. "It's not funny, Ryker."

"Am I missing something?" Ethan questioned as he cocked an eyebrow in confusion.

"It's nothing," I answered.

At the same time as Ryker said, "Kaiya's jealous that the waitress was checking me out,"

I narrowed my eyes and frowned. "I am not."

Ethan cleared his throat. "So, Kaiya, how did my brother manage to land someone as beautiful and sweet as you?"

My expression eased as I looked away from Ryker to Ethan. "Well, I started working out at his gym and ended up taking his self-defense class." Both corners of my mouth started to tip up as I remembered our first meeting. "He saved me from a painful treadmill death."

Ethan's eyebrows raised in intrigue. "Really? Oh, I've got to hear this."

I proceeded to tell the story of my graceful first encounter with Ryker, and Ethan was howling with laughter by the end of my mortifying tale.

"See, Ethan, I'm a regular knight in shining armor," Ryker joked.

Ethan was too busy laughing to respond to Ryker, and our whore of a waitress finally decided to come back and take our order. She continued to ogle Ryker, pissing me off more with every passing second.

Calm down, Kaiya, You don't want to make a scene.

Taking a deep breath, I stared her down, then placed my order as calmly as I could before placing my hand on Ryker's leg.

"And for you, handsome?" she flirtatiously asked Ryker as she batted her eyelashes.

The anger I was trying to temper threatened to boil over. Didn't she fucking see me sitting right next to him?

Ryker draped his arm over my shoulders and pulled me closer to him as he gave her his order. I watched her face fall in disappointment, causing a smug smile of satisfaction to replace my jealous scowl.

Yeah, that's right, he's mine.

I linked my fingers with Ryker's. "Thank you," I said dismissively after we'd all placed our orders. Her lip practically curled up in fury before she huffed under her breath and walked away.

"You know you have nothing to worry about, right, Warrior?" Ryker asked as he stroked the back of my hand with his thumb.

I felt a slight pang of embarrassment as I leaned my head against his shoulder. "I know." I squeezed his hand. "These pregnancy hormones are something else," I joked, even though I knew I would've felt the same way even if I wasn't pregnant. My insecurities and low self-esteem were hateful bitches that caused unwanted emotions and drama that I didn't need. I'd dealt with them my whole life, and I wished they'd just go away so I could live without the heavy weight of them bearing down on me constantly.

Yeah, wishful thinking.

Ryker pressed a kiss to my temple, then directed his attention back to his brother.

The remainder of our lunch was filled with conversations about Ethan and Ryker's childhood, my pregnancy, and sports. Thankfully, my past was never brought up. I discussed my demons enough in therapy with Kamden and I didn't want to think about Kaleb any more than necessary. Ethan knew about the shooting, so I assumed that Ryker had asked him not to bring up anything involving Kaleb, which I appreciated more than he would ever understand.

Once we finished our meals and paid the bill, Ethan gave me another tight hug and spoke low into my ear. "Thank you for whatever you did to bring my brother back."

My mouth slightly gaped open out of shock from his words. "I didn't do anything," I quietly replied back.

Ethan pulled away, keeping his hands on my shoulders as he smiled broadly at me. "Yes, you did." He rubbed my shoulders affectionately. "It was a pleasure meeting you, Kaiya."

I smiled back. "You, too."

He turned his attention to Ryker. "Sox game next Saturday, bro?"

They joined hands, then hugged. "For sure," Ryker answered as he threaded our fingers together. "Text me later."

I was exhausted by the time we got home, so I told Ryker that I was going to take a nap. He had some fitness plans to finish, so he headed to our home office to work on them.

I'd just laid down in Ryker's bed and turned on my side when I felt a jolt in my stomach.

Oh my God, is that?

Rolling onto my back, I placed my hand over the spot where I felt the movement. A few seconds later, I felt the twitching in my stomach again.

"Ryker!" I yelled out excitedly. "Come here! Hurry!"

I heard his footsteps pounding before he rushed into the room. "What is it? Is everything okay?"

I giggled. "Everything's fine. Come here." I patted the bed next to me.

He gave me a confused look as he sat down next me. I grabbed his hand and placed it on my belly where I'd felt the baby kick.

Ryker started to speak, "Wha—"

"Shh. Just wait," I whispered as I held his hand to my abdomen.

He looked down at my stomach. About a minute passed and I was about to give up and take his hand off when the baby finally moved again.

"Did you feel that?" I asked excitedly, unable to stop my lips from spreading into a huge grin.

Raising his eyes to mine, he gave me that beautiful smile of his and nodded.

I placed my hands outside his so that I could feel the baby kick again. "Isn't it amazing?"

We both stared down at my stomach in wonder for several seconds before Ryker answered, "You're amazing."

I looked up to see Ryker gazing at me. He kept his hand on my stomach and cupped my cheek with his other as he leaned in and kissed me.

He continued pressing kisses down my chest to my stomach. Lifting my shirt, he placed one last kiss in the center of my pregnant belly.

The baby kicked again. "I think he or she likes that," I said.

"Oh, yeah?" He raised an eyebrow as the side of his mouth lifted in a lopsided grin.

I smiled down at him and ran my fingers through his hair. "Yeah."

Keeping his eyes fixated on mine, Ryker kissed the middle of my stomach again, then all around my abdomen. The baby kicked a couple of times throughout, and each time made the smile on my face spread wider. "I was wondering when the baby would start moving. I was going to ask Dr. Wallace about it at my appointment next week."

Ryker sat up next to me. "It's next week already? We find out the sex of the baby at this one, right?"

I nodded. "I can't wait. I'm dying to know what we're having."

"Me neither." He placed a hand on my stomach. "I think it's a boy."

I looked down at his hand. "I don't care either way. I just want to start buying cute baby outfits already."

Ryker chuckled. "We can go right after the appointment. Start looking at cribs, get some clothes and other baby shit."

"Baby shit, huh?" I laughed.

"I don't know what things babies need, okay? Give me a break here."

"I have a general idea, but maybe you should ask Ethan," I suggested. "I'm sure he remembers what they had to buy for Tristan. Plus, Molly is pregnant again so it's probably on his mind anyway."

His brows furrowed. He didn't seem to like that idea. "Maybe." He took his hand from my stomach and rose off the bed. "Get some rest, Warrior."

Being reminded about my nap made my eyelids feel heavy. "Okay," I yawned.

Ryker gave me a loving smile before walking out and shutting the door behind him. I placed both hands on my stomach as I closed my eyes and smiled contently. It didn't take long for me to drift off to sleep.

Chapter Sixteen

Ryker

Time seemed to be moving backward as we sat waiting in the doctors' office. I had been dying for this appointment because we were going to find out whether we were having a boy or a girl. Since finding out about the pregnancy, I'd wanted a son, but now I didn't care either way as long as they were healthy.

Kaiya was flipping through a baby magazine as my leg bounced anxiously. She glanced at me out of the corner of her eye and suppressed a smile. "Nervous?"

I drummed my hands on my knees. "Nah, just excited. I wanna find out already."

Kaiya laughed softly. "Me too. The doctor shouldn't be too much longer."

About fifteen agonizing minutes later, the receptionist called us back. Then, we had to wait another twenty until the doctor and ultrasound tech finally came in.

Dr. Wallace gave us a warm smile. "How are you feeling, Kaiya?"

"Excited. I can't wait to find out what we're having," Kaiya replied enthusiastically.

The doctor's smile spread. "Any stomach pain? Nausea? Cramping?"

"No, everything's been good," Kaiya smiled as she rubbed the small bump of her belly.

"Great. Now, let's get to what you've been waiting for."

The ultrasound tech wheeled the cart next to Kaiya and got her prepped. The computer lit up with the image of our baby as soon as the sensor pressed against Kaiya's belly.

"There's the head. Let's move down a little to see if we can get a glimpse between the legs." The tech said as she moved the wand down. "There."

We stared at the screen where the mouse cursor was pointing at something. "Is that?" I started to ask.

The tech grinned. "Yep. Congratulations, you're having a boy!"

A boy... I'm going to have a son.

My chest swelled with pride and a huge smile spread across my mouth. I leaned down and kissed Kaiya's forehead. Her face beamed with joy as she gazed up at me when I pulled away. "I wanted a little Ryker."

The doctor handed Kaiya the sonogram picture after it printed out. Her smile was from ear to ear as she looked at the image. "Hayden."

"Hayden?" I repeated.

"That's the name that comes to mind when I look at him." She brought her eyes to mine. "What do you think?"

I rubbed the stubble on my chin. "I like it. Sounds strong."

"And it's not that common. I don't want him having a name that everyone else has, like John or Mike."

I smiled. "Hayden it is then."

We thanked Kaiya's doctor and the ultrasound tech before leaving. Kaiya linked our hands together and squealed excitedly. "I can't wait to go shopping!"

At class the next day, I planned to demonstrate another small circle hapkido technique. I'd been researching various maneuvers over the past couple of weeks, but had only been teaching the basics and integrating them into defenses that we'd already learned since many of the moves were very intricate. They weren't necessarily hard. They just required that everyone pay attention to detail.

After working on the bags, I gathered the class on the mats. "As you know, we've been going over the basics of small circle hapkido—all of the various locks and grabs. The reason for this is that I wanted to have a solid foundation to build on for the more intricate defenses. The first one I taught was a simple, introductory move to get your feet wet."

I motioned Mark to come to me. "Today, we're going to work on small circle defense against a lapel grab. This would even work against a frontal choke."

I walked the class through the steps of the maneuver before instructing them to get with their partners. Kaiya smiled as I approached her. "This one looks like it's going to hurt."

"All of them hurt, babe. That's why they're so effective."

She playfully rolled her eyes. "Okay, sensei, let's get started."

I patted the left side of my chest, over my heart. "Grab my shirt here." I waited for her to grip my tee before continuing. "Since you're holding me with your right hand, I'm going to bring up my left hand and grab your wrist with it. I can use my right hand to block if my attacker tries to punch me, or even to get some hits in to slow them down before I continue the technique."

I wrapped my hand around her wrist and brought my right arm up in blocking position. "I can do some jabs to the face, maybe even some sudos to the throat from this angle if I want. Then, I'm going to bring my hand over to the one you're holding me with, and grab your thumb." I gripped her thumb, using my fingers to push into the pad of her palm at the base of her thumb. "Now I slide my thumb onto the web between your index finger and thumb. Then, I secure it there before pressing down and away, prying your hand off of me while making a circular motion and bending the wrist at a forty-five degree angle."

Kaiya's face contorted and she hissed in pain as I executed the maneuver, but she didn't tap out; she rarely did. I still let go, not wanting to hurt her because of her stubbornness. "Once you get them to release you and into that position, you can throw in whatever you like since they will basically be at your mercy. A roundhouse to the ribs, maybe a side kick to the knee. You could even let go and finish with a back fist, followed by a ridge hand right to the face."

Kaiya rotated her wrist and rubbed it. "That hurt—even for me." That pretty mouth of hers curved up in a smirk. She tried to fight a laugh, but she couldn't hold it back. "You're going to tap out so fast."

I cocked an eyebrow and crossed my arms over my chest. "You think so, huh?"

She continued to giggle as she nodded. "Oh, yeah."

I narrowed my eyes in challenge. "We'll see about that."

She was probably right, but since she was talking shit, I had to prove her wrong. I grabbed the strap of her tank top with my left hand, knowing full well that I would definitely tap out if I used my right due to my injury from the shooting.

Kaiya initiated the move without my guidance. She had some trouble slipping her hand in the right place and securing mine, but with practice, I had no doubt she would be able to execute it efficiently.

"Need some help?" I teased as she continued to try and get her hand placed correctly.

She frowned and glared up at me, giving me her answer without words. I knew I was going to pay for that comment in a minute or so.

Kaiya's narrowed eyes spread wide in excitement when she finally gripped my hand right. She twisted it away from her in a circular motion, and I immediately wanted to tap out from the pain. I didn't understand how women were so damn flexible. I ground my teeth together to keep from tapping, my stubborn pride outweighing the worry of injury.

Our eyes met and the corner of Kaiya's mouth lifted before she let go. "I don't want to hurt you because of your stubborn pride."

I shook my wrist out and smirked. "It's called determination. You know I never back down from a challenge."

Her lips spread wider into a full, seductive grin. "I know."

We practiced a few more times before I ended class. Some students complained about the difficulty of the maneuver, but most enjoyed the technique and its simple effectiveness. Others preferred the larger body attacks and felt like they had more control and power with punches and kicks. I had to agree, but I still wanted Kaiya to participate in class, so compromises needed to be made.

After closing up the gym, I mentioned some thoughts I'd been having to Kaiya as we walked out. "So I'm thinking about doing small circle hapkido for one class per week, and then normal self-defense for the other two."

She nodded. "That sounds good. From what I've heard, most of the girls like the small circle hapkido, but prefer the regular self-defense techniques better."

"Yeah," I agreed, grabbing her hand as I led her to her car. "Some of the hapkido techniques can be very intricate and some people don't have the patience for that."

"I'm surprised you do," she joked as we reached her car. Turning around, she leaned back against the driver's side door and smiled knowingly. "You're one of the most impatient people that I know."

I placed my hands on the outside of her shoulders against the window, caging her in between my arms. "Depends on the situation." I leaned forward and barely grazed my lips over hers. "With you, I was definitely impatient. When I want something, I have to have it. But with self-defense," I said as I pulled back, putting some space between our faces, "you have to be calculated and precise. Any wrong move could mean injury or death during an attack, so patience is a must."

"Wise words, Master Campbell," she replied with a playful grin. Her stomach growled loudly, causing us both to look down at her baby bump and laugh. "I think Hayden is hungry," Kaiya giggled.

I took one of my hands off the car and placed it on her belly. "Well, he's a growing boy. Let's go get him something to eat."

Kaiya stood up on her tiptoes to kiss me. "I think we have some leftover Italian chicken and risotto from earlier this week." She looked down again at her stomach and smiled. "We both really liked that."

I gave her a kiss before grabbing the door handle and opening the door for her. "I'll meet you at home."

"Okay. Be careful," she replied as she got in.

"You, too, baby," I said, shutting the door.

Kaiya smiled at me through her window and started her car. She waved as I backed away toward my truck.

I followed Kaiya back to her apartment. We parked next to each other in front of her building before heading up the stairs to her place.

"Kam, we're home," Kaiya announced as we walked inside. All the lights were off, leaving the room completely dark.

Kaiya flipped on the light to living room and called out to her brother again. "Kamden?"

Still no answer. A month or two ago, this would have been typical, but since Kamden stopped drinking, he was usually home, either watching TV or working on his computer.

Kaiya dropped her purse and gym bag on the coffee table, then went into the dining room and kitchen, turning the lights on in each room. When she came back into the living room, there was no denying the look of worry on her face.

"What's wrong, baby?" I questioned as I scanned over her wide eyes and the tight line that had replaced her normal smile.

"There's an empty bottle of Jack on the counter, plus a bunch of empty beer cans."

Shit.

Kaiya whipped around and sped to Kamden's room. Seconds later, her shriek pierced my ears. "Oh my God, Kamden!"

Chapter Seventeen

Kaiya

Rushing to Kamden's side, I knelt beside his limp body on the floor. An almost empty bottle of Jack was next to him, along with a folded letter, envelope, and a handful of pictures scattered around the hardwood.

One photo caught my eye—Kamden and Kaleb back in high school with their arms draped over each other's shoulders and wide smiles on their faces.

"What is it, Ky?" Ryker asked from behind me.

I jerked slightly, startled by his voice, but I didn't respond. My fingers hovered over the letter and my eyes scanned the pictures. All of them were of Kaleb and Kamden, ranging from when they were toddlers to teenagers.

Where did he get these?

Snatching the letter off the ground, I unfolded it and started reading:

"Let these pictures be reminders of the horrible sin you committed. You're a murderer and deserve to suffer for what you did."

I stared at the paper in shock for several seconds before crumbling it into a ball with my fist. I threw it angrily across the room as tears streamed down my cheeks.

I grabbed the envelope and looked at the return address, even though I knew who the letter was from. My fucking mother.

There was no name, just a P.O. Box, but I knew it was her. No one else would be so heartless and have those pictures. Only her.

I dropped the envelope and focused back on my brother. A choked sob shuddered through my chest as I looked down at his face. "Please, God, no," I whispered as I reached out my hand toward him. Shaking his shoulder, I pleaded, "Kam, wake up." After several seconds, I shook more forcefully. "Wake up, Kamden!" I cried out desperately.

He was on his stomach, face down, and I couldn't tell whether he was breathing or not. I tried to turn him over, but he was almost as big and bulky as Ryker, so it was like a chihuahua trying to flip over a pitbull.

Ryker was next to me in an instant, helping me turn Kamden over onto his back. His skin was pale and cold, and I feared for the worst.

Please be alive, please be alive, please be alive.

As I pressed my ear against his chest, a chill ran up my spine. An overwhelming case of déjà vu came over me—I was doing the same thing less than a year ago when Kaleb had come for me.

Tears blurred my vision as I waited to hear my brother's heartbeat. I could vaguely hear Ryker talking on the phone, giving my address and describing the situation to whoever was on the line. "An ambulance is on its way."

I didn't reply, too focused on listening for Kam's heart to say anything. It felt like hours had passed when I finally heard the weak thump. I closed my eyes and sighed in relief. "He's alive."

I stayed by Kamden's side, holding his hand until the paramedics came. Ryker followed me in the ambulance to the hospital, and I had to be pried off of Kam when they took him back to work on him.

My eyes burned from the non-stop flow of tears as I sat in the emergency room waiting room. Ryker sat next to me and draped his arm around my shoulders, hugging me tightly to him and giving me the comfort I needed.

About an hour passed when a doctor walked into the waiting area. "Kaiya Marlow?"

I popped out of my seat. "That's me. Is my brother okay?" I urgently asked.

The doctor scanned my face. "We had to pump his stomach because of the amount of alcohol he consumed. We're replenishing his fluids, and he's in recovery now. We want to keep him for observation for twenty-four hours, but you can see him now for a few minutes if you'd like."

Some of the heavy weight bearing down on me receded. "Please," I croaked, my voice tangled up with emotion.

The doctor led us to Kamden's room, where he had a tube in his nose and an IV stuck in the top of his hand. He slowly turned his head to look at me through half-lidded eyes. "Hey," he rasped.

My bottom lip trembled, and my eyes become watery again. "Hey." I sobbed, making my way to his bedside.

I grabbed his hand in a death grip, fearing he would slip away if I let go. "You scared the shit out of me."

His face fell in shame as he looked away. "I'm sorry."

My fear and worry transformed into outrage as I raised my voice in anger. "How could you do that, Kam? You almost killed yourself!"

Fuck, I shouldn't have said that. He's vulnerable and needs my support, not my reprimanding.

He met my gaze with narrowed, bloodshot eyes, but didn't reply. The hurt in his clouded stare was apparent, and I wanted to do whatever I could to take his pain away.

"I'm sorry." I sighed, stroking the back of his hand with my thumb. "I'm just upset. I thought I lost you."

He squeezed my hand, and his face softened as he looked at me apologetically. "I know. I'm sorry. The letter hurt so much, and the pictures were the icing on the cake."

Thinking about what my mother had sent him made rage burn through my veins. "Fuck her," I gritted out angrily.

Tears welled in his eyes. "She's right."

I clenched his hand tighter. "Don't start this again, Kam. She's bat-shit crazy and has no fucking idea what she's talking about."

He glared at me stubbornly. "Facts are facts. I killed my brother, my own flesh and blood. That's a fucking fact."

I scoffed in exasperation before arguing back. "Protecting me! You did what you had to do to defend yourself. If you hadn't, Kaleb would've killed you, Ryker, and me. If anything, this is all my fault."

Some tears trailed down his cheeks. "I just want the pain to go away."

The anguish and sorrow present in his voice washed away my anger and replaced it with sadness. I didn't think I could loathe my mother more than I already did, but my hate for that bitch increased tenfold for the pain she was causing my brother.

I released his hand and leaned over, wrapping my arms around his neck and hugging him. He copied my actions, holding me tightly to him as he buried his face in my chest and sobbed.

My own tears poured from my eyes as everything overwhelmed me. Helplessness for not being strong enough for my brother, fury at my mother for her actions, guilt for causing this whole fucked-up mess, all combined with my hormones to create an avalanche of emotion.

Kamden was still crying after I finally stopped. I continued to hold him, hoping to guide him back from the limb of hopelessness he was balancing on. He needed me now more than ever, and I was going to be there for him.

"Tell me about your week," Dr. Lowell prompted at our next session following Kamden's incident. It had been almost a week since that night, and I'd made sure that he hadn't had anything else to drink. I felt like an overprotective mother. I knew I was annoying the hell out of him, but it had to be done.

Kamden let out a deep breath. "I relapsed. Ended up in the hospital with alcohol poisoning."

Dr. Lowell adjusted her glasses and sat up straighter, the concern obvious in her voice as she spoke. "What brought this on? You were doing so well."

Kamden ran his hands over his face, then his buzzed head. "I got a letter. Pretty sure it was from my mom, even though it didn't say it was."

Dr. Lowell wrote on her notepad. "Tell me more about this letter. What did it say? How do you know it was from your mother?"

"Are you sure that he should be talking about this so soon after? It was a traumatic experience for both of us. I thought… I thought he was dead when I found him. I was terrified."

Kamden placed a hand on my knee. "Ky, it's okay. We need to talk about it if we're going to move past it."

I searched his eyes. He still looked wounded, but strong at the same time, like he was ready to move on, but needed support to do so. And I would be that support.

I smiled proudly at him. "Okay."

Kamden gave me a soft smile back, then directed his attention to Dr. Lowell. "Along with the letter, the envelope contained pictures—pictures of me and Kaleb when we were younger. No one would have those except her."

The psychiatrist nodded. "And what did the letter say?"

Hearing Kamden repeat the words from the letter caused my anger to resurface.

How dare she? She just wants everyone to be miserable like her. Stupid bitch. Kamden was doing so well.

"What made you turn to the alcohol after so long?" Dr. Lowell asked.

The answer was obvious, and even though I hated the stupid questions that Kamden's therapist asked, I knew they were necessary to get him to open up and address his issues.

"I couldn't take it. The guilt was so overwhelming, and those pictures." He paused and exhaled a shaky breath. "Those pictures were branded into my mind. I couldn't stop seeing them even when I wasn't looking. I just wanted the pain to go away."

Tears rolled down his flushed cheeks, and I rubbed his back in an attempt to soothe him. "It was a stupid moment of weakness." He looked over at me and apologized. "I'm sorry, Ky."

His voice was meek and sorrow-filled. I gave him a comforting smile. "Don't apologize—it's not your fault. It's our bitch of a mom's fault."

His face hardened as his lips formed into a tight-lipped frown. "I should be stronger by now. I need to be stronger."

"It takes time to heal. There will be bumps along your road to recovery, but you will get there," Dr. Lowell said with an assuring smile.

Kamden nodded. "I hope so."

"You will. I have total faith in you," I interjected. "You've helped me through so many hard times, and I know you're gonna pull through this one."

My brother gave me a weak, but genuine smile. "Thank you, *sorella*. You don't know how much that means coming from you."

Giving him a perplexed look, I scrunched my eyebrows together and slightly pursed my mouth. I didn't understand why my statement was more meaningful than anything Dr. Lowell had said; she was the expert. "Why?"

Kamden's shoulders bobbed as he chuckled softly. "Ky, you've been through so much—things that would make some people go insane." He softly took my hand in his and looked into my eyes. "Hearing that you believe in me after what you've endured in your life is empowering. If you can overcome your demons and live with their scars, then I can do the same with mine."

I was so wrapped up in his words that I didn't notice I was crying until a tear rolled down each cheek. My throat was clogged with my emotion, preventing me from speaking, so I just threw my arms around my brother and hugged him tightly. Neither of us needed to say anything as an unspoken understanding passed between us. We were each other's support, beacons that guided each other through the dark, stormy times. Kamden had been mine for so long, and now it was my turn to be his.

It was Saturday, and I was absolutely ecstatic to finally go shopping for some stuff for Hayden. We hadn't been able to go the last weekend because of what had happened with Kamden. I'd been too scared to let him out of my sight once we had brought him home from the hospital, so I stayed in the apartment the whole time.

Ryker and I walked into the baby store, which heightened my excitement. I'd been a couple of times before to buy gifts for coworkers' baby showers, but this time was completely different, a whole new experience now that I was a first-time mom-to-be.

Many of the mothers at my work had told me not to buy things like bottles, diapers, bathing items, or baby toys yet because I would be getting a lot of that at my baby shower. I just had to pick the ones that I wanted and scan them onto my baby registry.

My heart warmed as I took in the rows and rows of baby clothes, strollers, car seats, and nursery furniture. Ryker looked overwhelmed, his eyes wide as he gazed around the huge store. "Wow." He whistled.

I laughed. "Lots of baby shit, huh?"

"No kidding. This is nuts." He chuckled.

I stopped near the baby registry kiosk and looked at Ryker. "We should probably do our baby registry while we're here. Nori told me she wanted to include it in our shower invitation, and she's going to be sending them out in the next few weeks."

"All right. You do the honors, Momma." He gestured to the kiosk area.

A smile crept over my lips, and my heart fluttered. He just called me Momma.

Oh my God, that's the sweetest thing ever.

I walked to the kiosk and started pressing buttons on the screen. After completing the registration and getting the price scanner, Ryker and I headed to the first section of the store and began scanning items.

Once we had made our way to the clothes section, we'd already picked out a bottle set, a baby bath tub and towel set, a mobile to hang above the crib, packs of diapers and wipes, and nursery items to match the adorable crib set we picked out.

I wanted to find the perfect outfit for Hayden to wear home from the hospital since it was going to be the very first outfit he ever wore, and I was definitely planning on keeping it.

We found some cute outfits that we put in our cart, but none that stood out to me as "the one." I was about to give up and leave when I caught sight of the perfect outfit.

"Oh, Ryker, look!" I cooed. Tugging his arm, I walked in the direction of the adorable clothes set.

The outfit consisted of a dark brown onesie with turquoise trim. A puppy playing with a red ball was centered in the middle and teal and brown plaid shorts with the same puppy on them complimented the shirt.

"It's so cute." I ran my fingers over the shorts. "Oh, look at the shoes!"

A matching pair of slip-on shoes, socks, and a beanie that looked like the top of a puppy head accompanied the set of clothes.

"This is it." I grabbed the hanger. "Can you get the shoes and socks?"

We headed back to the customer service desk to turn in our registry before purchasing the items we had chosen. Ryker carried our bags to the truck before helping me in—it was beginning to get awkward to step up into his lifted Chevy due to my size.

"Happy, Warrior?" Ryker asked as he started the truck.

The smile that had been on my face since we entered the store curved higher. "I've never been happier."

Chapter Eighteen

Ryker

Kaiya's birthday was in a few days, and I had finally decided what I was going to get her. Now I was standing in a pet store full of yapping puppies, meowing kittens, and screeching birds. Great fucking idea.

"Is there something I can help you with today, sir?" A blonde, teenage girl with braces asked. She smiled politely as she waited for me to answer.

I looked around the store before meeting her eyes. "Um, yeah, I'm trying to find my girlfriend a pet for her birthday."

The girl's smile shifted from professional to genuine. "Aw, that's so sweet. My name is Becca, and I can help you find the perfect pet for your girlfriend," she said before pursing her lips to the side in thought. "I, for one, love kittens. Most girls do."

I thought about having to deal with cat litter and claws scratching me, then furrowed my brows. I didn't think Kaiya would like that shit either. "I was thinking a puppy. My girlfriend is pregnant, and I think a litter box would be too much maintenance."

"Well, cats are very independent, but pregnant women aren't supposed to be around cat urine, so I think a puppy is a great idea." She walked and talked over her shoulder. "Let me show you the puppies we have available."

I followed her to the center of the huge store, which had a big sign in the shape of a dog over it. The barking got louder the further we walked into that section. Dog food, leashes, collars, chew toys, and every other kind of dog essential lined the shelves in that, and a glass wall with puppies was in the very back.

"Are you looking for a small or large dog?" Becca asked as I scanned over my options. I loved big dogs, but I knew Kaiya would think a little dog was cute and would probably dress them up and all that prissy shit. "Small," I answered.

The girl nodded with a smile. "Our smaller dogs are on this side." She guided me to the far left side of the transparent wall of puppies. Some were sleeping, others were playing around, and a few wagged their tails and barked at us.

"Ryker?"

I froze in my tracks. That voice was like nails on a chalkboard for me.

"Ryker, is that you?"

Fuck me sideways.

I turned to face someone I hadn't seen in years; someone I could have gone the rest of my life without seeing.

Molly.

"It is you! Fancy meeting you here," she commented as she approached me. "How have you been?"

Great until now.

I forced myself to respond. "Fine. How about you?"

"Good, thanks." She placed a hand on her small baby bump as her eyes ran up and down my body. "You look amazing."

Pushing the thought of her being pregnant and all the bad memories it caused to resurface, I crossed my arms over my chest. "What do you want, Molly?"

She shifted uncomfortably and a look of hurt flashed across her face. "I can't ask an old friend about how they've been?"

I scoffed. "Old friend? If you treat your friends like you treated me, I'd hate to be your enemy."

She stretched out a hand out to touch my shoulder. "Ryker, don't be that way."

Stepping back, I moved out of her reach. "What way, Molly? You want me to be happy to see you after what you did?"

She narrowed her eyes at me. "That was over five years ago, Ryker! Are you ever going to let it go? Ethan said you had, but that doesn't seem to be the case."

Let it go? Is she serious?

I turned and walked away. "Nice seeing you, Molly."

"Ryker, wait," she called after me. I could hear her heels clacking on the floor behind me. "Please. For Ethan."

Damn it.

I stopped as I thought about my brother and our mending relationship. I wanted to get back to how we used to be, and unfortunately, Molly was a part of that.

Fuck, fuck, fuck.

"Fine." Clenching my fists, I turned back around. "What do you want?" I ground out, pissed off about the situation.

She paused, giving me a hesitant look before finally speaking. "Well, I, uh, want us to be friends."

I cocked my eyebrow at her in disbelief. "Friends?" I repeated sarcastically.

Molly rolled her eyes. "Okay, maybe not friends, but I want us to be civil. Ethan is so happy that you're talking again and fixing your relationship, and I don't want your grudge against me to hinder that."

Damn it, she's right.

No matter how much I hated Molly, I loved my brother more, and I didn't want my stubbornness to fuck up the progress we'd made.

I dropped my arms by my sides and sighed, feeling somewhat defeated for having to give in to what Molly wanted. "You're right." I forced myself to say. The words left a bad taste in my mouth. "I'll try. For Ethan."

Molly's eyebrows rose. She must have been surprised that I agreed with her. "Great," she stammered, then smiled. "I'm glad you're going to at least try."

"I'm not making any promises."

She nodded. "I know, but I have faith in you." Turning around, she called over her shoulder. "I'll see you around."

I stood there, dumbfounded by what had just happened.

Did I just agree to be civil with Molly? Damn, I'm going soft.

"Sir? Are you ready to see the puppies?"

I'd forgotten all about Becca and where I was. Molly had a way of flipping shit upside down like that, and not in a good way. I turned to face the employee helping me. "Yes, sorry."

"No problem." Becca pointed at one of the sleeping pups. "This little guy here is a Maltese. Like all of our puppies, he has all of his shots and is free of any parasites and diseases."

The dog she showed me was completely white with long hair. I thought about the white strands being all over the place and the maintenance he would need to stay that clean and white. "Maybe something not so white and fluffy," I chuckled.

The teen smiled in understanding. "How about this one? She's such a sweetheart—very playful and loving."

Becca pointed out a tiny Chihuahua. Normally, I didn't think that the mascot of Taco Bell was cute, especially considering most Chihuahuas had bug eyes and yapped all the time, but this one was different. She didn't look like most Chihuahuas—she had chocolate brown fur and green eyes.

I moved closer to the wall of dogs and the small puppy started wagging its tail and scratching at the glass barrier between us. "She's cute." I grinned.

"Would you like to hold her?" Becca asked.

I hated handling small things—I always felt like I was going to break them somehow with my bulky, clumsy hands. But I definitely needed practice for when Hayden was born, and the little ball of fur in front of me might be perfect for the job.

"Sure," I replied, then hesitated. "Wait, she's not going to piss on me or anything, right?"

The young worker giggled as she took out a set of keys. "She shouldn't. We take the puppies out to relieve themselves every hour since they are still potty-training, and I took them out right before you got here."

I nodded. "All right, but if she pees on me, I'm sending you the dry cleaning bill," I joked.

Becca stuck one of the keys in a lock on the right side of the glass box that held the Chihuahua. "Come here, cutie." She baby-talked as the puppy bounded to her excitedly.

She turned around, puppy in hand, and extended her arms out toward me. "Here you go."

I awkwardly grabbed the pup and held her in my hands. She was wagging her tail so hard that her whole body shook with her excitement. She wiggled and stretched in my grasp, trying to get closer to me, so I pulled her against my chest so I wouldn't drop her.

"She likes you," Becca cooed as the tiny dog licked my chin and whined in excitement.

"Okay, okay, stop." I laughed, pulling my face out of reach of the pup's searching tongue.

"So, what do you think?" Becca inquired expectantly.

I looked at the squirming animal in my hands, whose tongue was now hanging out as she panted at me. I chuckled. "I'll take her."

I calculated that I would have maybe ten minutes to spare getting everything ready for Kaiya's birthday. I planned to surprise her with the puppy, then take her to meet Kamden and Nori at her favorite restaurant for dinner.

Becca, being the expert salesperson she was, talked me into buying almost one of everything in the dog section for Kaiya's new puppy: leash, collar, crate, food and water bowls, puppy food, shampoo, bed; you name it, I bought it.

I wasn't good at the romantic boyfriend thing, but I was trying my best to make Kaiya's birthday special. I wanted the puppy to be a complete surprise, so I got a cardboard gift box, poked some holes in the top, put the dog inside, closed it, and slipped a pink bow around it.

Becca had given me a puppy starter kit that had more essentials that we would apparently need for our new addition. I put everything I had bought and arranged it in the puppy's bed before hiding it in my closet.

About fifteen minutes before Kaiya usually got home, the puppy started whining and scratching inside the box. I decided to hold the box in my lap on the couch, hoping that would silence the puppy's cries.

The pup still whimpered, so I tried talking to her to calm her down. "Shhh, little one. It's okay. Just a few more minutes."

Thankfully, my plan worked, and Kaiya's present cooperated with me. "Good girl. Mommy will be home soon."

When I heard Kaiya twisting her key in the door, I stood with her present in hand. Her eyes immediately found me as she walked in. "Hey, baby."

I walked toward her. "Happy birthday, Warrior." I presented the gift to her. "I got something for you."

Kaiya smiled sweetly as she took the box. "Ryker, you shouldn't have. The flowers at work were enough, and I know you planned something with Nori."

I smirked. "Just open it, babe."

She rolled her eyes playfully and took the box over to the dining room table. She slipped the bow off and neatly laid it down before removing the top. I heard her gasp right before she squealed, "Oh my God, Ryker!"

I could see the puppy's head bobbing as it tried to jump out of the box. Kaiya scooped her up and hugged her to her chest as she twirled around and faced me. "She's precious!" The smile she had lit up her whole face, and caused a matching one to form on mine.

"You like her?" I asked.

Kaiya gave me a look of disbelief. "Like her? I love her!" She walked over to me and wrapped her free arm around my neck, squeezing me tightly to her. "She's adorable. By far, the best birthday present ever!"

That's what I was hoping for.

"What are you going to name her?" I asked as Kaiya pulled away.

Kaiya held the puppy out in front of her and looked her over for several seconds. "Brownie."

I snorted. "Brownie?"

Kaiya hadn't taken her eyes off the puppy. "Yes, Brownie. Look at her—her fur is the same color as a brownie."

My chest rumbled with soft laughter. "Maybe we should call her Princess Brownie."

Kaiya leveled me with an annoyed glare before turning her attention back to Brownie. "Aren't you just the cutest thing ever? Yes, you are. Yes, you are."

I chuckled before leaving the two divas to go to my closet. I grabbed everything I'd bought for Brownie and took it out to the living room. "I think I got everything we need for her, but we can always go back to the pet store and get more."

Kaiya scanned over the pile of items with wide, shocked eyes. "Wow, I can't believe you thought to get all of this."

I grinned. "I had help."

"That explains it," Kaiya teasingly replied as she sat down on the couch with Brownie. "Especially since everything matches."

All of the items that Becca had picked out had a pink leopard print design. "The girl that helped me said you would like it."

Kaiya rubbed Brownie's belly. "She was right. Now, all we need is to get some cute dresses. Isn't that right, princess?"

I smiled as I took Brownie's bowls and food out of the bed, then headed to the kitchen. I knew she would want to dress the dog up. "We need to leave in about forty-five minutes."

Setting the bowls on the counter, I turned on the sink and filled one of the dishes with water.

"Why?" Kaiya asked.

I ripped open the bag of food and scooped some of the contents into the other bowl. "It's a surprise."

"Ryker, wh—"

I interrupted her. "No questions. Now go get ready."

Her lips fought a smile as she bent over to put Brownie down on the floor. "Fine," she huffed playfully before standing.

Once I set Brownie's bowls on the tile in the kitchen, she scampered over to them and started eating.

"Babe, what should I wear?" Kaiya called from down the hall.

I left Brownie to finish her dinner and headed to my room. Kaiya was in the closet in only her bra and lace boy shorts with her back to me when I entered, causing my dick to twitch.

You don't have time right now.

I cleared my throat and focused on her question. "Whatever you want. You look great in everything."

That's the right answer, right?

Kaiya turned to face me and the right corner of her mouth lifted. "I mean, how should I dress? Fancy? Casual? Something in between?"

Duh, dumb ass.

Her sexy smirk made my cock harden. I crossed my arms over my chest to keep from walking over there and taking her against the door frame.

Focus on the question.

"Something in between."

Kaiya disappeared into the closet after I answered. I started to make my way back to the living room when a brown blur flew past my feet and into the bedroom.

I turned around to hear Kaiya giggling before speaking in a high pitched voice. "Hi, cutie. Is your belly full? Did you like your dinner?"

I entered the closet to see Kaiya squatting down and rubbing Brownie's exposed stomach. She continued to baby talk the puppy. "Who's the prettiest girl? Who's the prettiest girl? You. Yes, you are. Yes, you are."

I checked the time on my watch. "Babe, we have reservations."

Kaiya glanced up at me, then back down at Brownie. "Daddy's a party pooper, Brownie. He won't let us play."

A warm smile spread over my face as my stomach tightened from hearing Kaiya call me "daddy."

God, I love her.

Brownie rolled off her back and stood. Her butt shook back and forth from how hard she was wagging her tail. Kaiya patted her on the head and smiled. "Go play with Daddy. Mommy has to get ready now."

Kaiya rose back up. "Maybe you should take her outside before we leave," she suggested as she resumed her search through her clothes on the rack.

"Okay." I picked Brownie up and carried her to the bedroom door. "You better be ready by the time I get back," I joked.

"Yeah, yeah, whatever," Kaiya shouted as I walked down the hall. I knew she wasn't going to be anywhere near ready when I came back inside.

"Your momma is a smart ass," I said as I scratched our new puppy's neck. "But I wouldn't want her any other way."

Chapter Nineteen

Kaiya

I could hardly wait to see where Ryker planned to take me for my birthday. My family had never been big on parties growing up. As adults, Kam and I wouldn't do anything extravagant when our birthdays came around, much to Nori's displeasure. She'd always wanted to throw both of us a huge party, but we usually ended up just doing dinner and dancing for my birthday and barhopping for Kam's.

"Just tell me where you're taking me," I pleaded for the fifth time since we started driving. The anticipation was killing me.

Ryker chuckled. "Nope. It's called a surprise for a reason."

"Damn it," I mumbled under my breath before huffing like a bratty child.

Ryker placed his hand on my thigh, which was slightly exposed by my new dress. I couldn't figure out what to wear so I ended up going to buy one for the special occasion. "You'll like it, Warrior. Trust me." He grinned with a wink.

My lips curved up at his sexy smile. "Yeah, you do know what I like."

That was a big understatement—Ryker always knew how to please me. His smile morphed to a cocky smirk from my words as his fingers danced higher up my thigh. The tender skin tingled with pleasure until he reached the juncture between my legs and stilled.

His eyes were filled with lust as they locked on mine. My lips parted to release a small gasp as he started to rub his fingertips against my panties.

He moved to the edge of my lace boy shorts and snaked his hand underneath the fabric. His gaze left mine as he looked back at the road, but his fingers didn't stop their course. They slowly continued, tracing their way along my skin until they found my heated core.

Ryker played within the sensitive folds, massaging my clit using his expert touch. "Guess I do know what you like—that sweet pussy is soaking wet for me," he growled, his voice thick with lust.

Leaning my head back, I closed my eyes and bit down on my lower lip as Ryker slipped the tips of two of his fingers inside me and quickly dragged them out.

I squirmed as he toyed with my clit again, aching for him to sink his fingers deep in me again. A moan left me as he teased my entrance, knowing he was going to make me come completely undone before giving me release.

After several blissfully tortuous seconds, Ryker slowly pushed his fingers inside my pussy, causing me to cry out. I gripped the edge of my seat as he pulled them out again and groaned in protest, "Ryker, please."

"Not yet, baby. I'm not ready for you to come yet."

Damn it.

I hated and loved every second of Ryker's pleasurable torment. I wanted him to end it, yet didn't want him to stop. I didn't know how long he continued his heavenly ministrations, but after some time, he took his hand away and huskily spoke. "We're here."

My eyes snapped open and met his. "Don't stop," I whimpered as I writhed against the seat, wanting, no, needing release.

Ryker chuckled before sticking the fingers that had just been inside me into his mouth and sucking them.

Holy fuck. That's one of the hottest things I've ever seen.

I licked my lips, then closed my mouth, which had parted as I watched Ryker savor my arousal.

His eyes darted to my lips and back as the right side of his mouth curved up into a sinful smirk. "We'll be late if I don't stop," he said in a sensual rasp.

Sparks of lust flared in the silence that followed his statement, then our lips crashed together. Ryker gripped my hips as he lifted me over the center console of his truck and onto his lap. His hands roamed under my dress and grabbed my ass as I fumbled with his zipper.

A smack on the window broke us apart. "Hey! Quit that shit! You bitches have a party to attend!"

I turned my head to see Nori outside Ryker's door. A mischievous grin lined her lips as she took a drag from her cigarette and blew out the smoke from the corner of her mouth.

I buried my face in Ryker's chest, which moved up and down with his laughter. "Perfect timing," I mumbled against his shirt.

Ryker rubbed his hands up and down my back. "Guess we better go. Don't want to keep her waiting."

I groaned in protest, still craving release, but raised my head and opened the door to the truck. Nori snickered as I climbed down. "Sorry, I hope I didn't interrupt anything important," she teased before taking another puff of her cigarette.

Narrowing my eyes, I glared at her. "Cock block."

Nori laughed and flicked her cigarette to the asphalt. "Sorry, girl. You know how impatient I am, and I've already been waiting fifteen minutes for you."

I heard the truck door close behind me, followed by the beep of the alarm locking. "Hey, Nori," Ryker greeted once he reached us.

Nori smiled with amusement. "Hey. You were supposed to get her here on time, not be the reason she was late."

Ryker shrugged. "Sometimes I just can't help myself." His eyes ran over my body and a smirk tipped his lips. "Look at her."

I looked down at myself and scoffed. "I look like a fat cow."

Nori snorted as Ryker draped an arm over my shoulder and pulled me into him. "No you don't, Warrior. You're the most beautiful woman I've ever seen."

A small smile curved my lips. "You have to say that."

Ryker was about to reply when Nori interjected, "All right, lovebirds, let's go." She walked toward the restaurant, which I finally noticed was Luciano's now that I wasn't caught up in Ryker. I looked up at him and grinned widely. "Luciano's?"

Ryker led me behind Nori, keeping his arm around me as we walked. "Your favorite for such a special occasion."

I knew it wasn't anything major, but all the little things that Ryker did to make me feel special meant the world to me. No one had ever done so much to make me happy. I squeezed him around his middle. "Thank you."

Ryker kissed the top of my head. "Anything for you, Warrior."

My phone chimed as we neared the entrance. I pulled away from Ryker and stopped to fish my cell out of my purse. "Let me grab my phone real quick."

A text message popped up when I swiped my screen:

> Unknown: Happy birthday hope you get everything your heart desires

My stomach clenched as fear rooted deep throughout my insides. My head darted frantically around the parking lot, searching for anyone suspicious.

Who the fuck is this?

Ryker placed his hand on the small of my back, causing me to startle and jerk away.

"Whoa, babe, it's just me." Ryker calmly spoke as if talking to a spooked animal. "What's wrong?"

I gulped, then exhaled a shaky breath. "Nothing. I'm fine."

Ryker gave me a knowing look. He wasn't buying it. "Kaiya." His tone was like that of a disapproving parent who caught their teenager in a lie.

"Hey, I'm starving here. Hurry the fuck up," Nori interrupted.

Thank God.

I forced a smile. "I'm fine, really. Let's get inside."

He narrowed his eyes and reached out his hand. "Let me see your phone."

No. He can't find out. He'll be upset and even more worried.

"Can we not do this right now?" I deflected and crossed my arms over my chest. "It's my birthday."

His features softened as he sighed in defeat, then quickly hardened again. "We *will* be talking about this later." His tone left no room for argument.

Fuck. Shit. Damn.

"Okay," I replied in resignation, then walked toward the door, hoping that he'd forget by the time the night was over.

Wishful thinking.

When we got inside, we followed Nori to a table in the back of the restaurant where Kamden sat with a bunch of pink balloons and cupcakes.

"Happy birthday!" Nori and Kam shouted in unison.

My mood shifted, even though a tiny sliver of dread lingered in my gut. I buried it down, determined not to let some psycho asshole ruin my birthday. I'd dealt with that enough in my life.

Tears welled in my eyes from the thoughtfulness that had been put into this surprise. I knew I'd be crying more than once before the night was over. "You guys." My voice cracked as emotion clogged my throat.

"Geez, you're like a faucet lately," Nori joked as she hugged me. She pulled back and smiled. "It's your party, and you can cry if you want to?"

I snorted with laughter and swiped the moisture from my lashes. "Yeah. Thank you for all this." My eyes drifted from face to face of each of my loved ones. "All of you."

The night was filled with laughs and joyful banter. No talk of Kaleb, no talk about Kamden's drinking or rehab—just happiness. I prayed that we would have more times like this in the future, especially once Hayden was born.

Once we were almost finished eating, Kamden pulled out a small, wrapped box from under the table and presented it to me. "Happy Birthday, Ky."

I took the gift from him. "Kam, you didn't have to get me anything." Everything he'd done for me was enough to last me a lifetime.

"I wanted to." Motioning with his hands, he urged me to open the present. "Go on, open it."

Ripping the paper off, I revealed a small cardboard box. Inside that was a black jewelry case. I opened the lid and stared down at a necklace with two hearts; a large heart that had the word "*sorella*" engraved on it dangled from a smaller, open heart.

My vision was clouded as I looked up at Kam. His lips curved up slightly as he grabbed my hand. "The little heart is you—holding me up when I need it most. Thank you for being there to support me through everything."

I squeezed his hand back, unable to speak as tears trickled down my cheeks. After I wiped my face with my free hand and took a deep breath to compose myself, my words came out soft as cotton when I replied, "Thank you."

Kamden smiled warmly. "You're welcome. Let's see how it looks."

I took the thin, delicate chain out of the box and clasped it around my neck. I made sure it lay correctly against my skin before looking back up at my brother. "I love it, Kam."

"Good, I'm glad. Shopping for you was hard." He chuckled.

"It's perfect. You made a great choice," I replied genuinely.

"My turn!" Nori squealed as she handed me a card and a gift bag.

"Not you, too. You guys didn't have to do all this for me."

"Just shut up and open the damn gift," Nori playfully demanded.

I smashed my lips together, fighting the smile trying to break through. "Fine." I huffed as I tore the envelope open and slipped out the card that was inside. A gift certificate to my favorite spa fell out as I opened the card and read what Nori had wrote inside:

"We may not be sisters by blood, but you're the only sister I'll ever need. I love you and can't wait to be a part of this next chapter in your life. Happy birthday!"

My eyes watered again as they drifted up to Nori. She shook her head, fighting tears as well. "Cut it out, damn it. You're going to make me cry."

I chuckled and wiped my eyes before opening my arms to her. She leaned over and hugged me. "Happy Birthday, Ky."

I pulled back and smiled. "Thank you."

"Don't forget the gift," Nori reminded.

I took out the pink tissue paper and looked in the bag. I pulled the little baby outfit out and held it up. It had a bib, onesie, and pants; both the bib and onesie read "My aunt is cooler than your aunt."

I laughed as I showed Ryker, who snorted. "I love it," I said, hugging Nori again. "You're more family to me than my real family ever was. Well, besides Kam, of course."

She squeezed me tight. "I know, girl. Same here. I'll always be there for you."

When I pulled back, I looked around the table at the amazing people with me. My family. A smile spread over my face as I placed a hand on my bulging belly and gazed down.

I had everything I ever needed right there with me.

As soon as we set foot in Ryker's apartment, he questioned me. "What happened earlier?"

I played dumb, even though I knew he wasn't going to buy it. "When?"

He lowered his head to make eye contact with me, making me uneasy. My eyes flitted away, then back to his. "Don't act stupid, Kaiya," Ryker responded abrasively.

Shifting uncomfortably, I rubbed my hands up and down my bare arms. "It was nothing."

"Bullshit," he growled. His face was lined with anger. His jaw set, and his eyes burned with fury. "Don't fucking lie to me."

Damn it, how does he read me so well?

My brain raced as I held his gaze, trying to think of a believable lie. I'd lied to everyone about Kaleb for most of my life, so lying was a natural defense mechanism for me. I swallowed the lump in my throat as the perfect thing came to mind. "I just…" I started, then paused and sighed. "My mom text me."

His face fell as guilt washed over, making me feel like a piece of shit for lying. He opened his arms and moved toward me. "Baby, I'm sorry. I shouldn't have pushed you to tell me." His arms wrapped around me and pulled me against his strong frame.

Resting my head against his chest, I sighed, still feeling disgusted with myself. "Can we just forget about it? Please?"

Ryker rubbed his hands up and down my back. "Yeah, Warrior. We can."

Chapter Twenty

Ryker

Cheering sounded throughout the bar as Ortiz hit a home run with two players on the bases. I took a swig of my beer as my brother clapped wildly. "Go Sox!" he shouted before turning from the T.V. to face me. "Can you believe that hit? Two strikes in the bottom of the ninth and then he blows it out of the park to tie it up. Unbelievable."

"Yeah, it was a pretty good hit," I replied unenthusiastically.

Ethan's brows furrowed. "What's wrong with you, bro?"

My argument with Kaiya and encounter with Molly were still weighing on me a week later. "Just have a lot on my mind."

"Molly told me she ran into you last week."

I nodded. "Yep. It was awkward at best."

He chuckled. "Well, at least you're trying."

I took a long pull from my bottle. "Doing my best. I'm not gonna lie, it was hard to take that step."

He patted me on the shoulder. "It'll get better. Time heals all wounds."

I snorted. "We'll see."

"Have faith, bro." Ethan smiled warmly. "I do. You both love me too much to let what happened come between us again."

"The past is the past, right?" I asked rhetorically.

He raised his beer toward me. "Cheers to that."

I tapped our bottles together. "To moving on."

Ethan's smile broadened. "To moving on."

We both took a drink, then Ethan asked, "So does that mean we can all go out to dinner or something soon?"

I thought for a second before replying, "I'm not so sure about that yet."

"Come on, Ry. Kaiya's going to have the baby in a couple of months, and you've already gone through the worst part."

He had a point. I hadn't wanted to see Molly, but I'd gotten that confrontation over with, even though it was tense and awkward.

"I'll talk to Kaiya about it and let you know. Her baby shower is in a few weeks—maybe you can bring Molly and Tristan to that."

Ethan grinned broadly. "I'd really like that."

I left the bar feeling better, but I couldn't get the argument with Kaiya out of my mind. Even though she'd said her mom had texted her, which would have caused her to react the way she had, I had a sick feeling she was keeping something from me. My gut was usually right, just like with Molly.

Kaiya isn't Molly. She wouldn't do that.

The problem was that I wasn't sure. Doubt lingered in the back of my mind.

Old habits die hard.

My past had made me distrusting of everyone, especially women. Kaiya had broken through most of my walls, but the way she'd been acting over the past few months was making me want to build them back up again.

By the time I got home, I had enough time to think and had made myself even more conflicted than I already was. But as soon as I saw Kaiya napping on the couch with her hand on her huge belly, the love I felt for her quickly eradicated the negative emotions I was feeling.

Brownie was cuddled up in between her legs, but started moving when I shut the door. Her tail wagged as she stood up and paced back and forth on the couch, looking for a way to get down. Then, she started whimpering and scratching at the cushions.

"Shh, mommy's sleeping," I whispered, picking her up.

After putting Brownie down on the floor, I grabbed the blanket from the top of the couch and draped it over Kaiya, who stirred but didn't wake up.

As I turned around, I glimpsed Kaiya's phone on the coffee table. My eyes darted back and forth between her and the device several times before I finally picked it up.

I swiped the screen, but it asked for a password.

Since when does Kaiya have a lock on her phone?

I stared at the locked screen, which had a picture of us from her birthday party as the background.

What is she hiding?

I put her phone back down on the table before directing my attention to Brownie, who was pawing at the bottom of my jeans. "You need to go outside?" Her ears perked up. "Let's go outside."

I needed to get out and clear my head. I thought I was over the whole Molly thing, but Kaiya's mysterious calls and seeing Molly again triggered my doubt and caused a sick feeling of dread to settle in my gut. I'd been down this road before and Kaiya was acting the exact same way Molly had when we'd been together.

Brownie bounded to the door and circled in front of it happily. I took her leash off one of the key hooks on the wall and tried to get her to sit still long enough for me to attach it to her collar.

Once I did, I walked Brownie to the pet area. The thoughts swirled around in my head, creating a lethal mixture of paranoia and suspicion. The more I tried to block, defuse, and deny them, the more they screamed not to ignore them.

.When I went back to my apartment, Kaiya hadn't moved from when I covered her. After I removed Brownie's leash, she ran back over to the couch and attempted to get back on.

She hopped repeatedly, reminding me of a bouncing bunny as she kept trying to jump on the sofa. "Need help?" I chuckled.

I helped her get on, then she proceeded to slip beneath the blanket and curl up with Kaiya again. A smile curved up the right side of my mouth as I watched them.

My smile faded as the question I had from earlier resurfaced.

What is she hiding?

The following Saturday, Drew texted me, asking to meet up for a couple of drinks at our old bar. I hadn't been out with him since we found out that Kaiya was pregnant, so I decided to go, needing some guy time.

Maybe it'll help clear my head.

A knock sounded on the door, breaking through my thoughts. I heard Kaiya greeting Nori, who had come over to have a girl's movie night with Kaiya while I went out.

I checked myself one last time in the mirror before walking out to the living room, where Kaiya was scanning over the DVDs in Nori's hand.

"I brought *Steel Magnolias*, *Dirty Dancing*, and *The Sweetest Thing*. Which do you want to watch first?"

Kaiya gave her an 'are you serious' look. "Nobody puts Baby in a corner."

Both women burst out in laughter. A smile spread across my lips as I walked over to Kaiya and kissed her on the cheek. "You girls have fun."

Kaiya linked her fingers with mine. "You too. Be careful."

I squeezed her hand. "Always."

Letting go, I traveled the rest of the way to the door and left. I took out my phone and called Drew as I trotted down the stairs. "Hey bro, I'm on my way."

"You're always late." He chuckled. I could practically see him shaking his head at me through the phone.

"I know, I know. You there already?"

"Not yet. I knew you'd be late, so I took my time. I'm on the way, though," he answered.

I unlocked my truck and hopped in. "I'll be there in ten."

"All right, see you then."

Drew was already seated at the bar when I walked in. What I assumed was a Jack and Coke sat next to him on the bar top as he drank his beer. He tipped his chin up at me as I approached. "'Sup?"

I patted him on the back before taking the seat next to him. "Not much. How's everything with you?"

"Good." He paused and took a swig from his bottle. "Things with Nori are getting kinda serious."

I cocked an eyebrow. "No shit?"

His goofy, love-struck smile told me he was head over heels for her before his words did. "I think I love her."

Nori and Drew had been dating since right before the shooting. They'd been pretty casual the whole time, and it had been awhile since Drew and I had really talked, so I had no idea they had gotten serious. "Have you told her?"

He shook his head. "Nah. Everything has been going so well, and I don't want to jinx it."

I nodded. "I feel you. If it ain't broke, don't fix it."

He tipped his bottle to me. "And you? How are things with Kaiya?"

"Awesome." That was partially a lie; a lie based on me making assumptions, but still. "Only a couple more months till Hayden is born."

"Damn. I still can't believe it sometimes. After Molly, I never thought you would settle down." He made an 'oh shit' face, then rushed his next statement. "But things with Kaiya are totally different. She'd never do what Molly did."

I wasn't totally sure, but I agreed anyway. "Yeah. She wouldn't."

"When's his exact due date again?"

"August 2," I answered before taking the first swig of my drink.

"Damn, so two and a half months, huh? Bet you're excited."

"I am. Nervous, too."

"I'd be shitting bricks if I were you. I know nothing about babies."

"Thanks," I replied sarcastically. "That makes me feel so much more confident."

He slapped me on the shoulder. "I'm sure you'll be a great dad. That kind of shit comes naturally once the baby is born."

"I hope so. I'm in the same boat as you."

"Maybe you should buy some parenting books."

I gave him a look of disbelief. "You're kidding, right?"

A teasing grin lifted his lips. "Not if you're that worried."

I scoffed. "I'm not going to read a parenting book. I'm sure I'll be fine."

He shrugged. "Suit yourself."

I noticed a woman at the end of the bar eyeing me seductively. In the past, I would've have been all over her in a second, buying us a few rounds of drinks before taking her home later that night. But I wasn't that guy anymore. Instead, I ignored her signals and directed my attention back to Drew, who was back to analyzing his feelings for Nori again.

An amused smirk curved the corner of my mouth.

How things have changed.

After a few more drinks, I looked at my phone to see if Kaiya had text me. Nothing.

I wonder what she's doing.

My mind conjured up images of Kaiya in bed with another man, her girls' night with Nori just a ploy to get away from me without suspicion.

I pushed the thoughts back as I turned to Drew. "Hey, has Nori texted you?"

He took his phone out of his pocket, then looked at the screen. "No. Why?"

I laughed inwardly at my crazy imagination. Kaiya fucking another man with her huge, pregnant belly.

I slipped my phone into my back pocket. "No reason."

By the time we left, I had a nice buzz. "We have to do this again soon. It's been too long, bro. You're all domesticated and shit," Drew teased as we walked to the parking lot.

I punched his arms. "Just wait until you have a kid on the way, dick. Things will be different." We clasped hands once we reached our cars. "I'll hit you up next weekend."

No matter how much I tried, I couldn't completely push out the thoughts of Kaiya with another man as I drove home. The way she'd been acting lately, along with the lengths she was taking to keep her phone from me made me suspicious of her.

And the same question kept plaguing me.

What is she hiding?

When I got home, my muscles tensed in anticipation as the images of me walking in on Kaiya having sex with someone played in my head.

I exhaled and unlocked my front door before entering. I hoped that my fears were unrealistic, and that I wouldn't be made a fool twice.

When I walked in, I found Nori and Kaiya both sleeping on the couch. Brownie was balled up in between them on top of the blanket that covered their legs. Their feet were propped up on the coffee table and Kaiya's head rested on Nori's shoulder.

I laughed lightly at my ridiculous thoughts from moments before.

What was I thinking?

I turned the TV off, then carefully went to scoop Kaiya off the couch so I wouldn't wake up Nori. Neither woman stirred as I picked Kaiya up and carried her to our bedroom.

As I tucked Kaiya in bed, a new question surfaced as I stared down at her.

Am I really just imagining things, or am I too blinded by my love for her to see the truth?

I swallowed deeply and my stomach knotted uncomfortably. I didn't know the answer.

Chapter Twenty-One

Kaiya

Ryker's apartment was madness as I watched Nori and some of the girls from my office run around trying to get everything ready for my baby shower while I sat on the couch.

There was blue everywhere. And I mean *everywhere.* Streamers, balloons, banners, and other decorations were spread out over the living room, dining room, and kitchen. It was kind of overwhelming.

Finger foods were arranged on decorative plates on the counters in the kitchen, and presents sat on the coffee table in the living room. I snacked on some chips and dip as Nori set out the cake. "How you doing, girl? You need anything?"

I finished chewing my chip. "I'm good, just going to grab some fruit." I started walking to the fruit tray.

"I'll get it. You go sit down and relax," Nori ordered as she softly grabbed me by the shoulders and stopped me.

I rolled my eyes. "You sound just like Ryker and Kamden."

She gave me her take no shit look. "Go."

"Fine," I huffed before turning around and walking into the living room. My feet were already hurting anyway, so I didn't mind following Nori's demand. I needed to relax some before Ethan and Molly showed up.

I was so anxious about them coming over. I'd asked Nori a dozen times if my outfit looked okay, even though I felt like a walrus. I'd straightened my hair repeatedly, wanting my hair to look perfect for the occasion. Not to mention I couldn't stop stuffing my face with food

I'd met Ethan a couple of times before, but not Molly or their son. To be completely honest, I really wasn't looking forward to meeting Molly for obvious reasons. I already disliked her because of how much she hurt Ryker, but I was going to try to be as nice as possible for his sake. I wanted to give him all the support that I could.

Ryker wasn't too thrilled about having to deal with Molly either, but he was making the best of it to mend his relationship with Ethan. Both he and Molly were at fault, but Ryker had found that it was easier to forgive Ethan since they were brothers and put most of the blame on Molly.

I waddled over to the couch to sit down before they arrived. I felt like a bloated cow ready to be milked, and everything was swollen—my feet, my legs, my stomach, everything. I was more than ready for this pregnancy to be over with so I could finally hold Hayden in my arms.

Only nine more weeks.

Ryker brought me a bottle of water and sat next to me. "How you feeling, Warrior?" He gently rubbed my stomach.

"Fat," I answered with a sarcastic laugh. "I don't know how you can stand to look at me."

He tucked a strand of hair behind my ear. "I think you look beautiful carrying my son." His fingertips trailed along my cheek as he looked down. "How's my little man doing?"

I followed his gaze and smiled. "I think he knows we're having a party for him—he's been moving around a lot."

Ryker focused on my bulging belly. "Oh yeah? Where is he now?"

I grabbed his hand and moved it to the opposite side, right under my ribs. "He's been kicking me here for a while. It's so uncomfortable."

Ryker narrowed his eyes at my stomach. "Quit kicking Mommy, Hayden."

I couldn't help but giggle at how adorable he was. I caressed his scruffy jaw with my fingers.

God, I love him.

Ryker looked up at me and smiled. His rugged beauty still caused my heart to stutter when I looked at him.

How did I get so lucky?

Just then, the doorbell rang. Ryker glanced over his shoulder as he said, "That's probably Ethan." He stood and reached his hand out to help me up.

I stopped him. "Wait, do I look okay?" I asked as I ran my fingers through my hair and straightened my dress.

Ryker pulled me closer to him and kissed my cheek. "You look great. Don't worry." He led me to the entryway and opened the door. "Hey, come on in," he greeted.

Ryker closed the door behind the family that walked in. He came by my side and rested his hand on my back. "Ethan, you remember Kaiya, right?"

Ethan grinned and stretched his arms out towards me. "How could I forget? Nice to see you again, Kaiya."

I smiled and accepted his hug. "You too. Thanks for coming."

When he pulled away, he gestured to his family. "This is my wife, Molly, and our son, Tristan."

Molly had blonde hair and hazel eyes, and her pregnant stomach protruded from her tiny frame. She was about ten weeks behind me, but I looked a hell of a lot bigger than she did, even when I was at that stage in my pregnancy. That made me hate her even more. I knew I was being juvenile but I didn't care.

Tristan looked identical to Ethan, just like Ryker had said. I smiled as I pictured Hayden looking like Ryker. I definitely didn't want him looking anything like me or *him.* I wasn't sure how I'd cope with seeing a replica of Kaleb everyday.

I quickly swiped the thoughts of Kaleb away before they spun out of control, not wanting to ruin my special day because of him. He'd ruined too many days of my life, and now that he was gone, there was no reason to let him continue to do so.

Molly stuck her hand out toward me. "Hi, nice to meet you."

"Kaiya," I greeted as nicely as I could, with one of the most fake smiles I'd ever forced before. Inside, I wanted to rip her a new asshole and give her a piece of my mind for everything she had done to Ryker. But on the surface, I tried to stay calm and courteous.

"Ethan has told me so much about you." She sounded phony, like she was trying too hard to be enthusiastic about meeting me.

She turned her attention to Ryker. "Hey, Ry. Good to see you again."

Sure bitch.

Ryker gave her a strained smile before looking at Ethan. "Thanks for coming. We have plenty of food and drinks in the kitchen. Make yourself at home."

"Thanks, bro." Ethan replied before leading Molly and Tristan into the kitchen.

Ryker pulled me into his side and kissed the top of my head. I glanced up at him as he asked, "You okay?"

I breathed a sigh of relief, more comfortable now that Molly wasn't right in front of me. "Yeah. That wasn't as bad as I thought it was gonna be."

"Good. It'll take some time before things aren't so awkward, but we just took a big step."

I nodded. "You're right."

Leaning down, Ryker pressed his lips to mine and placed a hand on my belly. He couldn't seem to keep his hands off me, but I wasn't complaining; I loved it.

When he pulled away, he smiled down at me lovingly and caressed my stomach one last time, then led me back into the living room.

We mingled with some of my coworkers for a while before Nori dragged me away into the kitchen to get ready for one of the games she had planned.

Ryker was staring at me while Nori wrapped my torso with toilet paper. My stomach knotted as he gave me a seductive smirk.

"Hey." Molly drew my attention away from him.

What does she want?

Barely making eye contact, I forced a smile. "Hi."

Tristan was sleeping on her shoulder as she swayed back and forth. "He really loves you."

Nori glanced up at me as she continued to cocoon my abdomen.

What is she talking about?

"Huh?" I questioned.

"Ryker. He really loves you. I can tell by the way he looks at you."

Because you're an expert? Pffft.

I looked away from her to Ryker, who glanced away from Drew to me. He gave me another heartwarming smile as our eyes locked.

"He never looked at me that way," Molly added.

I didn't really care what she was saying because I was so caught up in Ryker. He patted Drew on the shoulder and told him something, then walked in my direction. My heart pounded faster with every step he took, and Hayden started kicking me again.

Molly was right about one thing—the way Ryker was looking at me displayed the love he had for me all over his face. He wrapped his arms around me when he reached me. "Hey, Warrior." He pressed a kiss to my forehead.

I smiled up at him. "Hi."

His hands came back around to my stomach. "Having a good time?"

"Much better now." I placed my hands on the outside of his forearms as I gazed up at him.

His eyes darted to my lips right before he leaned down and kissed me. The gentle press of his mouth on mine sent passion flaring through me. I shuddered a shaky breath when he pulled away.

Ryker smirked as he swept his thumb over my lips, then cupped my cheek. "I love you."

I nuzzled into his palm and closed my eyes. "I love you, too."

He looked down at my toilet paper-wrapped stomach. He grinned and raised an eyebrow in question. "Why do you have toilet paper wrapped around you?"

"For a game. People have to guess how many squares of toilet paper are wrapped around me."

He chuckled. "Weird."

I pulled him to one of the kitchen counter. "That's nothing. Check this out." I motioned down to the counter that had diapers with various melted chocolates on them. "People have to guess what chocolate it is by smelling it."

Ryker scrunched his nose in displeasure. "Gross."

I giggled. "It's just chocolate."

"Yeah, but it looks like shit."

"That's the point, genius," Nori teased as she interrupted.

Ryker scratched his forehead with his middle finger as he gave Nori a teasing grin.

Nori playfully returned his gesture, then looked at me. "Ready for the games?"

"Sure." I nodded and grabbed Ryker's hand. "Let's get started."

Nori made Ryker and me sit on the couch before starting the first game. Everyone was laughing and having a great time as we played the silly games Nori had planned for the shower.

By the time we had finished, my stomach was growling. I got up to go grab some snacks, then circulated around the apartment with Ryker to talk more to some of the guests.

"Time for presents!" Nori announced loudly as she came up to me. She grabbed my arm, then pulled me away from Ryker.

"Sorry, Ry," she giggled, leading me back to the couch, where she had arranged all the gifts on the coffee table.

Ryker sat down next to me as Nori handed me the first present. Kamden had a camera ready when I started unwrapping the gift.

Most of the presents were clothes and diapers, but we also got some bigger items from Nori, Kamden, and my boss. Nori had bought us a swing, Kamden had gotten the matching changing table to the crib set we had purchased already, and my boss had gifted us a set of bottles and the corresponding bottle warmer.

"There's one more gift," Ethan announced as he pulled an envelope from his shirt pocket. He handed it to Ryker, who gave him a quizzical look. Ethan chuckled, "Open it."

Ryker ripped open the envelope and took out a check. His eyes widened and his jaw dropped as he scanned over it, then looked at

Ethan in shock.

"That should cover what you needed for the house you wanted, right?"

I leaned over to look at the check in Ryker's hand.

Holy shit!

I blinked several times to make sure I wasn't imagining things.

Nope, still the same ridiculously large amount.

It was more than enough to pay for the remainder of the down payment that we weren't able to come up with for the house. And then some.

"Oh my God, Ryker," I gasped as I placed a hand on his leg. My eyes stung with tears when his eyes met mine.

"I... we... we can't accept this. It's too much, Ethan," Ryker said as he stood and handed the check to his brother.

Ethan put his hands up. "Nope. It's the least we can do after everything. Please take it."

Ryker looked at me, seeking my approval for what to do. That house was my dream house, so it didn't require much debate for me. Giving him a teary-eyed smile, I nodded enthusiastically.

He faced Ethan and stared at him for several seconds, then suddenly moved forward and threw his arms around him. Squeezing his brother tightly, Ryker's voice was drowned with emotion as he said, "Thank you. You don't even understand what this means to me."

A few tears spilled down my cheeks as Ethan hugged Ryker back. Even though what Ethan had done to Ryker was inexcusable, it made me happy to see them reconciling after so many years. Ryker would never admit it, but I knew he missed his brother greatly while they weren't speaking.

Ryker patted Ethan on the back before pulling away and looking at me. His eyes were glazed with unshed tears as he extended his hand to me.

Grabbing it, I linked our fingers together and stood by his side. He squeezed my hand and pressed a kiss atop my head.

My eyes found Ethan's. "Thank you so much. I don't think we can ever repay you."

Ethan smiled. "Just take care of my brother and nephew. God knows they need you."

My mouth curved up. Ethan had it backwards—I needed Ryker and Hayden more than he would ever understand. They were granting me a life that I never dreamed I could have, not to mention giving me a happiness I never knew existed.

I turned my head toward Ryker and my smile spread wider. Everything was falling into place for us, and for once, I couldn't wait to see what the future had in store for me.

The following Monday, I called our realtor as soon as her office opened to see if the house we wanted was still available. She'd sent us listings of a few more properties after, but none of them were what we wanted.

It had been months since Tanya had shown the property to us, but I was hoping that it was still available. We needed to find something soon—Hayden was due in a little over two months, and I didn't want to have to deal with finding a house and moving after he was born.

"Hello?"

"Hi, Tanya, this is Kaiya Marlow."

Her voice pepped up. "Hi, Kaiya. How are you? You're due soon, aren't you?"

I slipped off my shoes, hiding them under my desk. "I am—a little over two months now."

"Aww, I bet you're excited. I remember my first baby. I was so overwhelmed and excited all at once."

"Yep, I'm definitely getting more anxious each day. I can't wait to hold him." My heart warmed as I thought of holding Hayden in my arms. "I was just calling to see if that house we looked at back in March was still available. I know it's a long shot, but we we're able to get the money we needed for the counter offer."

"Let me check for you. I don't remember selling it, but that doesn't necessarily mean anything. I manage several properties at a time."

"I understand," I replied as a ball of anticipation tightened my chest.

Please, please, please.

I heard typing through the phone followed by the clicking of a mouse. "Do you remember the address or listing number?"

"9603 Briarwood Lane." I didn't think I'd ever forget that address.

More typing and clicking followed my response. "Here it is—looks like it's still on the market."

"Really?" There was no doubting the hope in my question.

"Yes. Just let me double-check something real quick…" After a few seconds of silence, her voice sounded back into the phone. "Yep, it's still available. Did you want to see it again?"

I couldn't stop the excitement that came over me. I sat up in my chair. "Can we just skip that and get to the paperwork?"

Tanya laughed. "I have to give your offer to the seller first. I'll do that as soon as we get off the phone."

"That would be great. Please keep me posted."

I could hear Tanya's smile in her voice. "I'll be in touch soon. You make sure that you stay well-rested for that baby."

"I will. Thanks again."

I text Ryker as soon as I hung up the phone to let him know the good news. Things were finally taking a turn for the better, and I wondered if they were too good to be true.

Chapter Twenty-Two

Ryker

"Where should I put this, babe?" I grunted as I hefted some chair that Kaiya had called a chaise through the doorway to our new house. It had taken about a month to get through the whole mortgage process, including extensive credit checks and employment verification, before we were finally able to move in.

Kaiya whipped around to face me, causing her ponytail to swing back and forth from the movement. "Um." She pursed her lips and walked toward me. "Right here should be fine."

I set the chair down where Kaiya indicated as she walked upstairs with a laundry basket full of baby clothes. I followed her with the box containing Hayden's crib, then put it down just inside his door.

I leaned against the door-frame and smiled as I watched Kaiya lay clothes on her enormous belly before folding them and setting them in the drawers of the dresser I had set up earlier.

I still had about two months left on my lease, so we were slowly moving stuff from both of our apartments into the house. We had also painted Hayden's room the week before, and Kaiya wanted to set everything up and have it ready before we moved in.

"Where do you want the crib?" I asked as I walked over to the cardboard. Gripping the edge, I started pulling at the top to open the box.

"Against that wall," Kaiya replied as she turned around and pointed across the room opposite of where she stood. "I want to put the rocking chair by the window."

I began to take the pieces out and arrange them on the floor so I could find them easily when I read the directions. After looking over the instructions a couple of times, I went downstairs to grab my toolbox out of my truck and get the tools I needed to assemble the crib.

Kaiya made several trips in and out of the room as I worked, bringing in the gifts we'd received at the baby shower and arranging them around the nursery. Everything was so surreal—moving into this house, becoming a father in just a month; basically settling down. If someone would have told me that this would be my life a year ago, I would've laughed in their faces.

Once I finished, I stepped back to survey my work. The crib looked just like the picture on the box. I gripped the edges of the crib and shook it a little to make sure it was sturdy.

"Finished?" Kaiya asked.

I looked over the crib again. "I think so." Bending down, I inspected the underside, then grabbed the legs and tested their stability. "Everything seems stable."

Kaiya came next to me as I stood and eyed the crib. "It looks good." She wrapped an arm around my waist and looked up at me with a loving smile. "Great job, Daddy."

I smiled from her words—I loved when she called me that. "Thanks, Momma."

Kaiya's mouth spread wider as she tiptoed up to kiss me. My hand automatically went to her stomach as our lips met; I loved feeling her belly and knowing that my son was inside her.

Or so you think.

My suspicious thoughts made me break the kiss and step back. "We have a lot to do. Stop distracting me," I deflected, hoping she wouldn't notice that something was bothering me.

She gave me a quick kiss on the cheek and smiled. "You're right. We don't have time to get carried away like usual."

Turning around, Kaiya grabbed the sheets we had bought for the crib and started putting them on the mattress. I went downstairs to get the rocking chair before bringing it up and putting it by the window where Kaiya wanted.

She walked toward me. "Thank you, baby." Sitting down in the chair, she looked out the window and sighed. "It's perfect."

I bent down and kissed her on the forehead. "I have some stuff to finish downstairs. Yell if you need me."

She smiled up at me. "Okay."

I ran my knuckles down Kaiya's cheek before walking out. Her phone rang as I walked out, so I stopped just outside the door to listen to the call.

The phone stopped ringing, but I didn't hear Kaiya answer it.

"Who was it, babe?" I asked as I stuck my head back in the room.

Kaiya jerked slightly before turning her phone over to hide the screen in her lap. The smile she gave me was forced, and I could tell she was trying to hide something. "Telemarketer."

Sure it was.

I nodded before leaving the room, trying to fight the sinking feeling that had crept in my gut.

Things between Kaiya and I had been getting tenser the closer she got to her due date. She was more irritable from the pregnancy hormones, and the suspicions I'd been having were growing the more I thought about them, making me trust her less and less.

I rented a couple of movies, hoping to relax and ease some of the tension between us. As we settled on the couch, my arm draped around Kaiya's shoulders as she curled up next to me, I could almost forget everything that had been bothering me.

That is until her phone vibrated and lit up during the first half of the movie.

Out of the corner of my eye, I tried to see the text message that had popped up, but as usual, she sneakily angled the screen away from me.

Anger lit my veins. We were a month away from having a kid together and she was hiding shit from me. Why would she be keeping things from me if she loved me and was about to give birth to my son. Unless…

He's not mine.

My mind ran a mile a minute, processing the revelation that dawned on me.

He's not mine.

The only reason she'd be so secretive was if she was cheating on me. If she really loved me, she wouldn't hide anything from me, especially weeks from having my kid. I knew the signs, and Kaiya had been flashing them brightly for months. I'd just been denying everything because I didn't want them to be true.

Then, another thing popped in my head. Whoever she was cheating with was the father. Not me.

He's not mine.

My heart felt like it was breaking into pieces, then being doused with battery acid. The pain that flooded me was unlike any other, and I knew there'd be no recovering from it. The wounds from Kaiya's betrayal would never scar, they'd be raw and open for the rest of my life.

Kaiya put her phone face down on the cushion next to her and focused back on the movie. Laying her hand on my chest, she snuggled closer to me, chasing away some of the harsh cold that had crept into my heart and replacing it with the warmth only she brought me.

No. Don't be weak. She doesn't love you. She's a cheating liar, just like Molly.

My teeth ground together as I thought about how stupid I'd been. Falling in love when I knew all women were the same. I needed answers; I needed to know why. "So, who is it?"

Kaiya kept her eyes on the TV. "Huh?"

Playing stupid, as always.

"Who are you cheating on me with?"

Kaiya sat up abruptly and looked at me with concern. "Ryker, what are you talking about?"

My heart pounded as my anger grew. "Don't lie to me anymore, Kaiya! Cut the bullshit and tell me!" I snarled.

Her eyes watered as she rested a hand against the middle of her chest. "Ryker, I would never-"

Unable to contain my rage anymore, I cut off her words, shouting over her. "Yeah, that's what she said! And look what happened!"

Tears poured down her cheeks. "I'm not Molly, Ryker! I'm not cheating on you!" she cried.

She's lying. Don't be fooled again.

I stood up and paced in front of the couch. "How do I know that, huh? You've been acting strange for the past few months. Secretly looking at your phone, angling the screen away from me so I can't see it, and getting calls from "wrong" numbers. Not to mention you added a password lock on your phone so I can't get in it."

Her face was blotchy as she looked up at me. "Here take it." She thrust her phone at me. "The password is Hayden's due date," she sobbed.

I stilled, starting to question my accusations.

Maybe she's not cheating. Maybe I'm just overreacting.

Don't be weak.

"It's too late for that now." I paused and took a deep breath before forcing myself to say the next sentence, even though it tore me up inside. "We're through."

The look of devastation that took over Kaiya's face constricted my heart, making me start to regret my words.

"Ryker, please. Let me explain," Kaiya pleaded desperately as she got up off the couch and grabbed my hands.

So she is hiding something. What else would there be to explain?

The coldness snaked back in as I steeled myself, preparing to do the hardest thing I'd ever done. I wasn't going to let her hurt me more than she already had. I was done letting my love for her blind me.

Forcing my steps, I made my way to the door. "Save it!" I yelled as

I grabbed my keys from the hook. "I don't want to hear your lies."

My chest tightened as I forcefully opened the door.

Don't go.

"Ryker, wait!" Kaiya started to beg. "Please don't g—"

I almost stopped, my love for her screaming for me to stay, to forget everything and take her in my arms, stop both of us from hurting. But I didn't. I walked out the door, slamming it behind me and cutting off Kaiya's sobs.

I had to get some air, and make sense of everything, make sure I was making the right decision.

You are.

As I got to my truck, I stopped. Every part of me, except my stubborn pride, told me to go back upstairs and quit being such a paranoid asshole.

Kaiya is eight months pregnant with your son. Don't leave her.

I almost went back, but what happened with Molly and me kept replaying in my mind. The way Kaiya had been acting over the past several months was similar to how Molly had acted before I'd found out about her and my brother.

I clenched my fists before punching the window of my driver's side door. Pain immediately shot up my arm, but I ignored it and got in my truck.

I should've never trusted her. I knew all women were the same.

I put the keys in the ignition, then stopped and gripped the steering wheel. Resting my head against it, I exhaled a heavy breath and closed my eyes.

Kaiya loves you. Go back up there and quit being a jackass.

Tightening my grip on the steering wheel, I started banging my forehead against it. "Fuck!"

You're letting your love for her blind you, just like you did with Molly. Don't be made a fool twice.

After starting my truck, I reversed and peeled out of the parking lot, ignoring pain in my chest and the knot forming in my gut.

Chapter Twenty-Three

Kaiya

Ryker's words held so much venom that I felt like my heart had been stung, injected with a lethal poison that was slowly corroding deep into my body and adding more irreparable scars to my broken soul.

How could he think that I cheated on him? I love him more than anything.

"Ryker, wait!" I cried out in despair. "Please don't g—"

I didn't get to finish my plea. The door slammed with his exit, and I felt like my heart had been smashed by it. All the pieces he had mended slowly fell apart again, shattering with every passing second that he was gone. Sinking to my knees on the floor, I sobbed into my hands as my world crumbled around me.

Why didn't I just tell him a long time ago? I'm so stupid.

I don't know how long I cried on the floor; it could've been minutes or it could've been hours, but when my tears finally ran dry, I was no longer upset. I was downright furious.

He wants to leave? Well, fine, I'm not going to sit around and wait for him.

Hefting myself off the floor, I stormed to the door, snatched my keys off the hook, and left.

How dare he accuse me of cheating? I'm pregnant with his son, for fuck's sake!

Tears resurfaced, streaming down my face as I went down the

stairs to my car. As I was about to open the door, a hand clamped down on my mouth and another came around my huge, bulging waist.

"I've been waiting for that meathead to leave you alone."

Bryce? What is he doing here?

I tried to pry his hands off of me but he tightened his grip. A feeling of dread permeated my stomach as I started to put two and two together.

Oh, God, no.

My words were muffled through Bryce's hand as he began to pull me away from my car. "What are you doing, Bryce?" My eyes darted around the empty parking lot, searching for anyone to help me.

"All those years, I was there for you. Every time you needed me, I was there. Then, you met him and threw everything we had away!"

His breath was hot against the side of my face, and it reeked of alcohol. "Bryce, please don't do this," I pleaded, even though I wasn't sure if he could make out my words since his hand was drowning them out. "I'm pregnant. I—"

He put more pressure on my stomach with his hand. "I see that! You barely know him, Ky. What were you thinking?" he spat.

More tears spilled from my eyes. I didn't know if they had even stopped from earlier. I struggled against Bryce as panic began to set in. He held me tighter to him and pressed me up against a car. His car.

I can't let him get me in the car.

I tried to scream, but with his hand over my mouth, I barely made a sound. I threw some back elbows into his ribs, but there wasn't much force in them because of how I was positioned. I managed to get a good hit in, forcing him to let me go briefly, but he pushed me by my chest against the car and held me there.

Bryce reared his fist back to punch me, but I turned and blocked it with both arms. Then, I gripped his forearm with my hands before throwing a back elbow into his chest. I used the momentum of the strike to force him to twist into the car, then pinned him there with my forearm on his throat.

Kneeing him in the groin, I caused him to clutch himself and drop to his knees. I screamed for help and turned to run away, but Bryce grabbed my ankle, sending me to smash my face on the hard asphalt.

Spots dotted my vision as the world spun around me. I felt Bryce pulling me into his arms as everything went black.

My eyes fluttered open to a ceiling. I was no longer outside. I was being carried inside somewhere.

Where am I? What is going on?

My head and nose throbbed with pain as I struggled to shake the disorientation clouding me. Then, I registered Bryce's face and everything came rushing back.

Oh my God!

"Help! Somebody help me!" I screamed as I squirmed in his arms.

Bryce clamped his hand over my mouth, muffling my cries. I bit down on his hand as hard as I could, causing him to pull his hand back and drop me. "You bitch!"

I fell to the floor and winced from the resulting pain. I glanced around, trying to take in my surroundings.

Shit.

I was in Bryce's apartment.

Out of the corner of my eye, I saw Bryce lunging toward me, so I turned on my side and kicked out, narrowly missing his knee and hitting his shin instead.

Get up. You can't let him pin you on the ground.

I rolled to the side and awkwardly stumbled to get up. I definitely wasn't as graceful as I used to be before I was pregnant. I got in my defensive stance as Bryce came at me again.

My techniques were limited since I was so large, and it was difficult for me to move fluidly like I needed to. I couldn't kick as well anymore, so I had to rely on my punching and hand techniques, which weren't my strong suit. I was at a huge disadvantage, but I wasn't going to give up. I had to protect my son.

Bryce threw punches as he advanced toward me. I backed up and blocked with my forearms, forgetting every thought except one:

Don't let him hit your stomach.

I kept retreating down the hallway as he advanced, blocking most of his punches, but not all. I was used to taking hits from all the sparring I had done, but each time he connected, the impact weakened me.

I backed through a doorway, then looked around to see where I was—Bryce had forced me into his bedroom.

Fuck, this isn't good.

I threw a palm strike toward his face, but he grabbed my wrist and jerked me forward. Wrenching my arm from his grasp, I stumbled backwards onto the bed.

I immediately sprung off and put my guard up. My eyes danced over Bryce as I tried to anticipate his movements.

In the brief time I had spent fighting him, I could already tell he preferred using his hands than kicking. Most men were like that, including Ryker, so I had experience against that style of fighting.

When I sparred Ryker, there was always one move that I got him with—a low high roundhouse attack. Unfortunately, I couldn't do the high kick anymore because of how big and off-balance I was, but I could still throw the low one.

Snapping my leg out, I caught Bryce in the thigh, but the hit didn't seem to faze him. He came in closer to me, causing panic to set in from his proximity. All I could think about was shielding my stomach from his hits.

I should've focused more on watching him and protecting my face. His hook caught me right on the jaw, causing fireworks to burst behind my eyelids before I crashed to the ground and darkness smothered me.

Chapter Twenty-Four

Ryker

I threw back another shot as I sat at the bar with Drew. Slamming the glass on the counter, I loudly ordered, "Another!"

Drew shook his head at the bartender, then looked at me. "Are you all right, bro? Shouldn't you be at home with Kaiya? The baby is due soon, right?"

Kaiya.

Hayden.

Home.

"Yeah. But I don't even know if he's mine," I lied. Deep down, I knew Hayden was mine. I was letting my stupid insecurities get the best of me.

"What are you talking about?" Drew looked at me skeptically, raising an eyebrow in question.

A glass of water was pushed in front of me, but I didn't take it. "They all cheat, you know. All of them."

Drew scoffed. "Are you serious? You really think Kaiya would cheat on you? Haven't you seen the way she looks at you? That girl has got it bad for you."

I didn't say anything for several seconds, trying to think of something to prove him wrong. My drunken mind came up with nothing. "I'm such an asshole."

Standing up, I wobbled slightly as I pulled out my wallet. I threw forty bucks down on the bar and rushed toward the door.

Drew quickly followed behind me. "What are you doing, bro?"

"Something I should have done hours ago. I need to get home to Kaiya." I pushed the door open before heading out into the warm summer night.

Drew stopped me by grabbing my arm. "You can't drive. You've had too much to drink."

I pulled my arm out of his grasp, and stumbled backwards. "I need to get home," I repeated more forcefully.

Drew tried to snatch my keys away, but I pushed him away. "Don't fuck with me, bro."

Drew put his hands up and took a step back. "All right, man. Be careful."

I walked away to my truck without a backwards glance, hoping I could fix the mistake I'd made.

I sped back to my complex, then sprinted up the stairs to our apartment. I fumbled to get the key in the lock as my eyes tried to focus on the knob.

Once I unlocked the door, I stumbled through and almost fell. "Kaiya," I called out into the dark room.

No response.

It's almost two in the morning. She's probably in bed by now, jackass.

"Warrior, I'm sorry," I apologized as I walked down the hall toward our bedroom.

The door was wide open. "Ky?"

Once I entered, I looked around the empty room, perplexed. Only Brownie lay sleeping in her bed in the corner.

Where is she?

I went into our bathroom and found the same thing. No Kaiya.

Damn it, where could she be?

I took my cell out and dialed her number. Her phone rang a couple of times, then went straight to voicemail.

Fuck.

Worry started to sink in. I tried to think of where Kaiya would go, especially since she was eight months pregnant. Then, the drunken fog lifted and the light bulb in my head went off.

I ran out of my apartment and didn't stop until I was banging on Kamden's door. "Hurry the fuck up, Kam! Open the goddamn door!"

The door abruptly opened, and I walked in, not waiting for an invitation. "Is Kaiya here?" I asked as I went down the hall toward her room.

I could hear Kamden's footsteps behind me. "No. I thought she was with you."

Shit.

Even though he just told me she wasn't there, I still went into her room. "What the fuck is going on, Ryker? Where's Kaiya?"

I turned around to face him and roughly ran my hands through my hair. "I don't know." I blew out a frustrated breath. "We got in an argument, and I left. She isn't answering her phone, and I have no clue where she is. I thought she'd be here."

Fuck.

Kamden's lip curled up angrily as he spat his words. "So, you're telling me that you got in a fight with my pregnant sister, then left her by herself, this late at night?"

"Look, I know I fucked up, but arguing about it isn't going to help us find her." I pushed past him to go back to the living room.

Where would she go?

Then, it hit me—Nori. "Maybe she went to Nori's," I said as I pulled out my phone and scrolled through my contacts.

Shit, I don't have her number.

I looked at Kam and asked, "Do you have her number?"

Kamden grabbed his phone from his back pocket and swiped the screen. He pressed it a few times before putting the phone to his ear.

I stuck my hand out. "Let me talk to her."

Kamden stared at me but didn't reply.

God, he's such an asshole,

I narrowed my eyes as anger simmered my blood. "Damn it, Kamden, give me the fucking phone!" I growled.

That motherfucker smirked at me, actually fucking smirked. He turned around as he greeted, "Hey, Nori. It's Kam. Is Kai—"

I ripped the phone from his hand, cutting off the rest of his sentence. He whirled around angrily as I put the phone to my ear. I gave him a warning glare as I spoke, "Nori, it's Ryker. Is Kaiya there?"

"No. Why would she be here?" She sounded confused.

"Fuck!" I yelled.

Where are you, Warrior?

"Ryker, what's going on? You're scaring me," Nori urgently replied.

I rubbed my hand over my face. "Kaiya and I got in a fight. I left the apartment, and when I came home she wasn't there. She's not with Kamden either. She isn't answering her phone."

I heard Nori gasp. "Oh my God, you don't think…"

"What?" I had no clue what she was talking about, but the fear and concern in her voice intensified mine.

When she didn't answer, I demanded, "Damn it, Nori, tell me!"

"You don't think the person who's been sending her those texts did something, do you?"

Now I was confused on top of being worried. "Wait, what?" I tried to make sense of what Nori was saying. "No, that was months ago, before Kaiya even found out she was pregnant. The texts stopped."

Nori sighed into the phone. "No, they didn't, Ryker. Kaiya just didn't want you to freak out and get yourself arrested over them, so she didn't tell you."

I slumped to the couch in shock. Those texts had been going on for over nine months and Kaiya had kept it to herself. No wonder she seemed so distant and off sometimes—she wasn't cheating, she was hiding the texts from me.

I wasn't sure if that revelation hurt more or less. I didn't fully believe that she'd been cheating on me, but keeping the texts from me was real. She didn't trust me enough to tell me what was going on.

Well, look how crazy you act.

I could hear Nori rambling through the phone, but I didn't care. All I cared about was finding Kaiya, and I had no idea where to start. And now I was terrified that whoever had been sending Kaiya the texts was somehow involved.

The phone fell from my hand to the couch. I bolted up and ran out the door, ignoring Kamden's shouts from behind me.

My apartment was still open since I'd left in such a hurry. I went inside and started looking around for anything that might tell me where Kaiya was. It was a long shot, but I was desperate.

I looked through our room first, but found nothing to help me so I went to the living room. I searched high and low, over every inch of the space, and still nothing.

Fuck.

Then, out of the corner of my eye, I could've sworn I saw a light flash. I jerked my head in the direction it came from, and then the small light flashed again from the couch.

Walking over to it, I found the source. There, barely sticking up out of the cushions, was Kaiya's phone.

I picked it and keyed in her passcode—Hayden's due date.

Why didn't you tell me what was going on, Warrior?

I went to her messages, hoping I could get some clues from the texts, and found the conversation with the unknown number.

The last text was sent at 10:33 PM, right after I had left.

Unknown: You're finally gonna be mine

My heart pounded with fear as my stomach clenched.

This is all my fault! Why did I act so stupid? Now Kaiya and our son are in danger, and I have no fucking clue where to find them.

I stared at the text, unable to take my eyes off it. Then, clutching the phone tightly in my hand, I reared back to chunk it across the room.

As I was about to let it fly, I stopped. I didn't want to destroy what little bit of a lead that I had.

"Find anything?" Kamden asked from the doorway.

I held up Kaiya's phone. "She left it here."

"Nori told me about the texts." He walked toward me with his arms crossed over his chest. "Any idea who sent them?"

"No," I sighed. "I didn't even know she was still getting them."

I scrolled through and read all the messages from the unknown number. Kamden was talking, but I zoned out everything he was saying, trying to pick out any detail that might point me in the direction of Kaiya.

Then, I stopped and zeroed in on one text.

No fucking way.

Kamden shoved me. "I'm talking to you, asshole!"

I clenched my jaw as I stared him down. "I found something," I gritted. I turned the screen to face him so that he could read it.

Unknown: Hope that meathead can protect you

Kamden's eyes met mine, then creased in confusion. He shrugged his shoulders. "What? I don't get it."

"You know who called me a meathead the last time Kaiya and I saw him?"

Kamden shook his head and raised an eyebrow. "No."

The rage coursing through me was evident in my voice. "Bryce."

After explaining to Kamden everything that had happened with Bryce, we got in my truck and took off toward Bryce's condo.

"I still don't think Bryce would do something like this. He and Kaiya have been friends for years."

I was almost positive that Bryce had something to do with Kaiya's disappearance. Not just because of the meathead text, but all of the messages combined. Especially the last one.

You're finally gonna be mine

Bryce had always wanted more than Kaiya was willing to give, and it seemed like he was going to take what he thought was his.

Too fucking bad—Kaiya is mine.

I was going to make him pay for taking her from me. Slowly and painfully.

Once Kamden navigated to Bryce's condo, I kicked down the door without even bothering to knock. Darkness blanketed the inside as I went in and switched on the light. "Kaiya!"

I surveyed the room, looking for any sign of Kaiya or Bryce. A chair was overturned and some picture frames lay broken on the ground. I searched the rest of Bryce's place and found more signs of a struggle, especially in the bedroom.

Pillows from the bed were on the floor, and the covers were bunched up at the foot of the bed. A lamp was turned over on the mattress and one of the nightstands was on its side.

I gripped the edge of the dresser as I fought to stay calm. I needed to be level-headed if I was going to find Kaiya, but the thought of Bryce hurting Kaiya, or worse, raping her, sent me over the edge.

I roared in fury as I swiped everything off the top of the dresser. Everything that was on top scattered to the floor as I turned and punched a hole through the wall.

Then, I saw something that made my heart sink—Kaiya's bracelet. It lay on the floor next to the bed. Kamden rushed in. "What? What happened?"

Ignoring him, I walked to the bracelet before bending over and picking it up. The link at the end of the chain was broken, probably during whatever happened. My eyes burned as I thought about Kaiya being hurt or worse, dead.

I closed my fist around the bracelet as a few tears fell down my face.

Not my Warrior. Please let her be okay.

A hand came down on my shoulder, and I turned and flung it

away, preparing to punch whoever touched me.

Kamden put his hands up. "Whoa, it's just me. As much as I want to kick your ass, we have other things to worry about. Like finding my sister."

He was right—I needed to focus on finding Kaiya and not get sucked into my emotions.

Where would he have taken her?

I put Kaiya's bracelet in my pocket before wiping my face. "Okay, let's search the house—maybe there's a clue as to where he would go."

We ripped the condo apart, looking for anything that would lead us to Kaiya. Bryce's office was where we had concentrated most of our efforts, but papers were strewn all over the floor and desk—it was like looking for a needle in a haystack.

Kamden sat in an office chair, going through papers on the desk. He huffed in frustration before throwing the papers down. "There's nothing here."

"Keep looking." I was searching through Bryce's filing cabinet when I came across a file of interest. It was labeled as "Real Estate Documents."

I pulled the file out and opened it. I began reading the papers, and finally found something that might help. I looked up at Kam, who had his elbows propped on the table as he held his head in his hands. "Hey, I think I found something."

His head jerked toward me, and he practically jumped out of the chair. "What?" he asked anxiously.

I scanned over the document one more time just to be sure before looking up at Kamden again. "Apparently Bryce has a house in Cape Cod."

"Do you think he might have taken her there?"

"I don't know." I took the paper and dropped the rest of the file on the ground. "But I'm gonna find out."

"Cape Cod is more than an hour away," Kamden pointed out as I started walking.

"Which means we better not waste any more time."

Chapter Twenty-Five

Kaiya

My eyes fluttered open slowly. Wincing from the pain swarming most of my body, I attempted to move, but couldn't. My hands were fastened to a chair behind my back and my ankles were tied together. Duct tape covered my mouth, stretching the skin around my lips uncomfortably.

My eyes darted around the room, attempting to take in my surroundings. I was in a bedroom, one that I'd never been in before. The walls were painted a light blue, resembling a springtime sky, and various beach décor adorned the room. The muted sound of waves barely registered, so I guessed that I was somewhere near a beach.

Where has he taken me?

Bryce didn't live near a beach, but I vaguely remembered him mentioning something about wanting to take me on a mini-vacation to a beach condo in Cape Cod. If he had brought me there, I was fucked. It was about an hour away from home.

Squirming, I tried to see if I could free myself and escape, but Bryce had firmly secured the knots restraining me.

Fuck.

I wasn't going to give up, though. The chances of someone coming out here to rescue me were slim, so I needed to figure out how to get out of here and back home.

Fumbling with the rope around my wrists, I attempted to loosen it but was interrupted.

"Ah, you're awake," Bryce spoke, drawing my eyes to the doorway where he stood.

I stilled as he approached me, not wanting him to see what I was doing. "Why are you doing this, Bryce?" My voice was muffled by the tape as I questioned him.

He circled around me. "Why am I doing this?" He responded rhetorically.

I tried to turn and follow his movement as he rounded my back, but I couldn't because of the way he had tied me to the chair.

His warm breath hit my neck, sending a chill over me as he spoke. "Because I'm finally taking what's mine."

Was he always this crazy?

No, you make people that way, just like Kaleb.

The pain of him ripping the tape off my mouth snapped me out of my thoughts. I screamed for help, but Bryce silenced me when he clutched my throat.

My heart started to pound as panic began to weave through me. I jerked my head back, but Bryce kept his grip on my skin. He wasn't applying enough pressure to block my air supply, but it was still uncomfortable.

"Bryce, please stop." I begged as tears formed at the corners of my eyes.

The pressure intensified for a few seconds before he let go and came around to face me. "I forgot that you hate to have your neck touched." His tone was mocking as he ran his finger over the scar on my throat.

My breaths were labored as panic ate at me and adrenaline rushed through my veins. Then, worry over Hayden's safety compounded my anxiety. I hadn't felt him move since back at the apartment. I knew the stress I was subjected to wasn't good for him, and I didn't want to go into early labor. I needed to calm down and find a way to get out of there.

I resumed messing with the ropes and locked eyes with Bryce. "Let me go, Bryce, please. I promise I won't tell anyone."

"Not even that meathead?" he replied snidely, his distaste for Ryker evident in his voice.

"I won't, I promise—he probably doesn't even know I'm gone. We had a fight and he left. He's probably not even home yet."

Bryce seemed to consider that for a moment as his eyes scanned my face. He looked like my old Bryce for a moment before his face shifted darkly, the way Kaleb's used to. His eyes narrowed menacingly at me. "I don't think so."

The tiny shred of hope I had evaporated. I knew that look—the one there was no reasoning with. I wasn't going to be able to convince Bryce to let me go.

The knots in the ropes loosened a little. I needed to keep Bryce distracted so I could finish untying the rope enough to escape. A few tears trickled down my cheeks as I held his gaze. "I'm sorry, Bryce. I never meant to hurt you."

He scoffed and shook his head. "I was there for you whenever you needed me. And how did you repay me?" He clenched his fists and raised his voice. "By kicking me to the curb for some asshole you had just met!"

"I'm sorry!" A sob broke through my throat as I looked into his wounded eyes. I felt bad for him for a split second, but pushed away the guilt and sadness, reminding myself of what he was doing to me. I tore my eyes away and steeled my voice. "I told you not to get involved with me, but you didn't listen."

"Oh, so it's my fault?" he replied incredulously. My eyes darted back to him as I heard his footsteps quickly approaching me, causing my body to tense in fear.

He lowered his face to my eye level. "You made me do this. I tried to make you see that I was the one for you. I tried to be patient. But after everything, I finally realized that when you want something, you have to take it."

I had almost unknotted the rope, but I didn't want to finish while Bryce was still in the room with me. I was in no shape to fight him off, and I wanted to escape with the least amount of confrontation as possible, preferably without him knowing.

He cupped my cheek, but I turned my face away, repulsed by his touch. Big mistake.

Out of the corner of my eye, I saw him rear his hand back. I flinched in anticipation before he backhanded me and bellowed in my face. "Look what you've done to us! I loved you!" His voice softened as he forced me to look at him by gripping my chin. His eyes were glazed with tears as he stared into mine. "I would've loved you forever, Ky."

I trembled as my gaze ran over his face. A face that used to be a source of comfort for me, but was now lost. He still looked the same, but the man I knew and loved was gone. I may not have loved him like he'd wanted, but I had loved him. And now I'd destroyed him, just like everyone else important in my life—Mom. Dad. Kaleb. Kamden… Ryker. Bryce had been one of my only friends, and I'd treated him like shit.

All I do is cause pain and ruin everything around me.

"You're right," I replied in a cracked whisper. "This is all my fault."

I hung my head as tears dripped from my eyes. My sight blurred as I looked down at my belly. I thought about the life inside me, something so perfect that I had helped create, something I'd finally done right. I wasn't going to let Hayden suffer from my destructive actions.

I kept my gaze downcast, hoping Bryce would think that I'd given up, then leave the room. Once he did, I could finish untying the ropes and get the fuck out of there.

"I'm sorry it had to come to this, Ky, but I can't live without you."

I felt him kiss the top of my head before the sound of his footsteps receding filled the room. The door closed and left me alone with just the dull murmur of the waves lapping up on the shore.

I waited a few minutes before straightening and working on the ropes around my wrists. My back was strained from the position I was in, making it harder for me to work on my task. Not to mention that I was utterly exhausted from everything that had happened.

My shoulders and arms burned after God knows how long. I was so close to untying the knots, but I just couldn't get them undone. I slumped in fatigue and sobbed, ready to give up.

I can't do this. I'm too weak.

Then, something amazing happened—Hayden kicked me, right when I needed it most. He reminded me of what I was fighting for, why I couldn't lose hope. Him.

I will get out of this. I have to

Sitting back up, I worked on the ropes again. I wasn't going to let Bryce win—I was going to escape and ensure my son's safety. Hayden was all that mattered.

After several minutes, the sound of a door crashing open halted my actions.

What was that?

Sounds of fighting, furniture breaking, and indistinct shouting followed. I strained to hear, but couldn't make out the voices through the closed door. All I could tell was that they were male.

What's going on? Who's here?

I started to get my hopes up that Ryker had come for me, but then I remembered our fight. He probably didn't even know I was gone. And if he did, he probably didn't care anymore.

His words replayed in my mind, making my heart sink back down into the pool of despair where my demons lay.

We're through.

The sting of tears assaulted my eyes as I thought about never seeing Ryker again, never feeling his skin against mine, or hearing him tell me he loves me.

The sound of doors opening roughly slamming into the walls broke through my thoughts.

"Kaiya! Kaiya!"

My breath hitched. I knew that voice.

Am I dreaming?

The voice became louder, sounding desperate and terrified. "Kaiya! Kaiya, where are you?"

The tears that had been pooling spilled over. "In here! I'm in here!"

Footsteps pounded down the hall, getting faster and louder as he neared. "Kaiya!"

I wriggled in the chair, trying to free my hands. "In here!" I screamed.

I didn't stop screaming until the doorknob jiggled seconds later. "I'm right here, baby. I'm gonna get you out of there."

Several thuds echoed off the door before it was kicked in. Ryker appeared in the doorway; his gaze immediately found mine, and in seconds, he was kneeling in front of me. Reaching behind me, he untied my wrists and slipped the rope off before unfastening my ankles from the bottom of the chair. He helped me stand, then wrapped his arms around me, holding me tightly to him. He expelled a breath of relief. "Thank God I found you."

My hands fisted the back of his shirt as tears ran down my face. "You came for me," I whispered in disbelief.

Ryker pulled back and framed my face in his hands. His eyes searched mine. "Of course I did, Warrior." He moved one of his hands to my belly. "I love you. You and Hayden are everything to me."

"But earlier you said th—"

"Fuck what I said. I was being a stupid asshole. I never should've said those things or left you. I'm so sorry, baby."

More tears flowed from my eyes. I should've been pissed as all hell, but all I felt was relief and my love for Ryker. He was, and always had been "it" for me. Nothing would ever change that.

I sobbed into his chest, my body shaking as reality sank in and overwhelmed me. The tears poured out of me and soaked Ryker's shirt as I held onto him for dear life.

Suddenly, my stomach was assaulted with the most intense pain I'd ever experienced. I couldn't stop the cry of agony that escaped me as my knees buckled, and I slumped against Ryker.

Ryker eased us down to the floor and cupped my face. "Ky, what's wrong, baby?" His eyes scanned over my face with concern.

Clenching my teeth, I gritted out my words. "I don't know." I clutched my stomach. "It just hurts."

Ryker draped my arm over his shoulders before lifting me up and into his arms. "I'm going to take you to the hospital."

Biting my lip, I buried my face back in his chest and fisted his shirt in my hands. Tears involuntarily streamed down my heated cheeks from the excruciating pain. "It hurts so bad," I whimpered.

"I know, baby. I'm sorry. I'll get you there as fast as I can." Ryker replied as he rushed through Bryce's condo.

"What happened?" Kamden urgently questioned. "Is she okay?"

"I don't know. She's having some stomach pain. I'm taking her to the hospital."

I cried out, unable to stifle the sound. The pain was too much. I felt like my insides were being shredded with a razor-sharp saw, and I worried for Hayden. I was still five weeks away from being full term, which wasn't that bad, but so much could go wrong, and I didn't want anything happening to him.

"Ryker, please," I whimpered. "Hayden."

We started moving again. "You coming or not?" Ryker gruffly asked my brother.

"What about him?" Kamden replied.

"Fuck him. All I care about is Kaiya and the baby. I'm leaving. You can stay if you want," Ryker abruptly retorted.

Even though my eyes were closed, I knew we were outside. The smell of the ocean wafted over me as the sea breeze cooled my fevered skin. I could hear the waves crashing against the sand as we continued walking.

Ryker laid me down in the backseat before climbing in next to me. He rested my head in his lap and another wave of pain slammed through me.

Fuck! It hurts so bad.

I arched my back as I writhed in the seat and screamed. Sweat beaded on my forehead and my body felt like it was on fire.

Ryker pushed some hair out of my face and yelled at Kamden in the front seat. "Drive! Fast!"

I closed my eyes again as Kamden and Ryker shouted back and forth about the closest hospital and what highway to take. Their voices faded out as darkness overtook me.

Chapter Twenty-Six

Ryker

Kamden drove to the nearest emergency room in Cape Cod. Kaiya had passed out when we started driving, and I hadn't been able to wake her.

Staring down at her, I was unable to take my eyes off her slowly rising and falling chest. I feared that if I looked away, she would stop breathing.

Stay with me, baby.

Kamden parked right in front of the emergency room doors. He had barely put the truck in park as I hurried to get Kaiya out of the truck and inside.

Cradling her in my arms, I rushed through the sliding glass doors and to the front desk. The nurse stood when I reached the counter. "What's your emergency?"

"My girlfriend started having stomach pains. She's thirty-five weeks pregnant."

"Okay, I need you to fill out this paperwork." The nurse handed me a clipboard.

Kaiya started to stir. She writhed in my arms and moaned.

Fuck I hate when she's in pain.

Tears flowed from her eyes, which were clenched shut in pain. Her cries became louder and her fingers dug into my arm and back. "Ryker!"

The agony in her voice sliced right through my heart. I directed my attention to the nurse. There was no mistaking the anxiousness in my tone. "Please get someone!"

"Sir, I nee-"

"Now!" My voice boomed through the room. "Can't you see how much pain she's in?"

Kamden reached for the clipboard. "I'm her brother. I promise I'll fill everything out, just please get my sister some help."

The nurse looked back and forth between both of us before handing Kamden the clipboard. Then, she grabbed the phone as Kaiya screamed out in pain again.

I pulled her closer against me. "It's going to be okay, Warrior. They're getting someone right now. Just hold on."

Sweat coated Kaiya's forehead as she buried her face into my chest. Kamden stood in front of me and stroked her hair. "Shhh, *sorella*. Everything's going to be okay."

Kamden began filling out the paperwork as I impatiently paced back and forth in the waiting area. After a few minutes, two medical personnel came through some double doors to our right. They wheeled a rolling hospital bed through and approached us. "Kaiya Marlow?"

I took a hurried step toward them. "Right here."

The male nurse quickly glanced up at me. "Lay her down gently."

I carefully lay Kaiya on the stretcher, but she wouldn't let go of my shirt. "Don't leave me," she pleaded.

I ran one of my hands through her hair. "I'm right here, baby. I'm not going anywhere."

She winced and squirmed on the bed as she pulled me closer to her. "Make it stop."

Fuck. Shit. Fuck.

I hated being helpless. Not being able to ease Kaiya's pain was killing me inside. I looked up at the female nurse across from me. "Please hurry. She's in a lot of pain."

She smiled sympathetically. "My name is Meredith, and that's Jake.

We're going to take care of her." She attached a medical bracelet to Kaiya's wrist and continued speaking, "We need to check the baby's heart rate. If he or she is in distress, then we'll need to do an emergency C-section."

I wasn't an expert on pregnancy, but I knew that Kaiya wasn't full term yet. "She's only thirty-five weeks," I replied with concern.

"I'm sorry, but if the baby is at risk, we have to deliver."

"No," Kaiya whimpered. "He's not ready."

I pried her hands from my shirt and held them in mine. "He's gonna be okay, Warrior."

Kaiya's eyes watered as she squeezed my hands. She gritted her teeth and groaned in pain again.

Jake and Meredith pushed the stretcher through the open double doors in front of us. Soon, we were wheeled down the hall into a room with an ultrasound machine.

After getting settled in the room, Meredith prepped Kaiya, attaching various wires to her chest to monitor her vitals while Jake grabbed a small machine from one of the cabinets—it looked similar to the one Kaiya's doctor had used when we listened to Hayden's heartbeat.

Meredith applied gel to Kaiya's stomach as Jake handed her the wand to the fetal doppler. Noise soon filled the room as Meredith moved the wand around Kaiya's abdomen. I immediately recognized the sound of Hayden's heartbeat, even though it was noticeably slower than the other times we'd heard it.

Meredith's forehead creased in concern as she stared at the handheld machine. "Eighty-five bpm. We need to get an OB in here stat."

"Wait, is that bad?" I questioned anxiously.

Kaiya moaned in pain as Meredith grabbed the phone. "I need an OB to room 103. I have a patient and fetal heart rate is 85 bpm."

Meredith hung up the phone, then grabbed some supplies from a drawer and swabbed Kaiya's inner elbow with an alcohol wipe. "Normal fetal heart rate is between one hundred twenty and one hundred eighty beats per minute. Anything over or under that puts the baby at risk."

My mind was all over the place, unable to register what either of them were saying. I finally was able to come up with a coherent thought. "Are they going to be okay?"

Meredith hesitated before answering, "They'll be fine. There are always risks when it comes to any surgery, but the sooner we act, the better. The doctor will probably want to get the baby out as soon as possible."

The doctor entered as Meredith wrapped a band around Kaiya's belly. Kaiya writhed in pain on the stretcher and moaned again. Meredith addressed the doctor. "Fetal heart rate is 85 bpm."

The doctor looked at the monitor that was hooked up to Kaiya. "Let's monitor for a few minutes. Start the IV and get some fluids in her."

Meredith inserted an IV into Kaiya's arm. She winced in pain. "Ryker."

Rushing to her side, I grabbed her hand. "I'm right here, baby."

"What's going on? Is Hayden okay?" She gritted out as she tightly squeezed my hand.

"He's going to be fine. His heart rate is a little slow so they may have to do an emergency C-section."

"What? No," She moaned. Suddenly, her grip on my hand loosened. "I don't feel good."

The monitor started beeping wildly. Meredith rushed to Kaiya's other side. "Blood pressure is dropping." Her voice was urgent.

Kaiya's skin went pale, and her eyes slowly closed. Her words were slurred and barely audible. "Ryker, I—"

Kaiya's head lolled to the side.

My heart dropped into my stomach.

Please, God, no.

I shook our joined hands, trying to wake her. "Kaiya! Kaiya!"

"Get her to surgery now. We have to perform an emergency C-section." The doctor said, then directed his attention to me. "Are you the father?"

I couldn't process what was happening. My eyes burned from tears as I stared down at Kaiya.

The doctor placed a hand on my shoulder. "Sir, we have to go now. Are you the father?"

I looked up at him, my sight blurred. "What?"

"Are you the father?

My voice cracked. "Yes."

"Do we have your consent for surgery? We need to get the baby out now."

I looked down at Kaiya, then back at the doctor, still trying to take in everything. "Do whatever you need to do. Please save them."

The doctor nodded, then walked toward the door. "Let's get her into surgery."

Jake pushed the stretcher as Meredith guided it out of the room behind the doctor jogged beside it, keeping Kaiya's hand in mine as we rushed down the hallway.

When we reached the set of double doors at the end of the hall, Meredith turned and looked at me. "There's a waiting area back down the hall, to the right. The doctor will come speak to you following the surgery."

My heart rate increased as anxiety set in. "I can't come with her?"

"I'm sorry, but due to the complications she's experiencing, no."

I reluctantly nodded my understanding before leaning down and kissing Kaiya on the forehead. I brushed the sweaty hair out of her face. "I love you, Warrior." My voice was strained by emotion.

"I'm sorry, we have to go now." The doctor stated impatiently as he went through the doors.

Meredith gave me a sympathetic look as she and Jake began to push Kaiya behind the doctor. "We'll take good care of her. Don't worry."

I nodded as tears fell down my face. I stared at Kaiya until the doors closed, taking her out of sight. I ran my hands over my face, then through my hair.

Fuck! This can't be happening.

I slammed my fist into the metal and pressed my forehead against the doors.

Calm down, everything is going to be fine. Think positive.

I let out a breath in an attempt to calm myself down. And then, for the first time since God knows when, I prayed.

I know I'm not one of your favorites, but please take care of them. I can't lose them.

I stayed there for a few seconds before I pushed off the doors and headed back to the lobby, unable to stop the anxiety that was overtaking me.

Ethan was talking to Kamden when I entered the waiting room. When he caught sight of me, he ran over, stopping right in front of me and meeting my gaze. "What happened? Are Kaiya and the baby okay?"

My vision blurred as tears stung my eyes. I took a deep breath and exhaled heavily. I hadn't explained the details over the phone when I called him; I just told him to get his ass to the hospital as fast as he could. "Kaiya was… attacked. The trauma sent the baby into distress, and as they were monitoring her, she passed out. They had to do an emergency C-section."

Ethan stared at me, apparently stunned by my words. He raked his hands over his face. "Oh my God, Ryker, I'm sorry."

I sat down next to Kamden. I held my head in my hands and bounced my leg anxiously. I was not prepared for this.

Please let them be okay. Don't take them from me.

Kamden placed a hand on my back. "They'll be okay. My sister's a fighter—always has been."

I couldn't speak because of the emotion threatening to choke me, so I nodded. I knew Kaiya was a fighter, but I still had a knot of worry balled deep in my gut that grew with each passing second they were in there.

Ethan sat on my other side and sighed. "I can't believe this is happening."

Me neither.

About twenty minutes passed before the surgeon came into the waiting area. He looked at the screen of an iPad. "Ryker Campbell?"

I stood up immediately and went toward him. "That's me—is Kaiya okay?"

Kamden and Ethan came up next to me as the doctor replied, "She's in recovery right now. The surgery went well—no complications."

I let out a heavy breath. "And the baby?"

The doctor smiled. "A healthy seven pound, three ounce boy. He's doing very well. You should be able see him soon."

Thank God.

I couldn't stop the smile that slowly spread over my face.

They're okay.

Ethan patted me on the back. "Congratulations, bro."

I looked at him, still in shock that both Kaiya and Hayden were okay after everything they'd been through in the last few hours. "Thanks."

Kamden started asking the doctor questions about Kaiya's surgery and recovery, but all I could think about was seeing her and Hayden. Images of what he looked like ran through my head.

"Are you ready to meet your son?" The doctor asked, breaking through my thoughts.

Son. My son.

I laughed. "Yes. Hell yes."

Chapter Twenty-Seven

Kaiya

"Wake up, my Warrior," a soft, deep voice spoke, sounding garbled as I teetered between awake and sleep.

My eyes fluttered open to a dimly lit room.

Where am I?

I tried to sit up, but I was too weak and everything hurt. I moaned in pain.

"Easy, baby. You just had surgery."

I gingerly turned my head toward the sound of the voice I loved so much. "Surgery?" I rasped, my mouth dry and cottony.

My eyes stung, and I was unable to focus on anything so I closed them as Ryker answered, "Hayden went into distress, and you passed out. The doctor had to do an emergency C-section."

"Is Hayden okay? Where is he?" I asked as my mind scrambled to make sense of everything. I strained to open my eyes, but the faint light hurt, forcing me to shut them again.

"He's fine, baby. He's right here. We've been waiting for you to wake up." He paused before talking again, this time in a gentler tone. "Ready to meet Mommy, Hayden?"

Tears leaked from my closed eyes. I fought to open them, anxious to see my baby and finally succeeded. My sight may have been blurred, but I knew I was looking at the most beautiful thing I'd ever seen as I laid eyes on my son.

Ryker stood next to the bed, cradling the tiny bundle in his huge, inked arms. So opposite, yet so perfect. He gazed down at Hayden lovingly before giving me the same look. "Wanna hold him, Momma?"

I weakly lifted my arms, but couldn't hold them up.

Damn anesthesia.

"More than anything," I whispered as more tears fell down my face.

"Relax." He shifted toward me and gently laid Hayden on my chest. I used every ounce of strength I had in me to bring my arms up to wrap around my baby.

My baby.

I softly kissed his fuzzy head as Ryker ran a hand through my hair. "You did amazing, Warrior. He's perfect."

He is, isn't he?

I stared down at my son, unable to take my eyes off of him. My eyes ran over every feature as my fingers traced over his velvety skin.

I can't believe I created something so perfect. I finally did something right.

I glanced up at Ryker, who was also gazing down at Hayden on my chest. I smiled as I continued to stare at the man I loved.

Our eyes met as one corner of his mouth curved up. "What?"

My lips spread wider. "Nothing."

He brushed his knuckles down my cheek. "Tell me."

"I just love you. I'm so lucky to have you."

"Nah, Warrior, you've got it all wrong." He looked down at Hayden and carefully rubbed him on his little back. "I'm the lucky one."

Chapter Twenty-Eight

Ryker

It felt amazing to finally bring Kaiya and our son home. The few days we had spent in the hospital seemed to drag, especially since Kaiya and I both hated hospitals. And to make matters worse, we had to deal with the police asking questions about Bryce. Bastards wouldn't even wait until Kaiya was discharged.

Kamden, Kaiya, and I had given our statements about the incident. The police had decided not to press any charges on Kamden or me for assaulting Bryce or breaking into either of his properties. The investigating officers had informed us that Bryce would be charged with assault and kidnapping and would face up to fifteen years in prison.

Kamden and I had done a number on Bryce, breaking four of his ribs, his jaw, and rupturing his spleen. I probably would've beat him to death if I hadn't been so desperate to find Kaiya.

Kaiya had broken down once the police finally left the hospital. Bryce had been one of her only friends, and what he had done hurt her deeply. But I knew she'd recover; my Warrior always did.

I carried Hayden in his car seat as I helped Kaiya inside the house. There were still stacks of boxes in every room that needed to be unpacked, and Hayden's room was filled with everything he needed and more.

I set down his carrier and all of Kaiya's bags, then led her to our bedroom. She was exhausted and had been fighting sleep to spend as much time with Hayden as possible, but now she was going to rest whether she liked it or not.

After carefully helping her get into bed, I covered her with the blankets before kissing her forehead. "You need to rest, Warrior."

"I don't want to rest—I need to take care of Hayden," she argued stubbornly, throwing the blankets and sitting up in bed.

I shook my head and chuckled. "I'll take care of Hayden—you sleep."

She yawned but still resisted. "But—"

"No buts. You've barely slept since he was born."

Sighing in defeat, she gingerly laid back on the bed. "Fine. But wake me up to feed him in two hours."

I wasn't planning to wake her up. Kaiya had already pumped some breast milk at the hospital, so I could feed Hayden myself. "Okay. Now get some sleep," I said as I backed toward the door.

She yawned again and closed her eyes. "I love you."

A smile tugged at my lips. I wish she knew how much I loved her, how much she and our son meant to me. They owned my whole fucking heart. "I love you, too."

I went back to the living room to check on Hayden. He was fast asleep in his car seat, so I decided to unpack some more of our things while he and Kaiya slept. We'd managed to get most of our large furniture in, but hadn't planned on Hayden coming early, so we weren't fully moved in yet.

After about an hour or so, Hayden started crying. Kaiya was still sleeping, so I grabbed a bottle of breast milk from the fridge and put it in some hot water to warm up before taking Hayden out of his carrier.

I was so fucking nervous holding him. He seemed so small and fragile, especially in my bulky arms. I was afraid I would break him, so I tried to be as gentle as possible whenever I handled him.

Laying him against my chest, I held his head steady as I went back to the kitchen to check if his bottle was ready. His cries had died down to a whimper now that I held him, but the sound still made me anxious, definitely something that would take getting used to.

I checked the temperature of the milk, but it was still too cold. I set it back in the water and patted Hayden on the back as I waited a few more minutes. I was thankful that the nurses in the maternity ward had shown us how to prepare Hayden's bottles and feed him because I would've been lost otherwise.

When the bottle was ready, I grabbed it and carefully carried Hayden to the bedroom. Kaiya had made me move the rocking chair from the nursery a couple of weeks ago because she planned to keep Hayden in our room for a few months.

I sat down with the speed of a turtle and cautiously positioned Hayden in my arms so that I could feed him. I started to rock him once he started eating, and I relaxed a little. Just like with his mom, I hated hearing him cry, and would do anything to fix what was causing it.

My eyes ran over his tiny form in my large, inked arms. So out of place, yet right where he belonged. He was perfect. His mom was perfect.

I looked up at Kaiya sleeping in our bed and smiled. I would've never guessed in a million years that we'd be where we are now. But I wouldn't change it for anything. Life had a way of sorting itself out, and every detour or obstacle was there for a purpose, getting us to where we needed to be. And I was exactly where I needed to be.

Epilogue

Kaiya

Four Years Later

Laying on the gym mat, propped up on my elbows, I watched Ryker and Hayden over by the punching bag. Ryker was trying to teach Hayden some basic punches, even though he had just turned four and had a short attention span.

Ryker lowered the bag all the way down so Hayden could reach it. He squatted next to our son and put his hands up in front of his face. "Put your hands up like this—always protect your face. Don't let anyone hit you."

Hayden put up his hands. They looked huge compared to his head with the gloves that Ryker had just bought him for his birthday. "Like this, Daddy?"

Ryker's mouth spread in a huge, proud grin, lighting up his whole face. "Yeah, just like that." He mussed Hayden's hair. "Now, hit the bag with your fist like this."

Ryker modeled a few punches that Hayden attempted to copy. I couldn't stop the smile that formed as I watched them. Hayden was the spitting image of Ryker, with the same brown hair and eyes. It was amazing how much they looked alike.

My two boys.

Ryker glanced over at me, giving me that look that still knotted my stomach. His love for me was evident all over his face, just like it was when he looked at our son.

After a few more punches, he scooped Hayden up and brought him over to me. "Mommy, did you see me?" Hayden squealed as he threw his arms around my neck.

I hugged him back. "Yes, baby, you did so great!"

Hayden pulled away and stood next to me before flexing his muscles. "I want to be big and strong, just like Daddy."

Ryker and I both laughed before Ryker said, "You will, buddy. And remember that you'll always need to protect Mommy and your little sister when she's born, okay?"

"I will, Daddy. I promise."

Ryker leaned over and pressed a kiss to my lips as he placed his tattooed hand on my bulging belly and softly rubbed it. "How's my little Warrior today?"

"She's been kicking a lot lately."

"Sounds like her mama—always fighting." He chuckled.

I set my hand on top of his and smiled. "I wouldn't want her any other way."

Ryker's Love Note to Kaiya

Warrior,

You're asleep on the couch right now. After putting Hayden down for a nap, you fell asleep with your head in my lap while watching T.V.

Looking down at you, I started stroking your hair and thinking about how much I loved you; how I couldn't imagine living without you. I don't tell you enough how special you are to me, and that's something I'm going to change.

Since its Valentine's Day, I thought it would be the perfect opportunity to start. I'm not that good at expressing myself, and there's really no words to express what you mean to me, but here goes.

You're the most amazing person I've ever met. We've been through hell and back together, and its made me love you more than I thought I was capable of. You've made me a better man, and I know I don't deserve you, but I'm sure as hell not going to take you for granted.

Our son is just ... perfect. I can never thank you enough for blessing me with him. Raising him with you has been the greatest experience of my life, and I can't wait to spend the rest of our lives watching him grow together. You are the best mother, and even when you're covered in spit-up or have baby food smeared on your face, you're still the most beautiful woman I've ever seen.

You've made my life so much better, Ky. There's nothing that I wouldn't do for you and our son. I love you with everything that I am, and everything that I'll ever be.

Happy Valentine's Day.

Love,

Ryker

Playlist

~ Gotten – Slash ft. Adam Levine
~ Say Something – Pentatonix
~ Addicted – Saving Abel
~ Wild Horses – Alicia Keys & Adam Levine
~ Stay – Rihanna ft. Mikky Ekko
~ All of Me – John Legend
~ All I Want – Staind
~ The Only Exception – Paramore
~ Look After You – The Fray
~ Breathe Again – Sara Bareilles

Acknowledgements

Wow.

I've finished my fourth book.

This is the first series I've completed, and its bittersweet for me. Kaiya and Ryker got the happily ever after they both deserved, but I don't think I'm ready to say good-bye to them—I'm not sure I ever will be. They'll always have a special place in my heart, and I'll never forget their journey.

The pressure to create a sequel worthy to The Scars of Us was overwhelming. I really hope that you enjoyed the way Kaiya' and Ryker's story ended—it was definitely an emotional roller-coaster for me to write.

Thank you to my beta readers, Vanessa, Natasha, Nicki, Andrea, Jennifer, and Erin for their feedback. I don't know what I'd do without your support. I love you girls!

To my editor, Ana Zaun, for once again pushing me and helping my writing grow. There were times I wanted to chunk my laptop in frustration, but I know your criticism was only meant to help better myself. Thank you for spending your time making my work shine.

To Kari at Cover to Cover Designs, thank you for making another beautiful cover. The *Mending Scars* cover is a perfect follow-up to the one you made for *The Scars of Us*, and I know readers will love it as much as I do.

To Simon Barnes for taking another amazing photo. Your work always impresses me, and I appreciate everything that you do. Your hard work and dedication is evident in every photo you shoot, and I'm grateful for every time I get to work with you and Andrew.

And most importantly, to my readers. I know it took me longer than I originally planned to release this book, and I thank you for your patience. Seeing your excitement and interest while I dealt with my personal issues meant so much and helped lift my spirits. I'd be nothing without your support, and you will never understand how much you all mean to me.

Scarred Remnants

Bonus Content

Prologue

Kamden

I will not drink.

I repeat that mantra multiple times daily, yet more often than not, I give in. I can't break the hold that alcohol has over me, no matter how hard I try; I always fail.

I'm too weak, just like my brother said … right before I killed him.

I stare at the glass sitting on the bar before me, enticing me with its addictive poison. The alcohol has corrupted me, turned me into someone that I hate.

Go home.

I hesitate, keeping my eyes on the glass before turning to walk away. I know that leaving the bar is only the beginning of the battle. The ugly truth is that I'll probably stop at the liquor store on my way home, then proceed to drink until I can't feel the relentless guilt gnawing at my insides anymore.

Coward.

I know I have to face my demons, but drinking them away is so much easier. Therapy isn't doing shit anymore, and I need something more.

Kaiya says I should go to AA, but that makes me feel like I'm some lowlife scum. Hell, maybe I am.

All I know is that I need to do something, before the guilt consumes me and it's too late for me to be saved.

Chapter One

Kamden

Awakening to the alarm on my phone blaring at me, I opened my eyes, then immediately shut them from the sun shining through the window.

"Ugh," I grumbled as my head began pounding. I squeezed the bridge of my nose with my fingers, hoping to relieve some of the pressure building in my skull.

Knowing it was useless, I grabbed my used glass from the night before and filled it with whiskey. I threw the shot back, then stood and walked to the kitchen.

After setting the glass in the sink, I headed to the bathroom to take a shower. The heated water helped ease the aching in my head, and made me feel refreshed. But that all went away once I got out and looked at myself in the mirror.

I always saw Kaleb. Now, I understood why it was so hard for Kaiya to look in the mirror; the reasons may have been different, but the source was the same. Kaleb had a way of rooting himself deep inside and never letting go, even though he was gone.

"I'm gone thanks to you, brother dearest," he taunted as I stared at him.

I shut my eyes and clenched my fists.

He's not real. Get a fucking grip.

"Do you miss me, brother?"

I don't have time for this shit.

I gritted my teeth and pushed away from the counter, leaving my brother behind. He never really left me, though; he was always there, a ball and chain weighing down my soul, not letting me move on with my life.

Once I got dressed and ready for work, I returned to the kitchen and poured myself a bowl of cereal, then grabbed a couple of bottled waters and protein bars to munch on later before walking out the door.

I was a construction foreman for a general contracting company based in Boston. We took on every contracting project imaginable, from hotels to stadiums to medical offices. One of our current projects was renovating a hotel right on the Boston Harbor, which my crew was working on.

It was a miracle that I hadn't been fired yet, especially since I was frequently late. My boss had been sympathetic after everything had happened with Kaleb, however, the constant frown he'd been giving me lately told me his patience was wearing thin.

Thankfully, I was on time that morning. After clocking in, I grabbed a cup of coffee before heading to my office. I needed to look over a few of the blueprints again because the hotel owner decided to make some additional changes that weren't in our original plans.

I sat down at my desk and flipped open my tablet. All of the documents, schematics, and other paperwork related to the project were in a file that I could access anywhere from my laptop, office computer, or tablet.

After opening the the file, I took a sip of coffee, needing it to kill the rest of my hangover.

Everything seemed to be in order—the project was right on schedule, even with the extra alterations the owner wanted. A few more weeks, and we'd be finished.

A knock directed my attention to the door. One of my crew members, Eric, smiled in the doorway. "All the trucks are loaded up and ready to go."

"Great," I raised my mug. "I'll be out there as soon as I finish my coffee."

"Okay, sir," Eric replied before turning and walking out.

I went through the file again as I finished my coffee, just to be thorough. My personal life may have been out of control and sloppy, but my work wasn't. Any mistakes on the job could jeopardize the lives of my men, and while I wasn't too concerned with my life, my crew's were a different story.

Setting the empty mug on my desk, I stood, tablet in hand. I headed outside to my company truck, where Eric and the other crew members were waiting.

I put my sunglasses on and pressed the unlock button for my truck. "Load 'em up, boys."

Eric climbed in the passenger side as two other guys jumped in the back seat. I made my way to the driver's side and got in.

The job site was only about ten minutes from our office, but sometimes the drive took longer depending on the downtown Boston traffic.

I turned onto the major street that led to the site, and cursed. Traffic was at a standstill. Eric craned his neck out the window. "Looks like an accident at the corner of Austin and Main."

I glanced at the clock radio. "Great," I sighed, then leaned my head back against the headrest. We'd already been late several times on this assignment.

The guys in the back started talking about the Celtics' game the night before. "Can you believe Thomas made that shot at the buzzer?"

"Thank God he did; we'd have lost the game if it wasn't for him."

Eric joined the conversation. "You got tickets for Sunday's game?"

"Of course. It's almost time for the playoffs," one of the guys answered.

"Crunch time," the other added.

"I got an extra ticket, Kam. You should come with us." Eric offered.

Crowds and I did not mix, especially if alcohol was involved. I tended to lose my temper a lot quicker when I drank.

It would be nice to get out instead of drinking alone like some loser.

I nodded. "Maybe."

The car in front of me finally moved. An inch.

Fuck my life.

When we finally made it to the hotel, we were about an hour behind schedule. The manager wasn't around, but his assistant was, and I knew she'd be letting him know about our tardiness.

"Time to put in some work, boys. That traffic put us back, so we gotta hustle," I ordered as everyone readied the equipment. We were adding a few penthouses to the top of the hotel, which was one of the last minute changes the owner had wanted, and those additions had increased our workload by almost double.

We had already put up the exterior walls and most of the interior walls, along with the outdoor courtyard and fountain that led from the elevator to the suites. We'd completed all of the original plans, so we'd made a substantial amount of progress, but the extra modifications delayed our completion.

Towards the end of our lunch break, the manager, Mr. Trong, made an appearance. And he looked pissed.

Shit.

I took the last bite of the sandwich one of my crew members had picked up downstairs as Mr. Trong approached. He was a short, Asian man with a heavy accent. I could barely understand him half the time he talked.

He stalked up to me, then angrily pointed his finger in my face. "You late again, Mr. Malow."

I finished chewing what was in my mouth and swallowed. "I'm sorry, Mr. Trong. There was an accident on Main, and-"

"I no care!" He poked me in the chest. "This fifth time you late. I call your boss." He turned and started to walk away.

"No, Mr. Trong. Please, don't." I followed after him. "I promise it won't happen again."

He ignored me, continuing his path to the elevator. His assistant followed, talking on her Blackberry about some gala happening that weekend at the hotel.

Once the elevator door closed, I let out a breath of frustration as I kicked an empty paint can across the work site. "Fuck!"

Every man in my crew looked over at me, eyeing me warily.

"What the fuck are you looking at? Get back to work." I shouted angrily.

They complied, cleaning up their lunch and heading back to their work areas. I started walking to the courtyard, deciding to do some damage control by calling my boss. The phone rang a few times before going to his voicemail.

"Hey, Robert, it's Kamden." I rubbed the back of my neck and paced around the fountain. "Mr. Trong will probably be calling you because we were late again. There was a big accident on Main, and it held us up. Just wanted to give you a heads up. Thanks, bye."

Ending the call, I exhaled. I was already on thin ice with my boss, and didn't need any help breaking it.

The rest of the day went by without any other incidents, except a dirty look from Mr. Trong as we exited the hotel. I felt relieved to be getting out of there, but was also dreading going back to the office. I hadn't heard anything from my boss, and I doubted that no news was good news in this instance.

As we were unloading the trucks back at the office, the intercom sounded with my boss' voice. "Kamden, can I see you in my office?"

Shit.

I glanced warily at Eric, who forced a smile. I knew he was trying to be reassuring, but it didn't make me feel better.

I made my way to Robert's office, then knocked on the open door. "You wanted to see me, sir?"

He glanced up from some invoices on his desk. "Yes, have a seat, Kamden."

I sat in the chair he gestured to, and nervously rubbed my palms on my pants as I waited for him to speak.

Robert straightened the papers in front of him. "I got your message, as well as the call from Mr. Trong."

I nodded, then explained. "Sir, it wasn't my fault. Like I said, there was an accident and-"

My boss held up his hand. "Kamden, you're the foreman of your crew. Therefore, you are responsible for anything that happens on the job." He turned to look at his computer screen, then clicked the mouse a few times. "That was the fifth time you've been late on this project, not to mention the countless other times you've been late to the office."

I bounced my leg anxiously. "I know, sir. I'm sorry."

He swiveled in his chair to face me again. "I understand that you've been through a lot, but that was over two years ago."

Two years, four months, and eleven days.

I clenched my fists, holding back what I really wanted to say. Instead, I said what I thought would get me out of there quickest so that I could go home and drink until I couldn't remember what happened. "It won't happen again, sir."

He smiled, but I knew he didn't believe me. He grabbed a small slip from one of the paper organizers on his desk. "I'm sorry, but I'm going to have to write you up. Another write-up and I'll have to put you on a one week, unpaid suspension." He scribbled on the slip of paper, then tore off the top copy and handed it to me.

That was my second write-up since the shooting. I should've had a whole stack by now, but Robert was a pretty cool boss for the most part. I sure as hell didn't think I would've been able to handle myself as an employee.

"Is there anything else you need from me, sir?" I asked. I was so ready to get out of there.

"No, that's all. I'll see you tomorrow."

I nodded and stood. "Have a good night."

I made my exit, heading back to the garage to see if my crew needed more help unloading. No one was around, so I went to close up my office before I left.

As I drove home, I made a detour to a bar near my apartment. After the day I'd had, I really needed a drink. Or ten.

Who am I kidding? I'd be here regardless of the day I had.

I parked and got out of my truck. Now that I didn't have work to focus on, my guilt and anxiety was beginning to build up inside, threatening to choke me.

When I got inside, I went straight to the bar and waved the bartender, Mitch, down.

He smiled as he walked over to me. "Hey, Kam. How goes it?"

I shrugged my shoulders. "Had a shitty day at work—got written up."

"Aw, that's too bad." He grabbed a glass and filled it with ice. "Nothing a drink can't fix, right?"

I gave him a quick nod. "I'll take a Jack on the rocks."

He'd already grabbed the bottle of whiskey and started pouring. "The usual, eh?" He slid the drink to me.

"Thanks." I sipped on the amber liquid as I took a seat at the end of the bar. "I'll take a shot straight up, also."

He grabbed a shot glass and filled it. "Take it slow, kid."

I motioned for the shot, and he slowly gave it to me. I threw back the whiskey, then enjoyed the burn that ran down my throat. That burn was the only thing I wanted to feel, not the guilt and self-loathing that plagued me daily. Alcohol was the only way that I could rid myself of those feelings, swapping numbness for the never-ending pain.

I winced. "Ah."

A few more rounds and it'll go away.

After I'd had three more drinks and five shots, I threw back another and slammed my empty glass back on the bar. "Another shot of Jack," I called out to Mitch.

Mitch threw his towel on his shoulder as he walked over to me. "I think you've had enough, Kam."

I scoffed and tried to make eye contact, even though I could barely see straight. "I'm not even close to being done."

Crossing his arms, he narrowed his eyes at me. "Well, you're done here. I ain't serving you anymore."

I abruptly stood, wobbling as I gripped the bar to stay upright. "Fine. I'm outta this place." I grabbed my wallet and fished out a few twenties before throwing them on the bar. "Keep the change," I slurred.

Mitch mumbled under his breath, but I couldn't make out what he said. I stumbled toward the exit, eager to get home to the bottle of Jack I had in the freezer.

"You want me to call a cab?" Mitch yelled after me.

I waved my hand at him without looking back. "Nah, I got it."

I may be a drunk, but I'm not stupid.

The bar was a couple of blocks from my apartment, so I typically walked. On the rare occasion that I drove, I left my truck there and picked it up the next morning. Some nights I didn't even remember how I made it home, or I would end up in some random woman's bed.

When I made it to my door, I fumbled with the keys as I tried to get the right one in the lock, which was difficult when I was seeing two keyholes.

Once I went inside, I headed straight for the kitchen, tunnel vision on the freezer containing my precious elixir.

I tossed my keys on the counter before opening the freezer and grabbing the bottle of Jack. I set it down and retrieved a glass from the cabinet, then filled it to the top. Some of the honey liquid sloshed over the sides as I brought it to my lips.

I raised the glass in the air. "My best friend."

I took another swig, then trudged to the couch with the bottle and glass in hand. I plopped down, spilling some of the liquor on myself and the sofa in the process. "Great. Just fuckin' great."

I drank what was left, then filled the glass again, not caring about the mess I'd made. All I wanted to do was drink until I couldn't feel anything anymore; until I couldn't see *his*face in my head.

After downing another glass, I closed my eyes as dizziness settled over me. Soon, the darkness would come over me and relieve me from the pain—temporarily. But any relief was better than none.

I leaned back on the couch and propped my feet on the coffee table. I loosely held the bottle next to me as I lay my head back.

Maybe I should just end it all. No one would care.

I thought about the gun under my mattress.

It would be so easy.

An image of my sister and nephew popped in my head. They may have been fuzzy, but they were there.

Kaiya would.

I pushed Kaiya out of my head and replaced her with thoughts of guzzling the bottle next to me, then following it with another. A quick and simple way to go. No more guilt; no more pain.

You killed your brother. You can kill yourself just as easily.

Then, that stupid asshole conscience of mine reminded of my sister again.

Kaiya would be devastated. You can't do that to her.

Kaiya's a big girl. She'll get over it.

Lifting my head, I attempted to pour another glass, but failed in even lifting the bottle; I could barely keep my eyes open.

Maybe I'll just sleep instead ... yeah, sleep sounds good.

I lay my head back and felt the glass slip from my hand. Seconds later, blackness blanketed me and pulled me under.

Made in the USA
Middletown, DE
19 September 2024